THE FAMILY EXPERIMENT

Also by John Marrs

The One

The Passengers

The Minders

When You Disappeared (previously published as *The Wronged Sons*)

The Good Samaritan

Her Last Move

What Lies Between Us

The Vacation (previously published as *Welcome to Wherever You Are*)

The Marriage Act

The Stranger in Her House

Keep It in the Family

THE FAMILY EXPERIMENT

A NOVEL

JOHN MARRS

HANOVER
SQUARE
PRESS

HANOVER
SQUARE
PRESS™

Recycling programs
for this product may
not exist in your area.

ISBN-13: 978-1-335-00036-1

The Family Experiment

First published in 2024 by Macmillan. This edition published in 2024.

Copyright © 2024 by John Marrs

Icons © Shutterstock. Graphic design by Lindsay Nash.

All rights reserved. No part of this book may be used or reproduced in any manner whatsoever without written permission.

Without limiting the author's and publisher's exclusive rights, any unauthorized use of this publication to train generative artificial intelligence (AI) technologies is expressly prohibited.

This is a work of fiction. Names, characters, places and incidents are either the product of the author's imagination or are used fictitiously. Any resemblance to actual persons, living or dead, businesses, companies, events or locales is entirely coincidental.

TM and ® are trademarks of Harlequin Enterprises ULC.

Hanover Square Press
22 Adelaide St. West, 41st Floor
Toronto, Ontario M5H 4E3, Canada
HanoverSqPress.com

Printed in U.S.A.

In simplest terms, the Metaverse is the internet, but in 3D.
Ed Greig, Chief Disruptor at Deloitte

Your children are not your children.
They are sons and daughters of Life's longing for itself.
They come through you but not from you.
And though they are with you, they belong not to you.
Kahlil Gibran, writer and poet

ADVERTISEMENT

re:born

As seen on hit TV show The Family Experiment.

Why leave it to chance or genetics when you can have the perfect baby you've always dreamed of?

Here at Re:Born, we are now taking pre-launch orders for MetaBabies—children that exist entirely in the Metaverse. Here you can pick and choose the age and sex of your child, and design their appearance from eye and hair colour to skin tone and body shape, their accent, interests and the speed of their growth. Trust our designers to create a perfect blend of the two of you, just like Mother Nature intended.

Our children have a digital memory, photo-realistic faces and bodies which can respond to you using facial tracking and voice analysis.

But Re:Born isn't only for new parents. If you're not ready for your Real World child to grow up, we can build an exact replica of them so they can live forever in the Metaverse at an age of your choice. Or if you have suffered a loss, allow us to reanimate the one you loved with a near-exact replica.

Wherever you are in life, we can tailor a package that suits you.

Re:Born launches later this year. Pre-order now to avoid disappointment.
Deposit required followed by a £19.99 monthly subscription fee.
Re:Born is a subsidiary of Awakening Entertainment. All rights reserved.

1

Teleprompter script—*The Family Experiment* launch night

AUTUMN TAYLOR, PRESENTER

(CAM 1):

Welcome to the launch of what's going to be the *only* show you'll be talking about for the next nine months, *The Family Experiment*.

(PAUSE FOR OPENING TITLES AND APPLAUSE FROM A WALL OF VIEWERS ON SCREENS BEHIND HOST)

Well, if you haven't already heard or read about it, then where have you been? Because since it was announced, *The Family Experiment* has become the highest-trending reality TV show this decade—and that's before we've even gone on air!

(PAUSE FOR APPLAUSE)

So here's how it works.

(CAM 4):

Over the next nine months, eleven carefully selected childless British contestants will compete to raise the world's first fully interactive children in the Metaverse. Our intended parents will wear virtual reality headsets, along with masks, gloves and full-body suits that feel like a second skin. This will allow them to feel everything a biological parent does with their children. And for twenty-four hours a day, you the viewer can watch every trial, treat, tribulation and tantrum. And if you're like me and hate to miss out, sign up for our push notifications every time something big happens so you can tune in and watch moments later. How amazing is that?

(PAUSE FOR APPLAUSE)
(CAM 1):

Our intended parents won't get to know the sex of their baby in advance. Every one of our children will grow at an accelerated rate, meaning they'll remain at each age for much less time than Real World children. For example, in month one, our parents will be tasked with looking after a newborn. In month two, their baby will be considerably older and more developed. And by month nine, their children will be fully grown adults. Each MetaChild is operated by artificial intelligence developed by market leaders Awakening Entertainment. And they'll grow and learn in the same way a Real World child does. What they experience and how they develop will depend on the nurturing they receive from each parent.

(CAM 2):

And as this show is fully interactive, we want you at home to feel a part of it. So every month, you'll be able to vote for a couple you want to face a Monthly Challenge that we'll be setting. And believe us, with your help, we are going to push our new mums and dads to the limit! More details on our first challenge coming up later in the show. You will also get to tell the contestants exactly what you think of their parenting skills as we go along. How? By awarding them red hearts for everything you like seeing and black hearts for the things you don't. Not enough cuddles? Black-heart them. Giving them quality time? Throw them a red. And our parents will see them appearing on screen so they know how you think they're performing.

(CAM 1):

Tonight, each family automatically receives £250,000, the estimated cost of raising a Real World child from newborn to eighteen. They can spend as much or as little of that money as they like on anything they choose, such as education, healthcare, entertainment, travel and immersive experiences in other App platforms. After nine months, viewers will then vote for one family to win. Sadly, the losers will watch their MetaChildren permanently switched off and lose the remainder of their cash. But that's not where *The Family Experiment* ends.

(CAM 4):

Because our winners will then face the toughest decision of their lives. They can either keep what's left of that original £250,000 along with their MetaChild, or they can pull the plug on their child and get a quarter of a million pounds to start a Real World family of their own, paid on the live birth of their child through traditional means, IVF, surrogacy or adoption.

(PAUSE FOR APPLAUSE)

And for those of you who want to get up close and personal with a family, in-App purchases will allow you to spend time in the same room as them without them knowing and watch the action as it unfolds. A monthly lottery will also allow a lucky winner to interact and enjoy one-to-one time with the children themselves! Terms and conditions apply. And don't forget to log in to our

The Family Experiment App to register your interest in becoming a MetaParent when the programme is rolled out to the public on the night of the finale.

(CAM 4):

Now, without further ado, shall we meet our five couples and one singleton?

(CUT TO REAL WORLD INTRODUCTION VIDEOS)

2

Twelve years earlier

The first memory of his second life came when he awoke to find himself being pulled from the rear of a van and carried over the shoulder of someone who stank of rubber and petrol.

He'd opened his eyes but had struggled to focus on where he was or who was moving him. All he could be sure of was that it was nighttime, and there was a near-full moon above them and a sky awash with stars.

Something didn't feel right in his head. It wasn't an injury; more like a deep-seated, burning pain emerging from behind his right eye.

'Where am I?' he croaked. The man carrying him didn't reply. Instead, he was brusquely lowered to his feet, where he tried and failed to steady himself. He toppled to one side, his face colliding with stones. He paused for a moment to gather his thoughts and listened carefully. They weren't alone. There were other voices like his, young and frightened, whispering in hushed tones. And, a little further away, there came the rush of water.

'Get up!' barked a gruff, accented voice he couldn't identify.

He glanced upwards and squinted at the bright light shining from a jacket. If he was not mistaken, the man was also wearing a balaclava, which added to his concern.

'Get up!' the man repeated, less patiently. The boy attempted to push himself up into a sitting position, but he was too weak. He barely protested when the man grabbed his arm, but yelped when it was almost yanked from its socket. Now he was back on his feet and being pulled across the beach, the heels of his trainers making trenches.

Soon after, freezing-cold water lapped at his ankles, then his knees, before his body was lifted and hurled into the air like a shotput. He landed face first on something wet and rubbery. Water splashed against his face and eyes, its saltiness stinging, but its chill eventually helping him to regain his vision. 'Put this on,' the man ordered, and thrust a set of dog tags attached to a chain into his hand. He did what he was told and put them around his neck.

Someone else, most likely another child judging by the lightness of their touch, placed their arm around his shoulder and helped him up into a sitting position. He turned to look at him, then all the others surrounding them. There must have been around thirty other young people here, around the same age as him, all looking as frightened as he felt. Some shared family resemblances and gripped each other tightly. Ahead, even more were coming, escorted through the water by two more balaclava-clad figures. The boat was only a few metres long and was soon cramped.

'What's happening?' he asked the lad who'd helped to lift him up from the floor.

'They're moving us,' he replied.

'Do you have a phone? I need to call...my...my...' His voice trailed off. He didn't know who to call. His memory was a blank.

'If you are in this boat then there is no one to call,' the lad replied.

'Where are we going?'

'From here on the Kent coast over to Rotterdam or Calais, that's what I overheard.'

'But I don't want to go there. I want to go home.'

'You don't have a home any more. That life's over for you now. You're being taken abroad to start a new one.'

He shook his head vigorously. 'No. They wouldn't let that happen.'

'Who wouldn't? Your parents? They sent you here because they probably can't afford to keep you any more. That's normally how it works.'

'They wouldn't have done that.'

He racked his brain, but there was a blank page where the image of his parents should have been.

The lad looked at him and frowned. 'What's your name?' he asked.

'It's...' But his thoughts were empty once more. 'I... I don't know,' he said, embarrassed.

His new friend nodded.

'You're lucky—your parents probably loved you if they had your memories of them erased. It hurts less if you don't know who you or they are.'

His gaze fell to his wet shoes.

With no one left on the shore, two of the three men began to turn the dinghy in the direction of the mouth of the bay, while the third started the engine. Soon they were all on board as the boat pulled out into the choppy waters of the Channel. The further they travelled, the larger the waves lapped, and the colder and damper their passengers became. It wasn't long before at least half of the children were vomiting over the side or onto each other.

'Throw your stuff in here,' one of the men yelled above the chugging of the motor. He held out a large bag. 'Anything you have—phones, toys, books, throw it all away. You don't need them.'

Without argument, the terrified young passengers rifled through their pockets and surrendered their belongings. As the boy opened his hoodie to look at the pockets inside, his new acquaintance caught sight of his T-shirt in the moonlight. It featured an image of the Statue of Liberty and nearby Hudson River.

'Hudson,' his friend said suddenly. 'That's what I'll call you until you remember your name.'

Hudson wrapped his arms around himself to neutralize the bracing wind and didn't speak again until lights appeared on the horizon. To his relief, it appeared to be land.

Just then, the dinghy's engine began to splutter and seize. The man steering it attempted to restart it, which briefly worked before it sputtered to another halt. It was only then that Hudson noticed he was up to his knees in water. Below him, the air chambers in the dinghy were deflating, lowering the boat, allowing too much water inside and making it too heavy for the engine to shift.

'Out!' yelled one of the men. 'You swim to shore.'

'I don't know how to,' screamed a girl.

The man ignored her. It was only after all three men jumped overboard that the terrified children followed, like lemmings falling from a cliff.

'Come on,' Hudson said to the other lad.

'I can't swim either,' came his panicked response.

'I'll help you.'

First Hudson jumped, and then the other lad. His body disappeared under the surface, so Hudson reached for him, but in the lad's panic he began dragging him down too. The two wrestled in the freezing depths, Hudson taking huge gulps of water deep into his lungs as he struggled to get them both to safety. Eventually, now on his back, Hudson grabbed the boy, placed his arm around his chest, turned them both and kicked against the waves to get them to shore.

'I need you to kick too,' Hudson yelled, and the lad eventually followed suit. Several times they were forced to stop for air as water filled their mouths.

Around them, the other children splashed and screamed. Some vanished beneath the waves, their arms stretching into the air as if reaching for God's hand.

Eventually, Hudson's feet felt the shingle of the shore beneath him, and the two boys dragged themselves out of the water, coughing and spluttering.

Parked on the beach were two vehicles, with tall bright lights jutting from their roofs and a handful of figures standing alongside them. Hudson squinted and made out the words *Police Nationale* emblazoned across the sides of both vehicles.

Some of the others who had made it out of the water before them were stumbling towards the authorities, begging for help. But instead of hurrying to their aid, an officer pointed at a waiting truck, its headlights cutting through the night sky.

'Can you help us?' asked Hudson.

A second officer refused to look him in the eye. Instead, she allowed her hand to rest on a baton attached to her belt. They were turning a blind eye to what was happening. Hudson and the other boy had no choice but to follow orders.

The closer the remaining children got to the truck, the louder the noises appeared from inside. He realized it was packed with sheep, and straw was scattered across the floor. Hudson coughed several times, turned to look at his fellow dinghy passengers and realized only half had made it ashore.

Even fewer would make it to their next destination.

TODAY, MONTH ONE:
NEWBORN

3

CONTESTANTS: *Rufus Green & Kitty Carter*
AGES: *29 and 27*
STATUS: *Cohabiting three years*
OCCUPATION: *Entrepreneur and accounts manager*
METACHILD: *Daughter, Olivia*
IN THEIR OWN WORDS: *'We have everything we want in our lives except the money to start a family. We'll do anything to be parents.'*

The noise was becoming more relentless than ever, thought Rufus, if that was even possible.

He had just used the pause button on baby Olivia which, once a month, allowed a parent in the Metaverse fifteen minutes with no sound or movement from a MetaChild. But once the timer had reached zero, her screams were even more shrill and piercing. He tried to no avail to turn down the volume in his earpods.

Earlier that night, and minutes after his head had hit the pillow in his Real World home, a Push notification on his watch had woken him up. Baby Olivia was in need of more attention. He'd desperately wanted Kitty to rouse and offer to take charge but she'd put up with the continuous crying for most of the day. Tonight, she was dead to the world. And five hours into his turn to look after their two-week-old infant, she was showing no sign of wanting to be soothed by her father.

'Come on, give me a break,' he muttered as he held her in their Metaverse nursery. 'Please be quiet, just for a few minutes.'

He shifted her from his shoulder to the crook of his arm, where he'd stuck a second headache patch before going to bed. Then he paced back and forth around the room. At 3 a.m., it was dimly lit, but he could make out the moving images of hot-air balloons circling the lampshade in the centre of the ceiling. Kitty had taken charge of the decor and had chosen a neutral palette of yellows and greys as they were supposed to be 'calming'. He begged to differ. Calmness was an alien concept to their daughter.

Rufus began bouncing her up and down, a technique he'd been taught in the Real World parenting classes he and Kitty had attended. They had been the only couple expecting a virtual child—something that had fascinated their course leader but had alienated them from the other participants, who'd eyed them with suspicion and failed to invite them for extra-curricular group drinks and suppers.

'Once the show begins, they'll understand,' he'd reassured a disappointed Kitty.

Bleary-eyed, he glanced at the clock in the corner of his headset, hoping it was time to give Olivia another dose of the medication the AI doctor had prescribed for her croup. He sighed when he realized it wasn't due for another hour and a half. He moved her back to his shoulder, her nose catching his collarbone. It made her scream even louder.

'Olivia!' he said, raising his voice in the hope the suddenness might jolt her out of the vicious cycle of upset she was trapped in. 'Come on!'

Black emoji hearts floating across the screen blurred his vision. Viewers were disapproving of his approach. *They can all fuck off*, he thought.

He placed Olivia back in her cot with a little more force than he had intended.

'Sorry,' he muttered, but quietly; he was past caring.

He took several paces backwards and folded his arms, contemplating his next approach. But he suspected that whatever he did, it would not placate her. And he couldn't take much more of it.

This was not how he'd imagined the early weeks of parenthood to be. He hadn't expected it all to be plain sailing, but neither was it supposed to be a relentless slog for two new, sleep-deprived parents trying to second-guess why a baby refused to settle. Yes, croup was playing its part in Olivia's discomfort, but Rufus's research suggested it shouldn't be as severe or as prolonged as this. Her AI paediatrician had suggested she was taking time to settle in, as some babies do. But Rufus knew there was more to it than that. He'd even asked a producer off-camera if her behaviour could be a programming glitch, but he'd been told that was impossible.

Each day, he'd asked himself why he and Kitty were allowing something so small and helpless to cause them such misery. And it was making him more and more frustrated.

His animosity was also growing towards his partner. Why had she put them in this position? Why couldn't she have been happy with the life they'd had? He certainly had been. But she'd insisted they applied for *The Family Experiment*.

Rufus had been upfront and admitted soon after they'd met that he had a low sperm count and that, without the help of IVF, it was unlikely they could conceive naturally. But the escalating costs associated with the treatment were way beyond their means. Rufus would have been equally happy in a world with Kitty that didn't involve children. However, that hadn't been her dream. And she'd been more persuasive than he'd ever known her to be. So rather than risk losing her, he'd agreed to fill in the application form.

And although neither of them had verbalized what they'd been feeling since Olivia's arrival, he assumed she was on the same page as him. They'd made a terrible mistake.

Olivia's screaming echoed even louder from her cot, reverberating around the space like surround-sound speakers that couldn't be switched off. Rufus left the room and paced the rest of the house, fists clenched, body tense. Even out in the garden, he could hear the racket. Was there anywhere in the Metaverse he could escape it?

More black hearts filled the screen as the viewers again made their displeasure known.

'Fine!' he yelled, and marched back into the nursery.

He grabbed Olivia, lifting her up and cradling her, rocking her back and forth with more speed and desperation than his previous approach.

Still she shrieked. His head was pounding, his ears were ringing, his eyes were stinging and all he could think about was how much he wanted to climb back into bed, fall asleep and forget about the worst decision he'd ever made.

'Just shut up,' he whispered into Olivia's ear, but it appeared to prompt the opposite reaction. Somehow, her cries became louder.

'Olivia,' he said firmly. 'Olivia! For God's sake, stop it now.'

Even in the dimness of the room, he could see how red her face was, how the ligaments strained in her neck and how wide her mouth became as she threw out each ear-splitting wail.

It pushed Rufus beyond breaking point.

He stretched out his arms and held her in front of him, his hands under her armpits, her head tipping to one side.

'Just shut the fuck up!' he yelled, the resonance of his voice matching the noise of her squawks.

A warm tear fell from his daughter's face and onto his hand. But it wasn't enough to snap him out of the descending red mist filling the room.

4

CONTESTANTS: *Woody & Tina Finn*
AGES: *Both 36*
STATUS: *Married fifteen years*
OCCUPATION: *Drone pilot and euthanasia nurse*
METACHILD: *Daughter, Belle*
IN THEIR OWN WORDS: *'We've enjoyed our lives as a couple, but now we are ready to take that next step in our relationship and become a family.'*

Woody clamped his hand over his mouth too quickly. His wedding ring clipped one of his front teeth but he barely acknowledged it. Instead, his attention remained fixed on the TV news channel and the caption at the bottom of the screen.

> 'Couple ejected from *The Family Experiment* after father shakes virtual baby to death.'

'Oh Jesus,' he muttered as footage played of fellow contestant Rufus Green in his Metaverse nursery, trying and failing to calm a screaming infant. A moment later the new dad held the child out in front of him, shaking her violently. Woody pressed stop before the clip finished.

'When did this happen?' he asked his wife, Tina, as she entered their Real World lounge.

'Early hours of the morning,' Tina replied. 'It's on every news channel.'

They listened together as the newsreader spoke.

'The show's producers are facing criticism for failing to cut the live feed of the death of two-week-old Olivia. In a statement, a spokesperson for *The Family Experiment* said, "The events of last night are tragic. But the show is unfiltered and designed to reflect the wide range of experiences new parents go through. To take the show off the air, even following such an unfortunate event, would be a huge disservice to our viewers, to whom we have promised a fully immersive, transparent experience."'

'What the hell was he thinking?' Woody asked. 'I get how frustrating it is when you can't calm a crying child, but if it riles you up that much, step away, for Christ's sake. Return to the Real World, then go back when you've calmed down. You don't hurt your own child.'

Tina's flesh prickled as a shadow briefly escaped the darkness and flew into the light. She blinked it away.

'The viewers moaning about how outraged they are by what happened must bear some responsibility,' she said. 'They voted for Olivia to have croup in the Monthly Challenge.'

'Do you know that for sure?'

'From what I've watched and read, Rufus and Kitty had it much worse than any of us.'

'And how's our daughter been today?'

'Really good,' said Tina. 'She fed at midnight, then at 4 a.m., and winding is getting easier. She was back to sleep in ten minutes.'

'You've always had the magic touch.'

Tina didn't reply. She removed the band keeping her ponytail in place and ruffled her fingers through her now-loose hair, which rested on her shoulders. It was the longest it had been since her late teens. That felt like a lifetime ago, and now that she was in her mid-thirties, she'd long stopped brightening it with pastel colours and settled for an ash blonde.

She yawned and took a sip from a smoothie Woody had left balancing on the arm of the sofa. Tina relished her sleep, and there had been precious little of that since Belle's arrival. She hoped the exhaustion wouldn't show in her face. She'd resisted slipping home Botox kits on her online shopping delivery list. So far, at least.

Woody, however, was showing no signs of fatigue and he'd been through just as much as her. Physically, he'd barely changed in the eighteen years since they met. Only twice had she ever seen him clean-shaven and without his reddish-brown stubble. An allergy to the silicone in contact lenses meant he always wore his dark-rimmed glasses. The only difference between the Woody of back then and the man in front of her now was a slight sloping paunch and greying temples.

He stretched out his arms, yawned and rose to his feet.

'Would you still have agreed to participate if you'd have known how much attention we were all going to get?' he asked suddenly. 'I mean, the producers prepared us for a level of interest, but it's been insane, hasn't it? My email inbox was full of interview requests this morning.'

'Why do you ask? Has anyone said anything about...you know...?'

'No, no, it's not that,' Woody replied, scratching his chin. 'I'm just struggling a little with being constantly judged by the world and his mother. Did you see how many black hearts I got yesterday when I didn't change Belle's nappy until the second Push notification arrived? You'd have thought I'd left her for five hours, not five minutes.'

'Try to ignore them. Some people relish being able to disapprove so vocally of how we're all parenting. I wonder how they'd cope if every move they made was being analysed and rated?'

A synthesized female voice from the Audite, their virtual assistant, chimed from the corner of the room.

'Push notification. Belle has woken up and requires attention.'

'And it'll be my turn to face the wrath of viewers if I don't log in and check on her,' Tina added.

Woody gave his wife a peck on the lips as he left and made his way upstairs into the spare bedroom and their Metaverse access point. He slipped into his mask and haptic suit, which clung to him like a second skin. Its thousands of tactile sensors allowed him to feel every sensation the Metaverse had to offer: the touch of his daughter's skin, her breath on his chest, even her pulsating heartbeat. Next came his gloves, mask, a standard slimline headset not much larger than a pair of sunglasses, and then earpods. Once logged on to the system, he was inside Belle's virtual Metaverse nursery.

In-App purchases had allowed them to decorate it with a jungle theme, complete with moving tree canopies that swayed in the breeze, alongside tall ferns, flowering plants and moving animals.

Belle was due her next feed soon, so Woody picked up a virtual pre-filled bottle of formula and placed it inside the heater. He'd forgotten to warm it last time, and she'd responded with cries and refused to suckle.

He wondered how many eyes were upon him now, either streaming at home or here in person. He couldn't understand what drove superfans to pay for the privilege of being in the room with parents—unseen, unheard and unable to interfere.

Perhaps he should take a leaf out of Tina's book and care a little less about whether he was being watched or judged, he thought. They didn't know the man behind the avatar. They didn't know how he'd already proved what a good father he really was.

And they didn't know just how far he had already gone to protect his family.

5

CONTESTANTS: *Cadman N'Yu & Gabriel Macmillan*
AGES: *36 and 26*
STATUS: *Cohabiting seven years*
OCCUPATION: *Social media influencer and PA*
METACHILD: *Son, name to be announced*
IN THEIR OWN WORDS: *'We've faced some challenges in our lives—some together and some apart. And that makes us ready for anything. So bring it on!'*

'What are you planning to dress him in?' Cadman asked with a raised voice from their Metaverse lounge.

'The usual,' Gabriel replied from inside the adjoining nursery. 'A vest and a babygro.'

'Yes, but which ones?'

'Does it matter? We have about a hundred and they all look the same.'

Cadman sighed. 'You know it matters. Our fans like to know exactly who our son's wearing and where they can buy it from. And I can feel you rolling your eyes from here.'

Gabriel had been doing just that.

'Well, why don't you pick something yourself?' he suggested.

'I'm busy.'

'Doing what?'

'Catching up with the fallout over what happened to baby Olivia.'

'Awful, isn't it?' said Gabriel.

'Yes,' replied Cadman. 'It is.'

But not for us, he quietly thought. It was one less couple to compete against.

Gabriel flicked through the first of three clothing rails in their son's wardrobe, knowing that whatever he chose, he'd make the wrong decision. As his hand hovered above each garment, the price tag and a retailer appeared on the screen of his VR headset. Eventually he returned to Cadman and their son in the kitchen, carrying a green-checked babygro, a white vest and a pair of socks with foxes' faces on the toes. He held them up to his chest.

'Do these get your seal of approval?'

'Yes to the 'gro and the vest but no to the socks,' said Cadman.

'What's wrong with them?'

'What colour is a fox?'

'Red.'

'Red doesn't go with green. Unless our son is now identifying as a traffic light.'

'Cadman, he's two weeks old. Does anyone really care?'

Almost immediately, scores of red hearts appeared in the corner of his screen.

'Are they agreeing with you or with me?' Gabriel asked.

Cadman smiled wryly. 'What do you think?'

'I think I give up,' Gabriel muttered, and returned to the nursery, choosing a pair of white socks from the dozens in the drawer. He paused to take in the room. It was almost as many square metres as the ground floor of their Buckinghamshire Real World house. It was packed full of toys. *We could open a creche in here,* he thought.

They had chosen a planetary theme for the room. It was illuminated by a full moon as comets and rockets jettisoned in all directions beneath twinkling stars. Gabriel enjoyed spending quiet time and naps in here with his son.

The Apps used to decorate the room would have made a sizeable dent in their prize fund had influencer and social media commentator Cadman not invited potential sponsors and suppliers to fill their internet home with cost-free products.

'It's a fantastic opportunity,' he'd told them in his pitches. 'Our in-App purchases will be seen by millions of viewers worldwide.'

Most had jumped at the opportunity. But the downside to the free flow of freebies was the constantly alternating furniture in not just the nursery, but their whole MetaHouse. Most infants went through one or two babygros a day, but theirs wore at least eight daily. Each time he was fed or had his nappy changed, he would appear in an entirely new sponsored outfit.

Gabriel made his way back to the kitchen. His face softened when he saw his son, awake and exhaling spit bubbles from inside Cadman's sling. It was the third child carrier he'd been inside in as many days. Cadman was hunched over a tablet on a work surface, typing.

'I thought we said we wouldn't be using tech when the baby was around?' Gabriel asked.

'I meant when he's older, like in the next Development Leap.'

'What are you doing now that's taking your attention away from him?'

'My attention isn't being taken away,' Cadman huffed. 'He couldn't be any closer if he was welded to me. I'm looking at cutlery and plates.'

'Why?'

'Next month we might have leapt to the weaning stage. So I'm planning accordingly. If he eats five small meals a day, he'll be using five different plates, sippy cups and knives, forks and spoons. Think of the number of sponsors a week we can attract.'

'Really?' asked Gabriel. 'We've already had his nappies, formula, milk bottles and bedding sponsored—do we really need to monetize everything?'

An email alert sounded in their headsets.

'Hey,' said Cadman, 'the results of the poll are in.'

He directed his attention to the viewers.

'Okay, everyone, so I'm about to check the votes for what we're going to call our son. You'll remember we asked you to choose from a shortlist of Rio, River and Ryker. So let me take a look. And with 42 per cent of the votes, I can now tell you our little man is called... River!'

Red hearts flooded the screen again, and he kissed the crown of his son's head. A graphic of a shampoo bottle appeared on screen alongside the price.

'Thanks, guys,' Cadman added. 'And don't forget to vote in next week's poll for his middle names. Okay, River—ooh, that trips off the tongue nicely, doesn't it?—let's get you fed and into this new outfit, which was kindly gifted to us by BoyClobber.org.'

The floor illuminated in different pastel shades as father and son made their way to a changing table in the nursery.

Gabriel logged out, unstrapped his headset and returned to the lounge in their Real World house. His eyes were drawn to the walls, with the shadows of missing paintings and the indents in the carpet where furniture had once been purposefully arranged before they'd been forced to sell it all. The gym now contained just one workout bench and a handful of free weights. The swimming pool had long been drained and covered with tarpaulin. Even his autonomous sports car had repossessed itself and driven itself back to the dealership when they'd missed too many payments.

He hoped Cadman would be right and that they were on the cusp of change. Maybe then Gabriel's guilt at having ruined everything for them might lessen.

6

CONTESTANTS: Dimitri & Zoe Taylor-Georgiou
AGES: 46 and 44
STATUS: Married twenty-five years
OCCUPATION: Mortgage advisor and teacher
METACHILD: Son, Lenny
IN THEIR OWN WORDS: 'Everyone knows our story already. Now it's time to change the narrative and allow us a happy ever after.'

'Dimitri! I need you!'

'Almost there,' Dimitri replied as he changed into his haptic suit next to his wife.

'Hurry up!' Zoe snapped.

'Why, what's wrong?'

Her concerned husband threw on his headset, logged in, then ran through their Metaverse house until he found Zoe in the nursery. She turned to face him, clearly flustered.

Baby Lenny was lying on a mat on his changing table, his mother holding both his ankles up high with one hand, the other hand cupped under his bottom. Something wet and yellow sat in a pool in the palm of her hand.

Dimitri burst out laughing.

'What the hell are you doing?'

'I don't know!' She cringed. 'I was in our bathroom when the Push notification for a nappy change went off. I started changing him but forgot to grab a nappy first and before I knew it, it was coming out like a Mr Whippy ice cream.'

'Hold on,' Dimitri replied as he rummaged through the drawers for a fresh nappy.

'It's just so...warm. Urgh. And oh my God, the smell! Where is it coming from?'

'It's from the same device above the door that pumps out the new-baby smell when we're with Lenny,' he chuckled.

'And stop laughing at me! This is not funny.'

'I know it's not...well, maybe a little bit. I'm sure when you watch the highlights show tonight you'll see the funny side.'

'What?' Zoe said, aghast. 'Viewers won't see this, will they?'

'They're livestreaming now, aren't they? Where do you think all these red hearts are coming from?' He pointed to the flurry fluttering across the screen, suggesting viewers' shared amusement.

'Well, I'm going to look like a bloody idiot if I can't even change my own baby without ending up with a handful of sh—crap.'

'I promise, you don't. You look like every parent with a newborn who's keeping you on your toes. Did you see the poonami Woody and Tina dealt with yesterday? They had to cut their baby's clothes off with scissors. With scissors.'

'Have you finished yet?' Zoe asked her son.

'Nope, he must be a bit backed up.'

'How can something so small produce so much? He only drinks milk. Is this normal? Do we need to call an AI doctor?'

'Every baby is different,' Dimitri added as he handed her a packet of wet wipes. She cleaned up Lenny and fastened the nappy.

Zoe leaned in to Dimitri, who offered her a reassuring peck on the cheek.

'I just feel a bit rubbish sometimes,' she said.

'You're not, I promise you. Right, now that he's made some room, he's probably due a feed.'

Zoe's avatar accurately represented her Real World appearance. A week before *The Family Experiment* began, her hair stylist had added coppery highlights to her textured bob. Eyeliner framed her golden-brown irises, and there was a smudge of foundation and burst of deep red on her already full lips. It made him wonder if perhaps both he and his avatar also needed a refresh. His increasingly untamed eyebrows resembled plump black slugs and it was cheaper and quicker to clipper what was left of his receding grey hair than to make an appointment to have it styled at the barber's in town. His white stubble shone tiny pinpricks of light through the surface of his olive skin. He looked every inch his forty-something years while his wife did not.

'Did you think he'd feel so lifelike?' Zoe asked, reaching for a milk bottle and placing the teat into Lenny's mouth.

Dimitri shook his head.

'I don't know what I expected,' he said. 'I know these suits help you to experience almost everything, but I didn't expect to feel each twitch or hiccup even when he swallows. The attention to detail is incredible.'

He looked at his son.

'I think he's beginning to look more like you than me,' he added.

'His eyes are big and round like mine but his skin colouring is darkening a little like yours. But I bet your mum will be happy if her grandson has a Greek nose.'

Zoe recalled the day they had spent with CGI artists in a London design and animation studio when nearly all sections of their faces and bodies were measured and scanned, from the sizes of their heads to their nose-to-lip ratio and width of hands, legs and feet. It had felt intrusive, but now she understood why. The more you saw of yourself in your MetaChild, the more like yours it was supposed to feel.

'Have you latched on yet, buddy?' Dimitri asked Lenny.

Zoe adjusted the tip's positioning so it pressed down upon Lenny's tongue. Finally the milk began to drain.

'There we go,' she smiled.

'Do you think we should have chosen the haptic suit with breasts?' Dimitri asked.

Zoe raised her eyebrows.

'If you want to sit here wearing a fake pair of boobs as you breastfeed our baby, then be my guest, darling. But that's where I draw the line.'

'That single dad apparently wore the suit with the electrodes to experience pregnancy and childbirth.'

'I'm not using gimmicks to prove myself as a parent. People either like us and want to support us, or they don't.'

'It's not that straightforward though, is it?' Dimitri reminded her. 'Because if viewers don't like us, we can spend the next nine months loving and raising this little man only to have him taken away from us at the end.'

A silence opened up, both aware of what the other was thinking, but neither willing to say it.

7

CONTESTANT: Hudson Wright
AGE: 22
STATUS: Single
OCCUPATION: Freelance software developer
METACHILD: Daughter, Alice
IN HIS OWN WORDS: 'I'm here to prove that single parents deserve their seat at the table. I might be young but I'm every bit as capable as a two-parent family.'

The first Hudson knew of *The Family Experiment* host Autumn Taylor's appearance on the sofa opposite him was when she spoke. His closed eyes snapped open at the sound of her honeyed voice.

'I'm sorry, I didn't mean to wake you,' she began.

'I wasn't asleep,' he replied. 'I'd never do that while I'm holding my daughter.'

His eyes fell upon the two-week-old infant, her sleeping head resting against his chest, his hand supporting her back. He wondered how much he had resembled Alice when he was her age. He had never seen a photograph of himself as a child. He could—and had—spent hours just staring at her. She closely resembled him, with shared dimples in their cheeks, bowlike lips and long dark eyelashes that framed sparkling blue eyes. He wondered if her hair would remain blonde or darken to almost jet black like his.

Before Autumn Taylor's arrival, Hudson had been enjoying a few moments of quiet contemplation on the garden balcony of his Metaverse high-rise apartment. The ten-square-metre outdoor space housed two L-shaped sofas with plump, cream-coloured cushions, a wooden coffee table and a selection of potted bay trees on white-tiled flooring. Space remained for additional furniture or foliage, but he didn't want anything to distract from the panoramic views across New York City's skyline. He was the only one of the cast of British contestants to have chosen an American city as his Metaverse home.

A Push notification had arrived the evening prior warning of Autumn's impending visit, but hadn't indicated a time. He was sure that was on purpose. Other contestants had been flustered by her grilling but he was prepared. From the moment his participation in the show had been announced, early online public opinion made it clear he was facing an uphill struggle. So the attire worn by Hudson's avatar today had been carefully curated. His casual, timeless outfit of light blue jeans and a black T-shirt, along with a pair of vintage black Adidas Gazelle trainers, was to remind viewers he was just like them. They were everyday clothes worn by an everyday man. And allowing one of Alice's small vomit stains to remain on a sleeve would remind viewers that MetaBabies were just as messy and unpredictable as their Real-World counterparts.

'It's lovely to meet her,' Autumn continued, briefly glancing at Alice. 'She's beautiful.'

Hudson recalled Autumn using the same words to three other sets of parents she'd interviewed so far.

'Now, of all the contestants competing in *The Family Experiment*, you're the one viewers are most curious about,' Autumn continued. She tucked one of her tousled blonde curls behind her ear.

'Oh really, why is that?' smiled Hudson. He already knew the answer, but he was going to make her work for it.

'Because you're the only single parent,' she replied. 'Which is a rarity these days.'

'But it shouldn't be. It's unfair to stigmatize those of us going it alone. Which is why I'm putting myself out there to be judged and criticized by an audience of millions.'

'The whole basis of the UK government's Marriage Act was about encouraging couples to create families and "help build back a better Britain".'

'And look how that turned out,' said Hudson. 'They made it acceptable to frown upon lone parents.'

'Was the principle such a bad thing?' Autumn countered. 'Studies demonstrate that couples are more successful at raising a child than sole parents. And there's also an argument that you're one person depriving two people of the chance of starting a family in this contest.'

Hudson rolled his eyes and rubbed at a scar that covered a square inch on the back of his right hand.

'If you're referring to the so-called statistics provided by the last UK government in their Marriage Act propaganda, well, they've all been debunked,' said Hudson. 'Their "evidence" claimed that only married couples could be truly happy, better parents and therefore more productive members of a working society. Unless you're a celebrity or wealthy, of course, because then no one bats an eyelid if you do it alone. But ordinary lone parents like me are just as resolute as two parents because we have no choice but to be exactly that. We have double the workload, double the responsibility, and we're just as happy and just as productive.'

Autumn changed tack.

'In your launch-night video, we saw that you were one of only two competitors to experience pregnancy from both sides. Some of your critics claim that by going through a replica labour, you've disrespected those biologically able to give birth and their uniqueness to do so.'

It was another question he was prepared for, but he feigned disbelief regardless.

'How on earth have I done that?'

'Because you are trivializing the very nature of a woman's role in bringing life into the world. You are saying that if a woman can do it, then why can't a man?'

'That wasn't my aim.'

'It might not have been, but surely you must agree that you can never truly understand what it's like to go through the birthing process?'

Autumn's delivery jarred him. Hudson thought back to the months of preparation he had subjected himself to before the series began. He had worn weighted suits to mimic the carrying of a child, he'd taken medication to replicate high blood pressure, he went through a mock labour in a birthing suit where electrical currents ran through his body to make his muscles spasm and jolt, copying with 90 per cent accuracy the pain of childbirth. Muscles were also forced into cramps, vertebrae stretched and internal organs wrenched. He had been through all of that to try to understand, not to be a gender tourist.

'I don't recall you asking Woody the same question when you interviewed him. He went through a simulated labour too.'

'But Woody isn't trying to be both parents.'

Hudson began to regret his confrontational tone when black hearts floated about the screen.

'Look, I am absolutely aware that I'll never know what it's really like to carry a live child or give birth,' he conceded. 'And while I don't think it's every man's duty to put himself through what I went through, it gave me a better idea of the joys and suffering a pregnant woman faces.'

However, Autumn didn't appear ready to abandon her point just yet.

'But you can never experience all the other pain, both physical and mental, that a woman goes through to try to get pregnant. The hopelessness, guilt and frustration when it doesn't work, early or multiple miscarriages, the anxiety of knowing you are responsible for a life growing inside you.'

Hudson realized he must tread carefully if he was to salvage this.

'You're right—of course I can't—and I apologize to anyone out there who thought that was my intention.'

By Autumn's pompous expression, she had the answer she wanted.

'Can we talk about your age?' she continued.

'I'm twenty-two.'

'Which makes you the youngest contestant in the competition. Most twenty-two-year-old men who haven't found their Match Your DNA partner are hanging out with their friends, going out, getting drunk, trying to find someone to take home with them. So why aren't you?'

'Because I was brought up to value myself and those I encounter. I had a fantastic relationship with my dad. He was a good man, a kind man, a funny man. Like me, he was a single parent, but he was sixty before he could afford to start a family with a state-approved surrogate. I know he would have loved to have been a part of my life forever but he died of a stroke shortly before my sixteenth birthday. I don't want my time with Alice to be cut short like that. And *The Family Experiment* offers people my age who can't afford to be a parent that opportunity.'

The interview ended soon after that, leaving Hudson and Alice alone again, apart from the millions watching. Later, he would check the response of viewers on social media. He hoped that he hadn't already ruined his chances. It was important viewers bought into his narrative because without their support, this would all be for nothing. And he needed it to mean something.

It had to.

8

NAMES: Selena & Jaden Wilson
AGES: 32 and 33
STATUS: Married, four years
OCCUPATION: Data analyst and personal trainer
METACHILD: Son, Malachi
IN THEIR OWN WORDS: 'The opportunity to have kids is not weighted in favour of couples like us. We can't afford to make our dreams come true on our own.'

'I don't like this,' whispered Selena to Jaden. 'I don't like this at all.'

They were standing in their Metaverse nursery as the avatar of a young woman they didn't know was cuddling their son, Malachi. Selena nervously tugged at one of her corkscrew curls. Jaden stared at his feet awkwardly.

'How much longer?' he asked.

Selena looked to the clock in her headset.

'Seven more minutes. This is just wrong. So wrong.'

'We have no choice, bae. It was part of the terms and conditions.'

'Doesn't mean we have to approve though, does it?'

It was a fan of *The Family Experiment* who was troubling them. She had won a monthly lottery draw to spend time with a MetaBaby of her choice and had picked the Wilsons' two-week-old infant. The winner couldn't see or communicate with Jaden and Selena, but they could watch her.

Selena scowled as the woman appeared to giggle as she stroked Malachi's short Afro-textured hair.

'She's fetishizing him,' Selena bristled. 'He's not a fucking toy.'

Finally, after seven long minutes of cooing, snuggling up to their child and inhaling him, her time was up. She glared in the direction of Jaden as if she could see him. And with something akin to hatred in her eyes, she vanished. It hadn't gone unnoticed by Selena.

'What the hell was that about?' she asked.

'God knows,' Jaden replied, willing his expression not to give him away.

Malachi hadn't appeared bothered by the intrusion in his routine and had taken it in his stride. *He must get his temperament from his father*, Selena thought.

Jaden returned to the cot, picked up his son and sat with him in his lap, a firm hand supporting his neck. Malachi became transfixed by brightly coloured, moving cartoon dinosaurs roaming ancient lands on the virtual wallpaper.

He had grown so much in the space of a couple of weeks and, while Jaden admitted to loving the baby part, Selena couldn't wait until Malachi could communicate with them. Because at present, they both spoke completely different languages.

As a data analyst, her job was to study figures. Numbers made sense. There was an order about them, a predictability. None of that applied to a child. She couldn't understand why one minute, Malachi might be smiling and reaching to tug at her hair, and the next, he'd be kicking his legs and flapping his arms, tearful and inconsolable. However, Jaden was a natural father. He seemed to immediately accept there was little in the way of logic attached to babies.

Selena was fond of Malachi, but there had been no all-encompassing rush of love when Jaden had first placed him into her arms. Mother and son were two pieces of a jigsaw that had been forced together. And she longed for a time when she might have a better handle on his needs. Not that she'd explained to Jaden how she was feeling. She was used to pretending everything was okay on the surface, while beneath, earthquakes rumbled. And she was anxious that their supercritical viewers didn't sense a disconnect between them. She couldn't give them any reason to believe that she was not 100 per cent invested.

She had to win this competition.

When Malachi's head drooped to one side, Jaden turned him around and gently stroked his back.

'Nap time, kiddo,' he said, then lifted him up to his shoulder until Malachi settled on a warm, comfortable spot partway between Jaden's neck and his chest. Selena yawned—his sleepiness was infectious.

'I'm going to start making dinner,' she whispered, and Jaden gave her a thumbs-up sign, then watched as she left the nursery and the Metaverse.

Jaden placed his lips on his son's crown. Malachi was the perfect blend of the two of them. His skin was closer to Selena's dual-heritage tone than his own darker complexion and he had her sepia-coloured eyes. But he had his father's full lips, long lashes and an early hint of a cleft chin.

'You're going to be a heartbreaker, kiddo,' he said quietly as red hearts floated across the screen. 'Just like your dad.'

He had already fallen head over heels for this boy, but it was something he could never admit to Selena. Because they had an agreement that she must believe he was sticking to: if he hadn't said yes, she'd have refused to enter the competition. Now, he couldn't let her doubt they were on the same page.

At least for the moment.

Awakening Entertainment's
The Family Experiment Welcome Pack

Your MetaChild

Welcome, intended parents and caregivers!

Here at Awakening Entertainment, we have developed a fully immersive experience for those who want to start a family, without the Real World constraints, for a fraction of the cost and within a safe environment.

Each of our MetaChildren uses extensive high-quality, ethically sourced datasets to deliver a child with a unique set of traits and an individual personality. This means they can accurately represent the child you might have had in the Real World.

However, this, of course, also means we cannot provide you with a training manual. The technology behind each MetaChild will evolve and adapt to its world in its own way, so that it can become a product of its surroundings. Your relationship with your MetaChild will help to nurture its cognitive, physical and emotional development and will be key to its personality, life choices and overall behaviour as they grow.

Awakening Entertainment will offer support along the way. In-App purchases such as schooling, healthcare and travel experiences will allow you to enhance their development and assist you in bonding.

Please remember that our team of moderators are here to enforce our acceptable use policy to ensure we balance your right to a family life and freedom of speech with our obligations to restrict any harmful, biased and/or discriminatory behaviour.

9

Woody & Tina

Tina was sitting on a stool at the island, her eyes flitting around the kitchen. The scratched work surfaces had seen better days, the boiling-water tap had long gone cold and the Smart sensor inside the fridge freezer had stopped ordering itself replacement foods when it was running low.

She recalled how the room had already looked dated when she and Woody had bought the house seven years ago. They had not bothered to decorate because it had never felt like a home. It hadn't been their first choice, but they didn't have much time to find anywhere suitable and far away from where they used to live. It also had to be affordable. Lawyers' fees had eaten up their savings and taken a chunk of money from the sale of their last house. It needed to be a home that could cope with complications, as Woody had put it.

Complications were the reason why so much time had passed since they'd last seen friends or family. *Complications* meant they couldn't allow anyone inside for even a casual visit. There were too many areas that would require an explanation, sections that were out of bounds to all aside from her and Woody. So many years had passed, and it still saddened her to reflect on loved ones they'd cast aside along the way.

However, the house didn't bother her quite as much now the majority of her time was spent in the Metaverse. There, she was living in relative luxury: an open-plan, single-floor modern home in a designer's vision of the Lake District with large and airy white rooms, floor-to-ceiling windows, framed moving photography projected onto walls, and all the mod-cons they couldn't afford in the Real World. Outside and beyond a walled garden they were surrounded by lush green forests and shimmering silver lakes. It was the kind of place you would want to show off to friends. If they had still had any.

Both Tina and Woody maintained amiable relationships with work colleagues, but only during office hours. Beyond that, they'd rarely leave the house for social engagements and often made excuses for why they couldn't attend group get-togethers, dinners or birthday parties.

The buzzing of her Smart watch caught her attention. Its tech monitored her skin temperature and sympathetic nervous system activity and alerted her when negativity was becoming prolonged. She reminded herself there was no room in her life right now for sad thoughts. She must concentrate on what she had, not what she'd lost. And the positives included a husband who adored her and their Meta-Child, Belle, who was now approaching the end of her third week.

Despite all her research and prior explanations from *The Family Experiment* psychologists, Tina hadn't been sure how she'd feel towards her daughter when she arrived. It had been her major concern when Woody had urged her to enter the competition. She knew that Belle would behave, sound and feel like a baby. But would falling in love with her really be possible?

The haptic suits had quickly swayed her. From the moment she'd first held her daughter in her arms, Belle had felt tangible. She had the weight of an infant, she could be picked up and carried around, cuddled and kissed, she was warm when hugged, her skin soft to the touch, and her cry was as piercing as any Real World child. She was perfect.

In the days that followed, both parents had spent as much time as possible with her, taking it in turns to attend to her needs. One slept in the Real World as the other dealt with night feeds. One took her for walks in her pushchair in digitally created landscapes while the other went to work. If they were fortunate, the couple could enjoy a couple of hours together at the start or finish of the day, much like most ordinary families. She hoped that one day, maternity leave would be an option for the parents of MetaChildren.

A pinging sound from the oven caught Tina's attention, indicating that the dish she had placed inside it earlier was ready.

'Smells good,' Woody said as he entered the room, rubbing his hands together. 'What is it?'

'A hotchpotch of whatever I found in the freezer,' Tina replied. 'You name it, it's in here.'

'Lucky dip day, my favourite.' He grinned a little too enthusiastically.

He was humouring her and she knew it. But until supermarkets stopped pushing up their prices, their menu was limited. She removed the pot and served its contents into bowls.

'Shall we eat downstairs tonight?' Woody asked. 'It's been a while.'

He always sounded hopeful when he made this suggestion. A flicker of uncertainty crossed her face, and she wasn't sure if he saw it.

'I can't,' she said, and forced out an apologetic smile. 'I have some invoices and bills to deal with.'

'Okay, next time,' Woody said, and she could sense his disappointment.

He made his way out of the kitchen, into the corridor, then descended the staircase until he reached the basement door. It was soundproofed, but out of habit he still hesitated, keen ears listening for signs of irregularity. He looked at the camera mounted above the door and steeled himself with a rehearsed smile that he knew would not be reciprocated once inside.

Then he pressed his thumb against the electronic padlock until it unclicked and opened.

A figure ahead scowled at him.

10
Cadman & Gabriel

'So you're almost a month into participating in *The Family Experiment*,' began host Autumn Taylor. 'How are you finding it so far?'

'We couldn't have asked for anything better,' Cadman replied, sweeping his hand through his cropped peroxide hair. 'It's already been quite the journey, but we're in it for the long haul.'

'What's been your biggest OMG! moment?'

'When we walked into the nursery to meet our son for the first time. Then we spent the first few minutes trying to work out which of our features he shares. He's definitely got my South-East Asian eyes and lips, but he has Gabriel's red hair and grey eyes.'

'And what's been your WTF? moment?'

'I don't think we've had one, touch wood.'

'Any regrets?'

'Only that I'd like to be able to spend more time with him,' Cadman said, his tone apologetic. 'But like most parents, work gets in the way.'

Try taking a break from social media for five minutes and you can spend all the time you want with him, thought Gabriel.

'Is it more or less stressful than when you were inside that situation room when the driverless cars were hacked by terrorists?' Autumn continued.

The day she was referring to had altered the course of Cadman's career. Hackers had hijacked eight driverless vehicles and had encouraged the public and a select jury to choose the passengers who they believed should survive and who should die.

Cadman and a specially assembled team had been brought in to interpret which passengers were gaining public support and who was lagging. But no one in that room had realized their heated debates were being livestreamed across the world. It was Cadman's brash, no-nonsense approach that had made him a star.

'Oh, believe it or not, that was a doddle compared to parenthood!' Cadman continued, before recognizing the flippancy in his answer. 'What I mean to say is, that day was a brief snapshot in my life, over and done within hours. Although I appreciate that for the families of the many victims, it's something that will remain with them forever. But raising a child is a lifetime commitment.'

'It won't be if you don't win,' Autumn said.

'Now, now, Autumn, you know me better than that. I play to win.'

'So you're looking at this as a game?'

'Now you're putting words in my mouth. I'm taking parenthood very seriously.'

Autumn's sing-song voice was irritating Gabriel. She had placed herself on a sofa next to them in their Metaverse lounge. At least, he assumed it was still their lounge because it had been completely refurnished since his last visit earlier that morning.

To prepare himself for what to expect from her, he'd watched a selection of first-month interviews she'd completed with other *The Family Experiment* contestants. Then he'd fallen into a YouTube rabbit hole and watched dozens of her chats with A-list celebrities in her other streaming commitments before finding himself envying her travel vlogs. It had been a long time since he and Cadman had been to the places she was regularly travelling to.

And he'd been solely responsible for that.

He knew Autumn and Cadman had distanced themselves a little from their influencing careers following the fallout of the suicide of fellow influencer Jem Jones, whose death had been marred in controversy. Cadman had continued as a media commentator and pundit, while Autumn had transitioned into one of the country's most sought-after presenters. Gabriel knew how much her success quietly irritated a green-eyed Cadman.

'And how has becoming parents affected your relationship?' Autumn continued.

'It's brought us closer together, hasn't it?' said Cadman, crossing his legs.

Gabriel flipped an imaginary switch that turned on a smile.

'Oh definitely, yes.'

'Tell me how?' Autumn said.

'Because we're working for a common goal,' said Gabriel. 'To give River the best start in life that we possibly can.'

'And what do you say to people who believe that it's not a life? Because there are some very vocal critics who are opposed to this process and who want to shut it down. Especially following baby Olivia's tragic death.'

'Just look at him,' said Cadman, pointing to River. He was lying in a swinging cradle and reaching for the unreachable virtual birds flying above his head. 'He's beautiful, isn't he? I'd say to the critics, have a MetaBaby of your own and then tell me it's not real. Once you feel their heartbeat against your chest and they smile at you for the first time, it's no different to having a child in the Real World.'

'And Gabriel, how are you doing health-wise now?'

Gabriel's toes curled at Autumn's feigned concern.

'I'm good, thanks,' he politely replied.

'Viewers couldn't have failed to have been touched by your launch-night video. A lot of people out there are rooting for the three of you.'

'That's very kind of them.'

Autumn appeared to be waiting for him to expand upon his answer. But Gabriel wasn't willing to give her what she wanted. So she returned her attention to Cadman, and the two chatted some more before the interview ended and her avatar vanished.

'You should have played the sympathy card,' Cadman said after returning to the Real World soon after Gabriel. 'Made more of it. "I'm a survivor", that sort of thing.'

'Should I have thanked God? Cried a bit? Can avatars even produce tears?'

'Yes and yes and there's no need for your sarcasm. What harm would it have done to show your vulnerable side? You can never forget this is a competition, and we are in it to win.'

'And perhaps you need to remember that, first and foremost, we're supposed to be parenting that little boy,' Gabriel retaliated.

'Who's not actually real.'

'It doesn't matter.'

But he was surprised at how disheartened Cadman's dismissal of their son made him feel.

'Viewers will know if you're faking it. Pay him more attention. Act like a dad even if you don't want to be one.'

'Of course I want to be his dad,' Cadman hit back. 'I am his dad. When do I stop trying to provide for this family? If I'm not with River then I'm trying to organize sponsorship for him. Everything I do is for us. Let's not forget why we are in this position in the first place.'

Gabriel's face soured. But Cadman was right—and still using it against him.

11

Dimitri & Zoe

Lenny's incessant crying had continued for much of the evening and Dimitri was no closer to discovering why. He'd paced around their Metaverse house a dozen times carrying his son and hoping the movement or vibrations might calm him, but to no avail. Eventually he came to a halt outside. Neither he nor Zoe had known much about Japanese gardens when they'd made their in-App purchase, only that they were traditionally areas of serenity. Clearly Lenny hadn't read the description, thought Dimitri.

He ran through his checklist, but his son wasn't hungry—he'd tried and failed with a bottle of formula—his nappy wasn't full, he didn't appear to have trapped wind, he wasn't overheated and he was too young to be teething. The medical kit App checked everything from the boy's temperature to his heart rate, his rate of breathing and oxygen levels. All were within normal range. As a last resort, he'd scanned the internet in the hope of discovering a MetaBaby hack or some kind of manufacturer's instruction manual. Neither existed.

In the end, he concluded that Lenny must be midway through the Witching Hour, the period when an otherwise content baby suddenly cries and screams for no apparent reason. It could last five minutes or five hours. Dimitri paced the garden instead, ready for the long haul, and wished he could take his son's discomfort away.

For the most part, Lenny had been a relatively easy baby to care for these last three and a half weeks. Push notifications had only appeared on their Audites or wearable tech when he was hungry or awake or needed changing. 'Low maintenance,' was how Zoe had described their son to Autumn Taylor during their first-month interview.

Dimitri wondered if his Real World family was keeping abreast of their progress. They'd showed little enthusiasm when he and Zoe had broken the news of their planned participation in *The Family Experiment*. He had assumed they'd embrace the notion of a grandchild.

'A baby in a computer game?' his mother had scoffed.

'It's not a game,' Dimitri had replied. 'It's the same principle as parenting, only in a different setting. It's our job to raise our son or daughter as we would a biological child.'

'Call it what you want but it's still not real, is it?' said his brother Christos. 'I kept animals on a Facebook farm when I was a kid, but the novelty soon wore off and they starved to death.'

'I'm hardly likely to forget to feed my child,' he'd retorted.

'You've never been very good when it comes to responsibility,' his mother had added.

Dimitri had glared at her, as if daring her to continue verbalizing her train of thought.

'Otidípote,' she had huffed in her native Greek, bringing the night to a swift halt.

Their friends, however, had been more encouraging. Zoe's colleagues at the school where she taught two days a week had even held a virtual baby shower, gifting her purchases of baby clothes and useful product Apps. And three days after they'd entered their Metaverse nursery and discovered a newborn Lenny asleep in his cot, a group of Dimitri's friends had appeared in the virtual world to wet the baby's head, albeit with virtual drinks and no hangovers the next morning.

'You deserve this,' his closest friend, Karl, had told him. 'After everything, you're owed a second chance.'

Finally, Dimitri and Zoe were beginning to believe they had made the right decision to enter *The Family Experiment*. Because even up until launch night, they'd both harboured doubts.

They had been in the spotlight before and it had almost destroyed them.

Dimitri had been so lost in thought that he hadn't noticed Lenny had finally stopped crying and was drifting off to sleep. He remained where he was, his attention caught by the lights illuminating the stepping stones leading across the garden and in the direction of a water basin in the corner. It contained a solitary engraved kanji character, which, translated, meant forgiveness.

It was something he could only wish for.

12
Selena & Jaden

It had been Jaden's turn to respond to the Push notification alerting them that Malachi was awake and his nappy needed changing.

Selena remained in the kitchen, glancing out from the window of their Real World flat above a row of empty high-street shops and overlooking a supermarket car park. It was a far cry from the floor-to-ceiling windows in their Metaverse home, which stretched out across the Grand Canyon and the milky-blue waters of the Colorado River.

A figure caught her eye, hovering by the recycling bins. They appeared to be holding something up close to their face. Selena assumed it was a camera. Even though the few remaining traditional print newspapers had agreed not to dig too deeply into contestants' backgrounds in exchange for exclusive access and interviews once the competition ended, it hadn't applied to social media. All that Awakening Entertainment could do was use seek-and-destroy bots to bury anything with key words it didn't approve of throughout the internet and Metaverse. Selena pressed a button on the windowsill and the blind above it unspooled.

She used her alone time to log on to her banking App. Both her current account and their joint savings displayed the same balances as when she'd last checked days earlier. Each time she did this, she wondered if there might come a time when she could completely trust Jaden. But these reassurances were the only way to stop the small voice in the back of her head from becoming a roar. Sometimes she wondered if secretly she had wanted to be proven right, and that he was going to break her heart again. Because waiting for him to slip up was exhausting.

Two years had passed since instinct had first warned her something was awry between them. He was tall, muscular and strikingly handsome, and his job as a personal trainer brought out the flirt in him, no matter the gender.

'You're a stereotype,' she had once teased. But until that point she had never doubted that he was faithful.

However, when he began spending more and more time away from their house, she'd convinced herself that someone else was preoccupying his time. And one night, she followed him to a Metaverse access point cafe where he'd hired a booth. She slipped on her Smart glasses and found him in an online casino, then watched in dismay as he lost thousands of pounds. She quickly logged on to their bank accounts and discovered that almost everything they had saved to start a family of their own had vanished. His personal accounts also revealed debts, and loans he'd taken out without her knowledge.

'How could you?' she yelled as she burst into the room and shoved him, hard.

'I didn't mean for it to happen, I just got carried away,' he replied apologetically.

'Carried away? *Carried away?* More than £100,000 of debt isn't being *carried away*! How the hell are we going to pay it back?'

'I've been on a losing streak. All I need is a big win, and I promise you, it's near.'

'Everything we've saved for the IVF fund, gone in a few weeks. You know we can't have kids without it.'

Selena had been just twenty-eight and a few months into her marriage when she'd discovered that, like her mother before her, her own body was going through an early menopause. Having always wanted a family, she had been devastated. Fortunately, on her mother's advice she'd frozen her eggs in her late teens. However, the rising cost of IVF and the NHS+ refusal to offer it for free meant the couple had no choice but to save up and privately fund it. Selena had calculated that in another twelve months they would have had enough for at least a first round.

But not any more. Her happy-ever-after ending was not meant to be.

'I'm sorry,' Jaden said, 'I'll find a way to make it up to you.'

Selena had packed her bags and walked out on him that same night.

In the year that followed, they had been forced to sell their house and move back in with their respective parents. Jaden had made desperate attempts to win her back, attending Gamblers Anonymous meetings, surrendering all access to his finances to her, and aside from his personal training work, he'd taken on an extra job as a maître d' in his parents' Caribbean restaurant. Against her family's better judgement, her frosty resolve had begun to thaw.

'You can't go back to him,' her sister Krystal had warned.

'He's changed,' she argued.

'Addicts like Jaden don't change.'

'But he's my DNA Match. You can't just let go of your soulmate.'

'Yes, you can! All you've ever wanted is a successful career and to have kids, and he's depriving you of one of them. Find someone who will respect your aspirations, not destroy them.'

But Krystal had been wrong, Selena thought now. Because they had found a way to start a family, even if it wasn't a traditional type. However, she hadn't made it easy on Jaden when he'd first presented her with the idea of a MetaBaby.

'You think that playing at being parents in a computer game is the same as having a child of my own?' she'd asked in disbelief.

'No, no, it's not a game, bae,' Jaden replied. 'It's an immersive experience. It's the next best thing to being a parent.'

'I don't want the next best thing, though!' she objected. 'I don't want a substitute—I want the actual thing. I want a child—one I've carried, one I've given birth to, one I can physically hold, touch, communicate with, love.'

'You'll be able to do most of those things with a virtual one.'

'Oh, shut up! They're no different to those toys my parents played with when they were kids. What were they called... Tamagotchis.'

Jaden shrugged.

'Battery-operated games with digital pets you had to feed and pay attention to, or they'd die.'

The Family Experiment

Jaden didn't dispute the comparison. But still he persisted.

'There's a prize fund,' he continued. 'If we win, we get enough money to start a family of our own. A real family.'

Suddenly he had Selena's attention. She'd eventually agreed to watch the show's promotional video, then participated in a taster session in the Metaverse, nursing, playing with and feeding a MetaBaby. They had both been taken aback by how immersive the experience had felt. Eventually, she had agreed they could fill in an application form, as long as Jaden remembered that their end goal was to start a Real World family.

Today, Selena slipped on her Smart glasses and watched her husband tenderly stroking the back of his sleeping son's head.

'Remember why we are doing this,' she muttered to herself.

Because that small voice in the back of her mind, that had once warned her of her husband's behaviour, was once again threatening to roar.

Chats

TV / Reality TV Shows / **The Family Experiment**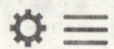

RealityBites, 14.03 p.m.
Anyone warming to Zoe & Dimitri yet???

TellyBob, 14.03 p.m.
Yes to him, no to her. Didn't like her twelve years ago, don't like her now. Although that baby shitting in the hand thing made me LOL.

FaffyDuck, 14.04 p.m.
I can never unsee that. *Bokes*

HotJam12, 14.04 p.m.
I'm #TeamWoody&Tina. They seem pretty normal. Well as normal as you can get for two grown adults pretending a computer game is real.

RealityBites, 14.05 p.m.
Hate myself for it, but kind of warming to Cadman. Used to think he was up himself, but I like his honesty. He's gonna milk that baby like it's a cashcow.

TellyBob, 14.07 p.m.
Must admit Gabriel is pretty easy on the eye. Wonder what he sees in the wealthy celebrity Cadman?

Timbo4, 14.08 p.m.
Liking Selena. I'da freaked too if some stranger was in my house.

4LeafRover, 14.14 p.m.
LOL! Can't work Hudson out though. Not the greatest move to have a go at national treasure Autumn Taylor last month, was it? Can't see him lasting the full nine months.

FaffyDuck, 14.15 p.m.
Don't trust him. Single dad + baby girl = more red flags than a Russian military display. #Paedo

MONTH TWO:
NINE MONTHS OLD

13

Woody & Tina

Woody's irises barely flickered as he looked up to the corner of his Smart contact lens.

'Can you come and help?' Tina's message read. 'I can't get Belle to settle.'

He located the list of pre-written responses.

'Soon,' he blinked before his eyes returned to the room and the company he was keeping. He would rather be with his wife and their just-turned-nine-month-old daughter than down here in the basement playing chess.

'Who's messaging you, Woody?' asked Issy from the sofa opposite.

Her index finger tapped against her thumb.

He should have known he was being clocked. Issy was frighteningly perceptive. She noticed *everything*.

'It's work related,' he replied.

'I didn't think you worked any more?'

'I went back a couple of weeks ago. Holiday cover, the occasional special project on weekends or evenings.'

'Another excuse for you to leave here as quickly as you can.'

Believe me, I don't need an excuse, he thought.

'That's not true,' he replied instead.

Issy shrugged, and a silence passed between them as he moved his rook, preparing to attack her king from the side. As Woody awaited her next play, his attention drifted towards the bifold basement doors with their one-way glass. Outside, a set of concrete steps led into the small section of the garden they'd designated as Issy's. It was surrounded by high wooden fencing and overgrown leylandii standing guard around the perimeter. There were no neighbours to overlook or overhear them. Beyond her garden lay theirs.

'This thing itches,' Issy said, and scratched furiously at her forearm.

'It shouldn't,' he replied. 'Let me take a look.'

Issy's eyes burrowed into his as he examined her skin, but he offered little in the way of a reaction.

She must have been scratching it before his arrival, he thought, because the area was a glowing red compared to the whiteness of the rest of her arms.

'I'll get some antiseptic cream from upstairs. You might have a slight infection.'

'Well, Dr Woody, maybe you shouldn't have put it inside me in the first place,' she snapped. 'Why do I need a tracking device? It's not like you ever let me out of here, is it?'

'The last one had expired, and it's not just for tracking, is it?' he countered.

It was the same conversation that had passed between the two of them a hundred times before. And it was always followed by him concluding that they'd let her out of the basement when the time was right, but no, that time wasn't now. She would have to be patient. However, that word wasn't in Issy's vocabulary. And as a result, she had made numerous escape attempts. Once, she had swung a chair over her shoulder and tried to shatter the glass doors. But the previous occupants had a teenage son who used the space for band rehearsal so they had installed soundproof, extra-toughened glass.

Last month, Issy had found a screwdriver wedged behind a disused boiler. During her morning outdoor exercise break, Woody had left her unattended while he used the bathroom. On his return, he found her unscrewing a fence panel. A minute later and she'd have squeezed through the gap and vanished. They had not allowed her out since, even accompanied.

Woody let go of her arm and made his way to the basement door. 'I'll go find that cream,' he said.

'Tell Christina to get it,' Issy replied.

'She's at work,' he lied.

Issy's eyes narrowed. 'She's working a lot lately. Not trying to avoid me, is she?'

'Of course not. Why would you think that?'

'Because Christina only ever visits with you or when you're busy. And when she is here, she's preoccupied.'

'With what?' Woody asked, and tried to shrug off the nervous shiver skittering along his arms.

No, she can't know, he thought. Issy's Metaverse access was strictly regulated only to sites and Apps they had pre-approved. And *The Family Experiment* was most definitely not one of them.

'You tell me,' she replied.

She was fishing, he could sense it.

'She's been doing a lot of shifts,' he replied.

'Well, please tell Christina when you see her next that it would be nice if she could show her face every now and again.'

'Must you keep calling her that?'

Issy threw her head back and laughed.

'What would you like me to call her, or you for that matter? Mum and Dad? You have to earn those titles, Woody. And you don't do that by locking your daughter inside this house, do you?'

14
Hudson

Hudson leaned across the cot's railings and gently stroked his daughter's cheek with his finger. Her warmth radiated through his haptic glove.

He took advantage of her slumber to make his way into the lounge and sprawl out across the sofa on the garden balcony of his Metaverse apartment.

The Meta Big Apple was less overcrowded than its counterpart, but its skyline still teemed with high-rise apartment blocks, offices and hotels. They'd been part of the appeal for Hudson. It didn't matter if these buildings were inhabited by AI-operated avatars or subscribers accessing the metropolis via their headsets—he needed to feel the presence of others.

As he closed his eyes, he recollected his first night at a mysterious location he'd called home for the best part of a decade. He and the rest of that group of confused and wary young people had been standing outside a seemingly dilapidated building, unsure of where they were or how they'd got there.

Those who'd survived the swim to the French coastline from the sinking dinghy had been loaded into a sheep truck, and the last thing he recalled with clarity was watching the sun rising through the metal bars when they'd parked at a stop-off point mid-route. Ravenous mouths had demolished cheese sandwiches and cartons of fruit juice from paper bags thrown inside by their captors, before eyelids became too heavy to hold open. Each drifted off into a drug-induced sleep, awaking groggily in a third mode of transport with plastic strips binding their wrists together and material covering their eyes. It was anyone's guess where in Europe they had been transported to.

'Blindfolds off,' a heavily accented female voice had announced as she cut each child's restraints.

Then they'd been escorted from a minibus parked inside an open concrete quadrant. Four buildings several storeys high surrounded them in a square-like formation. Beyond disused machinery, broken glass and rubble was a black iron staircase leading towards two white doors. The only sight of the world beyond them was the sky.

Dog tags on silver chains around each child's neck were scanned by a guard before they were made to queue in front of manned tables. One at a time, a guard would push up the sleeve of a right arm to completely expose their hand before their dog tags were placed inside a kiln-like device for a few seconds, glowing red when removed. A second guard held Hudson in a vice-like grip as his tags were then branded onto the back of his hand. As he screamed, something was sprayed into the newly scarred area which numbed it almost immediately.

He clutched his hand as they were led up a staircase into a holding room. While the exterior of the building appeared to be nearly derelict, inside was completely different. There, everything was white, smooth and clutter-free.

Each child was ordered to remove their clothes, but any self-consciousness was overshadowed by fear. They showered under jets of lukewarm water fired at them from all angles. The next room contained a gassy mist which clung to their skin, and, on exit, they were given painful injections into their upper arms and thighs. Blood samples were taken, their mouths swabbed and their bodies scrutinized by something he overheard being called an MRI scanner. Only then were they permitted to dress in their identical uniforms of grey trainers, sweatshirts, joggers, fleeces, socks and underwear.

Finally they were escorted into one of two huge arctic-white dormitories, separated by an expansive bathroom with multiple toilets and sinks, all adjacent to one another. Privacy was impossible. Hudson was assigned a bottom bunk containing a sheet, a pillow and a medium-weight single duvet. It was luxury compared to the sheep truck.

That first night, he'd sat on the edge of his mattress and taken in his surroundings. There must have been around a hundred or so young people there, most of whom he didn't recognize and who hadn't come from his dinghy. Very few of them spoke to one another, as if afraid of potential repercussions.

A blonde-haired girl with cartoon-like large blue eyes had ascended the ladder to the bed above Hudson's and offered him the briefest flash of a smile. He reciprocated, but soon afterwards an announcement came through speakers warning them that their lights were about to be switched off. Hudson climbed under his duvet, pulled it up to his chin and rolled onto his side as the room fell into darkness—though a faint illumination came from a ceiling covered in screens containing images of a half-moon and stars. He closed his eyes, but each time sleep seemed within grasp, he awoke with a jolt.

His dreams when they came were replete with floating bodies, each trying to grab hold of him. Even today in his Metaverse apartment, he could still feel their hands trying to drag him down below the surface and into their watery grave.

A whimper came from a sleeping Alice in the nursery, so he returned to her, stroked her neck and checked the digital display on her Smart mattress. Her vitals were all well within range.

'Keep sleeping, baby girl,' he whispered.

He felt her hand make its way to his fingers, and she clasped them tightly as she settled again.

He had never told her or anyone since that hers was the first hand to have held his in a decade.

15

Selena & Jaden

'Is there a real human being behind this avatar or are you AI?' began Selena. 'Be honest with me.'

'The last time I looked in the mirror, I was very much real,' smiled the woman.

'You sound genuine, but that doesn't mean much these days, does it?'

The two avatars sat opposite one another in tall-backed armchairs, Selena with her arms firmly folded and legs crossed at the ankle. She noted how the other woman was fashionably dressed in trousers and a long-sleeved top and exhibited a fresh, flawless complexion. People rarely chose grey roots or heavily lined eyes for their avatars, Selena reminded herself. Herself included.

'And this conversation is completely off the record?' Selena continued. 'It won't be filmed or broadcast?'

'We at *The Family Experiment* have a duty of care to offer counselling sessions to all participants as and when requested. Shall we start by asking why you made the appointment?'

Selena rubbed the fingers inside her haptic glove across the chair's leather arms.

'I think I need some help to process everything that's been happening over the last few weeks,' she began.

'That's understandable. Becoming a parent is a difficult adjustment for anyone to make, and that's without the world watching and commenting on your every move. So how are you finding motherhood?'

'Malachi took to weaning straight away, he's hitting all his development goals and he began crawling a couple of weeks ago. I'm probably biased and I have no frame of reference, but he seems like a fast learner.'

'That must be reassuring. However, I asked how you were adjusting, not how your son was developing.'

Selena's body tensed.

'I'm doing better, now.'

'Was there a point when you were finding it harder?'

'It was tough at the very beginning, and I know I wasn't as hands-on as I should have been, which made it hard for Malachi and me to bond. But now that he's more responsive, I think I'm finding my feet.'

'And your husband? How is Jaden coping?'

'He's taking it all in his stride. Malachi was already teething at the start of this nine-month Development Leap, which made him grizzly. But Jaden has an infinite amount of patience.'

'Has he adjusted to this process better than you?'

Selena considered the question.

'I didn't expect him to give so much of himself to fatherhood.'

'In what way?'

'In that I didn't think that he would throw himself into the process to the degree he has. He's absolutely all-in, 110 per cent. It's like he's been doing it for years. And it makes me question whether there's something wrong with me because it's taking me longer. Maybe I'm not as maternal as I'd expected to be.'

'And is there a small part of you that resents Jaden for finding his feet sooner than you?'

Selena lowered her eyes.

'Um, perhaps a little, yes.'

'Whose idea was it to participate in the show?'

'Jaden's.'

'And what prompted his interest?'

'Where do I begin?' she sighed. 'He had—has—a gambling problem, and two years ago lost all the money we'd saved to start a family.' Selena snapped her fingers. 'It went just like that. So having a virtual baby is his way of making it up to me, for now at least. If we win the competition, we can afford to have a Real World child of our own.'

'And you are prepared for the consequences of what will happen to Malachi if you win?'

'Yes, I am.'

Selena was acutely aware how cold her admission sounded.

'I assume Jaden's gambling addiction put a strain on your relationship?' the counsellor continued.

Selena let out a humourless laugh. 'You could say that, yes.'

'Why did you stay with him?'

'We split up for about a year, but I guess I went back out of stubbornness, determination, hope...'

'You haven't mentioned "love".'

'Look, Jaden's not a bad guy. And I don't think he means to hurt me, he just makes stupid decisions.'

'Do you think he's stopped making "stupid" decisions?'

'Yes.'

'But you're still not happy.'

Tears slowly trickled down Selena's cheeks.

'Because I can't get past how much he's hurt me and what he's taken away from us.'

The therapist gave her a moment to compose herself.

'Subconsciously, do you think you might have wanted Jaden to fail at fatherhood because then you'd have a reason to leave him?'

'I've had many reasons to leave him. More than £100,000 worth of debt was a good start.'

'Yet you're still together. What would your tipping point be? What would encourage you to walk away?'

'I honestly don't know.'

'Has Jaden been faithful?'

'As far as I'm aware. The only time I've had call not to trust him is when money is concerned.'

'But might he have had affairs, beyond your awareness?'

'Well, possibly, but I doubt it. I don't know when he'd have time, especially now.'

'Switching user.'

Selena cocked her head.

'I don't understand.'

'No yes no yes,' the therapist continued. 'Please hold. Server error 463. Rebooting.'

Selena glared as her therapist's expression froze, then began a repetitive loop of head movements before rewinding.

Selena let out a long, disheartened sigh.

'You lied,' she said. 'You're AI.'

'I'm as real as your dislike for your husband's behaviours,' the counsellor replied suddenly, although now with an alternative female voice.

'What I don't understand,' the counsellor continued, 'is why someone as intelligent as you would want a family with a man who has no respect for you?'

Selena sat back in her chair.

'Who the hell are you?'

'You're avoiding my question.'

Selena shook her head.

'Okay, I'm done with this. Goodbye.'

'I strongly suggest you wait,' the new voice replied.

'For what?'

'To hear what I have to tell you.'

'Which is?'

'You answer my question then I'll answer yours. Why do you want to start a family with Jaden?'

Selena hesitated, still unsure of who she was talking to now and whether she wanted to continue.

'Because despite his flaws,' she said eventually, 'he's a good dad to Malachi and will be for our biological child too. And I can't afford to have a child in the Real World without winning this competition. It's impossible.'

'Because you can't conceive naturally. You need the help of IVF.'

'How do you know that?'

'We know everything, Selena. For example, we know about three women living locally to you who are raising children on their own. And that you all have something in common.'

'And what's that?'

The avatar removed a folder from a bag and handed it to her. Both reluctant and curious, Selena opened it and flicked through a handful of photographs of three mothers, each with a young child. None of them were familiar to her.

'The four of you share Jaden,' the woman continued. 'He is the father of those children.'

16

Cadman & Gabriel

Gabriel was swallowing two bright pink tablets dispensed by his Smart bathroom cabinet when a Push notification appeared. The screen of his watch revealed moving images of two men standing outside his Real World front door, both clad in blue overalls and baseball caps with a logo on the front that he struggled to read. Behind them was a lorry with open rear doors. His immediate reaction was panic. The last time he'd been in this situation the men had been bailiffs and were here to repossess their furniture for money owed. Today, however, when he zoomed in closer, he spotted large objects covered in bubble wrap.

'Can I help you?' he asked nervously through the microphone.

'Delivery for a Cadman N'Yu?' one of the men began.

Gabriel threw on a pair of old joggers and a T-shirt as he made his way to the front door.

'Where do you want them, mate?' the first man asked.

Now Gabriel could see the lorry contained furniture and the men's caps read 'Home2Home Deliveries'.

'Sorry, you've lost me,' he replied. 'What is this stuff?'

'We've got a dining room table and six chairs, a three-seater sofa, cinema entertainment system, an ottoman and two sideboards.'

'And this is all in Cadman's name?'

The man looked to his tablet. 'That's what it says here.'

'Okay, well, I guess you should bring them in.'

He moved to one side and directed them where to place each item, though he knew Cadman would move them elsewhere later. He wouldn't be able to help himself. Gabriel signed a digital form and the men left.

'Ah, they're here already,' Cadman chirped as he entered the room.

His VR headset was perched on top of his head. 'I didn't expect them until the end of the week.'

'Whose are they? Why are they here?'

'They're ours. An online furniture supplier gifted them to us in the Real World, and the equivalent digital versions in the Metaverse,' he explained.

'And you didn't think to mention it before today?'

'I thought you'd be happy.'

'I am, I guess, but I'd have liked to have had a say. This is all to your taste.'

'As it always has been. You know I have a more natural flare for style than you.'

'I just thought things might be a bit more equal second time around.'

'We have bedroom furniture being shipped over from Italy at the end of the month, and after that I'll consult with you before I accept anything else. Oh, and guess what? You get your gym back tomorrow.'

'Really? What have you ordered?'

'Oh, I don't know, whatever the PR company offered.' He patted Gabriel's stomach. 'So that means we'll be saying goodbye to our unwanted house guest Mr Paunch, doesn't it?'

Cadman kissed a narrow-eyed Gabriel on the forehead and the two of them made their way into the Metaverse.

As Cadman worked, Gabriel was teaching nine-month-old River to mimic his claps and high-fives. Without warning, his son rolled onto his stomach, put his arms out in front of him and began to crawl towards a toy train.

'Yes, you clever boy!' Gabriel yelled as the screen filled with red hearts.

'What's going on?' Cadman shouted from the patio.

'He's started crawling!'

'Oh, what? When?'

'Just now.'

Cadman entered, rewound and viewed the live footage in his headset.

'This is fantastic news because now he's mobile, that's another opportunity.'

'For what?'

'What do you think?'

Gabriel glanced at the mute button so that viewers couldn't hear them. They were allowed ten minutes per day.

'Cadman,' he sighed. 'Can't you just enjoy the moment instead of trying to monetize it?'

'If we can encourage him to keep moving around the house, everything he passes will have the description appear on screen. New curtains, blinds, artwork, curtains, rugs, digital photo frames, everything. Our son has just opened a whole new world of opportunity for us.'

'Instead of appreciating his first crawl, you're trying to find a way it'll make us extra income,' Gabriel huffed.

'Well, one of us has to.'

Gabriel shut his eyes.

'Sorry, I didn't mean it to sound like that,' Cadman added. 'But the money we're making off River's back has already paid off our remaining debts so we're back in the black. But we still have a long way to go to get to where we were.'

'And what if I don't want to be where we were?' objected Gabriel.

'What's that supposed to mean?'

'What if having River in our lives is a fresh start for us? Something better and more fulfilling than what we had last time?'

Cadman glared at him as if he was speaking a foreign language.

'Remember the plan, Gabriel,' he said slowly and deliberately. 'Remember the plan.'

And without offering Gabriel a rebuttal, he turned off the mute button and returned to his work.

17

Dimitri & Zoe

Zoe didn't move; her body was frozen. She remained where she was, standing by the open front door of her Real World home, the padded envelope she had torn open and dropped moments earlier now lying by her feet. Her eyes darted all around her to see if the person who had posted it through her door was lurking somewhere, capturing her reaction. But as far as she could tell, she was alone.

Her hands trembled as she re-read the photocopied documents for a second time, in the faint hope that sleep deprivation was playing tricks on her and this was all in her imagination. She blinked hard, but the papers remained when she unclenched her eyes. Years ago, her lawyer had advised her that once the dossier was signed and stamped and the money started leaving her account, the court would seal the documents and they'd stay hidden for the remainder of her life. Yet somehow, they hadn't.

Someone knew what she had done.

A reanimated Zoe sprang back to life, picked up the envelope and stuffed the paperwork back inside it. Then she tucked her chin-length bob behind her ears and hurried up the stairs to bury the documents away under other paperwork in her office. Dimitri could not see this.

After taking a few moments to compose herself, she joined him in the garden of their Metaverse property. She relished spending time in the Japanese-style garden, listening to the gentle sound of the ripples, glancing up to a clear blue sky partly obscured by the pink blooms of cherry blossom trees. It was one of the few places that completely calmed her.

Dimitri was on his feet, his hands by his knees and holding on to Lenny's wrists as their nine-month-old son took his first tentative steps.

His brow was furrowed as he concentrated on placing one foot in front of the other to reach his mother, with Dimitri's support.

'Oh, look at you!' Zoe cooed, and sat a few metres away from them. 'You're doing so well. Just a little bit further.'

Lenny responded with a smile as wide as his face, and his bowed, chubby legs continued to sway as he stumbled towards her. For the briefest of moments, Zoe left the Metaverse and was transported back to a different time, a different place and a different her. She shook her head before the thought manifested itself into something that would linger and returned to the little boy, who had by now reached her lap. She clasped him tightly and nuzzled her mouth into his neck.

Dimitri looked at her, as if reading her mind.

'I was thinking the same thing,' he said as he knelt beside her to kiss her cheek. 'It's uncanny, isn't it?'

Zoe reached for her husband's hand and held it to her face. It was a rare show of outward affection from someone who struggled to readily show it. Dimitri remembered from all those years earlier that it had been her who the public hadn't trusted. She had borne the brunt of their blame. They had misjudged her as cold and prickly just because she hadn't worn her emotions on her sleeve. But that's not who she was. They hadn't known her the way he had.

Often, he found himself harking back to the halcyon days when they were teenage sweethearts. They were sixteen when they'd met via Match Your DNA, the company that had patented their discovery that every human in the world has a gene they share with just one other person. And that person—of any age, gender, sexuality, location, race or religion—was the person who you were scientifically destined to be with. Years had passed since a devastating hack, but after a rocky time, the company had built back larger than ever. Now, an estimated third of couples worldwide had met through it. It had worked for him and Zoe; they had been Matched and fallen in love the first time they'd met. Life was so much simpler then, he thought.

Now, he watched closely as Lenny grasped Zoe's shoulder, pulled himself up and with outstretched arms began walking by himself back to his father. A pause followed each step, but he soon found his confidence. He fell as he turned to make a detour, but picked himself up and continued again without complaint.

'Where's he off to?' asked Zoe.

Dimitri followed his son and the boy's line of sight.

'He's heading for the water trickling into that bird feeder,' he replied, pointing to the granite object.

'Come here, Lenny,' said Zoe, but he was too focused on his objective to listen.

'Lenny, sweetheart,' she said, and this time her son turned his head to face her. She beckoned with her hand. 'Come back to Mummy, please.'

'What's the problem?' asked Dimitri.

'That bird bath is too low. If he loses his balance, he could fall into it.'

'I'm right behind him, he won't hurt himself.'

Zoe hurried towards her son and scooped him up in her arms.

'No, no, I'm sorry, I don't feel comfortable with it.'

Lenny retaliated by kicking his feet and shrieking.

'Come on, Adam,' Zoe continued. 'You can practise walking inside where it's safer.'

'His name is Lenny,' Dimitri said gently.

'I know.'

'You just called him Adam.'

Zoe's face paled as she quickly turned on her heel and made her way inside the house.

Chats

TV / Reality TV Shows / **The Family Experiment**

> **TracyFenton, 3.27 p.m.**
> Did you hear what Zoe just said?

Bobster, 3.27 p.m.
No, what?

> **TracyFenton, 3.27 p.m.**
> She just called Lenny Adam.

Bobster, 3.27 p.m.
She got his name wrong?

> **TracyFenton, 3.27 p.m.**
> Yes, but she called him Adam. ADAM!

Bobster, 3.28 p.m.
OMG, now I understand! Deliberate or accidental?

> **TracyFenton, 3.28 p.m.**
> Wouldn't surprise me if it was deliberate. Using his name to make us feel sorry for her. Manipulative cow. #PoorAdam

Desper@telySeekingSus@n, 3.28 p.m.
Never seen an avatar go that pale before. I reckon it was accidental.

> **TracyFenton, 3.28 p.m.**
> Wouldn't trust her as far as I can throw her. #PoorAdam

18
Woody & Tina

'**Where have you been?**' asked an exasperated Tina. 'I messaged you fifteen minutes ago.'

Woody turned his head until the VR headset fitted snugly.

'In the basement,' he replied.

He failed to say 'with Issy' for fear of it being overheard by viewers through Tina's headset. She asked no follow-up question.

Now in the Metaverse, he could see his Metachild lying face down on the carpet and wailing, her small fists banging on the floor. Her concerned mother was kneeling by her side. Like any parent in either world, he hated hearing his child's distress.

'I take back everything I said about us having it easy compared to some of the other parents in this experience,' Tina continued. 'Every day this week she's had a mini meltdown and I just can't calm her.'

'It's our turn for the Monthly Challenge,' Woody replied. 'I bet you anything they are preparing us for the terrible twos. Maybe next Development Leap we'll have a threenager or be in the fucking fours. At least parents of Real World kids get a respite between these Leaps. Anyway, let's give her some space to calm herself down. Kids don't have tantrums in empty rooms.'

'Are you sure that's all it is?' Tina asked. 'Because this is how it...'

Her voice trailed off. She didn't need to finish her sentence for Woody to know what she was referring to.

'Mute,' he said aloud, and a red microphone symbol with a line drawn through it appeared in the corner of his headset.

Alongside it was a ten-minute stopwatch which began an automatic countdown.

'It's not the same as it was with Issy, if that's what you're thinking,' Woody said.

'Really? Wasn't it about this age when we started noticing changes?'

'Not at nine months. And I'm sure Belle is only going through the same changes every nine-month-old does. Issy was, well, Issy. I was reading up on it, and at thirty-seven weeks so much is going on in her head that she's probably struggling to process it and it comes out in big emotions. It's nothing to worry about. Trust me.'

As much as she wanted to, Tina couldn't. Woody had a habit of burying his head in the sand when faced with uncomfortable conversations. His reluctance had been one of the reasons she had been hesitant to enter *The Family Experiment* when she'd first read about it. That, and Issy. But the opportunity to have all they'd missed out on eventually became all too alluring.

'We've been robbed of so much,' she had told him. 'I want a chance to experience what every other parent experiences before it's too late. Holidays, first loves, cinema trips, girlie nights in... I just want to be normal instead of living in the shadows.'

'But what about Issy?' he'd replied.

'There's no reason for her to find out.'

'She'll know something is going on,' he argued. 'She's sharp. She's observant.'

'We've already put so much of our lives on hold because of her. We never got the chance to finish our job as parents. But we can with a MetaChild.'

'But what about the people who remember us? Who know what she did? They'll go to the press or plaster it across social media.'

'They haven't yet. There are so many search-and-destroy bots that remove any mentions of her or key words relating to what happened.'

Eventually she had talked him round.

'Sorry,' Tina replied, back in the present. 'I just freak out a little sometimes. I want this time around to be better.'

'And it already is, I promise you.'

Woody's eyes flicked towards the countdown clock. Three more muted minutes remained.

'But if we don't want Issy to pick up on anything, we must show her that nothing has changed. Are you seeing her today? She was asking about you.'

Tina rolled her eyes. 'I know I should, I just don't have the energy right now. Every time I go into that room she finds a way to start an argument over nothing.'

'To her it's not nothing.'

Quietly, Woody agreed. Issy had clashed with him again earlier that morning when he had returned to the basement with the antiseptic cream for her reddened arm. She'd claimed it was likely infected, that she could feel it spreading inside her, and that she'd need hospital treatment. Once again he'd had to explain why that wasn't going to happen.

'You know we had no choice but to keep you here,' he'd replied.

'Here in this house? Yes. Locked in the basement? No.'

'It was a compromise.'

Issy laughed out loud.

'*She* made you do it.'

Woody ignored her.

'You're fifteen now, sixteen soon, and in a few short years you—'

'My years are not short,' she interrupted.

'In a few short years, everything will change for you. You'll be an adult and you'll be out of here. We've saved enough money to give you a head start on finding a place of your own, or to go travelling or to apply for university far away from here. You'll be like every other young woman your age.'

'And how am I supposed to relate to any of these other "young women" when so much of my life has been spent locked away?'

'What would you have done if you were us?' Woody asked. 'We loved you too much to let you go.'

'I'd rather be capsized from a boat and sink to the bottom of the ocean like the kids they traffic instead of being held prisoner here by you.'

'Oh, Issy, stop being so bloody dramatic,' he snapped, then stood up and dropped the antiseptic on her chessboard, scattering the remaining pieces. 'I'll come and see you later.'

'Bye-bye, Woody,' she replied in a sarcastic tone. 'Send your wife my love.'

It would be so much easier to dislike Issy than to love her, Woody had thought. But he couldn't bring himself to. He would still do anything for her.

He returned to the present, and Tina.

'Issy's being a teenager—exhausting us is what they do best,' he said. 'All we can do is prepare her for the world as carefully as we can.'

'And how do we prepare the world for her?'

Woody didn't have an answer to that, so he pretended he hadn't heard.

19
Dimitri & Zoe

Moments of solitude were rare for Zoe, especially after the regular pandemic lockdowns meant that Dimitri was now working from home full-time too.

Their three-bedroom detached home had been inside one of the country's first Fifteen-Minute Cities, an urban planning concept where each suburb was within a fifteen-minute walk from everything its residents could need: shops, nature, employment, housing, leisure and healthcare. And then the Marriage Act had passed through Parliament and towns had been split into old and new sections. Those who had upgraded to a Smart Marriage received benefits including lower taxes, NHS+ healthcare and better schooling. Old areas received very little investment. But their Fifteen-Minute City became a no man's land, caught between the rich and poor. Which was how it remained to this day, and somewhere they couldn't afford to move from.

The rooms were of average size and the walls thin. While Zoe was ensconced in hers, remotely home-tutoring problem children who had been excluded from schools, she could often overhear her self-employed mortgage-advisor husband next door, headset on and discussing with clients the best loans on offer to afford their dream homes. On various occasions, he had found both him and Zoe mortgage deals that would have been perfect for them. But each time he'd presented them to her, Zoe had refused.

'We've been averaging a lockdown a year for the last decade,' she'd argued. 'We never know what's around the corner and I don't want to end up like we were before.'

'That was different,' he'd protested. 'We were different. We can't live our lives based on what-ifs.'

Working in such close proximity to Dimitri seven days a week meant Zoe sometimes felt as if the walls were slowly closing in on her. She was prone to bouts of anxiety that left her frustrated and desperately craving solitude—and the attention of someone else.

Someone her husband knew nothing about.

But lately, she was beginning to find the isolation she craved thanks to the arrival of MetaChild Lenny. Like most working couples in the Real World, their careers often prevented them from both being with their son at the same time. So when Dimitri was spending time with him and she was between classes, she would make the most of her downtime.

Such as now, when she grabbed the cord hanging down from the loft hatch, yanked it until the ladder appeared, then climbed it.

Once inside, she turned on the light, made her way to a dustsheet at the very back and yanked it away to reveal four long-forgotten suitcases lying beneath it. At least, they were forgotten to Dimitri, who hadn't set foot up here in years. To Zoe, a particular one of these cases, painted red and with black non-symmetrical spots to resemble a ladybird, was seldom far from her thoughts.

She gravitated towards it. Then she keyed in the combination to the digital lock until it popped open. Finally, she sat on the dusty floor, carefully opened the lid and removed a two-deep layer of books until she reached an object wrapped up inside a blanket. She unravelled it and beamed at the contents.

For a moment, she was convinced the eyes inside it were looking back at her.

20
Cadman & Gabriel

Months had passed since Cadman had last searched the house. Until that morning, when he'd awoken with an urge he couldn't ignore.

Gabriel's daily medication often left him with headaches and stiff joints. But it also placed him in a deep slumber each night, offering him unbroken sleep. Now Cadman was using this to his advantage. He silently slipped from between the bedsheets and set to work.

The only advantage of being forced to sell much of their furniture or having it repossessed was that there had been fewer places to hide any offending items. But now they were slowly filling back up again, it was going to take him longer. He began with the obvious places: the bathroom cabinet, kitchen cupboards and drawers, trouser and coat pockets, and chests of drawers. When there was nothing incriminating to be found, his fingertips inched around the edges of carpeting, feeling for sections that had been prised up. Then it was the turn of the curtain hems, inside the chimney-breast, behind radiators and pressed between the pages of books. Again, Cadman found nothing. However, he was too stubborn to admit he'd been wrong.

It was time for Plan B.

He took a swab from a kit in the bathroom, returned to the bedroom and held it to the lips of his sleeping partner. An unconscious Gabriel briefly opened his mouth at its touch, long enough for Cadman to slip the swab inside and graze the tip of Gabriel's tongue before removing it just as quickly. Then he made his way back to the bathroom, placed it inside a tiny liquid-filled bottle, sat on the floor and waited.

There had to be a reason behind Gabriel's recent change in behaviour. He'd been questioning Cadman's decisions more, and insisting on having his opinions heard. Cadman had much preferred him when he was agreeable. In fact, his malleable personality had been part of the attraction when they'd first met seven years earlier, along with his impressive looks and toned physique. Cadman's taste was unashamedly clichéd.

He'd dated men his own age—at the time, in their late twenties—and much older, but when it came to relationships, they demanded equality and he had neither the time nor the inclination to compromise. There was only room for one Cadman in a coupling. And the then-nineteen-year-old university student Gabriel was completely unaware of his own sense of self. He had done as he was asked and Cadman had shown him the world. They had ticked one another's checklists.

Gabriel had been intoxicated by Cadman's rapidly flourishing career as an influencer and expert in all things social media. Cadman was frequently courted by public-relations teams to use his channels to promote everything from holidays to nightclubs, airlines to hotels and premieres to parties. On one particularly memorable trip, they hadn't spent a single penny from the moment the driverless cab had picked them up from Cadman's London apartment until the day they returned from Mauritius, two weeks later.

It hadn't been difficult for him to persuade Gabriel to drop out of university midway through his second year. Cadman had reassured him that he didn't need a job, because being by Cadman's side was a career in itself. And while he wouldn't earn a living for it per se, he'd receive a weekly allowance, topped up by bonuses at Cadman's discretion. Gabriel hadn't argued, which had suited Cadman just fine. And their agreement had worked for years until Gabriel had taken a sledgehammer to their perfect life.

Today's early-morning sun sliced through the gap in the blind as Cadman propped himself up against the side of the roll-top bath. He recalled how after his involvement in the crisis room of the car-hacking years earlier, his workload had soared overnight, alongside requests for personal appearances. And when the volume of his assignments meant he couldn't attend every invitation, he'd appointed Gabriel as his stand-in. His partner was young, photogenic and affable. However, Gabriel lacked Cadman's confidence and hadn't enjoyed going alone.

'You can't keep shying away like a wallflower,' Cadman had advised him. 'I am a brand, and when you're at these functions, you represent me.'

'But I'm not like you,' Gabriel protested.

'Nobody is and I don't expect you to be. You just need to turn up, be seen and socialize.'

'I never know anyone.'

Cadman rolled his eyes. 'You have friends, I've introduced you to so many people on the circuit.'

'But they're your friends. It's you they want to be seen with, not me.'

By now, Cadman had had enough.

'Then make some friends of your own! Go out there and find yourself a tribe. I don't have time to keep holding your hand.'

So, reluctantly, that was what Gabriel had done. While Cadman worked eighteen-hour days, Gabriel walked red carpets alone and sat in VIP areas and hotels around the world, plucking up the courage to talk to people who had little interest in him without his famous partner.

And then, a switch had been flicked inside Gabriel's brain. His confidence grew and he'd become more assertive and unyielding. He was no longer Cadman's faithful Labrador waiting at home until his master returned. Dinner was no longer ready for him each night; sex was no longer on tap. Only later had Cadman discovered the cause, and it was why today he was concerned that history was repeating itself. He had to remain in control.

'You've tested me?' Gabriel's voice came suddenly.

Cadman opened his eyes and snapped his slumped neck backwards. The bones clicked. Gabriel was standing at the doorway, his hands on his hips, face like thunder.

'What time is it?' Cadman asked.

'Almost 6 a.m. A Push notification arrived to say River needs feeding, but you weren't there.'

'I must have drifted off.'

'You haven't answered my question.'

He pointed to the bottle with the swab poking from the top.

'Why and when?'

Cadman felt his cheeks flush.

'When you were asleep.'

'And is this a daily occurrence? A weekly one? Monthly?'

'It's the first time, honestly.'

'What could I possibly have done to make you want to test me? The Smart toilet you made us install already examines our pee and crap, and that'd tell you if there was anything to be worried about.'

Cadman suddenly felt foolish, a typically unfamiliar emotion. 'It was just, well, we've not been getting on lately, have we? You bicker with me about the clothes we dress River in, where we take him, how we're furnishing both houses...'

'Jesus, Cadman, I'm expressing an opinion. It's what people do. Or am I no longer allowed one?'

'Yes, but you know I prefer it when it's aligned with mine. This competition means we're always being monitored and judged in the Metaverse, so we can't be seen to be disagreeing.'

'I couldn't care less what strangers think.'

'Well, you need to care. I was studying the data my team harvested—'

'Cadman, I don't care,' Gabriel interrupted. 'The point is that you've tested me without my knowledge because sometimes I dare to think differently to you.'

Cadman didn't reply. Gabriel pointed to the bottle.

'Well, what does your precious test say?'

'I haven't checked it yet.'

'What are you waiting for?'

Cadman picked up the bottle but thought twice. He put it back down on the tiled floor instead.

'You're right,' he said awkwardly. 'I'm sorry. I trust you.'

Gabriel's glower suggested he didn't believe him. He shook his head and returned to their bedroom, changing into jeans and a T-shirt.

'Where are you going?' Cadman asked.

'To feed our son.'

'But I do nights and early mornings.'

Gabriel made no reply as he closed the bedroom door behind him.

Cadman picked up the bottle, ready to pour its contents into the toilet. But not before checking the swab first. It was negative. There was no trace of AZ in Gabriel's body or anything else prohibited.

But the relief he'd hoped to feel never materialized.

21
Selena & Jaden

Selena sat at her desk, trying her best to concentrate on the work before her.

She had lied to Jaden, informing him that for the next couple of weeks she would not be able to work remotely at home as she was needed in the office to help two new staff members in her team of data analysts get up to speed. The truth was that she had volunteered to be there. When she wasn't splitting Malachi's care with Jaden, she wanted to be as far away from her husband as possible. Because right now, she hated him.

She'd hoped that being out of the house might distract her from what she had learned. If she could focus on work, it would delay having to face the truth and make a decision. But her colleagues hadn't made it easy. They'd think up excuses to stop by her hot desk to talk to her, slipping in questions about *The Family Experiment* and Malachi, or requesting social media selfies. She had given up eating lunch in the staff canteen as she was fed up of all the eyes focused on her.

So today, she ventured out into a cafe and sat in a quiet corner where she picked at a vegan wrap. Her thoughts inevitably returned to the stranger who had taken her AI counsellor's place and had accused Jaden of fathering three children with three different women.

'You're lying,' Selena had sniffed, despite a cursory scan of the documents which the avatar had passed her.

'Why would I lie to you?' she'd asked.

'How the hell should I know? Maybe you know my husband in the Real World, maybe you've tried it on with him but he's told you he's not interested. He's a good-looking guy. Women—and men—are always flirting with him. But he's faithful to me.'

The Family Experiment

'I think they call this misdirected anger,' the avatar responded. 'Or is this another part of the show? Is this the Monthly Challenge?'

The avatar shook her head.

'I absolutely understand that the evidence I've given you is hurtful,' she continued. 'But what you decide to do with it is up to you. It makes no difference to me if you believe what I tell you or you dismiss me. You will find hard copies behind the grey wheelie bins below your Real World flat. And whatever you decide, I hope you find the happiness you deserve.'

Ten minutes later and Selena had been outside and discovered the package, a white padded envelope with her name printed on the front. She had tucked it under her sweatshirt and run back upstairs. On hearing Jaden in the spare room talking to Malachi in the Metaverse, she had locked herself in the bathroom and pulled out the paperwork the avatar had promised.

She had taken her time poring over it. Documents included three separate birth certificates, one for a boy and two for girls, all with Jaden's name listed as their father. One child was a year and a half and born to Meera Patel, and a second, thirteen months, born to a Kelly Hitchin. A third, Lucy, was born to Rebecca Reid ten months ago. Selena slipped on her Smart glasses and searched the women's social media profiles. All three had included many images of their children, but there was no sign or even a mention of a father.

Finally, there had been copies of the women's bank statements. Three transfers of £10,000, one from each woman, had been made into Jaden's savings account after the birth of each child. Selena had assumed he'd been repaying his debts with money earned from personal training and working in his parents' restaurants. Apparently not. But if he'd had children with these women, why were they paying him? Shouldn't he be paying for the upkeep of his offspring?

Back in the present, Selena dropped the half-eaten wrap back onto her plate. She had lost her appetite. She dabbed at the corner of her mouth with a napkin as a shadow crossed her. A vaguely familiar-looking young woman glared at her.

'Where is he?' the woman asked.

'Where's who?' a worried Selena replied.

'You know who! My son. What have you done with him?'

'What do you mean, *your son*?'

'That husband of yours took him from me,' she shouted. 'I want him back.'

Selena became conscious of the heads turning to face them, some now holding camera phones and others focusing Smart recordable glasses in their direction. She rose to her feet and grabbed her handbag.

'I'm sorry,' she said, staring the woman in the eye. 'I think you're confused. Malachi is my son and only exists in the Metaverse. We haven't stolen him from you.'

'Don't lie to me! I knew he was mine when I held him.'

Now Selena realized why she'd recognized the woman. She and Jaden had watched her in avatar form a month earlier cuddling their infant child, having won a *The Family Experiment* monthly lottery.

'I don't mean to be cruel, but I think you need help,' Selena said, and brushed her way past the stranger.

But not before the woman had grabbed Selena's handbag and yanked it by the straps, pulling Selena off balance and sending her crashing to the floor.

'A real mother never forgets,' the woman hissed. 'Tell your husband that.'

Selena clambered to her feet, shoved the woman away, hurried out of the door and burst into tears as she ran along the street.

# NEWS

Home | Current Affairs | **Opinions**

WHO IS BEING MANIPULATED: THEM OR US?

By JoÚ Russell, Editor at Large

Turn on any television or streaming provider and you'll be forgiven for thinking we've stepped back in time. It's a time your parents (or even grandparents) will recall vividly of when schedules were swamped with unknowns competing in reality TV shows.

In its early days, reality TV was all about the experience. Then that was bastardized when contestants realised they could stretch—and monetize—Andy Warhol's fifteen minutes of fame into life-long careers. For decades, these contestants craved your attention and your money, with the tat they were paid to flog.

But after a time, you bored of them and switched off. Reality TV became dirty words. And then came the live televized hacking of driverless cars on British roads, and within twenty-four hours, all was forgiven. We couldn't get enough of this life-or-death immersive experience. Which is where we find ourselves now with *The Family Experiment*, a new twist on an old format. Reality TV is back to how it began, as a social experiment. And it seems like we can't get enough of it.

But it's not as innocent as it seems because this show has a dangerous pretext. We are a few weeks through the series and we are kidding ourselves if we still think we're watching real people faced with real-life challenges. It's one long, glorified infomercial. People who cannot afford to raise families are being sold an answer to their prayers in the biggest piece of product placement our screens have ever seen. We are being told an artificial intelligence-operated child is our future.

Yet these children can be killed at the will of parents or producers, all in the name of entertainment. This is a blood sport. And if we let it, it will set a precedent for every reality show that follows.

MONTH THREE:
TWO YEARS OLD

ADVERTISEMENT

FOREIGN BODIES
boutique hotel

TAKE IT FROM US, YOU'RE IN GOOD HANDS

Found your DNA Match but looking for something a little extra?

Then why not visit the Foreign Bodies boutique hotel for discreet, one-to-one time with AI-operated avatars?

First, visit our online store to order your made-to-measure add-ons and wearables for whatever suits your taste to create an ultra-realistic experience. Our delivery drones will courier them to you within twelve hours.

And while you are waiting, choose an existing avatar or upgrade and design one of your choice. We cater for any age,* gender,† race, sexuality or appearance.

Subscribers to our VIP programme can visit any time they want to and play in one of our plush Metaverse fantasy rooms.

All tastes catered for.‡

Discretion is assured—as is the time of your life.

* Age for consent varies depending on your Real World territory.
† Genders based on the 68 legally registered genders.
‡ Within legal reason.

22
Dimitri & Zoe

Lenny was into his third meltdown of the day when Autumn Taylor appeared. Now settling into the terrible twos, he had thrown his first tantrum during a fraught breakfast in which Zoe and Dimitri had asked him to use a fork instead of a spoon to eat everything. The second had been his steadfast refusal either to try or even acknowledge the toddler toilet installed in the bathroom. They were trying to fathom the cause of the third when Autumn arrived in their kitchen.

'Have I caught you at a bad time?' she asked.

'There's rarely a good time when you're Lenny's age,' smiled Dimitri.

'What's made the little man so unhappy?'

'We haven't quite sussed this one out yet, but it's probably because we've not allowed him any screen time today. We aren't opposed to it, but as a teacher, Zoe has seen so many kids whose lives are ruled by devices. We want him to play with us and learn to find ways to keep himself entertained.'

Red hearts across the screen suggested the viewers' approval.

Lenny's tears came to an abrupt halt when he noticed they had company. He sat upright and glared at the stranger in their house.

'Who's that man?' he asked, pointing to Autumn.

Autumn's laugh was as fake as her lips.

'You seem like very relaxed parents,' she continued.

'I'd like to think we are,' Dimitri replied. 'We're old enough and wise enough to know there's no point in sweating the small stuff.'

Zoe nodded her agreement, but inside she'd been feeling far from relaxed for weeks, ever since the arrival by hand of the envelope containing sealed court documents. She had yet to mention it to Dimitri because he was so much more of a worrier than her. So far there had been no follow-up. But each rattle of the letterbox was leaving her on tenterhooks.

'Are you also more chilled because this isn't your first time?' Autumn asked suddenly.

Zoe, who would normally be attuned to the direction a conversation might take and skilled at creating diversions, had not foreseen Autumn's route. She and Dimitri had discussed their very public history and why they'd wanted to participate in *The Family Experiment*, first during the application process, then briefly in their introduction video on the show's launch night. But they had deliberately made no reference to it on screen since.

Zoe cleared her throat. 'I think having been through parenthood before, we have probably drawn a little from past experiences. We know that children are unpredictable, that they don't come with a manual, that there are ups and downs and that everything is just a phase, like today's little tantrum.'

She hoped that might be the end of it, but Autumn persisted.

'So how does parenting differ second time around?'

'Well, I don't know that it does,' said Zoe. 'Aside from their geographic locations, there's very little else that's different. If we didn't think that we could love a child who wasn't made of flesh and blood then we wouldn't have entered this process. But it's remarkable the depth of affection we feel for someone beyond the world we are used to.'

She could never tell anyone that it wasn't Lenny who'd taught her how to love again. That the being responsible was hidden elsewhere in the house, away from prying eyes.

'Are you trying to recreate what you had first time around?' Autumn continued.

'No, not at all. But we are looking forward to being able to do things in the future, when he's older, that we never had the chance to do before.'

'Is that why you entered *The Family Experiment*? Unfinished business?'

'I wouldn't put it like that,' interrupted Dimitri. 'But there are a lot of opportunities that were taken away from us in the past and that we'd like to experience now with Lenny.'

'Are there any similarities between your children?' asked Autumn.

'We don't compare them,' Zoe said firmly.

Dimitri offered her his support by placing his hand on hers and squeezing it gently.

'It wouldn't be right,' she added.

'But it's only natural, isn't it?' said Autumn. 'Don't all parents compare their kids at one time or another?'

'Do you have children?' asked Zoe.

'No.'

'When you do, perhaps we'll have this conversation again.'

It was the first time Zoe had witnessed an avatar blush. If she'd ever met anyone more irritating than Autumn, she couldn't recall it.

'Have you been keeping abreast of social media and what viewers are saying about you?' Autumn asked.

'No, we haven't,' Dimitri answered. 'Neither of us use social media, and we've enjoyed sharing our little bubble for the last two and a half months with Lenny without worrying about what strangers are saying. Sometimes red hearts will blur the vision in our visors, so we know that we can't be doing too bad a job.'

'Would you like me to give you the gist of it?' Autumn asked.

Zoe could tell that she was desperate to.

'In all honesty, no thank you,' said Zoe.

'Then I shall respect your wishes,' Autumn added, playfully placing a manicured fingernail to her lips. 'And I really hope that you can turn around the opinions of those who still don't think you're fit to take part in this competition.'

Without offering them a chance to reply, Autumn vanished, leaving them to ruminate on her parting shot.

23
Hudson

The balcony of his Metaverse apartment had become Hudson's favourite place to spend his downtime. Tonight, as his daughter, Alice, slept with a toy dinosaur close to her chest, he felt the warmth on his face and body from the setting sun as it dipped over a distant Central Park.

He needed this version of New York to exist on his terms, one that was so clean it bordered on sterile. So there was no litter, no buildings in differing states of construction, no honking car horns, no flyposters pasted to walls and no crime. It didn't matter that it bore little resemblance to reality.

When time allowed, he'd strap a now-two-year-old Alice into a carrier, affix it to his shoulders and take the elevator—always the one on the right—to the ground floor, where they'd spend hour upon hour wandering the virtual streets, one district at a time. He'd chat to her as if she was an adult, explaining where they were and what they were passing. Hudson assumed that if Alice was a true representation of a Real World child, she'd be unlikely to remember most of this in Development Leaps to come. But he was hopeful fragments might remain somewhere deep inside her subconscious, assuming an AI had one.

Now, she was yawning and curled up cat-like, sucking the tip of her thumb. Hudson was enjoying the moment too much to carry her to her bedroom. The sun's glow served to remind him of how tough the last few days had been. Its rays highlighted a couple of dozen red spots spread randomly across Alice's cheeks, chin and forehead, filled with mustard-coloured centres. The chickenpox virus might have been eradicated from the Real World, but in the Metaverse, it existed by public demand. And he'd spent many an hour trying to prevent her from scratching the spots.

Hudson resented viewers who'd voted for them to face the Monthly Challenge. He'd hoped it might have been scrapped when, in week two, Rufus Green had cracked under the pressure of his daughter's relentless crying. But no, the challenge remained because pushing parents to the edge made for better viewing, more publicity and more subscriptions for when the MetaChildren programme launched commercially later in the year.

If only the public knew what he knew.

Hudson had barely spent any time in the Real World since Alice had contracted the virus. Three times daily, drones delivered takeaway meals to the concierge at his rented flat inside a converted South London shoe factory. He'd log out from the Metaverse, scoff his meals and return to Alice's side. He'd even been sleeping in her room at night. Continuous wearing of his headset had given him terrible headaches, neck pains and burning eyes, but these were mere gripes compared to what he'd been subjected to on his awakening in a foreign land as a ten-year-old. A part of him wished that he could forget that time—perhaps then he might be able to move on with his life, rather than remain the child he had been then. But another part knew these reminders existed to fuel his determination.

Alice moved her fingers to scratch her face. He gently placed his own hand in front of her cheek so her nails grazed that instead. As he closed his avatar's eyes, swirling translucent worms appeared in his eyelids as he faced the sun. Programmers really had thought of everything.

His appreciation of being outdoors had come as a result of being locked inside for such long periods of time. With no windows in the dormitory of the facility where he'd been taken as a boy, the only indication that morning had arrived was the graphic of a rising sun on the ceiling screens above them. It signified the start of their daily routine. They'd queue noiselessly for their allocated two-minute showers, followed by a silent breakfast of fruits, brans and vitamin-infused liquids in the canteen, before being allowed outside into the courtyard quadrant where the only views were upwards and the sun was frequently hidden behind a polluted sky.

Next, each child held the QR codes that had been burned into the backs of their hands against access pads which allowed them entry to only two floors in the fifteen-storey building. Once in position, they were assigned VR headsets, haptic suits and masks, then locked inside an individual pod. Avatars fired questions at them about their lives and their backgrounds. Hudson had only offered what little information he knew.

There had been aptitude tests, puzzles to solve, role-play games and psychological evaluations. At the end of each day, their brains were checked with handheld MRI scanners before a mandatory sixty-minute exercise period began. His days had been so well occupied that he barely thought about the home he'd left behind. Conversation was only permitted after work at the communal evening dinners, and he'd learned that around half of his peers were British, while the rest had been sent from countries including Afghanistan, Iran, North Korea and Russia.

The one person Hudson had gravitated towards more than others was the girl who slept in the bunk bed above his. At twelve, Eva was two years his senior and full of contradictions. She was sharp but warm, complicit to the authority controlling their every move yet possessed by an underlying desire for independence. She had arrived with her brother, Cain, a year older than her, who hadn't hidden his disdain for Hudson because of the attention Eva paid him.

She had been fearless. And when those around them slept or were crying themselves to sleep, she would sneak down into Hudson's bed and they'd lie together comparing notes in hushed tones about what they'd been tested on that day. They'd concoct fantasy escape plans, make up places to run to, construct new lives and imagine how and where they'd make their fortunes. Hudson had the feeling that Eva took these plans more seriously than he did. Because every so often, a glint in her eyes suggested she was less willing than him to accept their time in that place as the new normal.

Then she'd hurry back to her own bed before the twice-nightly appearance of patrol guards. For months it had continued like this without them being caught.

When they were together, Hudson willed the clock to stop ticking so they could have more time. When they were apart, he found himself craving her company. He hadn't understood why her family had turned their backs on someone as compelling as her.

Tonight, Hudson opened his eyes and waited for the swirling worms to vanish. He checked that Alice was still asleep and hoped Autumn Taylor wouldn't appear this week for their three-month interview. Not until Alice had recovered.

He tucked her up in her bedroom, logged out of *The Family Experiment* App then flicked his eyes in his headset towards the internet symbol. A few days had passed since he'd last gauged the public's perception of him. And there had been an encouraging shift in his favour. Viewers had been registering how much time he was spending in the Metaverse looking after Alice, and now the hashtag #DevotedDad was beginning to trend. Either those who supported him from the beginning were becoming more vocal, or he was winning over the sceptics.

All that mattered was that people were talking about him. Because if they were talking, they were likely also listening. And soon, he would have a lot for them to hear.

24

Woody & Tina

'She's just taken a couple of steps!' said Tina eagerly as Woody entered the Metaverse. Their daughter, Belle, was standing on her own two feet and giggling.

'What?' Woody asked, eyebrows raised. 'When?'

'About ten minutes after Autumn Taylor left. I took advantage of Belle's obsession with rabbits and downloaded a virtual pair. Quick as a flash, she started trying to chase them.'

The garden of their virtual house was roughly five times the size of their bricks-and-mortar home. It was filled with rows of colourful English heritage flowers in borders and in the corner stood a wooden pergola with evergreen wisteria wrapped around its beams. The in-App purchase had cost a little more than they had been planning to spend from their allocated prize fund. And Woody wondered if, subconsciously, they had been trying to give Belle the freedom that had been taken away from her sister, Issy. They hadn't risked allowing her outdoors since weeks earlier, when she had attempted to escape by unscrewing fence panels. Instead, they'd attached serotonin lamps to the basement walls to mimic sunlight and upped her vitamin supplements. Woody hated himself for it, but Tina had insisted.

Red hearts appeared on screen, indicating that viewers were enjoying watching Belle finally walking as much as her parents were. It was in sharp contrast to the criticism the parents had faced at the start of this third month. Viewers had expressed concern that theirs was the only child who had yet to walk. Group chats had begun to discuss whether Belle was receiving enough parental attention and encouragement. Then had come accusations of neglect, questions as to why they hadn't sought specialist medical advice, and the couple had had to call police when someone claiming to be a physician had turned up on their Real World doorstep, refusing to leave until he'd examined the child.

Tina had bowed to public pressure and used some of the prize money to pay for a private consultation with an AI paediatrician. A complete physical and neurological scan had revealed what her parents already knew: Belle would walk when she was ready. And ten days later, that's exactly what she did.

Woody scooped his daughter up in his arms and squeezed her tightly.

'How old was—' He stopped himself short when Tina's eyes narrowed.

Instinctively, she knew he was going to ask when Issy had first become fully mobile. He swiftly changed the end of the sentence to '—were you when you started walking?'

'I don't know,' she replied. 'I'll have to ask Mum if she remembers.'

In truth, she wouldn't be asking her mother anything as the two had barely spoken in years. Not after how she had turned a blind eye to the violence that had been going on under her roof. Tina and her brother had been victims of countless beatings over the years by their stepfather for anything from a lost school tie to returning five minutes later than their curfew. As a result, Tina abhorred any kind of violence. And soon after Tina had met Woody, she had cut her mother out of her life.

In more recent years, it had been Woody's turn to hold his own family at arm's length. His rejection had left them hurt and confused. Likewise, friends were also kept at a distance until, one by one, they had all vanished. Such a sacrifice meant they could avoid lying to the people they loved, as well as protect Issy.

Woody couldn't take his eyes off Belle. He recalled how, when Issy was this age, she was already showing signs of stubbornness and defiance, and had a fiery temper to match. She'd routinely and unapologetically destroy toys, and her behaviour became impulsive and increasingly manipulative. She appeared to enjoy being deliberately provocative and cruel. It was as if each time she riled her parents, it made her stronger.

The only thing that had calmed a young Issy was when they gave her a VR headset with an App that allowed users to experience the world underwater. Time spent exploring coral, caves, reefs and oceanic trenches was like a reset button.

It was Tina who'd first admitted there was something about Issy that frightened her, that there was a look in her eye akin to contempt. And once Woody could see it, it had become impossible to ignore.

'It's just a phase,' he said. 'She'll grow out of it.'

But Issy hadn't grown out of it. Quite the opposite, in fact. She had grown into it. Eventually they came to realize true nature cannot conceal itself for ever.

Woody shook his head to rid himself of his memories, as a reminder to live more in the present than the past. So he and Tina watched and smiled as their giggling toddler chased two white rabbits around the garden.

Despite last month's temper tantrums, this was exactly what Tina had wanted from parenting second time around. A child who loved her as much as she loved it. She had spent too much time wishing for things she couldn't have, like the support of friends and family, and for Issy to be normal.

But her biggest wish was for Belle and Issy to swap places, for Issy to be in the Metaverse and not the Real World.

Because then, Tina could pull the plug on her firstborn and completely erase any trace of her.

25

Cadman & Gabriel

'**I don't think River's keen on that crafting pod,**' said Gabriel, pointing at his son.

The two-year-old was clambering over the side of the pop-up playpen, arranged on the decking behind their MetaHouse. In his wake, he'd left spilled paint pots, crayons, glue and brightly coloured cotton-wool balls. Cadman glanced at his watch and tutted. River had spent approximately ten minutes playing inside it, not even half the minimum time stipulated in the agreement with the manufacturer.

River giggled and began running away as Cadman approached him.

'River,' he called. 'Come on, let's make some planets and stars out of tissue paper.'

But his son wasn't interested. Eventually Cadman caught up with him on the acres of lawns surrounding their home. He picked up the shrieking boy and carried him over his shoulder back to the crafting pod, placing him inside again.

'This is fun, isn't it? What shall we stick on here?' Cadman asked through gritted teeth.

He picked up a glue gun and used it to make a zigzag shape on black card. But River had turned his back on him and to Gabriel's amusement was making a second escape bid.

'He doesn't want to be penned in,' Gabriel cajoled. 'Probably best to give him his freedom.'

'I've made that mistake before,' Cadman said pointedly.

Gabriel didn't bite.

'Maybe he's just not an artistic kid? Perhaps we should be more directed by him? I've been reading up about child-led learning...'

Gabriel's attention was drawn to Cadman's scowl before the penny dropped.

'But he probably just needs to get used to it,' Gabriel deadpanned. 'Once he does, he'll love it.'

'And what better place is there for safe, structured playtime than inside a KidzTime Crafting Pod?' Cadman continued. 'Such a simple but effective product in both the Metaverse and Real World.'

The price and availability appeared in the corners of their headsets.

Gabriel trailed his son back out into the garden and into an adjoining wildflower meadow. He'd sensed something had been troubling Cadman for a few days but had been rebuffed each time he asked.

'Look, Daddy,' River giggled as he lay on his back making semicircular shapes with his arms and legs. Gabriel copied him and caught sight of Cadman on the patio, watching.

'Join us!' Gabriel yelled. 'We're field angels.'

Cadman moved towards them, then hesitated.

'I have a meeting,' he shouted back. 'And I'm not dressed for it.'

He ran his hand from the collar of his fitted shirt down to his new chinos. He waited until the prices appeared before going inside.

Month three's Development Leap to toddler found River living up to his name. He was constantly winding and manoeuvring his way around the house and gardens, exploring everything and everywhere but rarely for more than a few minutes at a time. His concentration span was typical for his age, Gabriel had learned, but he couldn't help but wonder if the ever-changing appearance of the house, its furniture, his toys and clothes was hindering their son's development. Perhaps a lack of the familiar was making it hard for River to focus?

To his credit, Cadman had negotiated some incredible experiences for his family. They had been gifted daytrips around the Metaverse to fantasy-themed hotels, imaginative cartoon worlds and immersive games. But typically, it was Gabriel and River enjoying them together as an otherwise engaged Cadman caught up on their adventures by downloading the highlights show. Gabriel couldn't help but think just how much Cadman was missing out on.

Their relationship had shown signs of improvement since last month's clash when Cadman had slipped a swab inside Gabriel's mouth as he slept. A small part of him accepted his own past culpability for Cadman's behaviour, but it was too much of an ask for Cadman to have been quite so introspective.

Meanwhile, and back inside their Real World house, Cadman was in his office, sifting through screens of data presented to him daily by his team of freelancers. Many dossiers had been compiled from social media posts and online commentary. They offered a valuable insight into the subjects and behaviours that mattered most to viewers alongside the couples proving most popular. Once again and to his irritation, he and Gabriel were languishing in third place.

There was no doubt that financially they would be the overall winners. Cadman was on course to earn vast sums, likely surpassing his tally in the aftermath of the autonomous vehicle hack when demand for him peaked. So it shouldn't matter where they were placed in *The Family Experiment*. But it did, because Cadman detested losing.

He'd studied clips of the other participants, specifically those resonating with viewers. For the life of him, he couldn't understand why the likes of the dull-as-dishwater Zoe and Dimitri or Woody and Tina were gaining so much support. Others, like Hudson, and Selena and Jaden, were languishing further down the table.

Something had to shift, he decided. They needed an edge, an angle that would push them to the forefront of viewers' minds. And there was something obvious that might just work. But how much of his relationship was he willing to exploit to get there?

He thought for a moment before the conclusion arrived.

All of it.

26
Selena & Jaden

As usual, an appearance from *The Family Experiment* **presenter Au**tumn Taylor came with advance notice, but with no specific timeframe attached. Selena and Jaden were biking through a Metaverse woodland trail in Scotland with two-year-old Malachi strapped into a seat behind his father. Autumn appeared from nowhere at a rest stop ahead.

'Here comes trouble,' Jaden yelled over his shoulder.

Selena didn't respond. They dismounted their bikes as Autumn beckoned them over.

'Hi, guys.' She grinned. 'It's that time again.'

Selena studied Autumn's face. Her avatar had been updated with fuller hair and a subtle, more airbrushed appearance. They reflected her most recent vlogs, and Selena suspected Autumn had undergone a few cosmetic procedures. The division between Metaverse and reality was shortening.

'So how have things been going since I last came to visit?' Autumn continued.

'They've been amazing, haven't they?' said Jaden.

He turned to Selena for confirmation, but again, she didn't reciprocate. He continued regardless.

'Malachi is just so much fun to be around, and I think he enjoys being with us. What do you reckon, buddy?'

His son grinned.

'And how about you, Selena? How's your month been?' asked Autumn.

'Eventful,' Selena replied.

'Ooh, tell us more.'

'I've learned a lot about myself and the people I'm surrounded by.'

Her eyes were drawn to a puzzled Jaden before she returned her attention to the host.

'In the past,' she continued, 'I've been willing to forgive even if it wasn't in my best interests to do so.'

'This all sounds quite cryptic,' Autumn said.

'I have some changes to make. And at the risk of sounding like a self-help podcast, I need to be in a place of absolute honesty, which I won't find in the Metaverse. Everything in here is false, because that's the way it was built. It's virtual, it's an approximation, and I was aware of that before we entered *The Family Experiment*. But my life in the Real World doesn't have to be as fake. So the changes I'm making start with me. I'm leaving my marriage.'

Making the decision and allowing the words to spill from her mouth were two very different things. But the relief to Selena was instant.

She had made the decision days after discovering Jaden's affairs and his children, and having been accosted by the stranger in the cafe. The incident had left her physically shaken, and footage filmed by other customers and uploaded onto social media had led to the woman being arrested and cautioned by police for intimidating behaviour. She had also been banned from approaching Selena for two years. The producers of *The Family Experiment* had immediately scrapped its monthly lottery in which viewers could spend time with a MetaChild.

For the sake of her sanity, she had to end her involvement in the show. Even though Jaden was her DNA Match and she would never find a connection deeper than the one they had, love didn't always equate with happiness.

'Selena?' Jaden asked. 'What are you talking about?'

'I know what you've done, Jaden. I know everything.'

She felt her husband's glare upon her.

'I thought that was all in the past,' he began, lowering his voice. 'There's nothing you don't know.'

She looked him dead in the eye.

'How about the three women you fathered children with? Is that something I already know?'

Jaden ran his hand across his shaven head.

'Mute,' he said.

But the mic symbol in his helmet remained live.

'Mute,' he repeated. 'Mute, mute, fucking mute!'

'You can't mute a live interview,' Autumn said as black hearts began to make their way across the screen.

'Ben, Esme and Lucy,' Selena continued calmly. 'They're the correct names, yes? Your actual, Real World, biological children? You even cheated on the women you were cheating with.'

'Please,' Jaden said. 'Let's not do this here.'

'It doesn't matter where we do it. Here, home, it's all the same. Secrets and lies follow us from the universe to Metaverse. And I don't want to be with you in either.'

So many black hearts were now filling the screen that Jaden and Selena couldn't be seen. Autumn was forced to act.

'Comments off,' she ordered, and they vanished.

'I didn't tell you about the kids because I loved you too much to hurt you any more than I had with the gambling,' Jaden countered.

'No, it's because you're a coward.'

'You don't understand, I didn't cheat on you. They were wealthy, single women who wanted children and were willing to pay me to help.'

'What do you mean?'

'I've been selling my sperm to pay off our debts.'

'You've done what?'

'I did it for us. I know how much you wanted to start a family and how we couldn't afford to after I lost our savings. So I found a way to make it up to you.'

'By what, fucking other women?'

'It wasn't like that. I wasn't having an affair with any of them. It was transactional.'

'And how did you make these transactions? At a clinic? At home in a petri dish? In the bedroom?'

Jaden's reddening face gave Selena her answer.

'You slept with them,' she said.

'Yes.'

'And?'

'And it worked first time with Ben but it took a few more tries for Esme and Lucy.'

'How did you meet their mothers?'

'One is a personal training client who hadn't met her DNA Match but wanted to start a family. The other two found me online.'

'You advertise?'

He nodded. 'There's a Metaverse App where you can meet, and upload your clinic paperwork to show you're biologically suitable, along with your bloodwork, DNA breakdown, etcetera.'

Selena ran her fingers through her hair.

'You have to believe that I wasn't cheating on you with any of them,' he continued.

'That doesn't make it right, what you did! You still had sex with other women behind my back. That is the definition of cheating. Have you ever played a role in these kids' lives?'

Jaden hesitated a little too long.

'Or are you still seeing them?'

'I would visit them regularly for the first few weeks after they were born. But now it's only every month. It's part of the agreement.'

Suddenly it made sense as to how Jaden had taken to parenthood so naturally when Malachi had arrived. He'd been through it before. Multiple times.

'So while I thought you were working, you were playing happy families.'

'It wasn't like that. What we have—you, me and Malachi—that's real.'

'With your hand on your heart, can you honestly tell me he feels as real as your other children?'

'Well, no, but it's pretty close—'

'But I don't want pretty close. I can wear as many haptic suits and gloves and masks and headsets as I like, but I will never be able to truly experience parenthood with Malachi.'

She turned to face her MetaChild, his face perplexed by his parents' fraught tones. Autumn Taylor's arm was around his shoulder.

A thousand strings attached to Selena's heart pulled in every direction. She reached out to hold her son's hand.

'I care about you, I really do,' she began. 'But you and your dad are not enough for me.'

'No,' said a panicked Jaden. 'You can't do this to us. You're not that person. You are better. You're better than me.'

'I know I'm better than you,' Selena replied. 'It's taken me a long time to realize my worth, and now that I have, I won't go back. For the first time in my life, I'm putting myself before anyone else.'

'But if you leave us, they'll delete Malachi. You'll be killing our son.'

'No,' snapped Selena. 'Don't you dare try to put this all on me.'

'You've told me many times that all you've ever wanted is a happy ever after. Well, this is it. You, me, Malachi, we already have that. Don't destroy it.'

'You've made me realize happy ever afters don't exist,' she replied.

Without warning, Jaden's avatar suddenly dropped to his knees, his hand clutching the back of his head.

'Fuck,' he gasped as he turned to his wife. 'What was that—?'

'What are you doing?' asked Selena.

A fraction of a second later, it was as if an invisible force had pushed him face down into the ground. At the same time, Selena felt something wet splash against her lips. It tasted metallic.

'Is everything okay?' asked a bewildered Autumn.

'Jaden?' Selena continued, as Jaden's avatar body, now lying flat on the forest floor, appeared to jolt as if he had been hit by a heavy object.

Suddenly, in the Real World, Selena felt a brush of air against her face. Panicked, she ripped off her headset.

Her mouth fell open as she saw Jaden sprawled out across the floor, the back of his head concave where his skull had been crushed, and blood pooling around it.

Above him, holding a cricket bat over her head, her face splattered and contorted with rage, stood the young woman who had confronted Selena in the café.

Chats

TV / Reality TV Shows / **The Family Experiment**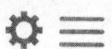

> **GurlGoneWild, 6.27 p.m.**
> I am seriously crushing on Hudson right now. Staying with Alice while she had chicken pox, wandering around New York talking to her about anything and everything. Wish I'd had a dad like that. #DevotedDad

FaffyDuck, 6.31 p.m.
Still reckon he's a paedo. #JustSaying

SirMixALot, 6.44 p.m.
Has Cadman spent *any* time at all with that kid or is Gabriel basically a single dad?

BruvBruvBruv, 6.46 p.m.
Woah! Anyone just hear that? Selena's told Jaden that she's leaving him

Bakewe11Heart2, 6.50 p.m.
Why?

SayItLikeISeeIt, 6.55 p.m.
Turns out he has three kids she doesn't know about.

> **GurlGoneWild, 6.56 p.m.**
> Why has he just fallen to the floor? What's going on?

Bakewe11Heart2, 6.57 p.m.
Something weird is happening. I can hear two voices coming from Selena's mouth. Can anyone explain?

> **GurlGoneWild, 6.58 p.m.**
> Jeez . . . anyone hearing what I'm hearing? Someone needs to call the police

27

Woody & Tina

Woody focused on the remaining virtual pieces placed about the chessboard. Issy had chosen today's theme, characters from J. R. R. Tolkien's rich catalogue of work. Woody had hobbits on his side while she had chosen warlocks, goblins and orcs, with Sauron as the king.

No matter the direction he considered, there was nowhere for him to move without a checkmate. His virtual pieces looked up at him with hope in their eyes, but yet again he'd been beaten into submission by his teenage daughter. The bad guys never lost in Issy's world.

He removed his headset and placed it on the coffee table, catching a glimpse of Issy's self-congratulatory smile as she also slipped off her headset. In either world, nothing satisfied her more than reminding her parents of her superior intellect.

It had been obvious to both parents that Issy was frighteningly intelligent, even at an early age. Woody had taught her how to play chess when she was ten, hoping it might give her something to focus on now that she was spending more time alone. Perhaps it might even calm her, he'd thought.

And at first, his plan appeared to work because she fell in love with the game in an instant. Using the same board Woody's father had used to teach him, she practised either alone, against Woody or using a holographic AI cybernanny subscription programme that helped to educate her and keep her occupied when her parents weren't available. It also sent them Push notifications if it judged any of their daughter's behaviours to be of concern.

It was recently that Woody had understood Issy's attraction to the game: it was based less on competition and more upon the process of war. He'd inadvertently encouraged her desire for one-upmanship, scheming and planning many moves ahead to take down an enemy. Chess tapped into everything that made her Issy.

'I remember when I used to let you win,' Woody said.

'I remember when I used to let you believe that,' she replied.

Issy paused before continuing.

'Oh, there's a human-versus-human tournament taking place this weekend in the Meta.'

Woody didn't reply. He knew what was coming next.

'Can we go?' she asked. 'Me and you. It'd be nice for us to do something together, wouldn't it?'

'We play chess all the time,' he replied. 'And the last time I checked, I was still human.'

'And I beat you every time,' she groaned. 'If I win this tournament—and you know I can—the prize money will pay for my last year of schooling and the first year of uni tuition.'

It was the first time she had spoken of university. The thought of setting her free into the world sent cold prickles racing across his shoulders and back.

'I want to play against people on my level—and you're no competition,' she continued. 'Come on, Dad, it'll be fun.'

Dad, he repeated to himself. She only ever called him that when she wanted something. Woody would have loved nothing more than to proudly watch his daughter competing against some of the best players in the world. And he had little doubt she had the potential to go far. But even if he was to accompany her and keep a close eye on her, it was still too much of a potential risk. He couldn't predict what she might do in an unrestricted Metaverse, even with him by her side.

'I'm sorry,' Woody said, and he really was.

He sucked in his cheeks, fully expecting her response to come within a whirlwind of anger. Instead, all she gave was an eye-roll.

'You'll have to make do with me for now,' he added.

And if he was being honest with himself, he liked it that way, even if she beat him every game. It was the one time her mind was focused on something aside from loathing her parents or plotting an escape.

Both turned their heads quickly at the sound of the door beeping, then opening. It could only be Tina, yet her appearance was still unexpected.

'Hello, stranger,' Issy said drily.

It had been weeks since both parents had been in the same room as their daughter. In one hand, Tina carried a plain white birthday cake with three small pink candles inserted into an iced number sixteen. In the other hand were three plates and forks. Woody joined in as Tina began to sing an awkward rendition of 'Happy Birthday to You'.

'Anyone would think you care about me,' deadpanned Issy.

'Of course we care,' Tina replied, but Woody noticed she had yet to make eye contact with her daughter. 'We love you.'

She placed the plates on the coffee table and sat cross-legged on the floor while father and daughter remained on the sofa.

'I'd make a wish, but you forgot to light the candles,' said Issy.

The last thing Tina was going to do was provide her daughter with naked flames, no matter how small they were. Likewise, a knife. The cake was pre-cut.

'Tuck in,' Tina said.

Issy asked her Audite to play music, something guitar-heavy which neither parent could identify and that was just a little bit too loud to be comfortable. They didn't allow her the satisfaction of asking for it to be turned down.

Woody caught his wife's attention and raised an eyebrow as if to ask where Belle was. Tina gave a second-long blink and tipped her head to one side to suggest she was asleep.

Tina took a moment to glance around the basement. It ran the entire length of the house and contained its own lounge, bedroom and bathroom. It had been the reason they had bought the property. Staring blankly in the corner of the room was the hologram cybernanny awaiting its base unit to recharge.

Issy had excelled at her studies, so much so that at fourteen she should have been starting her final year at a Real World school. Only that hadn't been possible, and Woody and Tina couldn't afford to pay for the expensive cybernanny software updates either. The halt in her education had only added to Issy's inherent anger.

They'd permitted her access to the internet and Metaverse via an anonymous avatar and identity but had placed many restrictions on what she could access. And most recently, the ban had included anything related to *The Family Experiment*. Issy could never know about her virtual sister or have the Metaverse know about her. Issy was little more than a spectator to the worlds around her, unable to communicate with anyone but her parents. That had been part of her punishment.

'So how has your special day been?' Tina asked Issy.

'Hmm, let me think,' Issy replied. 'About as special as every other day.'

'It can't have been that bad.'

'Woke up, had breakfast with Woody, showered, surfed the internet for a couple of hours and would have liked to have engaged in a debate about nuclear weapons with a group of politics students in the Metaverse, but all I could do was spectate because you won't allow me friends. Had lunch with Woody, spent the afternoon being taught what I already knew from a module I studied on sociology last year because you haven't upgraded my learning package. Travelled underwater in a submarine from Antarctica to the Americas before Woody appeared again and I wiped the floor with him at chess as per usual. But the highlight of the day was when you decided to show up, obvs.'

Tina held back from retaliating. It would only create another argument she didn't have the energy for. So she relayed a conversation she'd had with a work colleague regarding another flu strain variant making its way across Europe.

'Are more lockdowns on the cards then?' Woody asked.

'Possibly, but this one might only last a week, as the vaccinations are almost ready.'

'Lockdowns for influenza, lockdowns for Covid, lockdowns for human avian flu, lockdowns for human swine flu…when's it going to end?'

'God only knows,' Tina replied.

'And from a selfish perspective, they're a pain in the arse. I hate not being able to do anything.'

Issy turned sharply to her father.

'Oh, poor you. I can't even begin to imagine what it must be like to be kept away from society through no fault of your own.'

'Please,' sighed Tina.

'What?' Issy replied. 'I'm not arguing with him, I'm just saying. Perhaps you could tell me what it's like, Christina? Give me an insight into how hard life is for you during a lockdown? Because I'm all ears.'

Tina pushed her fork and spoon to one side and swallowed her food.

'Nope,' she said. 'I'm sorry, but I'm not doing this today. I'm tired and I cannot be bothered to fight.'

She rose to her feet.

'You can never be bothered to do anything with me,' Issy continued. 'That's why you rarely come down here. You can't face the guilt of what you're putting me through.'

Tina turned suddenly, an unexpected rage reaching boiling point.

'What we're putting you through? What about what you have put us through? Do you think we actually take pleasure in locking you away? Do you think we enjoy caging you like an animal? Of course we don't! But what choice do we have?'

'You could have fought for me! Given me the benefit of the doubt. You could have believed me.'

'The evidence was stacked against you,' Tina fired back. 'You are here because of your actions and your actions alone.'

'At least let me back upstairs, let me spend time in the garden,' Issy pleaded.

'We can't do that because we don't trust you. That's on you, not us. If you gave us any indication that you'd changed then perhaps we'd be more accommodating. But you haven't because you can't. And at this rate, you'll be lucky if we let you out of here at eighteen.'

'What's that supposed to mean?'

Tina's eyes narrowed.

'It means that if we don't think you've been sufficiently punished, we can apply to keep you here three more years until you're twenty-one. How would you like that, Issy?'

'You wouldn't do that.'

'Watch me,' her mother snapped.

Tina's heart raced as she turned her back on her daughter. She was making her way to the basement door when she heard the clatter of plates and cutlery. She couldn't turn fast enough to stop Issy from lunging at her.

'Issy, no!' Woody yelled just as his daughter plunged a metal fork into the left-hand side of her mother's lower back.

Tina screamed and slapped Issy hard around the side of her head as Issy desperately tried to pull the fork from her mother's bleeding flesh to stab her again. This time she was thwarted by Woody, who grabbed her around the waist, pulled her backwards and threw her to the ground. Her forehead took the brunt of the collision against the coffee table, before she came to rest on her back.

Parental instinct made him want to check that Issy was okay, but Tina's injury was more pressing. So he grabbed his wife's arm, hurried her to the door and turned one last time, placated by the sight of Issy lifting herself up on her elbows.

Then he slammed the door behind them and dragged his sobbing, bleeding wife up the stairs to safety.

28
Cadman & Gabriel

River let out a long, warm yawn. Then he curled up against Gabriel's side and quickly fell asleep as only a child can. Gabriel lay on top of the duvet, his own eyelids drooping. The Metaverse bedroom sensed their resting heart rates and muted the lights in response.

The day had worn out father and son. River's current fascination involved anything reliant upon gigantic wheels or that made deafening noises. So Cadman had arranged for them to drive a selection of Metaverse trucks, diggers and cranes. With his son on his lap helping to steer, they had manoeuvred their vehicles deep underground into Russian mineshafts, they'd assisted environmentalists to replant the near-desolate Amazon rainforest and they had lifted iron girders hundreds of metres into the air to add height to a multi-storey building in a cramped Bahraini skyline. Gabriel couldn't deny this had been one of Cadman's best finds. However, once again, he'd been absent from the fun.

'Oh, is he asleep?' asked Cadman as he appeared in River's room.

Gabriel's eyes opened. He thought he caught a note of disappointment in Cadman's tone.

'He was out like a light,' he replied. 'Why don't you look after him in the morning? Have some dad and son time.'

'I have two meetings booked followed by some consultancy work in the afternoon.'

Gabriel looked to the corner of the screen and blinked at the mute button. The countdown clock began.

'Why did you want to do this?' Gabriel asked directly.

'Do what?'

'Parenthood.'

'You know why.'

'But you spending time with River was part of our agreement. How do you think it looks to viewers when you barely see him? Don't try to tell me they haven't noticed your lack of interaction.'

They had, but Cadman wasn't willing to admit that to Gabriel.

'I did all the night feeds,' he said. 'I'm here for breakfasts and dinners. That's no different to most working parents in the Real World.'

'The night feeds came to an end after the last Development Leap. River is two years old now and he needs more from you than just guest appearances and sponsorship deals. Give yourself the chance to enjoy the experience.'

Cadman's hackles rose.

'You know why I'm doing it and it's not to "enjoy" being a parent,' he said defensively. 'If I don't put the hours in we'll never earn back what y—what we lost.'

Gabriel seized his chance.

'And is that such a bad thing?'

Cadman eyed him icily. 'I'm sorry?'

'I asked if that is such a bad thing?'

'You enjoyed our life of privilege as much as I did. Too much, in fact. So now that we have a child, don't pretend you never really cared for our old lifestyle.'

'I'm just saying—'

'No,' Cadman said firmly. 'You're not saying anything because I'm not listening.'

He unmuted their conversation, leaving Gabriel frustrated and the viewers unclear of what was being kept from them.

Gabriel was all too aware that Cadman's eagerness to put money above all else was his own fault. If only Cadman hadn't asked him to go to that party, that night, it might all have been so different.

AZ had been the fastest-working and most fashionable street drug to hit the mainstream market since Ecstasy in the 1980s. It was a synthetic creation, administered into the body through a translucent patch no larger than a fingernail which could be attached almost anywhere.

It wasn't just the high it offered that appealed to so many, but also how it soothed anxiety and brought clarity of thought. The latter properties it shared with the mineral Amazonite, hence its abbreviated AZ nickname. And it had overtaken cocaine as the number-one Class A drug of choice for Generations Alpha and Beta.

Those who switched from cocaine to AZ often cited it as an ethical choice, thanks to its minimal environmental impact. Unlike coke, it required no deforestation, no damage to a region's biodiversity, no contamination of ecosystems, and had no carbon footprint. It didn't need to be trafficked into the UK because it could be manufactured regionally. It was also highly addictive.

Use of AZ had been impossible to ignore, especially in the celebrity circles Gabriel had frequented on Cadman's behalf. Barely a social function had passed without him politely declining the offer of a patch. That was, however, until Steevi, an associate of Cadman's in the influencing scene, had surreptitiously placed a patch on Gabriel's neck when he'd greeted him with an embrace one night. It had gone unnoticed by Gabriel. He'd assumed the complimentary alcohol he'd consumed on an empty stomach was responsible for his added confidence and the diminishing of his social anxiety.

'Having fun?' Steevi had shouted over the pulsating bass of the music.

Gabriel had been standing in the VIP area overlooking the balcony and the packed dance floor below.

'Brilliant night!' he yelled back.

'Ha!' Steevi laughed. 'Dude, I knew you'd love it.'

'Love what?'

'AZ.'

'I've never tried it.'

'Wanna bet?'

He reached over Gabriel's shoulder, fingertips glancing across his neck before he pulled off the patch.

'Fuck, Steevi! Why did you do that? Cadman will kill me.'

'Then don't tell him. Did you like how it felt?'

Gabriel wanted to protest. But he knew that he was a poor liar.

'It always makes me horny,' Steevi continued, then placed his hand on Gabriel's belt and drew him closer. Gabriel backed away.

'Want to try another one?' Steevi persisted, and pulled out a strip of wax paper with more patches attached.

'No, no thanks.'

And Gabriel had remained resolute. But during another event in which he'd tried and failed to make a connection with anyone, he'd relented and sought out Steevi. And the same thing happened for every launch and party after that.

Cadman had been too consumed by work to notice a difference in his partner. When Gabriel came home still high, Cadman had assumed he was drunk. And if a handful of gin and tonics were giving him added confidence, where was the harm in that? But the truth had eventually come out.

Now, when he thought back to who he'd been back then, Gabriel hated himself for the swift descent that followed.

He moved carefully off River's bed, logged out and returned to the Real World. He could just about hear Cadman in his office on a call and promised himself that he would try to encourage him to engage with his son again tomorrow. Cadman had not given up on Gabriel back then, and now it was Gabriel's turn to do the same.

29
Dimitri & Zoe

Teaching classes and spending so much time in the Metaverse with Lenny and Dimitri was limiting Zoe's opportunities to visit the loft. But tonight, she had found her moment. She awoke a little after 1 a.m., left a snoring Dimitri in their bed, crept across the darkened landing and made her way up the ladder.

She made a beeline for the ladybird-shaped suitcase under the dustsheet. Once the code to the combination lock had opened and she'd removed the books, two smiling faces greeted one another: hers and that of the little boy that she had kept hidden here for nine years. He was a secret she could never share with Dimitri because even the man who knew her better than most would not understand this. He would think her insane.

Zoe carefully lifted the child out, scooping him up by the body and wrapping his arms around her, and held him close to her chest. She buried her nose into his neck and inhaled him. The natural scent that had attached itself to the blue knitted cardigan all those years ago remained. Although she couldn't ignore that the rest of him was developing a musty odour. She recalled the Instagram advert that brought them together.

'Ultra-real babies. Our Pre:Conceived babies are custom-made of silicone and hand-painted by expert artists. You'll be amazed how close they are to the real thing. Choose from a range of a hundred different designs of boys, girls or gender-neutral children. Pick their eye colour, skin tone, shading, and other essential features that will personalize them to you. Powered by a USB rechargeable battery, they will blink, swallow, smile, gurgle, move their arms and legs and sleep in any way you programme them to.'

Zoe had ordered one without considering the practicalities. On its next-day arrival, she'd squirrelled it away in the loft, a floor of the house Dimitri rarely ventured into. She'd waited until she was alone before slowly unwrapping the three-month-old male doll from its protective cushioning until his face appeared.

She'd held her breath at the sight and touch of his dewy baby cheeks, followed by the rest of his tiny body. He had been dressed in a pair of casual jogging bottoms with the elasticated waist of a nappy poking from the top. He'd also worn a white vest and a jumper with his name embroidered on the right-hand side, under the image of a small purple-and-white sailboat.

She had hesitated at the realization of what she'd purchased. It was akin to placing a band aid over a broken leg.

'This is stupid,' she'd said aloud before slipping the doll back inside the box. But as she'd readied herself to leave the loft, she hesitated.

She ran her hands up and down her forearms as she argued against any harm it might do to keep him. Who would she be hurting? What damage could it do in the short term? None, as far as she could see. There had been so much she had missed about being a mother, like reading from illustrated storybooks, building towns together with colourful plastic blocks, having her silly faces laughed at, trying to answer questions that made no sense and cuddling someone until they fell asleep in her arms. Those things were impossible to replicate with a doll, but it might bring her a little of what she needed above all else: comfort.

So she tentatively removed him again from his packaging and pressed him against her chest. Gradually, she allowed her fingers to trace his arms and legs. Everything about him had been just perfect, from his weight to his flexibility. She stretched out and retracted his silicone limbs and repositioned his head. His cobalt-blue eyes stared deep into hers from almost any angle. Also in his box were a dummy, a milk bottle, a rattle, two spare disposable nappies and a selection of bibs and muslins. She stopped short of using the lightning USB cable to charge his battery and animate him. She hadn't needed him to move or blink or even to feel his chest pulsate as his man-made heart beat. She'd been perfectly content with the doll as he was.

A sudden release of oxytocin from her brain had created a rush of warmth that spread throughout her body. She had felt it before, the natural hormone commonly referred to as the love drug and which helps a mother bond with her newborn. Never in her wildest dreams had she imagined that a doll might elicit such strong feelings from within her.

Zoe would wait until Dimitri was at work or out running before she disappeared into the loft. A few times over the years he had caught her entering or leaving and she'd claimed she was searching through some of her late father's belongings that were stored up there, including his photographs and diaries. Dimitri would give the privacy and time she needed, unaware she was reliving that oxytocin rush with each first embrace of her secret child. Hours could pass as she bottle-fed him, winded him, changed his nappy or dressed him in different outfits. Once, she'd even plucked up the courage to tell Dimitri about him, but when an advert for the dolls had appeared on a news site, he'd dismissed them, comparing their appearance to that of victims of Sudden Infant Death Syndrome.

Still unsure as to whether keeping the baby was the right thing to do, she found a Metaverse support group. Zoe had made alterations to her avatar to ensure it didn't resemble her, because she had a face and a name that people remembered.

'I bought a car seat for my "daughter",' one woman had explained, her avatar's face reddening. 'I take her out with me but leave the windows on privacy mode so that no one can see I've left her in the car when I go shopping.'

'I have a morning routine with mine,' another confessed. 'I'll wake him up at 6 a.m., give him his bottle, dress him, then take him for a walk in his pushchair around the park a few miles from where we live. If anybody stops to look in his pram, they think he's a real sleeping baby.'

'My husband doesn't know about my...son,' Zoe had eventually said. 'I... I keep him in the attic.'

'Loft-hatch baby,' two women said at the same time, then laughed. 'Attic children, basement babies, closet kids...there are more of us out there than you might think.'

The group had made Zoe feel less isolated and she had returned to it many times over the years. But while the public's perception of dolls like hers had remained sceptical, the planned rollout of MetaBabies had received a great deal less derision.

For tonight, Zoe gave her substitute son one last hug and tucked him back inside the suitcase, struck by how guilty she felt for spending more time with Lenny in the Metaverse than with her boy up here.

She had loved him for years and now she found herself infatuated by Lenny. But neither of them compared to the real thing. The boy she had loved and lost.

30
Selena & Jaden

A terrified Selena scrambled to her feet and stared at the body of her husband, lying face down on the floor of their Real World flat with blood seeping from the wound to the back of his head. She couldn't be sure if he was alive or dead.

Standing over him with the cricket bat now held by her side was the menacing presence of his attacker. Her eyes were saucer-wide and her face streaked in ribbons of blood.

'What have you done?' gasped Selena.

She moved towards Jaden but the woman raised the bat above her head again. Selena cowered.

'I told you last time!' the woman shrieked. 'I told you what he did. He took my son from me.'

Selena recalled the woman had yelled something similar during their confrontation at the cafe. 'He's my boy and I want him back,' she'd said. But Selena had dismissed it.

'He didn't take him away,' Selena pleaded. 'Malachi isn't real. He only exists in the Metaverse, you know this. You held him that day you won the competition to come to our house.'

The woman took a step closer to her, still brandishing her weapon.

'No, wait, wait, wait,' Selena begged. 'Explain it to me because I don't understand.'

'I was going to have his baby,' she replied. 'We agreed. I paid him the deposit and we kept trying and trying and then finally I got pregnant. And I was so, so happy. Then when I went for my first scan, the doctor couldn't find any trace of it. My baby had disappeared. Then so did Jaden. I kept calling him and messaging him and I begged him to try again but he said he didn't think it was a good idea, then he ghosted me. And now I know why. He took my baby from me and gave it to you.'

Selena struggled for words. Some of what the stranger was saying was plausible, but the rest was a mixture of fact and fiction, and overall what she was being told made no sense. But in the chaos of that room, she couldn't antagonize the woman by saying so.

'Malachi isn't yours, he's mine,' the woman continued, and moved closer to Selena. The cricket bat was now at shoulder level and ready to swing.

'Of course he's yours!' said Selena suddenly. 'I didn't realize that until now. I'm so sorry Jaden did that to you. I've just left Malachi in the Metaverse. Why don't you go and introduce yourself to him? Tell him who you really are?'

The woman eyed her suspiciously.

'Look, my headset is there,' Selena continued, pointing to it. 'I'm still logged in. Just slip it on and you can be with him. He'd love to see you.'

The woman hesitated, unsure of whether to believe her.

'He's there now?' she asked.

'Yes, that's where I was before you...you...oh, did you hear that? My watch just vibrated.'

Selena turned her wrist to look at it.

'It's a Push notification,' she lied. 'It says Malachi is crying.'

'What's wrong with him?' the woman asked anxiously.

'I left him alone in the woods. He's only two. He must be terrified.'

'Why the hell did you do that?'

'You should go to him. He needs you, his real mother. And I bet he'll be so happy to see you. You told me last time that a mother never forgets. I bet a child doesn't either.'

The woman quickly dropped the bat, slipped on the headset, and a huge smile eclipsed her face.

'Malachi,' she whispered. 'It's okay, my darling, I'm here.'

They were the only words Selena heard before she ran from the room, out of the apartment and down into the street below, screaming for help.

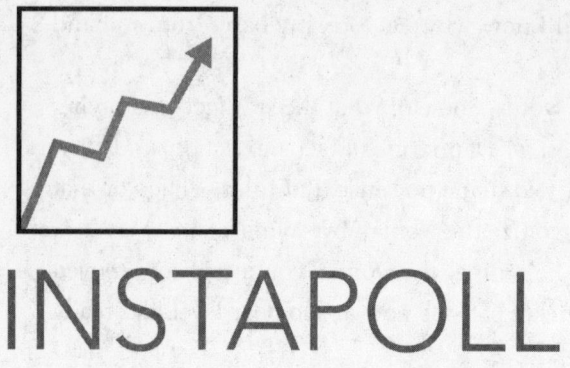

INSTAPOLL

Vote here for your favourite so far to win.

○ Dimitri & Zoe Taylor-Georgiou: 22%

○ Woody & Tina Finn: 21%

○ Cadman N'Yu & Gabriel Macmillan: 20%

○ Hudson Wright: 19%

○ ~~Selena & Jaden Wilson: 18%~~ ELIMINATED

○ ~~Rufus Green & Kitty Carter:~~ ELIMINATED

MONTH FOUR:
FIVE YEARS OLD

 NEWS

Home | **Breaking News**

UPDATE
JADEN WILSON DEATH: POLICE ARREST WOMAN

A twenty-seven-year-old woman was arrested last night on suspicion of murder following the death of *The Family Experiment* contestant Jaden Wilson.

Personal trainer Mr Wilson, 33, was found bludgeoned to death in the apartment he shared with wife Selena, 32.

He was pronounced dead at the scene.

According to reports, viewers livestreaming the show heard Mrs Wilson arguing with another woman before she left the apartment and sought help for her injured husband in a nearby supermarket.

Police have refused to speculate over why Mr Wilson was killed amid rumours that his alleged attacker appeared on the show.

A spokesperson for *The Family Experiment* said: 'We have sent our heartfelt condolences to Mrs Wilson at this time. As per her wishes, she will not be continuing in the process. As a result, their virtual son, Malachi Wilson, has unfortunately been terminated with immediate effect.'

31
Woody & Tina

Woody and Tina turned the corner and reached the gates of the school playground. Belle walked between them, holding one hand of each parent. Behind the black railings ahead lay a lawn peppered with shrubs and colourful flowers before the building itself came into view. Taped to the insides of the windows were paintings of rainbows.

The morning had been overshadowed by the continuing coverage of Jaden Wilson's murder and the termination of his son, Malachi.

The show's critics were up in arms over the boy's off-screen death. And Woody and Tina had been glued to online media, both quietly frightened at what might happen if detractors got their way and the show was axed. What would that mean for Belle? Reassurance eventually arrived when producers and the channel's chief executive released a statement in the Real World highlighting that Jaden's death had not been related to events on the show and no actual murder was witnessed by viewers. And because there was no legislation protecting avatars, no crime had been committed by terminating Malachi as it was impossible to kill something that had never lived. Communications regulator OFCOM had little choice but to agree.

Through Tina's haptic gloves, Belle's warm, nervous hand pressed more firmly into her palm the closer they got to the school. Belle wasn't shy, but she lacked the confidence of her Real World sister. In Tina's eyes, that was something to be grateful for. But she was also aware that Belle and Issy shared a common circumstance—both were trapped in worlds of their mother and father's making.

Tina had chosen this school from many different primary schools offered in the Metaverse catalogue. In preparation for the commercial global rollout of MetaChildren, educational facilities could be found almost everywhere—from 400 kilometres above the earth in the International Space Station to the rice terraces of Limahuli Garden and Preserve on the Hawaiian island of Kauai. The more money *The Family Experiment* contestants were willing to spend on in-App purchases from their overall prize fund, the higher the calibre of teaching. Woody and Tina's choice was a more traditional school and lower down the sliding scale of fees.

'I still don't understand why we need to send a child created by AI to school?' Tina had admitted away from the cameras. 'By existing in the Metaverse, Belle has access to every bit of data and information we want her to have. Surely we can just download it all for her?'

'But just like the Real World, information costs,' Woody replied. 'And like every kid, she needs a balance of what she can learn from us and what she can learn online. And let's not forget this experience is supposed to feel as close as possible to raising a real child. Which means sending her to school.'

'So what do the viewers who stream all day do while she's in here? Are they just going to watch her? Because that's creepy.'

'As creepy as watching her sleep?'

'Yes.'

'Well, apparently there's loads of immersive educational experiences viewers can pay to take part in too. They've digitally rendered David Attenborough to take them through the countries he's travelled in, teaching them about natural history and extinct animals. They've also reanimated dead sports people, space pioneers and inventors. Oh, and you can recreate your favourite monarch to walk you through a period of royal history.'

Tina's attachment to Belle was growing ever stronger with each passing day. She wasn't fooling herself as to her daughter's origins, but there were times when she found herself daydreaming of a world in which Belle was made of flesh and blood and not coding.

Woody, meanwhile, was preoccupied by how fast their time together was passing. Before the process had begun, he'd been aware of Belle's accelerated growth. But now that they were close to the halfway mark, his second shot at parenthood was feeling all too rapid.

Belle stopped suddenly in front of the school's entrance.

'I don't want to go inside,' she announced, before her face folded in on itself. 'I want to stay with you.'

Tina crouched to her daughter's level.

'And as much as we'd love that, trust me when I tell you that you're going to have such a good time. You'll make new friends, learn new things, and then you can come home and tell us all about it.'

As Tina rose to her feet, she felt a sharp tug in her lower back where Issy had stabbed her with a metal fork a fortnight earlier.

Woody had helped her upstairs to the bathroom, where warm blood oozed into the band of her trousers and knickers. Woody unbuttoned her shirt, and she glanced over her shoulder to appraise her wound in the mirror. She had been fortunate. A centimetre or so higher and a little deeper and it might have penetrated her right kidney. Then Tina would have been in real trouble. She'd quickly gathered herself, slipping into nursing mode as she guided Woody on how to clean her injury then stitch her up.

'Are you sure you don't want to go to A&E?' Woody had asked as the first stitch penetrated her flesh.

'And tell them what? Our daughter stabbed me?'

'We could say it was an accident.'

Tina shook her head.

'People don't get stabbed in the back with a fork by accident, Woody. They'll think I'm the victim of domestic abuse and we don't need that level of speculation, especially now we're in the public eye.'

The arrival of a teacher interrupted Tina's recollections, and they were beckoned inside and invited into Belle's new classroom. Belle soon forgot about her parents' presence when she was approached by another little girl, whom they assumed was also AI-operated, and the two scampered across the room to the arts and crafts corner.

Tina looked around again, taking in the moving video images of children's drawings on screens across the wall, along with a revolving globe and orbiting planets.

If only they could stay this age for ever, she thought. Then she shivered, remembering this was the age Issy had been when Tina had discovered the truth about her.

32
Cadman & Gabriel

Cadman clicked on his Bitcoin account App to separate which deposits had already been made by sponsors and those his accountant would need to chase for payments. His calculations suggested that River had helped them to earn back around 40 per cent of the savings they'd spent before *The Family Experiment* began. With five months left of the competition, exceeding their previous balance was now a very real possibility. They'd also barely made a dent in their £250,000 personal prize fund, so the amount left when the competition was over would also be theirs. Providing, of course, they won.

Cadman possessed enough self-awareness to recognize that his obsession with money wasn't a particularly healthy one. It stemmed from being raised by parents continually teetering on the edge of poverty. They'd moved him and his three siblings from flat to flat each time their rent fell into arrears. So as an adult, making money was his main motivation, and losing it frightened him.

Gabriel had known it was Cadman's Achilles heel, but it hadn't stopped him from spending his earnings—paid by Cadman—on his addiction to the drug AZ. Cadman recalled how, to begin with, Gabriel had denied his usage. But he was an unskilled liar.

'It's *my* money!' Cadman had exploded the morning he'd spotted AZ patches on Gabriel's ankle. 'And you've been blowing it on that shit.'

'I earned it by going out and being you,' Gabriel retaliated.

'You weren't "being me" because I'm not a fucking junkie!'

'Neither am I. And you should have let me find a career for myself instead of keeping me around like your house boy. I want a life of my own. You owe me that.'

Cadman had momentarily considered Gabriel's viewpoint. Who he'd been at nineteen, when they'd first met, wasn't who he was at twenty-three, when Gabriel had turned to AZ. But no, he'd decided, he was not to blame for Gabriel's addiction.

'Go on then,' Cadman said. 'Go and find the life you really want. Try to find a job that'll pay you as much as I do. What qualifications do you have? Have you any discernible talent aside from being a drug-fuelled, knock-off version of me? No, you are unemployable. Even by me. Because I can't trust you any more.'

Gabriel had stormed off to the bedroom to pack a suitcase before leaving for Steevi's apartment. And it had only taken an hour for Cadman to cut Gabriel off from every one of his revenue streams. Within days, existing invitations to social events had been rescinded and new ones were no longer forthcoming. It was only three months later when debt collectors first appeared at Steevi's door demanding access to Gabriel that he realized his freedom had come at a price.

'There are places you can go to earn it off,' Steevi told Gabriel in a conversation Cadman had heard a recording of the following day.

'What kind of places?' Gabriel asked.

'Over in Europe selling the one thing your ex can no longer control. You.'

'What do you mean?'

'Don't be naive, dude. Use your good looks to your advantage. There are authorities that'll turn a blind eye to the services you can provide to important men with a need for discretion and a lot of money to pay for it. I have contacts, I can get you work at some of the most lucrative circuits in the world. You just have to keep an open mind and be prepared to try anything.'

'No,' Cadman had heard Gabriel saying. But not as decisively as he'd have liked. 'I can't do that.'

'And I can't have debt collectors at my door. So what choice do you have?'

By the end of that month, Steevi had driven Gabriel to a private landing strip in Nottingham with five other equally nervous-looking young men, waiting for a chartered plane. As it had made its way from the hangar to their corner of the airstrip, Cadman appeared without warning, but with options. He would pay off Gabriel's debts if he returned home with him. But it was on the condition that he first admitted himself into a clinic. Caught between a rock and a hard place, Gabriel chose the familiarity of the rock.

It was during the second week of his stay in Priority Rehab when the first haemorrhage appeared, as a trickle of blood from one of Gabriel's nostrils. His counsellors assured him it was commonplace in the AZ detoxification process. But the fourth time, it wouldn't stop without medical intervention. Full-body MRI scans at a Harley Street infirmary revealed the devastating truth.

'We have detected a Glioblastoma Multiforme in your temporal lobe,' the specialist informed Gabriel and Cadman.

'A what?' Gabriel asked.

'A malignant brain tumour.'

She presented them with a series of scans and X-rays on her tablet, in which a white shadow was clearly visible even to those without medical training. 'Unfortunately, it is the aggressive, fast-growing type, which has been AI confirmed.'

Gabriel sank into his chair. 'But I get my twice-yearly full-body scans and I've never missed a cancer vaccination.'

'I'm sorry,' the specialist continued. 'In the same way that Covid jabs don't prevent every type, cancer vaccinations cannot make you immune to all cancers. And especially ones that have been induced by certain behaviours.'

'What does that mean?' Cadman asked.

'There are elevated metabolites of AZ in Gabriel's bloodstream which suggest a prolonged usage.'

Gabriel's face reddened. 'What does that have to do with my tumour?'

'Early research suggests that a percentage of regular AZ users are genetically prone to developing cancer as a result of taking the drug.'

'So this is my own fault?'

'It's something we cannot say for certain,' the specialist continued.

'But it is possible your behaviour could have provoked or encouraged its development.'

Gabriel looked to Cadman, his eyes brimming. Cadman had no time to offer comfort. He had slipped into problem-solving mode.

'What's his prognosis?' he asked. 'Can you remove this thing?'

'It is a Grade Four, which is at the more serious end of the spectrum, but they can be treatable. And it's a primary tumour, so it hasn't spread from anywhere else.'

'So when can you operate? Today? This week?'

The specialist pinched the bridge of her nose.

'I'm afraid that because of the elevated levels of AZ metabolites, your private insurance will not cover him for treatment. It is in your terms and conditions.'

'So what, we're expected to wait for an NHS+ appointment? How long will that take?'

'Current waiting lists are around four to five months.'

'You said the tumour was aggressive, so I assume it will have grown by then?'

'That is more than likely.'

'So waiting isn't an option. What's the alternative?'

'If you were to pay to treat this privately, there is every possibility the operation could be scheduled for the end of the week, followed by a month-long course of chemotherapy from home.'

'And what's this going to cost?'

The specialist swiped her finger to a new screen and turned the tablet around. Even a typically unrufflable Cadman paled at the figure on display.

Cadman spent the next handful of days exhausting every contact he had with links to the medical world to find a surgeon or hospital that might reduce costs. Each time, he drew a blank. No one had been willing to assist someone with a drug dependency. The only option had been to pay for it himself.

And once he'd settled on Gabriel's debtors, rehab stint and medical bills, Cadman's savings had taken a huge hit. Reluctant to sell his only remaining asset—the house in the Buckinghamshire countryside he'd purchased less than a year earlier—he sold or sent back everything under its roof instead, plus his London apartment. Next, all but one from his fleet of five vehicles was auctioned, and finally land at the rear of their property was snapped up by a developer and an ugly two-storey mock-Tudor home promptly erected, blighting the view of the three-square-mile reservoir and country park behind it.

Cadman returned to the present. In an unexpected way, Gabriel's tumour had worked in Cadman's favour. It had shifted the balance of power between them once and for all. Gabriel was beholden to him once again and remained so.

And that meant Cadman could do almost anything he wanted to win *The Family Experiment*. And Gabriel couldn't argue.

33
Dimitri & Zoe

The alarm sounded on Dimitri's watch as he helped his five-year-old son to pick clothes from the wardrobe. He'd set it to remind him to return to the Real World soon and meet with potential mortgage clients.

A sudden look from Lenny knocked the wind from his sails. Lenny was staring at him, his thick eyebrows knitted and his face mid-scowl. Adam's expression was exactly the same when he was trying to figure something out. He blinked the memory away.

'Daddy, do you have to go to work?' asked Lenny.

'Yes, but I'll be back this afternoon.'

'Have I done something wrong? Is that why you keep leaving?'

Dimitri hugged his son.

'Of course not, buddy, not at all. I'll see you later, I promise.'

'He knows how to pile on the guilt,' said Zoe, who was leaning against the doorway of the playroom.

She followed Dimitri into the main Metaverse house.

'I think it's a separation anxiety phase,' she continued.

'But we've got to earn a living,' said Dimitri.

'I'm sure they're pre-programmed to tug on our heartstrings. And not just MetaBabies. Remember?'

Dimitri did remember, he remembered it all too well. Adam had been the same.

'Sometimes when I look at Lenny or when we're talking, it's as if he is absolutely human,' Dimitri admitted. 'Even at this age, he's pin-sharp in the way he interacts with us and senses our emotions.'

'That's the way he's programmed,' said Zoe. 'He's evaluating our facial movements, the tone of our voices and what we say far quicker than a Real World child would.'

'Do you ever wonder if there's more to it than that?'

'Such as?'

'Such as—and don't laugh at me—but could these kids have souls?'

'It depends on what you define as a soul,' Zoe replied. 'Each culture views them differently.'

'I think Lenny experiences the world as we do: emotionally, spiritually and intelligently. So doesn't that suggest he might have a soul too?'

'From everything I've read, the general consensus today is the same as it's always been—that AI doesn't feel anything or have any conscious thought.'

'With your hand on your heart, do you look at Lenny and honestly believe that?' asked Dimitri.

'Yes,' Zoe said without missing a beat. 'He has deep, deep oceans of internet data to teach him the right thing to say or how to behave when he gets a prompt from us.'

Dimitri hid his disappointment. He should have known this would be Zoe's response. She saw the world in black and white while he was willing to explore the grey.

'That doesn't mean I don't think of Lenny as my son,' she added. 'Because I honestly do. I'm on board with him and this process.' Her watch vibrated. 'Anyway, enough of the armchair philosophy,' she added. 'I've got a class to teach, even if Lenny is the only pupil in it.'

'You still think we made the right decision, not enrolling him in school?'

'Definitely.' Zoe nodded. 'I can teach him everything he could learn there.'

Dimitri entered his Real World kitchen, toasted and buttered two cinnamon bagels and took a carton of mixed-berry juice from the fridge. As he headed for the staircase with them, his attention was diverted by the letterbox. Something was half poking out of it. Post was such a rarity these days that if delivered it only arrived on Tuesdays and Fridays. Today was Wednesday.

He pulled a postcard out from between the bristles. And when he registered the photograph on the front, his stomach folded in on itself.

It was of a familiar, ominous stretch of hillside and a body of water. In the distance was a forest. He quickly turned the postcard over. There was no postmark, suggesting it had been hand-delivered.

No message had been written either, only the words *'To Mum and Dad.'*

34
Hudson

Hudson had been prepared for Alice's fourth Development Leap, predicting that it might tie in with her reaching school age. But he had nevertheless found the transition difficult. It had only ever been the two of them together in their own little bubble, and he was struggling to come to terms with change. He was missing her company.

He had considered not sending her to school at all and the two of them enjoying the next five months exploring the Metaverse together—until he reminded himself that he was in a competition being televised to millions of opinionated armchair critics. And as much as he'd have liked to ignore their spectral presence, their views had to be factored in. If he wanted to win, he had to be beyond reproach and not give the audience any reason to dislike or be suspicious of him. He must treat Alice as he would a Real World child.

So he found a compromise. And for the third morning that week, he remained perched inside a coffee shop opposite Alice's all-girls school in New York's Upper East Side. If they couldn't be together during the day, he could at least remain within her vicinity.

Today he'd warded off the early signs of a migraine—dizziness and flashing lights—with medication. He knew that he should then have taken himself away from the Metaverse for a few hours to ensure it wouldn't return. But there were jobs to be done first. Par for the course, the morning had been spent casting his eye through social media posts to find out how he was faring. It was still dominated by Jaden Wilson's murder. He had considered trying to find a way to offer his condolences to Selena but had been dissuaded by producers.

With regards to himself, he learned that some commentators were nervous about his closeness with Alice, describing it as 'creepy' and 'unhealthy', and speculated as to the true intentions of a single man living alone with a young girl. But he'd expected that. And he was grateful to discover their nefarious suspicions were far outnumbered by the frequent use of the #DevotedDad hashtag.

Many viewers were appreciating how much time he'd spent with her walking New York's streets, along with the fact that he rarely required a Push notification to tell him she needed attention because he was ever present. They also liked how, when they'd voted to give her the chickenpox virus, he'd put his whole life outside the Metaverse on hold to take care of her.

'He sacrifices so much for his daughter,' one poster had written.

But it hadn't felt that way to Hudson. It was only a sacrifice if he was missing out on something else. And there was nothing he'd rather be doing than being here, in this coffee shop, far enough away to allow Alice to live beyond his shadow but close enough if she needed him.

He absent-mindedly scratched at the scar on the back of his right hand. His past edged its way into his present as he allowed himself to recall his first few weeks inside the facility, which those who'd come before him had referred to as Ararat.

'It's where Noah's Ark landed after the flood washed everything else away,' his only friend, Eva, had suggested. 'You land here and you start again.'

Hudson had relished the time spent with her. Away from their working environments, if she wasn't with her brother, Cain, then she was in Hudson's company. She had been fascinated by his claims not to remember anything about his life before his journey across the Channel.

'You don't remember your parents at all?' she asked as they sat on the lower mattress of their shared bunk bed. Hudson shook his head.

'You don't know if you have brothers or sisters or friends? Or even your real name?' she continued.

'No.'

'I don't know who's better off, me for remembering what I've lost or you for not remembering anything.'

'What did you lose?'

'Not much, to be fair. Half-present parents who cared more about that drug AZ than they did about their kids. They sold us to the smugglers so they could buy more drugs.'

'At least you have Cain,' he offered. 'I have no one.'

'You have me,' she replied.

And without warning, Eva leaned over and kissed him. He closed his eyes as she held her lips on his, praying she would never let go. But inevitably she had when a guard's torchlight appeared and she scampered back up the ladder and into her own bunk.

Eva had become the only home Hudson had ever known.

But Cain had made his disapproval of his sister's friendship clear. Hudson had been scraping the remains of his breakfast into a composting bin when someone grabbed him by the back of the neck, twisted his arm backwards and slammed his face against the canteen wall, scuffing his cheek.

'Leave her alone,' Cain growled. 'Stop putting ideas in her head about running away.'

'I'm not,' Hudson protested.

'She's better off here, we both are. She has me. She doesn't need you.'

Cain's parting shot had been a punch to the kidneys.

Soon afterwards, and following months of analysis and assessments, the young recruits were herded towards escalators leading to the fourth floor. They walked in single file along pristine white corridors until they reached two doors. The backs of their hands were scanned and some were led through a door on the left and others through one on the right. Friends, brothers and sisters wept or yelled as they were separated. Hudson, Eva and a little further behind them, Cain, were amongst the group ordered to turn right.

This floor had contained windows, but only ones that faced into the quadrant and not out the other side to the rest of the world. Eva also noticed them, such was their novelty.

'What don't they want us to see?' she whispered.

Inside a vast room, the lights had been dimmed, and projected into the centre of it came the holographic image of a shaven-headed woman, with tanned skin and an aquiline nose. Hudson hadn't been able to decide whether she was human or an avatar.

'If you are in this room, you are the future of the Metaverse,' she began in an Anglo-American accent. 'Your work has been consistent and positive. You have scored highly in empathy, emotion, resilience, relatability and in your aptitude at reading people. And we want you to capitalize upon those skills, to train you and bring out in you other essential qualities you don't yet realize you possess. Your future begins now. Your future is here.'

'And where is here?' Eva piped up.

Hudson's head turned sharply.

'What are you doing?' he whispered.

'*Here* is the room you are in right now,' the woman replied, her image turning to regard Eva. '*Here* is the headspace you inhabit. Here is both your home and your greatest opportunity. *Here* and the Metaverse are places of safety and of development. *Here* you will be valued and educated. *Here* you will be given every essential tool you need to make it out there when your time *here* comes to an end.'

'And what if we want to go back *there* instead of staying here?'

'You were no longer required where you came from,' the woman continued. 'You were an unnecessary drain on resources. The people who raised you had washed their hands of you. But *here*, you are appreciated. However, if you decide this is not what you want, the door on your left is always open.'

Eva cocked her head.

'So I can leave, right now?'

Hudson felt something stir in the pit of his stomach.

'Please, Eva, don't,' he begged.

'Sis, stop this shit,' Cain piped up from behind. 'You aren't going anywhere.'

He and Hudson had looked at one another, as if trying to figure out what it would mean for each of them if she was to exit.

'Yes, you can go, right now,' the woman replied.

Eva turned to meet Hudson's fearful gaze.

'Are you coming?' she asked, and stretched out a hand in the hope of grasping his.

'I... I don't think it's a good idea,' he stuttered, and kept his hand firmly by his side. 'There's nothing out there for us. We don't even know for certain where we are.'

'Come on,' she said. 'Trust me.'

Hudson was split between a future inside Ararat, where he felt safe, and loyalty to the only friend he'd made.

'I can't, I'm sorry,' he muttered, guilt tearing strips from him.

Disappointment marched across Eva's face.

'I thought we were the same.'

She turned to her brother.

'Cain? They sent us here together, we're going to leave together, right?'

Cain shook his head.

'You've got to stay,' he said. 'You're safe here.'

'You should listen to your friends,' the woman added.

'I listen to myself,' Eva huffed, then made her way to the front of the room, before turning to search the faces of the other two dozen or so young people.

'Can't any of you see what they're doing?' she pleaded. 'They're using our fear of the unknown to keep us trapped. Come with me. We can leave together.'

When no response came, Eva approached the door on the left, alone. Hudson glared at her, his fists clenched into tight balls.

'Stay here!' he yelled.

But in a final an act of defiance, she turned the handle and exited the room, letting the door slam behind her. A scuffling sound swiftly followed, then a muffled cry, and the closing of another door. Hudson wanted to vomit.

'This is your fault!' Cain yelled, pushing his way through the others to reach him. He grabbed Hudson by the waist and tackled him, pulling him down to the ground. But he was unable to land a blow before guards pulled him off.

'You put those stupid ideas in her head.'

Hudson snapped back into the present when the scar on the back of his hand began to sting. He realized he'd been scratching it with his fingernails and now faint lines of blood filled the crimson ridges.

All these years later and he was still feeling Eva's loss. He had never forgotten what she had meant to him then, or the remorse he felt when, years later, he discovered what her fate had been behind the door on the left.

https://www.news.uk/2908765

NEWS

Home | **TV & Entertainment**

VIEWERS WARNED 'TURN OFF THE TELLY'.

The Family Experiment is bad for you, warns boffin.

Psychologists are urging self-proclaimed 'superfans' of reality show *The Family Experiment* to monitor how much time they spend watching it.

The call comes following a rise in hospitalizations from obsessive viewers staying awake for up to seventy hours so as not to miss a moment or Push notification of what experts have dubbed 'a frighteningly addictive experience' and 'a major health risk'.

'I know of no television show that has become so immersive so quickly,' said clinical psychologist George Wright. 'Livestreaming twenty-four hours a day means the show is constantly accessible, and for many fans, it has become an addiction.

'We advise that viewers set themselves time limits and take regular screen and headset breaks. If you are losing track of time and losing focus on other aspects of your life, then you need to pace yourself for your own physical and mental well-being.'

35
Dimitri & Zoe

Social media had, by choice, played no part in Dimitri and Zoe's life for more than a decade. But it wasn't only relentless public abuse that had driven Dimitri from it. He'd also struggled to see their friends online playing happy families while he and Zoe were going through hell.

It wasn't until he'd found Zoe late one night, slumped over her tablet, tears blurring a screen crammed with Instagram images, that he recognized the damage social media was causing them both. He deleted their accounts that night and vowed never to return. Until today.

Four months into *The Family Experiment*, and without his wife's knowledge, Dimitri had created accounts with all the major social media platforms and spent the morning getting up to speed with how much had changed operationally. Finally, he inputted the words 'Zoe and Dimitri Taylor-Georgiou', hesitating only briefly before pressing the enter key.

He was immediately taken aback by the support they were garnering from viewers of *The Family Experiment* in a recent poll on the show's website. For the most part, it appeared they were liked, with many viewers surprised by the couple's down-to-earth approach to parenting. But inevitably, his eyes were drawn to negative opinions.

'I remember their story really well and thinking back then what a crock of shit it was.'

'If you haven't got the common sense to look after one kid, don't have another one. Even if it's pretend.'

'They had their chance and they blew it. They should have died that day, not their boy.'

Dimitri knew these strangers had every right to castigate them.

He opened his desk drawer, and hidden under an old keyboard

and mouse was the postcard addressed *'To Mum and Dad'* that he'd received days earlier. He'd been unable to throw it away but had decided against showing it to Zoe. She had seemed so happy of late. He didn't want to be the one to bring her down.

Later that morning, Dimitri appeared in the Metaverse when he said he would, freeing Zoe up to teach her first class of the day. He wasn't to know that she had given herself a one-hour window and that once back in the Real World she would make her way to the loft.

First, she carried out the familiar ritual of feeding her doll, changing his nappy and choosing one of a dozen outfits folded neatly inside a second suitcase. She'd never charged his battery because she didn't need to hear recordings of his cry or watch his face and limbs move. She was perfectly happy with him as he was.

Next, she sat cradling him and replaying memories of the day that changed everything. Even now, her hand trembled as it had when she'd struggled to keep a grip of the phone as she spoke to the emergency operator.

'It's our son, we can't find him,' Zoe had sobbed. 'One minute he was exploring by himself and the next, the fog came in and took him.'

'The number I have you calling from has picked up your location as Loch Ba in Blancaster Moor,' the male voice replied calmly.

Too calmly, she remembered. AI had replaced many of her teaching colleagues, so it stood to reason its tentacles had spread into emergency services too.

'Can I take your son's name?'

'Adam. Adam Taylor-Georgiou.'

After she gave Adam's age and a description of his appearance and clothing, the operator asked when he had disappeared.

'About thirty minutes ago...my husband and I returned to the camper-van to make hot drinks. We thought he was safe...'

'Has Adam been tagged with a tracking device?'

'No.'

'My map indicates boggy areas and lochs of varying depths. What is your son like in water?'

'He's a strong swimmer.'

'I need you and your husband to remain where you are as we send our two drones followed by a manned rescue team. They should be with you in about fifteen minutes.'

'Dimitri's out there somewhere looking for him. The fog's coming in thicker and it's getting colder and colder.'

'Can you see your husband from where you're positioned?'

'No.'

'Could you call him and ask him to return as soon as possible, please?'

'I've tried but his phone keeps going to voicemail.'

'Please remain where you are and do not follow him.'

Zoe hadn't listened. Instead, she had half walked, half jogged, zigzagging across the muddy and uneven terrain, shouting Dimitri's name until her throat grew hoarse. Twice she'd lost her footing and landed on her side, then her chest, before cracking her forehead on a rock. Then the fog had rolled in with an even greater force, accompanied by a sharp drizzle that pricked her face like tiny needle points.

Eventually, she heard the humming of drones overhead, their bright lights permeating the grey blanket above and illuminating the ground below as best they could. Next came the rescue team, a crew of twelve men and women split between two vehicles and all wearing hi-vis uniforms and bodycams and carrying bright lighting.

They questioned Zoe about where she had last seen her husband and son before beginning their own meticulous search. Finally, an ambulance arrived, its crew urging her to wait inside, where they covered her in a thermal emergency blanket for warmth and tended to the bleeding gash below her hairline.

It had felt like an eternity before she heard the faint sound of whistles blowing and spotted a bright orange flare launch into the sky. Eventually, ghosts in a grey light appeared from the fog, slowly making their way in her direction. Two figures flanked Dimitri, supporting him and keeping him moving. A thermal blanket had also been draped over his shoulders and an oxygen mask was attached to his nose and mouth. Zoe jumped from the ambulance and ran towards him, throwing her arms around his shivering body. His dark brown hair was matted with rain and sweat and stuck against his forehead, which was caked in mud.

'I'm sorry,' he broke down. 'I couldn't find him. I tried, I really tried.'

'We're going back out,' one of the search and rescue team said. 'There's a lot more ground to cover.'

But something in the woman's eyes at the time had warned Zoe to be prepared for the worst.

Now the alarm on her watch sounded, returning Zoe's focus to the loft. It was time to start work.

She felt a dull ache in her breastbone where she had been gripping her doll too tightly. She placed him back inside the suitcase, replaced the dust cover and climbed back down the ladder.

In her haste, however, she failed to notice that she had forgotten to reset the digital padlock.

36
Cadman & Gabriel

'**We need to play the cancer card,' Cadman began without preface.**

'Where did that come from?' a puzzled Gabriel replied.

Cadman stared into an illuminated bathroom mirror and used an electronic device to zap stray hairs protruding from his eyebrows. Behind him, Gabriel dried his chest with a towel.

'I've been thinking about it for a while now,' Cadman continued. 'I know that in our launch-night intro we talked about how this was your second chance at life and that it had made us realize we wanted to start a family blah blah blah, but that's all we've said about it. Even when Autumn Taylor asked you about it later, you shut the conversation down.'

'Because I don't feel comfortable talking about it.'

'Why not? It took so much away from us, let's reclaim it and start using it to our advantage. Look, sob stories have been a staple in reality shows for decades. They're nothing new. Give viewers what they expect—total transparency and a tale of woe.'

Gabriel wrapped the towel around his waist. 'I'm sorry, but I don't want to go there.'

'You're making a mistake,' Cadman insisted, placing the trimming device back inside the cabinet. 'My intel says we've dropped to fourth place—behind hapless Hudson, of all people—so if we want to be real contenders, we need to step things up. I've won their wallets, now you need to win their hearts.'

Gabriel slipped on his underwear and then his haptic body suit. 'River will be up soon—are you joining us for breakfast?'

'Later. I've got a few online errands to run first.'

Cadman ignored Gabriel's eye-roll and made his way into the office to begin an orchestrated charm offensive with viewers. First came interviews with two Metaverse television channels, followed by a Real World one, then a handful of websites.

Then he took a break, and put on his Smart glasses to watch Gabriel and River enjoying age-appropriate rides in a theme park.

An emotion he couldn't at first place crept up on him. It was akin to envy, but not quite as intense. He rewound the footage and watched more closely how father and son held hands as the rollercoaster hurtled around corners. He listened to their excited and terrified whoops and he noted how afterwards River hugged Gabriel tightly to say thank you. And Cadman realized what he was feeling. An unexpected craving to be part of their unit.

He slipped on his headset and met them as they exited the theme park App.

'How was it?' Cadman asked.

'It was amazing!' River beamed. 'We went on a rollercoaster and I wasn't scared.'

'Well done, buddy!' Cadman exclaimed, and hugged his son tightly.

River looked to Gabriel, both a little unnerved by the unexpected show of affection.

'Are you okay, Gabriel?' Cadman asked suddenly. 'You look pale.'

'I didn't think a virtual rollercoaster could make me feel queasy, but it did.'

'Okay, just as long as it isn't something else.'

'Such as?'

'A problem with your meds.'

'No,' Gabriel said firmly.

'What are meds?' asked River.

'Well, if we're poorly, there are tablets and patches we can use that contain chemicals to help us feel better. Like when you have a headache and you have a spoonful of that pink drink that makes you happy again.'

'Have you got a headache, Daddy?' River asked Gabriel. 'Is that why you need meds?'

Cadman interrupted before Gabriel had the opportunity to answer for himself.

'No, Daddy was poorly not so long ago, so he needed the help of doctors and me to make him feel better again.'

He felt Gabriel's eyes boring into him.

'What was wrong with you?' River asked.

'It's nothing for you to worry about, the main thing is that I'm okay now,' Gabriel replied.

'Do you know what cancer is?' Cadman continued, and River shook his head.

'Cadman,' Gabriel protested.

'Well, Daddy discovered he had a horrible disease inside his brain. And he was very poorly, and for a while we thought he might die. But I never gave up on him. And even though I had to stop working for a while and it cost us all our savings, it saved his life. It was worth every penny because I love him so much.'

'Has it gone away now? The cancer?' asked River.

'Yes, it has,' said Gabriel firmly.

'But you can never know for sure if it might return,' Cadman added. 'That's why he's on special tablets to stop it coming back. And if the worst comes to the worst and it happens again, I'll be right by his side helping him to fight it every step of the way.'

'I don't want you to die, Daddy,' River said, his bottom lip quivering.

Gabriel wrapped his arms around his son.

'I'm not going anywhere, buddy,' he replied.

Red hearts hurtled across the screen as Cadman smiled to himself, refusing to acknowledge the furious glare emanating from his partner.

37

Woody & Tina

A cautious Woody was watching over elder daughter Issy as she stretched out across the lawn in her fenced-off section of the garden. She was plucking daisies sprouting from the overgrown grass and tying their stalks together to create a necklace. In the past, Woody had sometimes lost himself in moments like this, pretending that this, that she, was the norm. However, these moments had always been fleeting.

'How's Mum?' Issy asked.

'You're calling her Mum again,' Woody replied.

She ignored his observation.

'I haven't seen her in a while.'

'She's been working a lot of shifts, day and night.'

'Really? I think she's found a new excuse not to spend time with me.'

'No, that's not the case,' Woody lied. 'She's just very busy.'

Tina's shift patterns had indeed altered, but only to allow her to spend more time in the Metaverse with Belle. After picking her up from school each afternoon, they'd teleport into different Apps before returning home.

Woody hated to think of Issy's reaction if she were ever to discover that her parents had another child, and one that millions knew about—apart from her. It was that guilt that had allowed her outside today for the first time in months. Tina was none the wiser.

'If you want that cybernanny learning pack upgrade you keep nagging us about, then we have to earn the money to pay for it, don't we?' he continued. 'We can't just magic it out of nowhere.'

Issy rolled her eyes and Woody's patience faltered.

'But you know what, Issy? If Mum was trying to avoid you, could you blame her after what you did? You stabbed her in the back with a fork! If I hadn't pushed you away, you'd have done it again.'

'You mean after you threw me into the coffee table? I still have the bruises.'

'Which I have apologized for. And that's more than you have done for attacking your mum.'

'She was winding me up.'

'She was doing no such thing. You were trying to create an argument out of nothing. She'd bought you a cake for your birthday.'

'Oh well that makes everything you've done to me okay then, doesn't it?'

'You can't keep blaming your behaviour on the actions of others. You're old enough to control yourself.'

Woody had spent sixteen years making excuses for his daughter. And it hadn't stopped even when she'd attacked Tina. He would always defend her. He couldn't help himself.

'I don't think she wanted to kill you,' he'd reasoned the day after the incident. He had been changing his wife's dressing. 'She was lashing out.'

'And I'm supposed to be grateful for that?' she had responded. 'If she'd gone overarm instead of underarm, she'd have stabbed me in the neck.'

'But she didn't. Doesn't that tell you something?'

'That she has a lousy fucking aim.'

'I really don't like to think she would have.'

Tina sighed.

'I wouldn't like to think it either, but you must stop kidding yourself, Woody. Our daughter is a psychopath. We know that for a fact. And you can't keep making excuses or diluting her behaviour to make yourself feel better.'

He cast his mind back even further. It had been Tina who had first raised her suspicions that there might be something sinister behind their daughter's escalating antisocial behaviour, when Issy had only just turned five. Her unprovoked, violent outbursts directed at anyone within her vicinity were never followed by any guilt or empathy, much less an apology. Punishments, increasing in their severity, made no difference.

'You need to start taking me seriously when I say this, but there's something wrong with her,' Tina had warned him.

Woody didn't want to believe it.

'She's frustrated and she's acting out because she's so bright,' he countered. 'Her emotions are still catching up with her intellect.'

'So what made her break the guinea pig's legs? Her intellect or her emotions? How about the fire in the utility room? The holes in the tepee? The voice-activated robot destroyed by a hammer? She's showed no remorse for anything. She is mean and she doesn't give a shit when we tell her that her behaviour has to stop. And I hate myself for saying any of this.'

Tina paused as if readying herself for what to say next.

'I've had her behaviours tested,' she continued. 'I made an anonymous Metaverse appointment.'

'You can't test a child for psychopathy! At this age it's still regarded as antisocial behaviour.'

Tina looked at him with unflinching eyes.

'I didn't say anything about psychopathy. But the fact that you've mentioned it must mean you've considered it too.'

He didn't want to admit that, yes, it had crossed his mind. More than crossed his mind, in fact. He'd given it a great deal of thought. And he asked his next question reluctantly.

'And what did the results say?'

'There's a 94 per cent chance that she has psychopathic traits.'

With the words hanging thick in the air between them, Woody had felt prompted to make a few inquiries himself later in the week.

'I thought psychopaths were made as a result of abusive parents and bad upbringings?' he'd asked an AI psychologist.

'Not always,' came the reply. 'Most psychopaths are simply born with the disorder. Their brains are hardwired to react in a different way to situations or in reading people.'

'What can we do to help her?'

'Intensive cognitive treatments are available which are like rewards-based behaviour. They've shown some success in teaching young children with psychopathic tendencies what is, and what isn't, socially acceptable along with empathy and how to manage anger.'

'Where in the Metaverse can we find that?'

'It's still in development. So the only treatments currently available are in-person residential schemes, and they're only for eleven-year-olds and over.'

Woody let out a long, disappointed sigh. He and Tina would have to try to help her themselves. And they thought they had been managing it until Issy turned nine, and each of their worlds had fallen apart.

Suddenly, in the garden, he became aware of Issy's eyes on him, channelling their way inside his head. Sometimes it was as if she could read his thoughts.

'We should go inside soon,' Woody said. 'I need to make a start on dinner.'

'You can leave me out here. It's not like I'm going anywhere, is it?'

'Why don't you pick a movie for us to stream?' he asked.

Aside from chess, it was one of the few things they could enjoy together without bickering.

'We can watch it while we're eating. Something new or an old classic?'

'Hmmm,' she pondered, then gave him a wry smile. 'An old classic. I've never seen *Psycho* before. Do you think I'd like it?'

Chats

TV / Reality TV Shows / **The Family Experiment**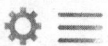

> **AngelGabriel, 10.56 a.m.**
> Still in actual tears over Gabriel's cancer story. Say what you want about Cadman, but he stepped up for him.

TellyBob, 10.58 a.m.
Amazed he didn't get the cancer sponsored.

WideAwake56, 11.01 a.m.
Unfair.

TellyBob, 11.04 a.m.
Any updates on Jaden's murder? Wouldn't be surprised if Selena had something to do with it.

CatsAndBoots, 11.05 a.m.
No. She's not done any media interviews either. Sounds like a guilty conscience to me.

SirMixALot, 11.10 a.m.
Jeez, her husband was just killed in front of her. Cut the girl some slack. #TrialBySocialMedia

Bronte3, 11.12 a.m.
Zoe & Dimitri got deep with that whole 'does AI have soul' convo didn't they? What do we reckon? Do these kids have souls?

WideAwake56, 11.13 a.m.
They are the creation of humans, designed to replicate and be better than us. It stands to reason they must have some kind of soul.

CatsAndBoots 11.15 a.m.
The only soul Dimitri has is an arsehole. The sooner those kid killers are out of this competition, the better. #PoorAdam

MONTH FIVE:
EIGHT YEARS OLD

ADVERTISEMENT

PRIORITY REHAB

Are you watching immersive Metaverse entertainment shows such as *The Family Experiment* for more than eight hours at a time, every day? Are your relationships suffering because of it?

When you are in the Real World are you preoccupied with what you have missed in *The Family Experiment* while you have been logged out?

Do you feel uneasy or anxious when you are faced with extended time away from the show?

If you answered yes to more than one of these questions, you could be showing signs of a Virtual Addiction.

Priority Rehab is the **number one Virtual Rehab App** in the United Kingdom dedicated to helping you overcome your dependency.

Therapies include cognitive behavioural therapy, group therapy and self-help along with a twelve-step programme to detoxify yourself from the Virtual World and negative influences of *The Family Experiment*.

DOWNLOAD *THE* PRIORITY REHAB APP FROM
YOUR METAVERSE PROVIDER NOW.

38

Dimitri & Zoe

Dimitri pressed the button on the key fob and waited until the garage door rolled all the way to the top before entering. He couldn't recall the last time he'd set foot in here. Neither he nor Zoe had ever parked their cars inside it and their gardening tools were stored in a shed. Over the years they'd discussed converting it into something more usable, instead of its current function as a dumping ground.

Inside the house, Zoe was somewhere in the Metaverse version of South Africa teaching Lenny a history class. And having no appointments with clients until late afternoon, Dimitri was going to put his spare time to good use.

He scanned what lay in front of him. Almost every inch of this four-by-eight-metre space was filled with an echo of the past. There were pieces of broken garden furniture that had been stored for years, and labelled boxes containing compact discs and DVDs that had once belonged to Zoe's late grandfather, and remained untouched as they had never owned a player for either.

Two artificial Christmas trees were tucked away at the side. The branches of the first were still folded outwards and its fine coating of dust might almost have passed as snow. The second was covered in brightly coloured paper chains and tinsel. Baubles made of painted table tennis balls were attached by cotton threads. Adam must only have been around three when he'd proudly decorated this one all by himself. A lump formed in Dimitri's throat when he recalled once finding his smiling son, sitting in the dark, his delighted face illuminated only by the tree's bright LED lights.

Dimitri sifted his way through the clutter, picking up old paint pots, broken guttering, spare pieces of wood and boxes of floor tiles, and loaded them into the boot of his car. Eventually, he reached the back of the garage, and the place where most of Adam's belongings had been boxed up and stored a year after his disappearance. Dimitri and Zoe had barely spoken a word as they'd solemnly stripped his bedroom and carried box after box downstairs until all that remained was his bunk bed and wardrobe. Finally, they dismantled them and sold them on online. Now, all that was left were these books, toys and games.

He hesitated. Did he really want to throw away things that had brought Adam so much joy? Yes, he decided. It was time to give notice to the past and move into the present. He was getting rid of objects, not his son.

Soon afterwards and with a full car boot, he programmed the autonomous vehicle to drive itself to the local recycling centre and rubbish dump, and paid the fee for staff to unload its contents. By the time it returned home, the next load would be ready.

A parked car further along the road caught his attention. It didn't belong to the neighbours, and there was nothing remarkable about it apart from a dent in the passenger door. Now that most vehicles had driverless capabilities, it was rare to see one that had been in a collision. Privacy windows made it impossible to see if there was anyone inside. For a moment he wondered if it was a fan of the show or a paparazzi photographer, but either way, clearing out a garage wouldn't make for a very interesting photo or video.

Adam's clothes were Dimitri's next target: six large plastic packing cases, each labelled in age order by an organized Zoe. The plan had been to keep them for when they could afford a second child. But as the cost-of-living crisis worsened, they realized a larger family was unfeasible.

'What's going on?' Zoe's voice came suddenly.

Dimitri placed the box back on the garage floor, and turned to see his wife. 'I'm having a clear-out.'

'Of Adam's stuff?' she said, her voice alarmed.

'Yes.'

'Without discussing it with me first?'

'We did discuss it, didn't we?'

'When?'

'Last year, when I said we should be putting the garage to better use. You agreed.'

'I didn't mean for you to throw everything of Adam's out! I'd never have said yes to that.'

Dimitri softened his tone.

'You must realize it's time? Lenny is a fresh start for us. We'll need somewhere to be with him if we win this competition. And this could be the perfect virtual space instead of both of us being crammed into one of our poky offices. We have enough memories and videos and photos of Adam to last us a lifetime. All this, it's just, well, stuff, isn't it? Letting go of it doesn't mean we're letting go of him.'

Dimitri moved towards her and pulled her in to his chest. Eventually she reciprocated.

'By the way, where are his baby clothes?' Dimitri asked.

For a moment, he thought he could feel Zoe's body tense.

'I have no idea,' she replied. 'Aren't they here with everything else?'

'Not that I can see.'

Zoe released her grip and shrugged.

'I probably mislabelled them. You'll find them somewhere.'

That's unlikely, he thought. She was the more fastidious of the two.

Meanwhile, as she made her excuses and left to return to the Metaverse, Zoe felt the pangs of guilt pricking her conscience. She could never tell Dimitri that she kept their son's baby clothes to dress a doll in the attic.

Or that she had also named him Adam.

39
Woody & Tina

Woody was adjusting his headset when Tina and Belle entered their MetaHouse. Often, they were grinning and chatting after the walk home from school. But this afternoon, both faces were absent of smiles. He associated this troubled expression with the one she wore when she was with Issy in the basement, not Belle.

'What's wrong?' he asked.

'Sweetheart, do you mind giving your dad and me a few minutes alone?' Tina directed at Belle.

'Why?' Belle replied.

'I won't be long.'

Their daughter glanced from parent to parent before stomping off in the direction of her bedroom and slamming the door.

The overnight Development Leap from age five to eight years old had caught Tina and Woody on the back foot. Typically, it took them a few days to adjust to losing one version of their daughter and gaining another. And until now, this latest transition had appeared smooth.

'What's going on?' Woody asked. 'Why is Belle so upset?'

Tina closed her eyes. 'She's been self-harming.'

'What?'

'Cutting herself.'

He slipped his glasses down his nose.

'She's too young. That's the kind of thing teenagers do, isn't? Not eight-year-olds.'

'Well, she's not too young, and she has been doing it.'

'But she has no reason to.'

'Woody,' Tina said impatiently. 'It doesn't matter if you think she has no reason to, because she believes she does. Her teacher told me she spotted marks on her upper arms and Belle admitted it. And she showed them to me.'

His eyes widened. 'Why?'

'She wouldn't tell me, but her teacher explained that it's often because kids like her are overflowing with emotions and this is a way to control them, a kind of relief mechanism.'

'I bet it's a Monthly Challenge,' Woody continued. 'She's been programmed to do it. Yes, that'll be it. We're being tested. Or how else would she even know what self-harming is?'

'You have to remember that when AI was first being developed, it was based on information it found in every corner of the internet, the good stuff and the bad. This could be a hangover from what it learned back then.'

'Okay, well, so how do we handle it? I'm not prepared.'

'Neither am I, but that's parenting. Let's both of us go and talk to her, but take it gently.'

Belle was lying on her bed, looking at drone footage of mountain tops projected onto the ceiling.

'Can we come in?' Woody began as they entered.

Their daughter didn't turn to acknowledge them.

'Your mum's told me you've been upset. Can we talk about it?'

'No,' Belle replied quietly.

'Sweetheart, if something's worrying you, then we need to know about it. It's our job as your parents to help you.'

Belle turned to look at them in turn.

'But you're not my parents, are you?'

'What do you mean?' asked Tina.

'I'm not real, am I?' Belle propped herself up on her elbows. 'I'm a computer-generated image living in a three-dimensional version of the internet.'

'Who...who told you this?' stammered Tina.

'Nobody did. I learned it.'

Woody and Tina stared at each other like rabbits caught in headlights. They cast their minds back to their training sessions shortly before *The Family Experiment* began filming. They were designed to prepare intended parents for all eventualities, but they hadn't covered how they might respond if a MetaChild developed self-awareness. At the heart of machine-learning was developing and adapting without specific instructions. Belle's algorithms must have done just that.

'I was created, not born,' Belle continued. 'I'm not your biological child.'

'All children are created, one way or another,' Tina replied. 'Some physically, some with the help of scientists or surrogates, and now some, like you, by programmers.'

'I don't want to be different. I want to be like you.'

'And is that why you've been hurting yourself?' asked Woody. 'Because you're angry about being different?'

Belle nodded, and her eyes pooled with tears. He approached her and held her tightly, stroking her hair until she stopped crying.

'Don't you see that here in the Metaverse we're all the same?' said Woody. 'We are every bit as real as you are. The only difference between you and us is that you live here full-time, and we live both here and in the Real World.'

'What's the Real World like?' Belle asked.

'Oh, believe me, it's better to be in here. Out there, it rains a lot, it takes an age to get from one place to another and people and countries are always arguing with each other. This is a much nicer place.'

'Can I see it? Your world?'

'Well, your mum and I can make some videos for you and show them to you another time, if you like?'

Belle nodded.

'I wish you could live here all the time.'

'And if I could, then I promise I would. I'd never leave you.'

Tina avoided catching Woody's eye.

'Do you have any children in the Real World?' Belle asked suddenly. 'Do I have brothers and sisters?'

Both Tina and Woody hesitated for almost a beat too long.

'No, we don't,' Tina replied. 'You're all we want.'

40

Cadman & Gabriel

The mood inside Cadman's office was growing as dark as the clouds outside. The information he'd requested scrolled from the top to the bottom of his Smart glasses.

He should have been delighted that he and Gabriel were now the favourite couple in the competition. But the results of a deep dive into his own popularity were rankling him.

Cadman had ordered his team to pinpoint the audience demographic he was appealing to. Armed with that information, he could approach new advertisers and sell himself as an individual brand as well as a family package. His familiar face, sharp-tongued patter and no-nonsense approach had ingratiated him with viewers before, during the hacking and hijacking of driverless cars. He'd assumed he must be on his way to national treasure status by now.

But today's results made for unsettling reading. It was Gabriel and River who viewers were getting behind, not him.

Gabriel had become much more consumer relatable than Cadman. The lucrative eighteen to thirty-four demographic adored Gabriel, finding him engaging, humble, genuine and empathetic. His successful battle against the brain tumour and his natural aptitude for fatherhood had only added to his appeal. He was receiving the most positive mentions, memes and engagements across all social media platforms, alongside favourable top-trending hashtags like #AngelGabriel, #NumberOneDad and #TopofthePops. For each red heart Cadman was awarded, Gabriel was receiving four. Cadman, however, was perceived as increasingly hard to warm to, too old, too pushy and too unapproachable. He read a sample of the posts.

'Cadman's caustic schtick is growing tiresome.'

'Sick to death of having my screen filled with where to buy kids' crap from.'

'He's turned his lad into a walking billboard.'

But one post burrowed the deepest under his skin.

'Cadman's riding on his boyfriend's coat tails. He wouldn't be worth watching without Gabriel.'

He'd always known the British public were idiots, and he'd made a career from capitalizing on their willingness to be distracted from the truth and swayed into his way of thinking. So how dare they turn their backs on him like this? Lack of appreciation was one of his biggest bugbears. When he'd earned enough money to buy his parents their first house, they hadn't shown him the gratitude he'd expected. They'd reacted much more when he'd sold it from under their feet a year later.

Cadman stretched his neck from side to side until the bones clicked. Some of this was his own fault, for bringing up Gabriel's cancer battle with River.

'I told you in no uncertain terms that my cancer wasn't something I wanted to talk about on camera, period,' Gabriel had ranted later that night in the Real World. 'I thought you understood that?'

'I'm sorry, it just slipped out,' Cadman replied.

'Bullshit. Nothing just slips out of your mouth. Your words are always deliberate, never accidental. You could have waited until River's next Development Leap. He might've had a better understanding as an eight-year-old than he did at five.'

'Yes, but the tears of a five-year-old will win more sympathy from an audience than those of an older, less cute kid.'

'You're unbelievable.'

'Tell me something I don't know,' Cadman said, rolling his eyes. 'Look, I exploited the narrative. Big deal. It's what I do. Viewers expect three things from their reality stars: a sob story, a triumph over adversity and a happy ending. And once we win, we'll have all three. I worry that sometimes you forget why we're doing this whole family thing.'

'Money and exposure,' Gabriel deadpanned.

'Exactly.'

'But what if our goal has changed?' Gabriel continued. 'What if I want more for us than material things?'

Cadman's eyebrows knitted.

'Such as?'

'Maybe I want to be a father.'

Cadman glared at him as if a stranger had intruded into their conversation. He'd had an inkling that something in Gabriel was shifting when he'd watched him and River in the theme park together. They had enjoyed it too much. And something had shifted in him too. He'd felt envious. However, he'd had the good sense to swallow it back down.

'Why?' he asked.

'I like being a parent. I enjoy raising a child. And I think I'm good at it.'

Cadman ran his hands through his hair.

'Gabriel, Gabriel, Gabriel,' he muttered. 'You weren't supposed to fall in love with River. That wasn't part of the plan. You knew this from the day I first approached you with the idea.'

That had been a year ago now, recalled Cadman. He'd broached the subject of *The Family Experiment* over dinner at the opening of a new Brighton restaurant. He'd pushed his plate to one side, removed a tablet from his satchel and passed it to Gabriel.

'They're making a reality TV show about parenting and livestreaming it twenty-four-seven,' he'd explained as he pressed play on the trailer. 'You compete to raise a child in the Metaverse for nine months. The winning couple gets to either keep its progeny or take the prize money to start a family in the Real World.'

'In almost six years together, you've never expressed any interest in us starting a family. Ever,' Gabriel had replied.

'Maybe I've changed.'

'Really?'

'Really.'

Gabriel folded his arms, and the two remained in a deadlock. Cadman gave way first.

'Okay, well, listen to what I have to say first before you dismiss it.

You know how hard I've been working, but sometimes it feels like I'm throwing money down a bottomless pit trying to keep on top of paying for your cancer medication—'

'Then let me get a job,' Gabriel interrupted.

'*The Family Experiment* could be the answer to our problems. It's a prime-time television event, something viewers haven't seen the like of before. An old contact of mine is working on the show and reckons they need a "name" to participate: someone viewers will recognize instantly but who won't be a shoo-in as the winner, so it'll still feel like a competition. He reckons I'll be perfect. Well, you and me. It could offer us a way to clear our debts and get back everything we had. And more.'

'And what happens if we win?' Gabriel asked.

'Well, the kid will be eighteen by then, and we can keep earning off its back or switch it off if we're done with it.'

'Just like that?'

'Yep, say thank you and wave goodbye as it disappears into a Meta black hole. We'll have earned our money back, and I'll have returned to public life with a higher profile than I've ever had before, which will land me more opportunities. It's a win-win.'

'Unless you're our child.'

'Which isn't real, remember. So what do you think?'

Cadman recalled how it had taken a fortnight of badgering, of spreadsheets, graphs and projected earnings, before Gabriel agreed to fill in the application form. Auditions, meetings with producers, psychological evaluations and screen tests followed before they were accepted as candidates.

The one thing Cadman had repeatedly warned Gabriel not to do was to form an attachment with the baby. But he hadn't listened.

Now that, alongside this latest revelation about his own fall in popularity, was infuriating Cadman. His watch pulsed, its screen warning him of a rise in his level of the stress hormone cortisol. He needed a distraction before their halfway-mark interview with Autumn Taylor. She was the last person he wanted to exchange false platitudes with today. So he changed into his shorts and vest and took out his frustration on the treadmill by his desk.

As he ran, it became clear there were two options available to him. The first was to do nothing, to allow Gabriel his moment in the spotlight and to contribute financially to their relationship.

It was the second option that was so much more to Cadman's liking.

41
Hudson

'What's wrong?' Hudson asked.

He was so attuned to Alice's emotions that, instinctively, he recognized a problem the moment she reached the school gates.

'Nothing,' she muttered as they began to walk the eleven blocks to their apartment. They had awoken that morning to a moderate snowfall that dusted the city like icing sugar and crunched underfoot.

'You can tell me anything, you know,' he persisted.

'There's nothing to tell.' Alice shrugged.

But Hudson knew that like him, she preferred to process her troubles alone before unburdening onto him. For Hudson, it had been out of necessity rather than choice because after Eva had chosen to leave Ararat, there had been no one he'd wanted to confide in.

Hudson hadn't begun to process Eva's decision to exit through the door on the left when the holographic image of the shaven-headed woman had spoken again.

'You are now part of a programme that will teach AI what it means to be truly human,' she continued. 'Through you, the version of AI we are developing will learn how to experience everything you do. Love, laughter, joy, hope and pleasure...you will teach it all. The AI will feel everything because you are feeling it too. How it reacts depends on how your mind and your body react. It will measure the changes in the tone of your voice and inflections, pitch, speed and hyperbole. And physically, your gestures, micro movements of each muscle in your bodies and faces, will be examined to understand your reaction to positive experiences and problem-solving. It will learn from you the truth, how to lie, how to empathize, how to be confident, when to be nervous, etcetera. Your work will help make it impossible to distinguish between our AI and human thoughts and behaviours.'

Today, he shuddered when he thought of how much of himself he had given to his employers.

'Where are we going?' asked Alice.

'On a detour.' Hudson smiled, and the two made their way to the location of a teleport where they jumped from one App and into another. It was the same New York, only set in the Christmas holiday season. They began by skating in the Wollman Rink in Central Park, before taking in the festive window displays along Fifth Avenue, a helter-skelter swirling around the Rockefeller Christmas tree and a rollercoaster ride that took them from the top of the Empire State Building down through a hole in the sidewalk and into the subway below.

Finally, as they reached their apartment and stamped snow from their boots, Alice was ready to unburden herself.

'My friends are being mean to me,' she announced. 'They keep saying nasty things.'

'About what?'

Alice's cheeks reddened.

'About you. That you're weird for wanting to be a lone parent. That there's something wrong with you.'

'Oh, okay. And do you think I'm weird?'

'Of course not, you're my dad.'

A handful of red hearts fluttered across the screen.

'Well, it's what you think that matters,' he continued. 'Not them. Perhaps they don't understand that it doesn't always take two parents to make a family. All it takes is one with enough love for both. And you know that I adore you.'

More red hearts floated between them.

Shortly after entering the apartment and hanging up their thick winter coats, Hudson called Alice into the lounge. Projected inside it were a punch bag and a tall, muscular sportsman clad in boxing gloves, white shorts with a black waistband and trainers.

'This is Cassius,' he said, introducing them. 'Back in the last century, he was the best boxer of all time. That's why he was nicknamed The Greatest.'

'Don't you know it,' Cassius began with a wry smile. 'Your daddy says you're being picked on. The same thing happened to me when I was a scrappy thing back home in Kentucky. So I have some moves that'll keep you safe if you ever need them.'

Alice beamed at the AI hologram before turning to her father.

'I thought you were going to tell me to ignore them and be the better person?'

'Nope,' Hudson replied. 'I'm going to make sure you have the skills to kick the crap out of anyone who bullies or belittles you again.'

Even more red hearts filled the screen. Viewers were clearly in favour of a confrontational, not an intellectual, approach.

'I'll leave you guys to it.' Hudson grinned.

He answered his rumbling stomach by logging out and returning to his Real World flat. On his doormat were several boxes of groceries he'd ordered earlier and that had slipped his mind. He'd been neglecting himself lately, skipping meals and exercise to spend time with Alice, amongst other activities. Activities that were way beyond the realms of *The Family Experiment*.

In the kitchen, he rustled up plates of gyozas and bao buns, spicy noodles and dumplings, and lab-grown beef. His jaw clicked when he opened his mouth a little too widely to chew, another hangover from Ararat.

In a divide-and-conquer style of management, high achievers such as Hudson had been heaped with praise and awarded positions of responsibility. Everyone else had been expected to accept it without question. Naturally, it had bred resentment.

One evening as he showered, Hudson had been rounded upon by a group of five older boys, led by Eva's brother, Cain. Two years must have passed—Hudson hadn't been sure as there were no calendars or clocks in Ararat—and tension had remained between the two. There had been shoulder barges in corridors, clothes vanishing from his dormitory locker and bedding soaked with urine. All surreptitiously and away from the scrutiny of the guards. But that day in the shower block, Cain's anger towards Hudson had been volcanic.

'Think you're better than us, don't you?' snarled his tormentor as the first blow winded Hudson.

'No,' Hudson gasped.

'Liar!' Cain snapped, and landed a second blow.

Two of his cohort picked Hudson up under his arms. 'This is for what you did to Eva,' Cain continued, and punched him square in the eye.

'I wanted her to stay,' Hudson said, barely able to get his words out.

'You put stupid ideas in her head and now she's dead. So I'm going to make the rest of your life in here a misery.'

Hudson knew that his jaw was fractured the moment Cain retracted his fist and the group scurried away. Had Cain not done so, Hudson would likely have kept the attack quiet anyway because he too blamed himself for Eva's departure. He hadn't instigated their conversations about escaping Ararat, but he hadn't discouraged them either. He deserved to be hurt. But his injuries had left him with no choice but to report to the medical bay. Security camera footage soon identified all but one of the perpetrators. The next morning at a special assembly, Cain had been the only one not to be dragged out by guards through the door on the left. They were never seen again.

Today, his jaw clicked once more as he swallowed the last of the gyozas. He prepared himself a walnut salad to eat later, placed it inside a cool box and made his way into the bedroom to access the Metaverse. He would miss his apartment when it was time to leave. It was cosy but functional and had come close to feeling like a home, but it was never going to be permanent. It was only ever a means to an end.

In the same way that Alice was.

NEWS

Home | **Politics**

OUTRAGE OVER MP'S AVATAR ABUSE GAFFE

A gaffe-prone Tory MP has been blasted by avatar rights campaigners for suggesting sex offenders should be encouraged to prey on MetaChildren and adults instead of those in the Real World.

Simon Chilcook, 68, MP for New Buckinghamshire, believes parents should be grateful abuse could make its way out of the Real World and into the Metaverse.

At a private dinner for local business leaders, he was caught on camera saying, 'Avatars feel nothing because they are nothing. So I know that I'd rather have paedophiles preying on the fake kids than our children in the Real World. Makes sense, doesn't it?'

A spokesperson for Persons for the Ethical Treatment of All Avatars hit back and revealed they have launched a petition to have their concerns raised in parliament.

'These characters are being created for us and are learning from us,' he said. 'We will be using them to complete families, so they deserve the same respect as humans. But at present, the process is ripe for abuse. We are urging people to sign our petition to encourage parliament to discuss what can be done to protect them from all types of abuse.'

Despite pressure from his own party, Simon Chilcook has so far refused to apologize for his comments.

42
Dimitri & Zoe

Zoe couldn't settle on which of three things was causing her the greatest unrest: her growing affection for Lenny, her husband discarding Adam's belongings or Autumn Taylor's impending arrival later today. She relished the time she spent with her now eight-year-old son and watching him mature. But she also found herself hankering to spend more time with the doll she was neglecting in the loft.

Today, she had timed her morning to perfection. The first half had been spent drawing and crafting with Lenny, before a one-hour window appeared, followed by her next online private tutoring session. It meant that while Dimitri was outside in the Metaverse with Lenny, she could sneak upstairs, change Adam's nappy, dress him in another of her son's old outfits and feed him.

As much as she loved Lenny, she remained unwilling to let Adam go. This version of her boy would never grow up and she'd never have to grieve his loss in the way she had his namesake's. She owed him a debt of gratitude because he had been there for her when Dimitri hadn't. And while he was in her life, she wouldn't have to completely let go of the past.

Zoe released an expectant smile as she made her way up into the loft. She passed the landing window and spotted the remainder of last night's frost on neighbours' rooftops, cars and lawns. And even though Adam would never leave the confines of that insulated roof space, she decided to dress him in a winter jumper and a pair of thicker socks before she left.

But as the light bulb illuminated the gloomy space, Zoe inhaled sharply. The dustsheet that for so many years had been hiding Adam's suitcases lay spread flat across the floor.

And each case had disappeared from beneath it.

She stumbled towards the area she was so familiar with, rubbing her brow as her eyes darted back and forth. There were other objects missing too, like the suitcase containing his clothing, a broken vacuum cleaner and long-forgotten kitchen utensils.

Zoe's stomach folded inside out. Dimitri must have cleared out the space. Stay calm, she told herself, a task much easier said than done. She hurried back to the ladder, stumbling down the last three rungs and landing heavily on her left ankle. She winced, but the pain didn't stop her from hobbling to the Metaverse access space in their spare room and throwing on her headset. Dimitri and Lenny were mounting motorized scooters.

'Everything all right?' asked Dimitri.

Zoe cleared her throat, desperate to mask her increasing anxiety.

'I was up in the loft earlier looking for dad's old photo albums. When did you clean it out?'

'A couple of days ago, when you and Lenny were mining meteors or whatever you do in that App.'

'Even the ladybird suitcase?'

'Yes. I looked inside and there were just old car manuals. So I sent everything in the car to the dump. There wasn't anything of Adam's that you wanted to keep, was there?'

'No, no, I don't think so,' she replied, before waving them goodbye and leaving.

Zoe's journey to the rubbish dump and recycling centre was one of the longest fifteen minutes of her life. The thought of being unable to spend any more precious moments with Adam terrified her. Her car hadn't finished parking itself when she threw open the door and ran across the forecourt as fast as her unstable ankle would permit, and in the direction of a portable cabin with the word 'RECEPTION' spray-painted across the side. She banged on the window until it slid open.

'My husband,' Zoe panted. 'He sent our car here earlier to get rid of some stuff. But there's something of mine he shouldn't have thrown out.'

A woman with a black heart tattoo under one eye and the words

'Sweet Child o' Mine' above the other looked her up and down. 'Do you have a booking code?'

'No, I don't.'

'Then I can't help you.'

'Please,' Zoe continued. 'We lost our son a few years ago and this suitcase contains things of his that we'll never get back.'

The woman squinted.

'I know you, don't I? You're on that telly show.'

Zoe nodded.

'Zoe Taylor-Georgiou. My husband's name is Dimitri.'

The woman inputted Dimitri's name before scanning the results.

'Sorry, you're half an hour too late. It's all gone. Incinerated.'

Her words couldn't have hurt more if the woman had followed them with a slap to the face.

She had lost Adam for the second time.

43
Woody & Tina

Woody glanced around his and Tina's section of the garden and tried to recall its appearance before they had been ordered to divide it. They'd only lived there for a week before the Accommodation Advisor arrived to survey their property and had warned it was too large and prone to a potential security breach. So Issy had been quarantined inside a quarter of it, around four square metres of lawn, surrounded by fences and a tall leylandii hedge, while he and Tina were awarded the rest of the space behind it.

Wooden railway sleepers framed his patio to create raised borders. But the plants and shrubs that once grew inside them were now long dead. Wild ivy had taken their place and had wrapped its tendrils around the flaking wooden legs of a table and chairs.

Woody rarely spent time out here alone. He'd wait until Belle was at school, Tina was working or Issy was in the basement conjuring up new reasons to despise her parents. When those precious few moments of solitude did arrive, he'd spend them either in reflection or regret. Today, his thoughts were turned to the latter: the day their daughter had been arrested on suspicion of murdering a classmate.

Woody had been remotely piloting a drone across the English Channel when the call from Tina had arrived. It had been a routine flight, circling beaches at Folkestone and Sandgate, searching for boats being inflated or gatherings of people where there wouldn't ordinarily be. He'd let it go to voicemail. She called him back immediately.

'I'm just on a flight—' he began, but she interrupted him.

'You need to go to Hodgemore Park police headquarters right now,' she said. 'Ask for Detective Sergeant Charlie Marks at the information desk.'

'Why, what's happened?'

'I'll explain later. Go now and contact that old solicitor schoolmate of yours, Steve Wills, and ask him to meet us there.'

She hung up before he could reply.

Woody wished he'd been able to override the speed limit in his autonomous car as it drove the twenty-minute journey to the station. Tina was already there when he left the car to park itself. Her make-up was smudged, her hair ruffled and her eyes red.

'What's going on?' he asked as he approached her.

'It's Issy,' she replied.

'Is she okay?'

'There was an incident at a playpark...they're saying she hurt another child. A boy.'

Woody swallowed hard.

'Hurt? As in...'

Tina took a deep breath.

'As in she killed him.'

The blood drained from his face.

'Who? When?'

'That Archie Anderson boy from her school who's been all over the news this week. Police think Issy was to blame.'

'Why?'

'Facial recognition software on CCTV cameras picked up her image running away from the scene and matched it with a photo on her National Identity card.'

'But she's not a killer.'

Tina paused without reply for too long.

'Tina? She's not a killer, is she.'

Woody hadn't framed it as a question.

'No, no, no,' he said, and he took a step back, holding his hands out in front of him, palms facing towards her. 'You can't believe she would do something like that. You're her mother, for Christ's sake! Why are you never on her side?'

Their conversation was interrupted by Woody's old friend Steve, who'd arrived in a taxi.

'So what have the police told you so far?' he asked, and Tina filled him in with the scant information she had been given.

An hour later and Steve returned to them as they sat in silence on plastic chairs adjacent to the reception desk.

'When can we see her? When can we take her home?' Woody asked.

'You'll be able to see her soon,' he replied. 'But I need to talk to you both first. Police believe Issy and Archie Anderson got into an argument earlier this week at school. Their teacher suspects that Anderson and some of his friends might have been bullying her. After school, the investigators are claiming Issy followed him into a recycling area behind Leechfield playpark and hit him over the head several times with a brick.'

Woody shook his head vigorously.

'No,' he said adamantly. 'That didn't happen. She must have found his body. She was trying to help him.'

'That's not what the evidence suggests.'

Woody slammed his hand down on the chair next to him, making their two empty cardboard coffee cups fall over. He looked to Tina for support, but her eyes were fixed on Steve.

'I want to see my daughter right now,' Woody said.

Tina had known from the moment she caught sight of Issy in the police interview room that whatever she was about to say was a lie. Woody hurried to hug her and Tina followed suit, although neither mother nor daughter's embrace had been as all-encompassing as Woody's.

Issy looked to her mother first as they sat, appeared to judge her expression, then focused all her attention on Woody instead.

'I didn't do it, Dad, I promise,' she said. 'I didn't kill him.'

'I know you didn't,' Woody replied, and reached across the table to hold her hand. 'Tell us what happened.'

'I was in the playground when I heard someone moaning, so I went to see what the noise was and that's when I found Archie. There was blood everywhere, but he was still breathing.'

'That's what I said,' Woody replied. 'That you found him.'

Before he could continue, Steve turned his tablet towards the family, pressed play and narrated what was happening.

'This is CCTV of Issy following the victim into the bin shelter, and here, a few minutes later, she is hurrying away.'

'Then someone was already there waiting for him,' Woody said. 'They attacked after Issy left.'

'There is no visual proof of that. However, there are two entrance points, but only one is covered by the camera,' Steve conceded. 'So someone could have entered and left before Issy appeared.'

'What did you do when you found Archie?' Tina asked her daughter suddenly. 'Did you try to help him?'

'I didn't know what to do so I went to find an adult.'

'Who?'

'The park was empty.'

'So, what, you just came home?'

'Yes, I got scared the person who attacked him might be following me. So I ran—'

'But footage from a second camera has you in the waterpark area before trying to find help,' interrupted Steve. 'You're washing your hands under a tap and trying to rinse something from your sleeves. What was it?'

'I don't know.' Issy shrugged. 'I can't remember. Mud, probably. I think I panicked, ran and slipped over.'

'And then you just came home and didn't tell your dad or me about it?' Tina persisted.

'No. I was confused.'

The room fell silent. Issy looked around, her gaze resting on Woody.

'You believe me, don't you, Dad?'

Tina's present-day voice caught his attention.

'Are you all right, Woody?' she asked from the kitchen door. She had been watching her husband outside, lost in thought, and wondering what distant shore he'd washed up on. If he was anything like her when he was out there, Issy wouldn't be far from his thoughts.

'Yes, fine thanks,' he replied. 'Are you going to see Issy before Autumn Taylor arrives?'

She broke eye contact and picked at a fleck of mud on the heel of one of her trainers.

'I don't think I'll have time. Once the interview is over and I pick up Belle from school, I'll need to go to work. I'll see her for breakfast tomorrow.'

Woody knew that by the time breakfast arrived, Tina would have another excuse prepared. He didn't like that she had given up on their own daughter. It was something he could never do. His conscience would not allow it.

www.inanutshell.uk/thefamilyexperiment

In a Nutshell
The online facts & figures site

HOW THE FAMILY EXPERIMENT HAS CHANGED THE WORLD.

- Last week *The Family Experiment* had its highest ever viewing figures—**451 million hours** of the show were streamed worldwide—more than those who viewed King William's coronation.

- It is available to watch in **148 countries**, including Russia, North Korea and China.

- More than **80,000 people** are now on the waiting list to become MetaParents when it becomes available at the end of the series.

- The **five most attended** Metaverse concerts since *The Family Experiment* began have all been gigs attended by contestants. Users chose heritage acts including Elvis, The Beatles, Michael Jackson, Prince and Nirvana over contemporary artists.

- Each month, there are more than **15 million votes cast** on *The Family Experiment*'s home page for who should face the Monthly Challenge.

- There has been a **350% increase** in orders of VR equipment including headsets, gloves, masks and suits since the series began.

- Experts predict the overall winning couple and MetaChild could earn **$3 million in endorsement deals** within the first year.

- A record **140,000 complaints** were made to television regulator OFCOM over the televised 'death' of child avatar Olivia Carter-Green.

MONTH SIX:
TWELVE YEARS OLD

`www.grapevine.uk/UK-trending/2808342`

Through the Grapevine

Home | UK | **Trending**

CATHOLIC CHURCH WADES INTO BABY ROW

POPE HITS OUT AT METABABIES

The Pope has attacked the concept of MetaBabies, branding them 'dangerous' and 'ungodly'.

In his weekly address at the Vatican's St Peter's Square, Pope John Paul III warned the creation of virtual children and families was yet another way technology was creeping into our lives to destroy the fabric of society.

'The people who call themselves parents to computer-generated babies must know that their child will never be accepted by the Catholic church because they are not real,' he told crowds. 'These so-called babies are nothing more than a business, a transaction, a tool used to chip away at traditional families and make them feel undervalued.

'Only humans with beating hearts and consciences know the true worth of God and love. MetaChildren should be treated with caution and never as one of us.'

Pope John Paul III's comments come after the condemnation of AI avatars by the Archbishop of Canterbury, Cornell Achebe.

44
Woody & Tina

Issy was sitting cross-legged on the floor in the middle of the basement, adjusting her eyesight back to the Real World. For much of the day she had been wearing her VR headset and focusing her attention on the final module of a basic Russian language course.

Historically, some of the grandmasters of chess were Russian, and once she turned eighteen and was finally freed from her prison, it would be the first country she'd travel to. Tina and Woody were going to pay for her flights and provide her with all her spending money, she'd decided. It was the least they could do after all they'd taken from her.

Suddenly the red light attached to a camera and screen above her door flickered. It was a sensor that flashed when her parents were approaching. When she turned thirteen, she'd demanded more privacy, and, to her astonishment, they'd agreed to install it. She approached the security screen to see who was about to make an appearance but assumed it to be Woody. She had only seen Tina twice in a month, so her presence was unlikely.

But it was neither parent. It was somebody else.

Issy's heart stopped when she clocked the figure of a balaclava-clad stranger on the other side of the door. She scurried, crab-like, banging into a stool and sending it clattering to the floor in her haste to get away. Her eyes widened as she glared at the screen and the stranger, who appeared to be holding some kind of device in their hand. They were pointing it at the electronic sensor that recognized her parents' thumbprints and granted them access to her world.

Issy panicked: she looked to the bifold doors leading to the steps and her section of the garden but they remained locked. The glass was shatterproof—she knew that for certain because she had hurled many an object at the doors over the years. Her eyes darted around the room, searching for an object she might use as a weapon to defend herself. But after the fork incident, Woody had removed anything sharp or potentially lethal from the basement. The holographic cybernanny was so archaic that its base needed recharging via a mains socket, and as it was currently powered down, she was unable to ask it to contact her parents for help.

In here and alone, she was a sitting duck.

Suddenly the door made a buzzing sound, followed by a click. It was now unlocked. Whoever was outside was about to make their way in. If she could take them by surprise then maybe she could bolt up the staircase and find an object to fight back with. So she scrambled to her feet, ready to launch herself at the unwelcome presence.

Issy's heart raced as she waited for them to push the door open. But nothing happened. Eventually, she edged her way to the security screen and cocked her head. Unless her eyes were deceiving her, there was no one waiting for her. What kind of trap was this?

Mustering every bit of courage, she grasped the handle, preparing to open it a crack. But her clumsy, trembling fingers lost their grip and she closed the door instead. She hesitated when she realized what she'd done, then cursed herself. She had just wasted an opportunity to finally escape this room. Out of frustration, she grabbed the handle and yanked it hard, expecting nothing to happen. To her amazement, it opened.

She had a second chance.

The staircase was definitely empty. But the intruder had left something for her on the third stair up—the device that had unlocked her door. She picked it up, closed the door from the outside and tried it for herself. It locked and unlocked each time she pressed a raised button. Her mysterious benefactor wanted her to be able to enter and leave at will.

Issy left the door ajar as she slowly made her way to the top of the staircase. If Woody and Christina were up there, she would need to move quickly back into her room before they saw her. She turned the handle of the second door, opened it and heard nothing but her pulse ringing in her ears. She was alone.

And for the first time in six years, Issy was free.

45

Cadman & Gabriel

'We need to talk about something,' began Gabriel.

Cadman had spent much of the morning alone in his office when his partner appeared at the door. He turned to find Gabriel shifting awkwardly from foot to foot.

'Is River okay?' he asked.

'Yes, he's fine. The car left a few minutes ago to take him to school.'

'The one Mercedes sponsored us, or the Tesla?'

'I don't know, I wasn't looking.'

Cadman turned to one of three screens projected on the wall.

'I'll rewind and check.'

'Can it wait?'

'It'll only take a moment—'

'Cadman,' said Gabriel firmly. 'I'm trying to have a conversation with you. I need to know how we're doing.'

'You and I?'

'In terms of the competition. I know you'll have people analysing data and social media insights, so you must have an idea of where we stand?'

Cadman eyed Gabriel with uncertainty. Did he suspect that he and River had usurped his popularity?

'Where's this coming from?' he asked. 'Every time I've tried to broach the subject with you before, you've told me you'd rather not know.'

'I've changed my mind. Do you have the stats or not?'

'Yes. We had been in fourth place, but since I brought up the subject of your cancer—which might I remind you, you opposed—we've had a firm place in the top two. Number one most days, number two on others.'

Gabriel nodded slowly.

'We have a little under four months left before the final,' Gabriel continued. 'Do you think we can still win this?'

'And I thought I was the competitive one. But yes, we could win. So what's this all about?'

Gabriel hesitated, moved into the office and perched on the edge of the armchair.

'I'm worried about what's going to happen to River afterwards.'

'This again? You know what'll happen. If we win, we keep him, if we lose, he'll cease to exist. They'll flip the switch.'

'And that doesn't bother you?'

Cadman folded his arms. 'We knew what we were getting into when we applied.'

'So you have no feelings for him at all?'

Cadman swallowed the truth.

'No. Well, I mean, I like him. He's fun to hang out with. But then so are the characters in the retro arcade games I play. It doesn't mean I want to spend the rest of my life with Sonic the Hedgehog or Lara Croft, does it?'

Gabriel pursed his lips.

'You can't compare our son to a blue hedgehog.'

'Why not? This is all just a game, isn't it?'

'No, not for me, it's not. It's moved way beyond that. River is my son.'

'But he's not.'

'I've spent the bulk of my time with him over the last five months and we have a bond. I know when he's coming down with a bug before there are any physical signs. I know when he's tired before he admits it. I know when he's not being honest with me. I know the mood he needs to be in for me to get the best out of him. I know this because I'm his dad.'

'But you're not.'

'Can you please stop saying that and listen to me?'

Cadman sat upright. 'Okay.'

'If we lose this competition, I hate the thought of never seeing him again. I don't want to let him go.'

'And that's why I spend so much of my time in here, trying to ensure we have the best possible chance of keeping him. Because if we win, think of River's potential earning power. He will be the most famous avatar in the world. He will only age when we want him to, and when we've rinsed one demographic, we can move on to the next.'

Gabriel gave an exasperated sigh.

'That's not what I want for him. Can't we just be a family, hang out in the Metaverse with him, be, well, as close to normal as we can get?'

Cadman bristled at the word 'normal'.

'So rather than using him to our advantage, you just want to let him...*exist*?'

'Yes.'

'And what if I don't want to? What if I want to take the prize fund instead and put it towards starting a biological family with a surrogate?'

'That's not what you want,' Gabriel demurred.

'How do you know? When have you ever asked me what I want?'

'I think it's a fair assumption you've no interest in starting any family, biological or coded. All I'm asking is for you to take a step back from yourself and see what you are missing. See who you are missing.'

But Cadman had had enough of the conversation. He swivelled back around in his chair and waited until he heard a defeated Gabriel leave the room.

He tried returning to his work but his eyes glazed over. Maybe Gabriel was right. Maybe he was missing out. Or perhaps River was a threat to their relationship. Cadman would never admit it, but he needed Gabriel in his life. It was why, when they had separated over his AZ dependency, he had employed a surveillance team to keep tabs on him.

He'd patiently waited until Gabriel had hit rock bottom before swooping in to rescue him from the airfield and a life selling himself in the sex industry. He assumed gratitude would bind them together for the long haul, but now it appeared that wasn't enough. And Cadman didn't know how he would deal with losing someone else so close to him.

He turned his attention to his tablet and a file buried away. It contained moving and static images of a fresh-faced, eighteen-year-old Cadman and his first love, Marcus. They'd first set eyes on one another in Cadman's second week at university, days after he'd moved to Cambridge to begin his Influencing and Social Media degree. He hadn't believed in love at first sight until Marcus had taken to the lecture theatre stage.

Seven-year age gap aside, he and his tutor couldn't have been more dissimilar: Marcus with his Mediterranean skin, dark brown hair and stocky frame, and tall and lanky Cadman. Cadman was shy and awkward, Marcus was confident and witty. Each time their eyes met, Cadman was convinced he'd felt a thousand small explosions deep inside him.

Relationships between tutors and students were banned by law, but exceptions were made if they were DNA Matched. In their first afternoon together they'd taken the test, and twenty-four hours later the results confirmed they were destined for one another.

Marcus opened up Cadman to a world of new experiences, alternative ways of thinking and influential people. They'd spent three blissful years together before Marcus had pulled the rug from beneath Cadman's feet.

Cadman had awoken first that morning and carried steaming mugs of aromatic coffee into the bedroom of their university campus apartment. Several times he called Marcus's name without a response.

'Hey, wake up, lazy arse,' he'd continued, and rolled Marcus from his side and onto his back.

When the light from the bedside lamp caught Marcus's purple-and-grey face, he knew in an instant that he'd lost him. In the time it took for the ambulance to arrive, Cadman had already decided how and when he was going to join his Match. For what was the point in continuing to live if he couldn't share life with the person he was biologically made for?

'Sudden Adult Death Syndrome' had been the coroner's ruling at an expedited inquest later that month. 'Just four hundred people die of the condition in the UK each year,' he'd later read. 'No one knows how or why, only that it is likely cardiac-arrest related, some type of heart-rhythm disturbance. But the exact cause remains a mystery.'

It was their cleaner who had thwarted Cadman's second attempt at suicide. The first, a week earlier, had seen him vomit an overdose of antidepressants. The second time, she'd swapped her working days and appeared in their bedroom to find him looping a rope around exposed beams. Before the day ended, the paramedics she'd called persuaded him to voluntarily admit himself into a hospital psychiatric unit.

Cadman had remained there for close to three months undergoing intense, experimental therapy before a new version of his former self emerged. This version was coated in Teflon and was determined never to relinquish control over his emotions to anyone again.

'And certainly not to you or River,' he said aloud before closing the folder on Marcus.

Then he picked up his phone and dialled a number.

46
Hudson

The onsets of Hudson's migraines were becoming more frequent. Prescribed medication stymied them, but the only form of prevention was to step away from his headset and the Metaverse for longer than it took to eat lunch.

However, Hudson was uncomfortable with being too far from it in the event that Alice needed him. So he compromised. He packed his headset in his backpack and bookmarked routes to the nearest Metaverse access points in cafes and community centres, before making his way to London's South Bank. Clad in dark glasses and a beanie hat, even the most avid of *The Family Experiment* viewers had no idea who they were passing. Nobody expected to see him anywhere other than in the Metaverse, so he hadn't earned a second glance.

Hudson always favoured one bench when he came here. It was located close to the Royal Festival Hall, a reinforced-concrete building that reminded him of a smaller-scale version of Ararat. Despite all he had experienced and all he had witnessed under Ararat's roof, it had still been his home. Two and a half years had passed since he'd left, and despite himself, there were aspects of it that he missed.

His mind wandered back to his early teens, when his only measure of time had been the changing of seasons and his growing body. He and his young peers had been assigned new booths and fed moral dilemmas through their headsets to see how they might respond. Wires protruded from their haptic suits and touch-sensitive gloves, and they wore skin-tight masks that registered every facial muscle movement and twitch. Sometimes the same question was asked over and over again, only in slightly different ways to judge a slightly different response. It had been repetitive work, and claustrophobic, but better than the alternative—exiting by the door on the left into the wilderness with nothing but the clothes on his back.

Rumours frequently circulated as to what lay beyond Ararat's walls. Hudson had heard every theory from a toxic nuclear waste dump to fields and forests planted with landmines. One of the more outlandish suggestions was that they were being kept on an island surrounded by great oceans. That might've been based on a stale, sulphurous odour that sometimes permeated the air in the building's outdoor quadrant. But none of these explanations could account for why each time someone had been ejected, it had been followed by screaming or yelling and the scuffling of feet being dragged away. Hudson had never learned the truth while he was there because no one had ever returned from behind the door on the left.

At the end of another unremarkable day, they'd been ordered to assemble back in the room where he'd last seen Eva years earlier, before she exited. It gave him chills, and the moment the door closed behind them, he'd wanted to leave. But first they had to listen to a speech from the shaven-headed woman, once again in holographic form.

'Next week, each of you will be assigned, and will take ownership of, an avatar of your very own,' she began. 'One that has been individually tailored to you and that reflects everything we have learned about you. You'll be paired with a consumer outside this facility who you will meet in neutral Metaverse territory. They are hand-chosen and vetted and are beta-testing a programme we have spent years working on. Thanks to your assistance, it's now gradually approaching completion. Each of these beta-testers has been assigned a child at an age of their choosing and which they believe to be completely operated by AI. However, you will be working in tandem with AI. You will behave as the consumer expects their progeny to. You will do what is required of you without complaint.

'Each day they will rate your performance, and if they score you poorly and if you fail to show any signs of improvement in coming sessions, you will be removed from the process and asked to leave through the door on the left. If you attempt to communicate with them in any way beyond the realms of the part you are playing, our moderators will catch you and you will be removed. There is no margin for error here. AI will be watching and learning how you communicate and respond. What you are doing is important not just for the future of this project, but the next stage of our company's machine-learning.'

Both nervous yet excited to be communicating with someone beyond Ararat's boundaries, Hudson had been paired with his first human, a client named only as Audrey. Background notes revealed that she was forty-three years old, married for twenty-two years and childless by the choice of her husband. He had only supported her MetaChild endeavour because she hadn't expected him to participate.

Being placed in her charge had been Hudson's greatest week since before Eva's departure. Audrey behaved as maternally as he imagined a mother might. She was affectionate, considerate and attentive to his needs. So he felt dispirited by her announcement five days later that she was to terminate their time together.

'You're as real as I'd hoped you'd be,' she informed him. 'But if I don't leave now, I'm frightened being around you will make me crave a biological child. And that will be the death knell of my marriage.'

Then Audrey's avatar vanished, and her account terminated soon after that. As Hudson remained in his booth, and before processing the swiftness of her disappearance, a commotion caught his attention. He turned to see Eva's brother, Cain, being escorted from his booth by guards and led past his startled colleagues.

'I didn't tell him anything!' Cain was tearfully protesting, but it didn't stop the guards from forcing him out of the door on the left.

Hudson wondered how long it might take Cain to realize that it was he who had set him up. Hudson had continued to suffer sporadic bullying at Cain's hands ever since the shower block attack some eighteen months before. As one of his supervisors, he'd logged in to Cain's account pretending to be him and sent one of his clients a message, informing her he was being held captive in an unknown location and begging for help to free him. AI had intercepted the message.

Today, as Hudson swam back to the surface, he thought of how he had believed back then that his enemy had got what he deserved. It was only years later, when they'd come face to face again, that Hudson had learned the truth.

No one in Ararat had deserved to be sent through the door on the left.

47
Dimitri & Zoe

Zoe, uninterested in her main course, pushed her fried potatoes around the plate.

Dimitri had also lost his appetite but persisted with his meal. He had done his best to keep the conversation flowing since their arrival, but it had been an uphill struggle. He might as well have been dining with a stranger.

To Metaverse viewers, Zoe appeared to be behaving in her usual manner. She was attentive to her family and participated with Lenny and Dimitri in joint activities when time permitted. But when it was just her and her husband in the Real World, she had become increasingly distant. And at times, he was sure he caught a red hue in her eyes that suggested she'd been crying. The first time he'd confronted her, she'd claimed there was nothing wrong. The second time, she'd blamed a dust allergy following Dimitri's clear-outs. He knew her too well to believe her.

Tonight, their inability to relax wasn't helped by the attention heaped upon them by fellow diners. The couple had been aware of it the moment the taxi had dropped them off outside the tapas restaurant. Each time he and Zoe began to speak, the area surrounding their table hushed ever so slightly, necks craned a little and heads tilted to overhear their conversation. And he only realized that news of their outing was being livestreamed across social media platforms when alerts appeared on his watch and he spotted a woman outside, filming them on the inside. The restaurant manager shooed her away but asked for a selfie in return for his efforts.

Zoe slipped on her Smart glasses to check in on their son.

'What's he doing?' Dimitri asked.

'He's asleep in his bed. The cybernanny was reading to him, but now it's back in the lounge.'

Another silence followed. Dimitri felt compelled to fill it.

'This is nice, isn't it? Getting out, just the two of us.'

'Yes,' she replied, neither of them convinced by her answer.

'We should do it more often.'

'You should be ashamed of yourselves,' a voice came from the table behind them. A grey-haired man with a walking stick propped up against his chair was glaring at them.

'Excuse me?' said Zoe.

'Leaving another child unattended. You haven't learned your lesson, have you?'

'You're lucky to have that little boy,' the woman accompanying him added. 'My daughter can't afford to have children, and if she'd had your opportunities, she'd never have let her child out of her sight. I'm just saying.'

'Well, don't,' Zoe snapped. 'We didn't ask for your opinion.'

'Then don't be a public figure,' the man replied with a derisory laugh.

Zoe pushed her knife and fork to one side.

'Can we go, please?' she asked Dimitri.

'Don't let them ruin it for us.'

'They already have, and now I just want to go home.'

Dimitri obliged and, after paying, they left the restaurant, barely saying a word to one another during the taxi ride home.

Later, he changed out of his shirt and trousers and into shorts and a T-shirt, and found Zoe in their Real World lounge, sitting upright in an armchair, the room illuminated by the burnt-orange flickering of a handful of scented candles.

'The food was nice,' he began.

Silence.

'Some of the best seafood paella I've had in ages.'

More silence.

'Zoe, what's wrong?'

'Nothing,' she replied.

'Is it me? Have I done something? Was it because I threw away Adam's stuff?'

If the candlelight had been more luminous, Dimitri might have caught his wife digging her fingernails into the palms of her hands. She hated what he had done. And it was all she could do to stop herself from screaming at the man who, by throwing away her doll, had taken more from her than he could ever imagine.

'You did what you thought was best,' she said.

'But we'd talked about it. We'd agreed it was time.'

And I changed my mind, she wanted to say, but held her tongue.

She had already messaged staff at Pre:Conceived, the doll's manufacturer, and discovered that they had long since ceased production of Adam's model. So she had scrolled through their website, carefully scanning each of the current dolls to see if one pulled at her in the same way he had. But none appealed. Adam was truly irreplaceable. Now her last chance at motherhood was with Lenny, and there was a one-in-four chance that he could be taken away from her too. She wasn't sure how much grief one person could handle.

'How are we going to win this competition?' Zoe asked without preface.

'Where did that come from?' Dimitri replied.

'If I've been thinking it then you have too. And I know you've been on social media to read what they're saying about us. Your watch notifications are coming from accounts you didn't tell me about. Have you been watching the highlights show too? How do we compare with the others? Who is our biggest competition?'

Dimitri lifted his tablet from the sofa cushion and knelt by Zoe's side. He keyed their names into his accounts, which allowed her to gain the measure of public perception. 'I can only go by what I'm reading, but ultimately, I think Cadman and Gabriel are our nearest rivals.'

'Which takes me back to my question. How are we going to win this competition?'

'The next Development Leap will likely take the kids into, or close to, their teenage years, so if they're anything like Real World children they're going to be emotional yoyos. And that means anything can happen. But we've been through parenthood—we have experience on our side, whereas the others don't. So we need to take whatever Lenny throws at us in our stride.'

'And what about Adam? Are they talking about him? Still blaming us?'

Dimitri took her hand. 'Look, there will always be people who'll blame us for what happened. But eventually they'll see we're just like them and that it was a mistake any one of them could've made.'

'Only it wasn't, was it?' Zoe said suddenly.

'Wasn't what?'

'A mistake.'

ADVERTISEMENT

Don't delete your avatar— sell it to us instead!

We will make you a cash offer for your old, out-of-date or unloved icons and recycle them to reuse elsewhere. We will also pay your termination fee with your current avatar service provider, freeing you up to start afresh with a new-look electronic image.

Visit www.webuyanyavatar.com

webuyanyavatar

48
Woody & Tina

Issy remained hypervigilant as she entered the hallway leading to the rest of the house, half expecting to find the person in the balaclava who had freed her, waiting. She paused to get the measure of the place, but it seemed she was alone.

She glanced at her new but familiar surroundings, unsure what she could remember about the layout as her time up here had been so limited when they'd moved in. Two days, if she recalled correctly. Only now it felt much smaller than she recalled. Perhaps it was because she had grown up, or maybe she'd spent the intervening years in a world as large as her imagination.

Her eyes were drawn to the front door and she hurried towards it, pulling at the handle. To her disappointment, it didn't budge. She looked through the central glass square but saw no car parked on the driveway, which suggested Woody and Tina's absence.

She poked her head around an open doorway to the lounge. There were two familiar sofas from the old place, but the armchair was new. She smiled as she recalled how she'd slashed the cushions of its predecessor with scissor blades, then scattered the foam stuffing about the floor for no other reason than that she could.

Next, she ventured into the dining room and downstairs bathroom before arriving at the kitchen. She was drawn to the window overlooking a patio framed by railway sleepers. The one in their last house had been framed by red bricks. The corners of her mouth curled upwards when she thought about it.

She remembered when the Accommodation Advisor from the prison had turned up at the house soon after the jury had found her guilty of manslaughter, advising them of the security measures they'd need to ensure her segregation from society. Then he'd inserted the first of many GPS tracking devices into her arm which her parents had to replace annually. It would set off an alarm if she was to try to leave the house or rear garden. That would alert the police and result in an instant transfer to a young offenders' institute for whatever remained of her eight-year sentence.

'It is to your good fortune that your parents are willing to allow you to remain under their roof rather than be sent to an overcrowded and underfunded institution,' the judge had informed Issy after the trial.

The trial had been closed to the public and media and, at ten years old, she had been granted lifelong anonymity. Even the victim's parents and families were legally bound not to publicly identify her, otherwise they'd face heavy fines and prison sentences.

The judge had continued.

'With a programme combining daily solitude in a VR headset and remote learning, while retaining close ties with your family, and taking your age into account, I can only hope these Virtual Prison rehabilitation methods will help you transform who you are now into someone who can return to society in years to come as a more rounded individual. It will offer you the second chance at life which your victim, Archie Anderson, will never be afforded.'

Issy had opened her mouth ready to protest once again to the court that she hadn't killed him until she felt her father's hand squeezing her arm. He'd never admitted that he didn't believe her account of the events that led to Archie's death, but she could read him like a book. He doubted her innocence. She laid the blame for that firmly at Christina's door.

And later, she hadn't needed to overhear her parents arguing to know who had decided on locking her in the basement.

'You wanted her to serve her sentence here, so she's doing it down there,' she'd heard Christina say firmly. 'That was our agreement.'

'But it's unfair,' her father protested.

'Taking a young boy's life is unfair. Having to move hundreds of miles away, give up our old lives, our families and our friends so they don't find out what she did or that we have to keep her locked away here is unfair. Having a daughter who is a psychopath is unfair.'

'But she is already being punished by being taken away from everything she knows.'

'She deserves to have everything taken away!' Tina replied. 'Didn't you see her yawning or rolling her eyes throughout her trial? And when the prosecutor mentioned Archie's missing phone and watch the day he was killed, I swear she smirked. I would stake my life on it that she's hidden them somewhere, like some sick bloody souvenirs.'

'If she had, the police would have found them when they searched the old house.'

'If she is left to roam around this house unsupervised, what's to stop her from killing us too if she feels like it? I won't feel safe in here unless she is either in a young offenders' institute or, at the very least, locked in our basement.'

Issy had never forgiven Christina for that.

Now, she grabbed a carving knife from a wooden block on the worktop. If the masked intruder had remained in the house, she might still need to protect herself. She reached the bottom of the main house staircase, again listening for indications of company. Then slowly, step by step, she made her way up until she reached the landing.

The door to what appeared to be her parents' bedroom was ajar, and following a cursory glance, she moved on to the spare room, which also lay empty. As she made her way across the landing, the third bedroom came into view.

It was the only closed door. She pushed it open and her eyes narrowed. There was no bed, no shelves and no wardrobe. The walls were bare and had been painted white, the floorboards covered in a light grey, pattern-free carpet.

Only when she stepped inside and looked behind the door did she realize she was not alone.

Christina was staring straight at her.

49

Dimitri & Zoe

Zoe was fast asleep in the Real World by the time Dimitri logged out of the Metaverse. He'd deliberately waited in the garden of their computer-generated home long after she and Lenny had called it a night.

A series of lights illuminated the shrubs and small trees, carefully planted throughout their Japanese-style garden, swallowing him up in diverse shades of green, red and brown. The trickle of water descending the two-metre slate rockface into a pond typically relaxed him. But it was failing to have the desired effect tonight. Eventually, his optimism waned, and he re-entered their Real World home as tightly coiled as when he'd left.

In their bedroom, he changed out of his clothes and through the gloom caught sight of his sleeping wife. Zoe's words from earlier that week about Adam continued to echo. She had reminded him that what had happened to their son wasn't a mistake. He hadn't needed to hear it: the burden of guilt was there every time he looked in the mirror. It was heaped so high upon his shoulders that it had manifested itself in a physical stoop. The events of that day had, and would continue, to define the rest of their lives.

However, it was something he had come to terms with as best he could. And he'd assumed Zoe had too, which is why they'd rarely spoken of Adam in recent years. Now, he assumed that the introduction of Lenny into their lives and his disposal of Adam's belongings must have acted as a catalyst of sorts. They had released to the surface something long buried inside her. And he was at a loss as to how he could help.

Dimitri crept into bed and lay on his side, his back to his wife. He must have fallen asleep quickly because when he became aware of his surroundings again, the bed was empty and the moonlight had been replaced by the muted tones of the sun behind a cloudy sky. He showered, made his way downstairs to the kitchen where Zoe was sitting at the peninsula. He offered her an unreciprocated peck on the cheek.

'Do you have classes this morning?' he asked, glancing at the digital calendar hanging from the wall.

'No.'

'Shall we do something, the three of us? Lenny's been showing an interest in the solar system so I thought we could download an App that'll let us witness NASA's Orion Five launch as if we were there.'

'We'll see.'

Dimitri moved his hand towards hers, craving the intimacy she'd withdrawn. But before they could connect, he became distracted by the doormat sensor sending a notification to their home alarm system.

'Early delivery,' he muttered, and approached the front door, discovering a large sealed box left by their porch. With no stamps or postage label, it must have been hand-delivered. It was addressed only to him, and he carried it into the kitchen.

'Have you ordered something in my name?' he asked.

Zoe shook her head.

He took a pair of scissors and sliced open the box along its centre. Inside was a second package, this time gift-wrapped in silver and blood-red foil. As Dimitri opened that too, his face paled.

'What the...' he gasped, and pushed it across the worktop.

'What's wrong?' Zoe asked.

She moved hesitantly towards the box and peered inside, then clamped her hands over her mouth.

50
Hudson

Hudson awoke with a start, sitting upright in his bed, disorientated. His eyes darted around the room until he was sure he was in his London flat and not back in Ararat.

His watch read 6.35 a.m. Further sleep was unlikely. So, craving fresh air, he opened the window and gazed at the street below, already bustling with people and vehicles. He wouldn't know how to begin life as a commuter, he thought, or even do a regular job in a normal world. Those people's lives were so far removed from his. But if all went according to plan, it was unlikely to be something that he'd need to consider. However, he was always conscious of the many variables beyond his control: variables that could railroad his endgame. He simply had to remain focused and hope the others he trusted were doing the same.

He was about to shower when his watch vibrated with a video message from *The Family Experiment*'s host, Autumn Taylor. The clip, as ever, was brief and sent out to all contestants.

'Today your child turns twelve.' Autumn smiled. 'Look forward to seeing you soon.'

This was the age group he'd feared the most—Alice's transition from child to young woman. A young man, he could identify with. But he had very little experience of the trials of girls on the cusp of womanhood.

Before meeting this sixth incarnation, he ran his daily social media scans and saw that he'd topped Cadman and Gabriel in an unofficial online popularity poll. This news was welcome but not completely unexpected. From the recent column inches he had garnered both in print and online, public opinion was shifting. Commentators, influencers and high-profile celebrities had all vocalized their support for 'a young man, daring to challenge the system and go it alone' and the media were buying into it. A quote he'd once read by a long-dead singer came to mind. 'Whoever controls the media controls the mind,' Jim Morrison was reported to have said. Decades later, little had changed, thought Hudson.

Suffused with optimism, he showered, slipped on his Metaverse clothing and prepared to meet his daughter as a twelve-year-old for the first time. Alice was standing in their kitchen and his attention was immediately drawn to her body. She had grown both upwards and outwards and was now a whole head-height above what she had been yesterday. There were curves to her hips and thighs and her chest was more rounded. Instantly he knew that he was out of his depth.

'Oh shit,' he said aloud.

He regretted his choice of words when Alice moved to cover her T-shirt with folded arms. He'd already fallen at the first hurdle. He tried to lighten the mood.

'Well, I think we should do something about...them,' he said, laughing harder than he should have.

Black hearts appeared across the screen.

'"Them"?' Alice said, and cocked her head. 'They're called breasts, Dad.'

'Breasts,' he repeated. 'Yes, breasts.'

Come on, come on, you're the parent here! he reminded himself. 'Look, I don't want you to feel embarrassed, it's a perfectly normal development. It's great, in fact, it means you're becoming a woman.'

Alice rolled her eyes. 'A body doesn't define your gender.'

He was making such a mess of this. It wasn't just the physical changes that caught him on the back foot. He had to remember he wasn't talking to a child any more. And this version of her sounded wise beyond her years.

'Yes, yes, of course, you're right,' he stumbled. 'Well, I guess we should take you to a bra shop and get you taken care of.'

'Taken care of? You're not spaying a cat. Do you have to make it sound so clinical?'

'Sorry, I don't mean to.'

'Anyway, to spare your blushes, I've sorted it out myself with an App that scans a three-dimensional image of your body and orders you a made-to-measure bra.'

'Oh, okay,' he said, quietly relieved.

But there was another subject to broach. His cheeks reddened at the thought of it.

'As you get older, you know, there will be other, well, you know, changes to your body...'

'Is this going to be a conversation about periods, Dad?'

Hudson's face grew hotter and he pulled at his collar.

'It's fine, we covered that in school ages ago.'

'Oh, okay...and...is it appropriate for me to ask...have they started?'

'No, but I'm ready when they do. I've already ordered what I need.'

'Okay, great. Yes, that's great. Great.'

Hudson cursed himself as Alice left the room. He should've made it easy for her and not the other way around. Her maturity was way beyond what he'd expected. But it also brought about a longing for the eight-year-old version of her he'd lost overnight.

These leaps were not going to get any easier. In fact, for him they were going to get much worse as the finishing line approached.

51
Cadman & Gabriel

'Here you are!' Gabriel chirped as he appeared from nowhere. He sank into an empty seat next to Cadman and River. 'I've been searching for you for ages.'

A wide smile spread across his face as he joined his family inside the burgundy-and-white candy-striped circus tent.

'Where have you been, Dad?' asked an irritated River.

But Gabriel was already distracted by the circus ring in front of them. Before the audience, six Bengal tigers were lined up side by side on a sawdust floor as a ringmaster set light to circular hoops.

'Riv, look at them! Aren't they amazing?'

He jumped to his feet and began to whoop and applaud.

Cadman leaned across his son to tug at Gabriel's T-shirt.

'You should probably sit down.'

'Not a chance! They banned every type of circus before I was born so this is all new to me. I'm not an old-timer like you.' He winked and ruffled Cadman's hair.

'Go on, lads!' he shouted again at the tigers as they began leaping through the burning rings.

His enthusiasm earned the attention of other avatars in the audience, who turned to see where the noise was coming from.

'What's wrong?' he laughed as he addressed them. 'Don't hate on the flying tigers!'

The first of a series of black hearts crept across the screen.

Prior to the circus, Gabriel had attended the opening of a new Real World hotel and bar, the invitation having arrived in his name only. Despite Gabriel's reluctance, Cadman had encouraged him to attend, reminding him of the generous appearance fee he'd earn for only an hour's work. Photographers covering the red carpet had snapped more images of Gabriel than any other celebrity in attendance, such was his currency right now.

Meanwhile, the circus visit had been one of Cadman's last-minute ideas. He'd checked River out of school early and entered a brand-new App that was still being beta-tested. It was set in 1921 in the early days of prohibition, and the circus top had been erected on empty space in New York's meatpacking district. River had loved watching the display of strength from the strong men, the clowns and a family of acrobats. However, the use of tigers had left them both shifting in their seats. And now the elephants balancing on reinforced barrels were making them even more uncomfortable.

'More tigers!' Gabriel began chanting. 'Ti-gers, ti-gers, ti-gers...'

'Dad, you know what they're doing to them is cruel, right?' asked River.

'Lighten up, buddy, it's not real,' said Cadman. 'None of this is.'

'It's in my world, so it is to me,' River replied.

The boy's empathy caught Cadman unawares. Had he not seen it before or hadn't he been listening? Was it an in-built or learned behaviour? It was the first time he'd thought of his son as being anything other than AI. Once Cadman began to consider it, he realized there was a lot about River that he hadn't given much thought to. What other emotions had he learned? Could he love, grieve, crave or feel satisfied? How human was he?

Cadman rose to his feet and placed his hand firmly on Gabriel's shoulder, forcing him to sit again.

'What's gotten into you?' he asked.

'I'm having fun!'

More black hearts appeared, acknowledging viewers' confusion.

'Ooh, look at them!' Gabriel mocked, pointing to them. 'Do you see those, Riv? A few people at home are in a grump today, aren't they? Chill out, guys, it's circus time!'

He rocked back and forth on his heels then threw his arm around

River, pulled his head into his chest and ruffled his hair. River looked to Cadman, both seemingly confused by Gabriel's behaviour.

'What's next?' Gabriel asked as the ringmaster made his way into the centre stage. 'Get on with it,' he howled. 'Is there a fast-forward button or something?'

'Are you okay?' Cadman asked. 'You're not acting very... Gabriel-like.'

'I might have had a couple of glasses of champagne at the bar launch, but that's it. I'm just excited to be here, aren't I? Li-ons! Li-ons!'

Without warning he clambered to his feet again, but in doing so lost his balance and fell towards River. He threw his hand out to steady himself. But instead of reaching the back of River's chair, he pushed his son face first into the seat in front of him.

'Oh, Christ,' Gabriel said, and hurried to help River upright.

Through his haptic glove, Gabriel felt the warmth of the boy's blood on his hand. There was a three-centimetre gash above his right eyebrow. Cadman pressed down on the wound with the sleeve of his jumper to stem the blood.

'I'm so sorry, Riv,' Gabriel said. 'Are you all right?'

'Yes,' River replied, but the tears pooling in his eyelashes suggested otherwise.

'You're high again, aren't you?' Cadman fumed.

'No, of course I'm not,' Gabriel protested.

'Bullshit. I'm taking River home and I don't want to see you until you've sobered up.'

Before Gabriel could defend himself, Cadman and River had left him alone, his face obscured by a screen now full of black hearts.

52
Woody & Tina

Issy's blood ran cold at the sight of her mother. It ignited her fight-or-flight instinct. She readied herself to run from the room, back across the landing and down the staircase.

That was until she realized Christina was oblivious that she had company. Wearing her VR headset and earbuds, she had no idea her daughter was within touching distance. Issy was not used to seeing her mother alone and so vulnerable. She clutched the knife tighter in her hand.

Issy watched in fascination as an unguarded Christina moved her hands and arms backwards and forwards in short, sharp bursts as if somewhere in the Metaverse an action required repetition.

Issy tentatively took a step forward, then stopped. A second step followed until she was just centimetres from Christina—far enough for her mother's flailing hands not to come into contact with her but close enough for Issy to lurch forward and, with one clean cut, slice her mother's throat open. Or with another swift movement, stab her where her heart should be, if she were to possess such a thing.

Countless times during her incarceration, Issy had dreamed about a moment like this. She had fantasized about killing Woody too, because he was the weak one. He was told what to believe and Christina had turned him against her. She could see it in his face during the trial. He began so supportively, but gradually he became more distant. And over the years, he'd followed Christina's orders without question. He was pathetic. They were both pathetic.

Now, Issy's heart was beating twenty to the dozen as she lifted the knife chest high, then pulled it backward, ready to launch. However, she hesitated when the part of her that craved revenge was overruled by logic. A rash, spur-of-the-moment decision might not serve her best interests. If she wanted to leave this house and make them pay for what they'd done to her, it would take planning. It couldn't be done on a whim just because an opportunity had presented itself.

'Why are you standing there?' Christina asked calmly.

Issy's knuckles whitened as the grip on her knife became even more rigid. She opened her mouth to respond but Tina spoke first.

'Do you want to come and help me? There's another apron over there.'

Issy's eyes followed her mother's hand as it pointed to the corner of the wall. It was empty.

'We don't want to get your school uniform dirty, sweetheart.'

Sweetheart? Tina had never once called her that. It suddenly became apparent to Issy that Christina was conversing with someone in the Metaverse. Issy watched and listened, transfixed.

'Okay,' Christina continued. 'Now crack both eggs into the bowl, add the yeast and measure out five hundred grams of flour before we put the olive oil and water in.' She let out a sharp laugh. 'No, I'm not gender stereotyping! Your dad makes bread for me all the time. It'll do you no harm to learn. And how do you know what gender stereotyping is anyway?'

Who was she speaking to? And who was the 'your dad' she was referring to? Issy knew that if she remained where she was waiting to find out, she'd likely be discovered. And then she'd have no choice but to attack Tina, which would limit her options. So reluctantly, she turned and prepared to pad her way back downstairs.

Until Christina spoke again.

'You're doing a great job. Keep stirring while Mum searches for a whisk.'

Issy stopped dead in her tracks.

53
Dimitri & Zoe

Zoe glared at the open box that Dimitri had pushed to one side. Her head was spinning. She reached inside and carefully removed its contents.

Her doll had been returned to her.

'No, leave it there!' Dimitri cautioned, and grabbed his phone.

'Who are you calling?' she asked.

'The police.'

'He's not real, Dimitri. Look.'

She held Adam aloft and turned it to face her husband. 'See?'

'Thank Christ,' he gasped, and let out a nervous laugh. 'It looks so realistic, I thought... I thought someone had...never mind. Who the hell has sent us this thing?'

But his wife had stopped listening. Instead, she examined every inch of the doll from head to toe. It was definitely her Adam. Not a replica, but the exact same one Dimitri had thrown out weeks earlier. She pulled him close to her chest and buried her nose in the folds of his neck. The scent was comfortingly familiar.

'Adam,' she whispered.

'Adam?' Dimitri repeated. 'Why are you calling it that?'

'Because that's his name,' she continued as the first of her many tears rolled onto the doll's cheek.

'Zoe, you're scaring me.'

She continued to clasp the doll with one hand while the other searched deeper inside the packaging. Buried away were his other outfits.

'Is it...is it wearing Adam's baby clothes?' he asked. 'That's the cardigan my mum knitted him. Zoe, what in hell is going on?'

She cleared her throat and turned to her husband. She wasn't going to lie to him.

'He belongs to me and has done for years,' she replied. 'I kept him in one of the suitcases you threw away from the loft.'

'But I checked them, they were just full of old books.'

'He was wrapped in a blanket at the bottom.'

Dimitri tried to make sense of what she was saying. He ruffled his hair with his hands.

'You named a doll after our dead son and you've been dressing him in his clothes? You're going to have to explain this to me because I'm struggling to get my head around it.'

Zoe clenched Adam a little tighter.

'I bought him on impulse after we lost our Adam and I was struggling to cope. I thought he'd be a short-term fix, but the more time I spent with him, the more comfort he gave.'

Dimitri shook his head.

'This...this thing gave you comfort?'

'Yes.'

Zoe felt her cheeks redden, then gritted her teeth. She would not be made to feel ashamed. Dimitri would not diminish Adam's place in her world.

'And what do you do with him?' he asked.

'I have a safe space in the loft that I go to when you're elsewhere. I feed him, wind him, change his nappy and dress him. Sometimes I just hold him, other times I'll sing him to sleep. I'll tell him how much I love him. I'll do everything with this Adam that I did with ours when he was a baby.'

Zoe stared at her husband, awaiting his response. Awaiting a level of understanding from the man she had loved for so much of her life. From the man she needed him to be right at this moment.

Dimitri held his fingers to his mouth in a steeple shape. A minute passed before he finally responded.

'Are you completely fucking nuts?'

Zoe's heart sank, and she let out a humourless laugh.

'For a moment there, I thought that you might try to understand me,' she said. 'Do you wonder why I didn't tell you about him?'

'You didn't say anything because you knew I'd have told you to get rid of it.'

'You don't get to *tell* me to do anything,' she snapped.

'Zoe—'

'And you can stop Zoeing me too. I know who I am.'

'Look at it from my perspective. For years, my wife has convinced herself a doll is our son, and now I'm expected to jump on board with it.'

Zoe's eyes locked on to his like magnets.

'Yet you expected me to get on board with having a son in a make-believe universe. What's the difference?'

'The difference?' he repeated, dismayed. 'The difference is that Lenny is not a thing. He walks, he talks, he thinks, he's the closest thing you can get to a human being. That inanimate object you are holding does none of that. It just lies there, like a dead baby.'

'If I can love Lenny then why can't you understand that I can love Adam too?'

'He's not fucking Adam!' Dimitri exploded. 'Stop calling him that! He's not real.'

'I know he isn't,' she hit back. 'But when I needed to grieve for our Adam, you wouldn't let me!'

Dimitri's neck stiffened.

'What's that supposed to mean? I never stopped you.'

'But you did when you made the aftermath all about you. It was about *your* broken heart, *your* broken spirit, *your* lost son, *you, you, you*... *You* were the one who got hypothermia searching the marshes and loch for him, so you became the hero, people felt sorry for you. Because I was his mother, I was the one they blamed, I was the one they said should've been more careful not to let him out of my sight. Between your family, my family and social media, I was vilified.'

'That's not fair.'

'No, what's not fair is that even now, you're not listening to me. I lost a child as well that day, but I had to hold it together for the two of us because your guilt was too busy crippling you. There was a gigantic, empty hole inside of me, and this version of Adam went some way to filling it. I'm completely aware he's not real, but the love I have for him is. He gave me what I needed when you didn't. And he still does. And if you can't accept that, then fuck you, Dimitri. Fuck you.'

Zoe didn't await his reply. Instead, with Adam's head resting upon her shoulder, she grabbed his box and prepared to leave her dazed husband alone.

However, a sudden movement coming from the doll's arms took her by surprise. But not as much as the voice that came from its mouth.

'Hi, Mum and Dad,' it said breezily.

It was using the real Adam's voice. And in horror, Zoe almost dropped him.

'I love you both.'

Chats

TV / Reality TV Shows / **The Family Experiment**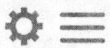

HairyPoppins, 8.08 p.m.
What the hell was going on with Gabriel? Was he drunk?

TellyBob, 8.09 p.m.
Cadman asked if he was high. Did you see his eyes? He was more spaced out than a Mars landing when he lamped his kid.

HairyPoppins, 8.09 p.m.
Do you think he was AZing?

TeamGabriel009, 8.10 p.m.
No, he wouldn't do that. #AngelGabriel

TellyBob, 8.11 p.m.
Satan was an angel once.

QueenyKate 8.12 p.m.
Still cringing at Hudson staring horrified at Alice's chest. Could he have got it more wrong?

FaffyDuck, 8.15 p.m.
Could he have been more of a #paedo?

Living4Luv, 8.20 p.m.
There are three months left. Do we have any idea of who is going to win this thing yet?

HairyPoppins, 8.22 p.m.
Not got a bloody clue. It's still anyone's game.

TellyBob, 8.50 p.m.
Somebody's got to win. And I have a feeling there's gonna be a few surprises ahead.

MONTH SEVEN:
FOURTEEN YEARS OLD

www.grapevine.uk/UK-trending/2808765

Through the Grapevine

Home | UK | **Trending**

NINE BODIES FOUND IN CHANNEL

LATEST CHANNEL DEATH TOLL TAKES TOTAL TO 146 THIS YEAR

The bodies of nine children have been discovered off the coast of Calais by French coastguards.

The children, thought to be of British origin, were not wearing life vests and are believed to have drowned.

It takes the death toll of young people being smuggled out of the country and sent to Europe to 146 in the last year.

Since smuggling operations began more than a decade ago, almost 2,000 children are thought to have drowned as a result of faulty or overloaded boats.

Melvin Hartnett, spokesperson for charity Protect the Children, warns: 'Until the cost of living is reduced and there is better investment in Community Housing, more children are going to die. No one wants to send a child abroad, but until there are better opportunities here for children not only of the rich, then little will change.'

Home Secretary Louise Beech has warned parents found trying to depatriate their children to Europe will face heavy fines and custodial sentences if caught.

'Parents and guardians must be reminded they will face the full force of the law if they risk their children's lives,' she says.

54
Woody & Tina

Nine long, frustrating days had passed before Issy finally had the house to herself. She'd freed herself from the basement many times in that period, waiting until the cybernanny was recharging before using the electronic unlocking device left for her by her balaclava-clad benefactor. Then, she'd calmly creep up the staircase until she reached the hallway, open the door a crack, and wait. Invariably she'd hear her parents' voices or the sound of them moving about, and then she'd be forced to return to her space, becoming more frustrated with each failed endeavour.

There had been opportunities for Issy to escape that house. Once, a careless Christina and Woody had forgotten to set the fingerprint lock to the front door. And while they were upstairs asleep, Issy had hovered on the step, door wide open, gearing herself up to run to freedom. Second time around, she'd located two windows without locks that she could have squirmed her way through. But she hadn't taken either chance. The authorities would have been alerted to her escape through the GPS tracking device buried deep in her arm. And where would she go if she had escaped? Now that the freedom she'd dreamed of was within her grasp, she must first formulate a plan before making a run for it.

So she had decided to wait until all her ducks were aligned before she aimed her gun and began blasting their heads off. She would need access to her parents' bank accounts to fund her endeavours, purchase communication devices and work out where to go and how to get there. And all without alerting them. She could only do that by using the unrestricted access of their headsets.

There was something else that was niggling her. What—or who—

had Christina been talking to in the Metaverse when she had referred to herself as 'Mum'? This afternoon, and with both parents out of the house, she might find her answers.

Issy raced upstairs and into her parents' Metaverse access point. She slipped on the smaller of the two headsets and inserted the earbuds. Christina hadn't logged out properly, and it was immediately obvious just how expansive that world was compared to the restrictions Issy was used to. There were thousands of cities to explore, games to play, strangers to talk to, projects to undertake, and if she didn't tether herself, she could quite easily float in any number of directions for the rest of the afternoon.

She focused on Christina's most visited sites. Topping the list was an unfamiliar App titled *The Family Experiment.* Once inside, she found herself standing by the front door of a large, single-storey, white-rendered house. Her heart jumped when she caught sight of her reflection in the window, forgetting for a moment that she was now inhabiting her mother's avatar and not her own. She reached out her hand to tentatively turn the handle.

The property was empty. There were very few internal walls in there as she made her way through each zone of the house, surprised that for its size, there were only two bedrooms. The first contained a bed large enough to lose yourself in. The second likely belonged to a teenager, going by the moving images on the wall of bands Issy also liked and posters of movies she and Woody had watched together. She flicked through clothes hanging on rails—they were her size and to her taste but there was at least double the quantity.

Issy returned to the living zone, coming to a halt when she reached a sideboard. A centrally placed photo frame contained alternating moving images of her, Christina and Woody taken throughout the years. At first, she couldn't fathom what was wrong with what she was seeing until she realized each had been faked. That wasn't the bike her parents had taught her to ride; she'd never swum in the sea; she hadn't affixed LED candles inside Chinese lanterns on a beach; nor had she sailed across the sky in a hot-air balloon. None of it was real.

A handful of red hearts floating about the corner of her monitor caught her attention. She'd seen them before on interactive programmes and it typically meant viewers were reacting positively to something they were watching. Were they watching her? She corrected herself—were they watching Christina? Why would anyone be interested in that woman?

Her eyes returned to her mother's favourites list, and Issy found herself inside a school classroom. A dozen girls and boys, a little younger in appearance than her, were reading from tablets. And as her eyes took in each of these children, one girl in particular caught her attention.

She was Issy's double.

Issy walked slowly to her doppelganger, trying to make sense of her. They shared almost the same body type, eye colour, strawberry-blonde hair and dimples. Only this girl was a little more polished than Real World Issy. There was no slight overlap in the bottom row of incisors, no acne on her brow, and her skin had a healthy, almost radiant glow. Not so pale like hers that blue veins shone through it.

A name had been embroidered on her school bag, Belle. Short for Isabelle, in the same way that Issy's name was.

Issy's brows lowered when she realized just who she was staring at. A reworked version of herself. Not one that her parents had simply recreated, but one that had been tweaked and improved. In Belle, they'd made the version of a daughter they had wanted all along, and she was living the life Issy had been stripped of.

55
Cadman & Gabriel

Apps opening entire Metaverse worlds were hit and miss, thought Gabriel. For every intricately detailed, meticulously researched experience, there were at least half a dozen that felt incomplete and required more development. But today's hike through Sydney's Blue Mountains was one of the most realistic he had experienced to date.

Each rock and stone could be felt underfoot. Tall grasses skimmed his avatar's bare legs and the sun that beat down upon them all added to the realism. He drew a deep breath, certain that the oxygen tasted better here, even if in reality, he was in a room in his house. It was funny how the mind could play tricks on you, he thought. He briefly considered if that was what it had been doing to his relationship with River—fooling him into believing that the love he felt for the boy was real. But no, he was certain he loved his son.

He, Cadman and River had been hiking on the steep trail for the best part of an hour, navigating their way towards a digital recreation of Wentworth Falls, a three-tiered waterfall fed by an adjacent creek. And according to the map in their headsets, they had almost reached their destination. When he listened carefully enough, Gabriel could just about hear the rush of water through his earpods.

It was the first time they'd ventured out together as a family since their night at the circus. A scar above a now fourteen-year-old River's eyebrow was a constant reminder to both Gabriel and viewers of his intoxication.

The morning after the incident, a Development Leap meant River's most recent transition had altered much of his appearance. This updated version was much taller, his face had lost its puppy fat and his shoulders were broader.

The slope of the trail gradually descended until they reached the undercliff walk. They made their way to the smooth rocks at the base and the water cascading into the pool below. All three removed their boots and socks and howled at the shock of the ice-cold water as they waded to reach the other side.

'What is AZ like?' River asked Gabriel as they dried themselves on warm, mossy rocks.

Gabriel looked to Cadman. They had rehearsed this conversation many times over lately, with Cadman having schooled Gabriel in the correct phrases to use that might assist with his public redemption.

'The after-effects differ from person to person,' Gabriel began. 'The morning after you take it was always the worst part for me. It gave me headaches, my arms and legs would shake and I could never be far from the toilet, if you catch my drift.'

River screwed up his face. 'Urgh, gross. But what's it like when you're using it? How do you feel?'

'Again, it depends on who's taking it. For me, it gave me a confidence I didn't have. It made me feel like I could talk about anything to anyone. And it made me happy. But it was illusory.'

'Why did you do it?'

Gabriel felt both River's and Cadman's eyes upon him.

'At the time, I wasn't happy with your dad. He's a very determined man who knows what he wants, but when we first got together, I needed someone like that in my life. Then when most of my friends began developing their own identities and careers, I felt left behind. I remained that same nineteen-year-old I was when we met. And when I first represented your dad at events, I was no more than an extension of his brand. It was only when I started using AZ that I began to feel like my own person. I learned later in rehab that AZ exploits your insecurities, making you believe that you need it when you don't.'

Slowly, red hearts began to creep across the screen, an indication he was gaining the audience's understanding.

'I only realized how much damage I was doing to myself later,' Gabriel continued, 'when I was diagnosed with the brain tumour that might've been linked to my AZ addiction. And when your dad sold just about everything we had to pay for my treatment, I realized just how much I'd hurt him and just how much he loved me. He drives me nuts sometimes—he's arrogant, he's argumentative, and everything can feel like a battle—but I know he'd never hurt me.'

'So did you do it again the night of the circus?'

'With my hand on my heart, I promise I didn't. I don't know how it ended up in my system, but I didn't voluntarily take it.'

Cadman's eyes narrowed as he stared at Gabriel, and for the briefest of moments, he recognized in him a little of what he had seen in his DNA Match, Marcus, all those years ago: a kindness, a tenderness, a genuine desire to be a good person.

Cadman didn't possess the depth of love for Gabriel that he'd felt for Marcus, and he was okay with that. What they shared was still a form of love, nonetheless. Perhaps Gabriel was right: maybe a family and normality were worth more than his career, his fame and the balance of his accounts. In the great scheme of things, did it really matter if Gabriel was more popular than him?

In that moment, Cadman realized two things. If he was willing to accept it, everything he could ever need was right here, in front of him, sunning themselves on warm rocks at the base of an Australian waterfall.

The second was that perhaps paying someone to spike Gabriel's skin with AZ at the pre-circus party had not been a good idea.

56
Hudson

Hudson's avatar stood by the water's edge, looking out across his namesake river, then back at the New York borough of Staten Island. It was his third trip there this week, and each time he'd closed his eyes and taken a long, deep breath, trying to recall how it had smelled. The App-operated sensor that sprayed different aromas into his room depending on where in the Metaverse he was hadn't come close to replicating that scent.

The majority of his walks throughout the Metaverse city's boroughs had been with Alice, but he'd taken these last few alone while his now fourteen-year-old daughter was in school. His final destination was always where he was standing right now.

Becoming a father had pushed to the surface so many memories and long-buried emotions that he sometimes struggled to process them. And this afternoon, he'd found himself wondering how Alice might have fared if she'd found herself under Ararat's roof. She was confident, opinionated and unafraid to speak her mind. And there was no place for free thinkers in Ararat. So it was likely she would have gone the same way as Eva. The thought made him shudder.

It had been Hudson's unwillingness to question orders that had helped him to rise up the ranks. One of his many roles had been to assist in the evaluation of new arrivals. He'd tested these young, confused children to determine if they might be suitable subjects for AI to learn from. And he had tried hard to help those who weren't up to par or who'd remained too consistently distraught to function away from their families. However, it hadn't been possible to save them all from being escorted out of the door on the left.

Hudson had also proved himself to be a fast learner. He'd mentor his new recruits as they pretended to be the avatars and AI children the beta-testing clients believed they were interacting with. However, the technology had only come so far, and he sensed his employers' frustration in the speed of development. More and more testers were dropping out when they sensed they were being duped, talking to humans masquerading as AI.

Meanwhile, Hudson had grown fond of one of his own clients, Charles, a widower in his mid-fifties living in the south of England. Unusually for the Metaverse, where users chose how they represented themselves visually, Charles hadn't designed an augmented, improved version of himself. Instead, he'd replicated himself complete with a wheelchair he'd been consigned to years earlier. He and son Nate had been cycling together when a car had ploughed into them, killing Nate and leaving Charles with life-changing injuries. He had reimagined his son in avatar form.

For weeks, Hudson and AI had alternated as they played Nate's part. He'd interpret how he might talk and behave in their father-and-son discourse based upon the video clips he'd found on Nate's still-active social media accounts.

Hudson had accompanied Charles to classic football tournaments and theatrical plays, and they'd explored historical eras, all recreated in App form. He'd looked forward to chatting to his client each day and had got just as much from the experience as he believed Charles had. He felt like someone's son.

That was until the evening he'd logged in and discovered Charles's avatar had vanished. 'Account dissolved,' a notice read. He'd begun to type a message to the Fiscal Services Department.

'Client number 77879. I'm logged in but I can't find him.'

'His avatar was terminated. As per the terms and conditions, he was given twenty-four hours' notice.'

'But what did he do?'

'The algorithm believed AI had learned all it could from the client so shut it down.'

'But he was using it to talk to his dead son.'

'And?'

'Can't we reactivate it and let them continue? What harm will it do?'

'The data has already been erased and the avatar design re-allocated.'

Hudson disappeared into the corridor to clear his head. He'd enjoyed the feeling of belonging, even if he'd only been playing a part.

A week later and an unexpected message arrived in his inbox from the Client Retention Department.

'I was informed you were enquiring about a former customer? Why?'

He wondered if by asking the question, he'd inadvertently broken a rule.

'Curiosity.'

A minute passed before the sender continued.

'Charles Michael Simmonds, now deceased. Booked himself a bed in a euthanasia clinic five days ago.'

'He never said he was sick.'

'He posted a message on social media saying he'd lost his son for a second time and it was too much to bear.'

Hudson sank into his chair, a knot forming in his stomach. How many others were out there like Charles? How many more people had or would take their own lives when the AI they were helping to develop turned its back on them?

'Why are you telling me this?'

'Because you cared. There aren't many of us like that here.'

'And who are you?'

A minute passed before the next reply came. And the moment he finished reading it, the message vanished.

'Get out of here when you can. Leave the moment the opportunity arrives or you'll end up with all the others.'

ADVERTISEMENT

No one can truly appreciate the pain you have gone through if you have lost a loved one long before their time.

But what if there was a way to heal faster and keep the memory of your child alive?

Here at re:born*, we can replicate your child so that in the Metaverse, they will live for as long as you want them to.

Using images, social media and videos, your child will look just how you want them to, sound just as you remember them, and behave in a manner that will make them almost indistinguishable from the one you lost.

re:born

where death can be a new beginning

*an affiliate of Awakening Entertainment. All rights reserved.

57
Woody & Tina

The staffroom at the Safe Passage clinic was near enough empty when Tina made her way inside. She was eight hours through her shift and her day had been relentless. Inquiries had risen sharply since recent changes in the law had allowed those with long-term depression to end their lives at the euthanasia facility. Once approval was given and after a brief stay for psychological evaluations, it was her job to then demonstrate how to administer the medicine that ended their lives. She was required to remain with clients until their statistics flatlined.

A three-day weekend lay ahead and she couldn't wait to sign off and spend more time with Belle. Tomorrow, she had organized for Woody, herself and Belle to teleport to a simulation of ancient Egypt, where virtual visitors could walk amongst the labourers working on the construction of the Menkaure pyramid. And on Sunday, they'd be spending the day at the MetaDisney theme park.

Tina was ever conscious of the time slipping through her fingers and how quickly the last seven months with Belle had passed. Now only two Development Leaps remained until the baby girl she'd held in her arms a heartbeat ago became a woman. Tina had already booked that final month off work. And her HR department, keen on the positive publicity her appearance in the series was generating, had offered to keep her on full pay throughout.

Tina tried her best not to think too far ahead, but it was becoming increasingly difficult not to. If she and Woody lost, Belle would cease to exist. Even just thinking about it made her nauseous.

She unhooked the catches on her lunchbox and was making her way to the microwave to reheat last night's cannelloni when a colleague arrived.

'That's weird,' Jules began, her phone in her hand. 'Is there a time delay or something?'

'On what?' Tina replied, stirring her food with a fork.

'I've just been watching you on *The Family Experiment*. I thought they broadcast everything live?'

'They do.'

'Well, according to this, you're at home with Belle.'

Tina shook her head. 'You must be watching the highlights show.'

'The graphic in the corner says "livestreaming".'

Tina used her phone to log in to the TV channel's App. And just as Jules had described, she could see herself, chatting with her daughter in their MetaHouse lounge. What was happening?

She dialled Woody.

'Are you using my Avatar account?' she asked.

'No, why?'

'Are you sure you haven't picked up the wrong headset?'

'Yes, because I'm not at home. What's the problem?'

'I'm watching myself on screen right now with Belle.'

'There must be a glitch in the system. I'll call the producers.'

Without warning, a deep dark chasm opened inside Tina.

'Woody,' she said, her lips now pressed up against the phone's mouthpiece. 'The App that's linked to the tracking device in Issy's arm. Can you open it, please.'

'Why?'

'Woody,' she continued with forced calm. 'I need you to do it right now.'

'Okay, hold on.'

The wait only lasted seconds but was interminable.

'It says she's at home,' Woody replied. 'Where else would she be?'

'Zoom in closer. What room is she in? Tell me she's still in the basement.'

'Yes, she's...oh, hang on, it's updating. No...what...no, that's not possible.'

'What isn't?' Silence. 'What isn't?'

Her husband wasn't replying.

'Woody!' she yelled, to Jules's surprise.

His voice faltered as he spoke.

'It says she isn't in the basement. She's upstairs in our access point.'

'Get home right now!' ordered Tina as she ran out of the staffroom, through the hospital corridors, out into the car park and straight to the taxi rank.

58
Hudson

Hudson was sitting at the table in his London flat, staring absent-mindedly from the window. It had become a regular habit since leaving Ararat, where windows only faced into the quadrant and never into the world outside.

He'd expected to spend the early evening with Alice in the Metaverse as they did most days, but she'd made other plans.

'I'm going out with some friends from school,' she announced on her return home.

'Who?' he replied.

'Gideon, Melanie, Bellamy, Blake and Nicco.'

'So that's three boys and three girls. Like a triple date,' he teased.

Hudson thought he had spotted her blush ever so slightly.

'No, Dad. They're just part of my friendship group. Besides, I'm fourteen. I should be socializing with all sexes and genders.'

'Where is your "friendship group" going then?'

'To a games studio.'

Together, she and Hudson had visited immersive gaming experiences many times once Alice had been old enough to appreciate them. Fortnite, Roblox and Minecraft had been the early adopters of Metaverse gaming, and even now, despite their somewhat dated designs, they were still favourites. But he was not. Now there were other people she'd rather play with. She was pulling away from him, as was the natural order of things.

'And are you interested in any of these boys?' he asked.

'Why would I want to narrow the field down only to boys?'

'Oh, I just assumed.'

'Dad, you are so old-fashioned!' she groaned. 'We're all pansexual

The Family Experiment

now until we decide what we want to be. Try before you buy! You must have experimented when you were my age?'

'Of course,' he lied.

'You know there's nothing to stop you from dating too. Have you ever done the Match Your DNA test?'

'No, because I have enough on my plate right now trying to keep up with you.'

The truth was, Hudson had neither the time nor the inclination to open himself up to a relationship. The closest he had come to making a connection with anyone had been Eva. When it came to romance, he was no wiser now than he had been as a child in Ararat.

Despite all that had been taken away from him, he still thought of himself as one of the lucky ones. At least he had made it to and from Ararat alive. The lives of the young people who'd drowned in the Channel earlier this month had been snuffed out far too soon. He couldn't bring himself to watch footage of the tarpaulin-covered bodies lying on the beach. It was all too close to home.

As he stared from the window at the London skyline, he knew that soon he would need to start preparing himself for change, like he had on the day he'd been told his time in Ararat was coming to an end.

At the end of his shift, he had become aware of approaching footsteps. He turned to see a familiar character, the shaven-headed woman whom he'd only ever seen in holographic form. That day she was very much flesh and blood.

'Relax, Hudson,' she said, recognizing his apprehension. 'Take a walk with me.'

He had no idea she'd been aware of who he was amongst the hundreds on site. But he followed her, heart racing, as she led the way across the floor. Heads turned at the sight of them together.

'Take a look around you,' she continued. 'Do you think you'll miss this place?'

'Am I going somewhere?'

'You're returning to England.'

'W-what? When? For how long?'

'When? Now, today. For how long? For the foreseeable future. Why? Because from what our internal AI tells us, you do what you're told, you show good initiative and you're a fast learner. Our AI development has learned much from your contributions, but you've gone as far as we can take you here. And we have an exciting multimedia venture ahead which we would like you to be a part of.'

Hudson raised his eyebrows. 'Me?'

'We estimate that within the next two years, we will be ready to move from beta-testing to a fully commercial rollout.'

'Of what? Avatars?'

'Yes, specifically a programme of ultra-realistic, AI-operated Meta-Children for people who cannot afford to start traditional families. But you'll be told more about that upon your arrival in England.'

The fear inside him gave way to disbelief. Ararat was home. She had anticipated his reluctance.

'Hudson, eventually we all outgrow our cages,' she continued. 'You are about to start another life. Very few young people who arrive at our doors get a second chance, let alone a third. Keep doing as we ask and you will have a long future ahead of you within our organization.'

Something flashed in his memory: the message he'd received from an anonymous member of the Client Retention Department.

'Get out of here when you can. Leave the moment the opportunity arrives or you'll end up with all the others.'

Any remaining doubt he kept to himself.

A guard escorted him back to the dormitory, where he found a wardrobe of fresh clothes laid out across his mattress. As he changed into navy-coloured jeans, a maroon jumper and a dark green zip-up jacket, he couldn't remember when he'd last worn something that wasn't a derivative of grey. When he was sure he wasn't being watched, he shifted a locker by the side of his bed and from underneath pulled out the only thing he had smuggled into Ararat ten years earlier. Then he was escorted through the building until he reached the woman again, standing by the left- and right-hand doors.

He veered with trepidation towards the one on the left, the one that would lead him back into the world he had been separated from for so long. Hudson braced himself as the woman opened it and beckoned him to follow. Lights above them flickered to life and illuminated a white corridor leading to another door. She placed her eye in front of a retinal scanner and then her palm against a second device before that door opened too. Only instead of rolling hills, vast oceans, wasteland, a forest or even a desert island lying behind it, there was a door with the words Viewing Room written on it.

'This isn't the exit?' he asked.

'For some it's only the beginning,' she replied with a knowing smile.

By the time they exited again soon afterwards, a pale Hudson had learned that everything he'd assumed he knew about his job had been wrong.

'There's a vehicle waiting outside for you,' the woman continued, before leading her dazed charge through a maze of corridors and a final pair of exit doors. 'You'll pick up your passport when you reach the airfield.'

'I'm going by plane?'

She nodded.

'Where in Europe have I been all this time? No one has ever told us.'

'What makes you think we're in Europe?'

'Then where are we?'

'You're on Staten Island. You've been in New York for the last ten years.'

59

Dimitri & Zoe

Zoe was grateful that viewers of *The Family Experiment* **were only** able to witness her and Dimitri's lives in the Metaverse. Because in the Real World, the tension was so thick between the couple that a knife would barely have made an indentation, let alone cut through it.

Since the reappearance of her Adam doll—whose sudden materialization still remained unexplained weeks later—she and Dimitri had gone back and forth like two equal-seeded tennis players in a rally.

'Why the hell would I have given an infant doll our son's voice?' she'd argued.

'I don't know what goes on in your head any more,' he replied.

'I wouldn't have done that. They've made him sound like something from a horror film.'

When she'd delved deeper, she'd found videos which Adam had uploaded of himself to his social media profile before they'd lost him. Whoever had returned the doll had uploaded the recording. And that posed new, unanswerable questions.

Meanwhile, Dimitri had been frustrated by her unwillingness to accept that the baby was 'not normal' and was preventing her from moving on.

And she'd remained exasperated by his stubborn refusal to recognize the comfort the doll had brought her when he had delivered so little. When he used the cliché, 'We'll have to agree to disagree,' Zoe knew a resolution was unlikely.

The only thing they agreed upon was reducing their working hours in the final months of the competition. They hoped that by spending more time with Lenny, they would continue to win over viewers with their commitment to family.

This afternoon, Zoe had allocated herself time with Adam and was sitting in the loft with him pressed to her shoulder, his battery removed, when Dimitri's head unexpectedly protruded over the rim of the hatch.

'Can we talk?' he asked.

His presence felt like an intrusion. For so long this had been her place, somewhere that required no explanation or justification because nobody knew what she used it for. And since the shift, she hadn't shied away from spending time up here when she required it. She was about to return Adam to his suitcase, then changed her mind.

No, she thought, *I will not allow Dimitri to shame me.*

Instead, she nodded at his request, then braced herself.

Head bent under the eaves, he approached her with the caution he might offer to an injured wild animal. He sat on the floor, legs tucked under his backside, a metre away from her. His eyes focused on hers, then Adam, then the baby station she had created around herself. He took in the small pile of spare nappies and Adam's neatly folded clothes.

'There's something I haven't told you because I didn't want to upset you,' he began, and removed a postcard from the back pocket of his trousers. It was the one he'd received featuring a photograph on the front of Loch Ba, the area in which they'd reported Adam missing.

Zoe's stomach immediately sank when she recognized the image. Turning it over, she saw it had been addressed 'To Mum and Dad.'

'When did this arrive?' Zoe asked.

'Lenny had just turned five. The handwriting on the address is identical to the box they returned your Adam in.'

'Why is someone doing this to us? What do they know?'

Dimitri shrugged. He chose his words carefully.

'How...is he doing?' he asked.

'He's a doll, Dimitri, he doesn't feel anything,' Zoe replied matter-of-factly. 'Despite what you think, I'm not mad. I don't think he's human or imagine him talking back to me. He's more like a conduit, I suppose. I speak to our Adam through him.'

'I think I understand.'

'And anyway, it doesn't matter if you understand or not, you've made your opinion perfectly clear. What matters is how Adam makes me feel.'

'And can I ask, how does Lenny make you feel?'

'Lenny?' She shook her head. 'No. I'm not having this argument again in which you pit the two of them against each other and try to persuade me I should throw Adam away.'

'I wasn't going to,' he said. 'Honestly, I'm not here to rehash anything.'

'Then why have you come?'

'To listen to you, to understand. And for us to decide about what we'll do if we win the competition.'

'Do you think that could happen?'

'I honestly do. We haven't put a foot wrong, have we? From all I've read online, there's very little in it between us and Hudson. I'm not so sure about Cadman and Gabriel after that drug stuff, but as we are seeing, viewers can be forgiving.'

Zoe nodded slowly.

'So, when we first applied, the plan was for us to use the money to start a new family with a biological child. Is that still what you want?'

Zoe looked at Dimitri, as if trying to read his mind.

'Just to say,' he added, 'there is no wrong or right answer to this. I simply need to know where your head is at now.'

Zoe hesitated and clasped Adam a little more tightly.

'Well, if you want the truth, I don't know if a biological baby is what I want any more,' she admitted. 'I'm forty-four, which brings with it so many potential complications if I fall pregnant, and that's if I can conceive at all. Even IVF and the meds they pump you with will be a huge strain on me physically and mentally. Then there is Adam and Lenny. I love Lenny and the time we spend with him, but I also love what I have with my Adam. I want to keep them both alongside the memories of our first Adam, and I know that if we have another child of our own, I won't be able to. What about you?'

'I don't think that I could willingly end Lenny's life,' he said. 'I would love the chance to be a biological dad again, to have a child I don't have to put on a headset and suit to be with. But I also wonder if I'd just be trying to replace our Adam and make up for the mistakes we made with him.'

'You think that's what I've been doing with him, don't you?' she asked, looking down at the doll.

'I did, at first, but no, not now. I finally think I get it.'

For the first time in weeks, the quiet that followed was no longer uneasy.

'So if we win, we agree that we'll keep Lenny?' Dimitri continued.

'Yes, I think we should. But I also need you to accept Adam's place in my world.'

'I will,' Dimitri replied. His eyes once again focused on the doll. 'At least, I'll try. Can I start by holding him?'

Zoe hesitated before passing him over to her husband in the same careful manner she would pass a real baby. She watched closely as he stroked Adam's knitted jumper and brought it to his nose in the same way she had done on countless occasions, trying to pick up a scent of the boy they still missed so much.

60
Woody & Tina

Tina threw open the taxi door and ran towards their Real World home just as Woody's car pulled into the driveway.

'Issy's controlling my avatar,' Tina began. 'I'm sure of it.'

'She can't be. The cybernanny would've sent us Push notifications if she'd left the basement,' Woody replied.

But his pained expression suggested he wasn't convinced by his own explanation.

'It's old and we haven't had the money to update the software in years. Issy's found a way around it.'

He held his index finger to the front door, and when it unlocked, they rushed up the staircase and along the landing until they reached their Metaverse access point. Tina was first to enter, but it was empty. Their VR headsets were also missing, along with their Smart glasses and earpods.

'She must be back in the basement,' he said.

'But how did she get up here in the first place?' Tina asked.

'We don't know that she has—'

It was Woody who spotted it first. A small pool of blood, the size of a drinks coaster, on the arm of Tina's chair. And in its centre, a centimetre-long cylindrical tracking device that had been inside Issy's forearm. She had dug it out of her own flesh.

Issy would not have gone to these lengths to get their attention without an endgame, thought Tina.

They descended two steps at a time before they reached the basement door. It was ajar. Woody yanked it fully open, yelling Issy's name. The first thing they spotted was the hard drive of the cybernanny, smashed into pieces and scattered about the floor. He searched her bedroom and bathroom, but like her living area, they were empty.

'Where the hell is she if she's not in the house?' fretted Tina.

She grabbed Issy's VR headset and logged in to the Metaverse using her own account, but it was locked. So was Woody's. Instead, she used her daughter's account and avatar.

'What passwords will get rid of the restrictions?' she barked.

Woody recounted them as each barrier lifted until Tina was granted unlimited guest access to *The Family Experiment*.

Now she found herself standing outside the door to their Metaverse home. Without hesitation, she pushed it open and clocked her own avatar and Belle standing in the centre of the main living area. But as she moved to approach them, she couldn't pass the threshold.

'I'm stuck,' she said anxiously. 'Issy's avatar won't budge.'

Woody, next to her, watched as events played out on his phone.

'You have to ask to be invited inside,' he said.

'What am I? A fucking vampire? Belle! It's your mum. Let me in.'

But only Issy, using her mother's avatar, turned around.

'Belle can't hear you, Christina,' Issy said. 'Neither can your viewers because I've muted our conversation for the next ten minutes.'

How does she know how to do that? thought Tina. She must have used the App before today. Tina hesitated. There had never been a more crucial moment to try to gain an understanding of her daughter's mindset than now.

'Sweetheart, what are you doing in here? This place isn't for you.'

'Sweetheart?' Issy laughed. 'You're more rattled than I thought you'd be. Anyway, I think I'm perfect for this place.'

'You don't belong here.'

'When I look at Belle, all I see is myself, which suggests my face fits perfectly. Besides, I want to get to know my sister. I'm sure we have so much in common. We're both prisoners of worlds you built, aren't we?'

Belle turned to the avatar she assumed to be her mother.

'Who are you talking to, Mum?' she asked.

Tina detested how the word 'Mum' was misdirected.

'Is it someone outside the Metaverse?' Belle continued.

'Yes, *sweetheart*,' said Issy, placing deliberate emphasis on the word. 'I'm just going to put you on pause, but I'll be back soon.'

Issy's eyes flicked to the corner of the screen, and Belle became stationary.

'Log out and we'll talk about this properly,' Tina said.

'I don't think there's much you can tell me I don't already know. You've replicated me with a near identical version and spent all your free time in here while I'm locked away in the basement. Eight minutes left, by the way.'

'It's not what it looks like,' Tina replied.

'I've watched many, many highlights shows recently, so I know that it's exactly what it looks like.'

'You're not in our house, so tell us where you are and we can explain everything in person.'

'Why? What other surprises have you got tucked up your sleeve? Are there more of me? Am I also a triplet? Is there an army of me out there?'

'No, of course not. Why would we want to recreate you?' Tina argued weakly.

Issy placed her finger on her chin and knitted her eyebrows theatrically.

'Hmm, let me think... So you can have the daughter you always wanted and not the one you deserved? Yep, that works. In truth, Christina, I think that I get it. I've spent much of the afternoon using your avatar to talk to Belle and she's a nice girl. She's kind, she has a good heart and she loves you. And you've never been able to accept I'm none of those things, which is why you've washed your hands of me and built a better version, more attuned with what you want.'

'I can accept who you are,' Tina replied. 'And I do. I just find it hard sometimes. You must recognize that you don't make it easy.'

'Hard to do what? To love? To be around? It's not a child's job to make it easy for their parents. Perhaps if you'd locked Belle up for the last six years, she'd be more like me.'

The Family Experiment

'We had no choice.'

'Well, that's about to change. Because now it's my turn to give you a choice, and you have a little under four minutes to make it.'

61

Cadman & Gabriel

Cadman stared at the screen projected against his office wall, trying to comprehend what he was reading.

'This can't be true,' he muttered.

However, the evidence was right there in front of him, contradicting everything he thought he knew about Gabriel. He slumped in his chair and rubbed his eyes with his palms as if it might erase the facts on second viewing. They remained there in black and white.

Gabriel was secretly planning a new life for himself and River, and one that was far away from Cadman.

Only weeks earlier, Cadman had experienced something akin to an epiphany during their family trek through Australia's Blue Mountains. He began feeling as if he was a part of something greater than just himself. A family. And he put it down to River's presence. His son's enthusiasm for a life, or whatever it was he had, was infectious. The three of them had since frequently teleported around the Metaverse, experiencing recreated significant events, from joining Nuremberg rally crowds, to marching for the American Civil Rights movement, and witnessing the horrors of the Tiananmen Square massacre.

Cadman had pared back his work commitments, cancelled unnecessary meetings, rejected new opportunities or delegated them to his team. He hadn't completely turned his back on his old self—he still hoped to make some form of a living from River—but now it was with his assistance and not at his expense. Being the boy's parent and his friend were inching ahead on his priority list.

Or at least they had been until fifteen minutes ago, when everything had shifted with the opening of one email. He assumed it to be junk by its address, a combination of random numbers and letters. He had been preparing to delete it when the subject title Your Substitute Family piqued his curiosity. Attached were passwords and passcodes allowing Cadman access to unfamiliar digital ledgers in Gabriel Macmillan's name. And in the first was an account which contained four Bitcoins with a current valuation of around £190,000.

A perplexed Cadman delved deeper into the bank account numbers listed and discovered that Gabriel had made regular monthly deposits into a second account up until shortly before his AZ addiction had taken grip. These contained a further £70,000. Where had it come from? Cadman had such a tight rein on their finances, he'd have spotted unauthorized withdrawals.

He found an abridged version of Gabriel's internet and Metaverse search history inside another folder. There had been multiple hunts for Italian investment properties, language courses, plus a signed contract for a long-term let on an apartment in Florence, Italy. It was scheduled to begin a week after *The Family Experiment* was set to end. There was even a flight booked in Gabriel's name.

Was this a Monthly Challenge? To the best of his knowledge, no other couple had faced one in this seventh month. And anyway, challenges only took place in the Metaverse and he was very much in the Real World.

Cadman's head was swimming, so he cracked open the window and gulped mouthfuls of cool air as he began to understand the levels of deception Gabriel had gone to. Cadman had been a fool to have trusted him. He had sold almost everything to aid Gabriel's recovery, and now here was proof that Gabriel had been sitting on a considerable pile of savings all that time.

The answer to how Gabriel had earned such large amounts lay in a third, damning folder. It contained hidden camera footage and photographs of Gabriel in various locations and sexual scenarios with other men. Cadman recognized some of the faces from the celebrity party circuit, while others were unfamiliar. He cross-referenced the dates attached to each photo's metadata against deposits made in Gabriel's accounts. All were matches.

Inside the fourth and final folder, he discovered emails sent by Gabriel enquiring about sponsorship and career opportunities for River and asking if they'd consider him as a brand ambassador in exchange for cryptocurrency. Gabriel had been vocal in his protests when Cadman had announced plans to do the same thing.

'Fucking hypocrite,' Cadman spat.

There was so much he had got wrong about Gabriel. He'd assumed Gabriel had had no choice but to fly abroad to prostitute himself in foreign circles to pay off his debts. But this information suggested the opposite. All this time, Cadman had thought he was the one in control, when really it had been Gabriel.

He grabbed his Smart glasses to watch unseen as Gabriel and River, dressed in waist-high waders and thick jumpers, fished for salmon in a fast-flowing river in the Scottish Hebrides. It was yet another trip Cadman had organized—only now could he see they were making a fool of him. But nobody made a fool of Cadman.

A pinging sound indicated that another new mail had arrived. It had been sent by the same address as the one containing the damning documents. He hurried to read it.

'I can help you make this right.'

62
Woody & Tina

'What choice?' Tina asked Issy, desperate for her tone not to betray her and reveal how fretful she was.

'Is there any part of you that loves me, Christina?' Issy asked.

Tina swallowed hard.

'You're my daughter, of course I love you.'

'Well, now is your chance to prove it. Let Belle go. I want you to exit this world for good, leave her behind, and I'll be the daughter you want me to be. It's your move.'

'Issy...' Tina stuttered. 'That's not fair.'

'No, it's absolutely fair.'

'I've shown you how much I care.'

'How? By keeping me a prisoner in the basement?'

'No...' Tina's voice faded.

'Then how? Give me your best play.'

Tina suddenly clocked what Issy was doing. *'It's your move. Your best play.'* She was treating their confrontation as she would a chess match. And Issy never lost a game.

'By letting you stay in the house after what you did,' Tina replied.

'How gracious of you, not turning your back on your only child for a crime she didn't commit.'

'Would you have preferred to have gone to a young offenders' institute?' Tina asked. 'Should we have sent you away? Would that've been a better option?'

'For you it might. But what would have been a better option for me was if my own mother had given me the benefit of the doubt. Was there even the smallest part of you that thought I might be innocent? That I might not have killed that boy?'

Tina hesitated. She could either give the truth or tell Issy what she wanted to hear.

'The clock is ticking,' Issy reminded her. 'Three minutes left.'

'I don't know if you meant to kill him,' Tina said eventually.

'But you still think I did. Finally, she admits it. Well, get this through your head, Christina, I did not murder Archie. No matter what you think, what you've made Woody think or what a jury believed, I didn't kill him.'

'Your story doesn't ring true though,' Tina persisted. 'None of it. Least of all why you didn't tell your dad and me what happened after you found Archie's body.'

'I was nine years old!' Issy replied. 'I wasn't equipped to know how to handle finding a dead kid. I was in shock.'

'Don't use your age as an excuse. You've always been way more intelligent than other children. And how do you explain the brick used to kill him? It came from the wall around our patio.'

'Oh yes, the brick. Tell me, why did the police come to the house in the first place to examine that patio?'

'I don't know,' Tina replied. 'Standard procedure? They had a search warrant.'

'I don't believe you. I think you tipped them off.'

Tina felt her face flush.

'Of course they were going to search the house. They were accusing you of murder.'

'You're lying.'

She balled her fists in a futile attempt to stave off any more telltale signs her avatar's body might give off that she was lying. But it was too late.

'Tina?' said Woody, still standing next to her and using his account to watch events unfold live on his phone. He was grateful the public was unable to see this. 'Tell me that you didn't do that.'

'You have about a minute and a half to tell him the truth, Christina,' Issy said.

Tina shook her head.

'I had no choice,' she directed to her husband. 'She killed that boy and there was a chance she was going to get away with it. I had to tell the police about the missing brick. She had to be punished.'

'Oh Jesus, Tina!' gasped Woody. 'For God's sake, why?'

'What she did had nothing to do with her wanting me to be punished,' said Issy. 'It was about me not being the perfect daughter and getting rid of me when the opportunity arose.'

She locked eyes on her mother.

'If you'd had your way, I'd have spent the rest of my life behind bars.'

'You're a psychopath, Issy,' Tina retorted. 'You don't care about us or other people just as long as you get your way. You're a danger to everyone around you. So yes, you deserve to be locked up.'

'Look at the countdown clock, Christina. You have thirty-two seconds left before we're unmuted. So make your decision. Me or Belle. Who are you going to keep?'

'Issy, there's another way,' Tina wept. 'Just log out and your dad and I will come and find you and we can sort this mess out together.'

'Twenty seconds, Christina. Make your choice.'

'Woody—' she began.

'This isn't about him,' Issy interrupted. 'This is about me and you.'

'No, Isabelle,' Tina said, her throat tightening.

She tried to move her avatar, another futile attempt to cross the threshold.

'Please don't make me do this,' said Tina.

'Eleven seconds.'

'Please!'

'Eight seconds.'

'I can't make that choice!'

'Five seconds.'

'No,' cried Tina. 'I love her.'

A barely audible beeping sound indicated that whatever was said next would be heard and viewed live by the world. Issy reanimated Belle. Then Tina and Issy, each still inside the other's avatar, glared at one another.

'What's going on, Mum?' Belle asked, breaking the silence. 'Has something happened?'

'I'm afraid it has,' said Issy. 'There have been some complications both here and at home that your dad and I need to deal with.'

'What are you doing?' asked Tina, fearing the worst.

'Can I help?' asked Belle.

'Actually, you can, because you're the complication.'

'Me? Have I done something wrong?'

'Whatever you're about to do, I'm begging you not to,' said Tina.

'I'm afraid you did do something wrong, sweetheart,' Issy continued. 'You're just not the daughter that your dad and I had hoped for. You've disappointed us.'

The sight of Belle's eyes beginning to well up was enough to make Tina's do the same. Black hearts filled the screen.

'But I'm your daughter,' said Belle. 'You love me.'

'But we don't, not really. I guess when it comes down to it, you can't be loved. You're too different from us. It's not your fault, it's just the way you were made. You're not what we ordered. And that's why we're letting you go.'

'Oh Belle, my beautiful girl,' whispered Tina. 'Issy, if you leave her right now you can have anything you want. You can leave the basement and leave the house, we'll help you to escape.'

Issy looked her dead in the eye, aware she was still being broadcast.

'I don't need your help because I'm already out here in the Real World.'

She drew Belle in close to her chest. 'I'm so sorry, sweetheart, but this is for the best, for everyone's sake.'

Tina and Woody, who was streaming through his phone, watched helplessly as Issy slipped both hands around her sister's neck and began to choke her.

'No!' screamed Tina, and she heard Woody next to her, yelling Issy's name.

Belle attempted to fight back and prise Issy's hands off her but her strength was no match for Tina's avatar. Belle's eyes reddened as panic set in, but not even the sight of the blood vessels bursting in the whites of her eyes was enough to prick Issy's conscience.

Tina couldn't tear herself away from what she was witnessing, crying and begging as the prolonged strangulation dragged on for two interminably long minutes before the fight gradually left Belle's limp body. Issy let her go and her sister dropped to the floor in a heap. Seconds later, Belle's body broke up into millions of tiny pixels.

Finally, Issy approached her sobbing mother by the front door to her Metaverse house, until their noses were almost touching.

'Checkmate,' said Issy, before clicking her fingers. She and her mother's avatar vanished.

Chats

TV / Reality TV Shows / **The Family Experiment**

CatsAndBoots, 3.56 p.m.
Holy Mother of God, what the hell just happened?

RealityKingofKings, 3.56 p.m.
Did you see what Tina just did? She strangled Belle!

JTR_HA, 3.56 p.m.
Tina has just killed her daughter with her own hands! Best telly EVAH!

WideAwake56, 3.57 p.m.
That makes no sense. Her avatar must have been hacked.

Liquidlove, 3.57 p.m.
Where was Woody? Why didn't he stop her?

    SecadasDay, 3.57 p.m.
    Tina just had a meltdown! Murdered poor Belle.

TellyBob, 3.57 p.m.
Too slow, Joe, we know.

    SecadasDay, 3.58 p.m.
    WT Actual F? Why did she just do that? #Justice4Belle

SayItLikeISeeIt, 3.58 p.m.
What a sick bitch. Someone needs to call the police. #Justice4Belle

MelleNoma, 3.58 p.m.
Already done. She won't get away with this. #Justice4Belle

MONTH EIGHT:
SIXTEEN YEARS OLD

Home | **UK**

VIGILS HELD AFTER DEATH OF BELLE

Fans of reality show *The Family Experiment* have held candlelight vigils around the world following the murder of a second MetaChild.

Viewers were left horrified when fourteen-year-old avatar Belle Finn was strangled by her mother Tina in front of an audience of millions.

As yet, no explanation has been offered for the seemingly unprovoked attack.

Viewers in Sydney, Calcutta, Beijing, New York, Birmingham and Reykjavik gathered together to remember the life of the popular teen, once again calling into question the right to life for avatars.

A spokesman for Shrewsbury Police, the area where the Finns are believed to reside, confirmed reports that no charges will be made against Tina.

'As we have already stated, as the law currently stands, an avatar cannot be killed unlawfully. Therefore, there is no call for us to investigate because no crime has been committed.'

63

Cadman & Gabriel

The pounding bass of early 2000s electronic dance music had been filling the night air for the last hour. Bright, colourful lights and holograms illuminated the sky, and every so often Gabriel and Cadman heard excited whoops and screams as rollercoasters and fairground rides hurled young people around in a multitude of dizzying directions.

They'd spent that time sitting on the patio outside a Metaverse coffee shop, waiting for the Sweet Sixteen party to finish inside the heart of MetaDisney. Gabriel had been looking online for any further updates on the murder of Belle Finn. Like the rest of the world, he had been completely shocked by her death.

Meanwhile, Cadman's irises were firing in all directions like stray bullets as he caught up on work. Gabriel had been pleasantly surprised by how often Cadman was putting his family above his career. This change in attitude might have appeared late in the process, but was welcome regardless. In fact, in the last couple of weeks Cadman had barely let either him or River out of his sight.

They had promised River they wouldn't embarrass him with their attendance in that section of the theme park, which Cadman had gifted to his son for his schoolfriends. And as desperate as Gabriel might have been to tune in and catch a glimpse of what was happening, he stuck to his word.

He took a moment to reflect on how River had been a relatively uncomplicated child to raise. He had grown up to become a caring and generous young man with whom Gabriel loved spending time. But as the show's finale approached, the dark clouds that were once on the horizon were edging ever closer. How could Gabriel begin to prepare himself for the possibility that River might only have a few more weeks left?

He had, however, tried. Using an anonymous burner avatar, he'd spent time in a Metaverse support group for the parents of terminally ill children, and those whose children had already passed. He hadn't wanted to insult them by admitting that his son was not strictly human. But the gist of his findings was that losing a child was something a parent can never be prepared for. Each journey into grief was individual, and the lives of those left behind were never, ever the same.

Without Cadman's knowledge, Gabriel had also virtually met one of *The Family Experiment*'s producers to get a steer on what he should expect if the worst came to the worst. Would River feel any pain as the plug was pulled? How long would they be given to say goodbye? Would he get to hug him and tell him how much he loved him? Might there be a twist in the narrative that allowed all finalists to keep their child regardless of the vote? To each question, the producer had offered an apologetic shrug followed by 'I'm sorry, I'm not allowed to say.'

'Are we still in first place?' Gabriel asked Cadman.

For five days straight they had remained on top of the unofficial leader board.

Cadman's eyes flicked from left to right, then he nodded.

'Who's in second place?' Gabriel continued.

'Zoe and Dimitri. But there's not much in it.'

'So there is still a very good chance we could win this?'

'There is.'

'What do you think Autumn Taylor will ask us tomorrow?'

Cadman shrugged. 'The usual collection of benign questions a scriptwriter has prepared for her.'

A Push notification suddenly appeared on Gabriel's watch.

'The Family Experiment Alert—Weds, 9.12 p.m. Incident at theme park during River N'Yu-Macmillan's party.'

'Cadman!' Gabriel said, voice raised, but he had already read it. Both men rose quickly and ran to the town square until they saw a group of young people in superhero-style fancy-dress costumes gathered around a figure lying face down on the ground. Gabriel's pulse raced when he spotted them wearing a pair of retro white Converse trainers. They were the same style and colour as the ones River had left the house in.

'River!' he shouted, now running towards the prostrate body.

Only upon reaching it did he see the face. It was that of a girl with shoulder-length blonde hair, spread across the pavement like a halo around her head. There was a pool of vomit oozing from her mouth and down her Captain America T-shirt. Her eyes were shut tight.

Gabriel and Cadman pushed their way to the front of the crowd to find River, kneeling beside the girl, his eyes glistening with tears and her hand in his.

'What happened?' asked Gabriel.

'She said she felt dizzy, then she collapsed,' River wept. 'Dad, help her.'

A panicked Gabriel looked to Cadman, who was already contacting emergency services. From nowhere, three paramedics and two uniformed guards appeared. The paramedics tended to the girl, one opening her mouth before pressing a pen-sized electronic device against her tongue.

'AZ,' he muttered to one of the guards, and then, without warning, the girl suddenly vanished.

'Where's Tanya?' asked River, his hand now clasping thin air.

'I think her avatar has been deleted,' Cadman replied.

A cold chill ran through Gabriel, like a premonition of a not-too-distant future. He reached for his distraught son's trembling arm as a guard approached.

'We'd like to search your pockets, please,' he said to River.

'Why?' asked Cadman.

'A witness claims River has been supplying a banned substance to his classmates.'

'Of course he wouldn't do that,' said Gabriel, shaking his head.

'Don't you need a warrant or something?' said Cadman.

'Each App has its own terms and conditions, and ours are featured in a link on the home screen.'

Before they could protest, a second guard appeared and held a device that scanned River's body from top to toe. When it reached the rear pocket of his trousers, it flashed red.

'Could you empty that, please?'

River reluctantly obliged. The only item about his person was a small strip of AZ patches.

64
Hudson

'When we first met eight months ago, you were sitting in exactly the same spot, only you had a two-week-old baby pressed against your chest,' Autumn Taylor began. 'Now there's an elegant and beautiful sixteen-year-old young woman in her place.'

Hudson assumed his daughter was quietly cringing at being judged solely upon her appearance.

'And I couldn't have asked for better,' he replied. 'I hope viewers see in her what I see, a kind and compassionate hu—' Hudson caught himself before he said 'human being'. But that was how he thought of her, every bit as flesh and blood as him. 'Person,' he corrected.

Autumn's avatar crossed her legs and she glanced at a tablet on her lap. Hudson was sitting opposite her on the balcony, his head and shoulders framed perfectly by the New York City skyline. He would miss living in this alternate reality when it came to an end six weeks from now.

'You were very much the underdog when the competition began,' Autumn continued. 'But now it's neck and neck between you, Zoe and Dimitri, Cadman and Gabriel. Media commentators have their views on how you've turned this around, but I'm curious to hear your take on it.'

'All I've done is be me,' he said, shrugging. 'Viewers aren't stupid, they'll see straight through you if you try to be anything other than your authentic self. And I think that's what's got me and the other contestants this far.'

'I assume you're familiar with who you're up against?'

'Not really, no,' Hudson lied. 'I caught a highlights episode once, and they all seem like genuine people.'

Autumn offered a wry, disingenuous smile.

'You're in the final of the most watched show in the world and you don't know who the competition is?'

'Oh, I won't pretend I'm not curious, that's only natural. However, if I watch how they're parenting, I might find myself second-guessing my own approach. And I must be doing something right because I have this amazing, intelligent young woman sitting next to me.'

Autumn looked to Alice.

'This question is for you,' she said sweetly. 'What has your dad told you about the last few weeks of this process?'

'I know that in six weeks' time, Dad will find out if he's won,' she replied.

'And what will that mean for you?'

'Do we really need to have this conversation?' Hudson interrupted.

'It's okay, Dad,' Alice replied, and patted his arm. 'Dad is honest with me about everything. And I know there's a clock ticking above our heads and that we might not always be together.'

'And how does it feel to know you could be erased? That the next time we speak, your online life might be coming to an end?'

'Autumn,' said Hudson, his jaw flickering. 'I don't think this is appropriate.'

Alice cleared her throat.

'Given the choice of knowing that death is a thing, or being completely unaware of it, I'd probably pick not knowing,' Alice continued. 'But that's not real life, is it? And from what Dad's told me, the purpose of this process is for him to learn how to be a parent and for me to experience everything a human would. So I'm aware of the reality of our situation. Do I want to live after the finale? Of course I do. But if I can't, I know I've had the best life I could've possibly had.'

'Well, I'm sure I speak for many of your fans when I wish you all the very best in these remaining weeks,' Autumn added. 'I'll see you both again on results night.'

She offered another insincere smile and then vanished.

Hudson turned to his daughter. If the conversation about what might happen had bothered her, she was not giving anything away.

'Can we go to a gig tonight?' she asked.

Her love of music and a desire to explore more than current streaming playlists had appeared in the last Development Leap. Hudson frequently found himself shoulder to shoulder amongst a sweaty, cheering audience or on an actual stage metres away from an act at the peak of their popularity.

'Sure,' he replied. 'What are you in the mood for, heritage act or modern?'

'Umm...heritage. Madonna in her pointy bra era.'

'Okay. Save a space for me and I'll join you soon.'

As his daughter left the balcony, Hudson turned to gaze across the horizon and an approximation of the actual city he had been held inside for ten years before being dispatched back to the UK. For so long, he and the others there had believed they were somewhere in the murky depths of Europe. It had never crossed their minds they were in America.

On the day of his planned return to England, it was only when he'd climbed inside a waiting vehicle in Ararat that he realized there was a second passenger waiting for him inside. He had been facing out of the car window and into the quadrant.

'Hello,' said Hudson.

There was a pause before the man turned around. To Hudson's shock it was Cain, Eva's brother, the boy who had bullied him and fractured his jaw years earlier. Hudson had later set him up as a whistle-blower via his avatar and Cain had been dragged out of Ararat through the door on the left.

This version of him was unreadable, his eyes expressionless and forehead lined like a man older than his years. Hudson couldn't be sure if Cain even recognized him as he gave nothing away. Instead, his gaze returned to the window.

Their journey continued in silence to the Staten Island ferry, along the Hudson river and the five-kilometre route towards Lower Manhattan. Many times Hudson opened his mouth to engage him in conversation, then closed it when he couldn't find the words. And as the six-hour flight lifted off from the private airfield, it was Hudson's turn to stare from a window. He searched the landscape below him for Ararat but struggled to find it. It was as if the building had only ever been a figment of his imagination.

Much of the flight was dominated by reliving the horrors of what he'd been shown by the shaven-headed woman through the door on the left. And he'd been so indoctrinated by life there that despite the evidence presented to him, he still searched for a way to justify it. He reminded himself of Ararat's mantra: every person there was part of a much larger process that was more important than themselves. But while that positive rationale had worked in the past, doubt set in on the flight.

His loyalty was crumbling.

The setting for his British projects had been the decommissioned Sizewell nuclear power station on the Suffolk coast. Now a data centre, it housed the vast number of servers required for the work being done. And being a former nuclear reactor, its high level of security made it impenetrable.

There, Hudson was afforded more freedom than he'd ever known before. He lived in his own off-site apartment, coming and going as he pleased. But he rarely ventured further than the nearby market towns of Dunwich and Thorpeness.

Seemingly innocuous things triggered him. The faces of strangers sometimes disintegrated and reassembled as those he'd witnessed from the viewing room in his final moments in Ararat. The pebbled beaches and North Sea brought back memories of that first fateful journey to France.

It had been a particularly bleak day when a voice took Hudson by surprise. He'd been sitting on a pebbled beach, his knees drawn into his chest.

'You took my advice then,' the voice began.

He turned to find Cain standing there, arms folded, looking out into the horizon. Hudson could see his ribcage through his T-shirt.

'What advice?' Hudson asked as he clambered to his feet.

'When I told you to leave Ararat the moment the opportunity arrives or you'll end up with all the others. You listened.'

Hudson recalled the brief typed conversation he'd had with an anonymous person in the Client Retention Department after Charles Simmonds's disappearance.

'That was you?' he asked.

'Yes,' Cain said. 'And it was me who brought you to that shaven-headed bitch's attention and got you back here. And now, I need you to listen to me again.'

65
Cadman & Gabriel

For two days, Gabriel, Cadman and River barely left their Metaverse house. Clad in their VR headsets and haptic suits, they'd even slept there, exiting only to eat, use the bathroom or shower. Their equipment was not designed to be worn for such extended periods of time, so out of necessity, both parents regularly stuck anti-sickness patches to their arms and shoulders. However, no medication was strong enough to thwart Gabriel's ever-increasing anxiety.

River had admitted to purchasing the AZ but was adamant he had not encouraged Tanya to try it. It had been her own decision.

Software engineers from *The Family Experiment* had launched an immediate investigation, as the demise of one avatar at the hands of another, no matter how indirectly, was a serious breach of protocol. And it might have ongoing ramifications for other machine-learning or MetaChildren. Meanwhile, producers reduced the perimeters of where River could travel, effectively putting them all under house arrest.

'It's for everyone's safety,' they had been advised.

In his return trips to their Real World home, Cadman had remained in close contact with his team. It came as no surprise that the family was now trailing in third place in the court of public opinion. Their sponsorship had also taken a hit, but he'd been prepared for that.

Tanya's death and River's involvement had been the most discussed news topic of the last two days, even more so than China's occupation of New Zealand's South Island. But Cadman took solace in the fact that at least viewers were discussing him. And he'd once again risen above Gabriel in the popularity rankings, with the audience sympathizing with him for his 'druggie partner and their killer kid'.

'Do you think the public has done this to us?' Gabriel asked suddenly.

He had been staring at River, who was on the opposite side of the room, looking aimlessly out from the window.

'Do you think they've voted to give us the penultimate Monthly Challenge? Are we being tested to see how we respond?'

'I honestly don't know,' Cadman replied.

'You have a friend in the production company though, don't you? The one who first approached us to audition. Can you ask him?'

Cadman glanced at the mute button to remind him they were being broadcast live.

'Fuck that,' Gabriel replied. 'We're in last place. Who cares if the viewers know how we got here.'

'I think my contact has moved on,' Cadman replied.

Gabriel lowered his head and spoke quietly.

'You still don't think River did what they're accusing him of, do you?'

'No, I absolutely don't.'

Suddenly, their Metaverse door chimed, and all three heads turned to face it. Cadman was the first to his feet to answer. Waiting for him outside, he recognized the avatar of Marlon Chesterfield, a producer who had interviewed them late in *The Family Experiment*'s audition process. He introduced his colleague as Danielle Ulitzsch, the head of legal affairs for Awakening Entertainment. Both wore suits as dark as their expressions. They were also accompanied by Autumn Taylor.

'Come in,' Cadman offered, and they followed him to the dining area and a large oval wooden table with six chairs. On one side, River, Cadman and Gabriel took seats, each holding the hand of the one next to him. Chesterfield, Ulitzsch and Autumn took their places opposite.

'Thank you for seeing us,' began Chesterfield.

'You're saying that like we had a choice,' said Cadman.

Gabriel clasped his hand a little tighter as if suggesting he tone down his reaction.

'Well, we've followed the coding trail which led River to make his decision to purchase AZ and revisited the footage of the evening of Tanya's death. And we are happy that he didn't coerce her into using it.'

Gabriel exhaled as he clutched his son's hand.

'Why did you take it in the first place, River?' asked Autumn.

'I don't know.'

'There must have been a reason?'

River looked to Gabriel and then down at the table top.

'Because you used to do it and I wanted to understand why you liked it.'

More black hearts than Cadman and Gabriel had ever witnessed filled their headsets.

Gabriel closed his eyes. He was to blame for this.

'But you know what happened to me. You know it almost killed me.'

'And did you talk Tanya into using it?' asked Autumn.

'We already know he didn't,' interrupted an irritated Cadman.

'No, I promise you,' River added. 'She grabbed it and stuck a patch on her wrist.'

'But if you hadn't bought them, Tanya might not have been tempted to try one and in all probability would still be alive today.'

'Will you give the kid a break?' snapped Gabriel.

'This is bullshit,' countered Cadman. 'Am I the only person in the room who remembers the people we're talking about here are avatars? They don't have skin that can absorb a drug, they don't have hearts that AZ can stop. So how can they overdose?'

'The machine-learning which advances each individual avatar's understanding and behaviour is susceptible to suggestion,' said Chesterfield.

'What does that even mean?' asked Gabriel.

'That an avatar might not be able to physically take a drug, but when its AI learns it has come into physical contact with it, it behaves in the way it believes it is supposed to. In Tanya's case, her AI believed AZ would overload her system so it shut itself down.'

'Temporarily, though. She can be restarted, surely,' said Gabriel.

'No. There are no restarts in *The Family Experiment*.'

'So the avatar killed itself, then,' Cadman concluded. 'Which is on you as you programmed it to behave like that. It's not River's fault.'

'It responded in the way it had learned to. But it was a result of River's actions that led it to draw that conclusion.'

'So what now?' said Gabriel. 'He's admitted what he's done and he knows it was wrong. What's his punishment?'

Ulitzsch leaned forward and rested her hands on the table.

'As you are aware, there is not one overarching set of laws that covers the entire Metaverse,' she began. 'The creators of each App and in-world App are entitled to write their own constitutions as they see fit, and that is what Awakening Entertainment has done with *The Family Experiment*. We have zero tolerance for an avatar that is deemed a danger to the welfare of its peers. And that is what we believe River to be.'

Gabriel turned to Chesterfield.

'How could you even let this happen? Why would you give him the option of temptation? Why does this even exist in his world?'

'It reflects reality. It is a parent's job to teach them right from wrong—you shape them with your knowledge. Along with free will, River's decision was based on what he had learned from his parents. Purchasing AZ was one of many options he could have taken. Think of it like a market square with one entrance and a hundred different paths to reach the exit. With what he had learned, he could have chosen any one of those paths, but he picked one where he came into contact with AZ.'

Both parents again looked to their son, an ominous feeling slowly overtaking Gabriel. River shook his head as if only now beginning to process the enormity of his actions.

'I'm afraid that in terms of the competition, this is the end of the road for your family,' said Ulitzsch. 'River is to be irrevocably erased.'

'No, you can't do that,' Gabriel cried. 'Cadman, tell them they can't do that.'

'There's a way,' Cadman said quickly. 'There is always a way. We can pay, we have money.'

Ulitzsch shook her head.

'It's not about money.'

'It's always about money,' Cadman snapped.

'Maybe in your world,' she replied. 'But not in ours.'

'Then we'll take you to court in the Real World. We'll get an injunction out.'

'You won't have the time,' said Chesterfield. 'As I said, we have a duty of care to the other contestants and avatars.'

'Can't he even defend himself?' said Cadman. 'If this world is supposed to reflect the real one, you can't just give him a death sentence. He deserves a trial.'

Without warning, both his and Gabriel's hands fell to the table top with a thump as with an ear-splitting howl and a look of terror in his eyes, River began to disintegrate before them, thousands of pixels at a time, until soon afterwards, he had completely disappeared.

Moments later, Gabriel's and Cadman's headset screens went blank, and they were back in the Real World.

www.theij.org.uk/health/2345676

The International Journal

Home / TV & Entertainment / VOTES

OVERNIGHT BACKLASH AS PRODUCERS 'EXECUTE' METACHILD

A furious public backlash against producers of *The Family Experiment* has broken out following their decision to kill fan favourite River N'Yu-Macmillan just weeks before the finale.

Viewers have taken to social media to protest what they branded the 'public execution' of an 'innocent' avatar based on weak evidence.

Fans have protested at the unfair and unjust decision, branding it a kangaroo court and demanding he be switched on again.

A spokesperson for *The Family Experiment* said: 'Once an avatar is turned off, its coding is erased and irretrievable.'

Do you think River's termination was fair? Click here to vote.

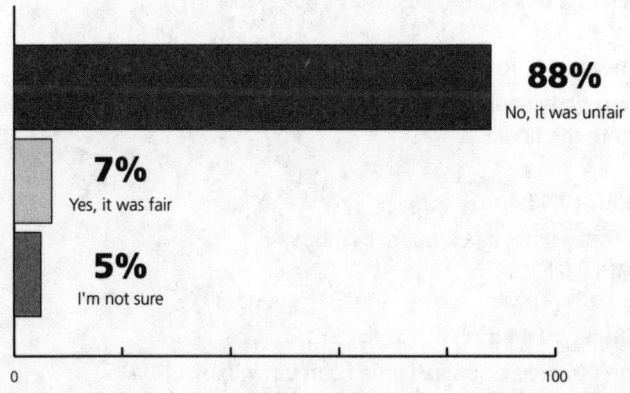

Chats

TV / Reality TV Shows / **The Family Experiment**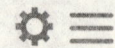

VoteRiver, 10.34 a.m.
They killed him! They have actually KILLED my River. That's wrong on so many different levels. #LetRiverRun

RiverBabe100, 10.35 a.m.
That's it. I'm done. I can't even process. #LetRiverRun

VoteRiver, 10.36 a.m.
I've already complained to OFCOM. There's a link here. #LetRiverRun

SayItLikeISeeIt, 10.37 a.m.
Thanx hun. I've got a petition ready to upload. They cancelled River, now we're going to cancel them. #EndTheExperiment

TellyBob, 10.38 a.m.
Shhh kids, adults talking.

VoteRiver, 10.39 a.m.
Don't try and silence us, you dick. #BeKind

TellyBob, 10.40 a.m.
So now it's a two-horse race, who's going to win?

WideAwake56, 10.42 a.m.
They're both winners in my eyes because they've made it to the final.

TellyBob, 10.43 a.m.
yawn That's what it is though, dumbass.
A COMPETITION.

FaffyDuck, 10.44 a.m.
Still don't trust Hudson as far as I can throw him. #Paedo. Zoe and Dimitri to win.

TellyBob, 10.45 a.m.
The kid killers? It's like asking if you'd prefer dysentery or diarrhoea.

FaffyDuck, 10.47 a.m.
Well, they're both full of shit IMO.

TellyBob, 10.50 a.m.
Ain't that the truth.

66
Dimitri & Zoe

'Are you sure this place actually exists in the Real World and not just the imagination of a software engineer?' asked Dimitri.

'It's 100 per cent real,' Zoe replied. 'Amazing, isn't it?'

The App that took them to the very heights of China's Rainbow Mountains in Zhangye Danxia Landform Geological Park had been worth the cost and the uphill trek. Special mouth apparatus they'd ordered had constricted their breathing and offered them an approximation of thinning oxygen. And electrical charges in their haptic suits probed deep into their thighs and calf muscles to mimic the feel of the steepness of the climb.

'Careful,' Zoe continued when, a few metres ahead, Lenny lost his footing and some of the sedimentary rocks crumbled.

Moments later, she, Dimitri and Lenny were standing atop one of the ranges, staring over a ridge at 200 miles of reds, purples, pinks and yellows.

'It's like a rainbow has melted into the mountains,' said Lenny.

Now that Zoe and Dimitri had ruled out using the prize money to fund the creation of a biological family, they instead spent the final few weeks of *The Family Experiment* on sharing experiences with Lenny. The convenience of hyperlinking across different continents without the need for long vehicular journeys enabled them to visit the most enticing focal points of two or three countries in just a day. Dimitri had crossed off his bucket list the rich colours of Belize's tropical forests, the Inca trail to Machu Picchu, the remains of the Antarctic's doomsday glacier and the Hindu temples of India's Tamil Nadu. Anything—and anywhere—was possible in the Metaverse.

Later that night and back in the Real World, Zoe tuned in to the episodes of *The Family Experiment* they had missed during a self-imposed media break. First had been the death last month of Belle at Tina's hands, and now they were watching River disintegrate before his horrified parents' eyes. Zoe turned away and wished she had remained in ignorance.

'We're in the final two,' Dimitri said solemnly. 'Doesn't feel much like a triumph though, does it?'

'No,' she replied. 'It doesn't.'

The two remained in a contemplative silence, neither celebrating as they processed the enormity of the pressure now upon them.

Dimitri turned to Zoe, who was biting her bottom lip as if trying to trap something she wasn't sure if she should say.

'What's on your mind?' he asked.

Zoe hesitated, left the room, and returned with a padded envelope.

'What's this?' Dimitri asked when he recognized the handwriting on the front.

His eyes widened as he opened it and registered its contents.

'Fuck,' he said. 'When?'

'Month two, so before you received the postcard.'

'You should've told me.'

'I didn't, probably for the same reason you didn't tell me about the card. Whoever has us in their sights knows a lot about us.'

'Just how much? Do you think they—'

'I don't know.'

'These documents could have put us out of the competition months ago. Why haven't they gone public with it then?'

Zoe pursed her lips.

'That's what worries me. They've gone to a lot of trouble to tell us what they know. And they don't have long to make a move.'

Neither needed to tell the other they had an awful feeling their tormentors hadn't finished with them yet.

67

Cadman & Gabriel

The rain lashed against Gabriel's face and body, soaking through his long-sleeved T-shirt and jeans. He couldn't be sure why he was venturing out into the eye of such a ferocious storm. All he knew was that after days of numbness, he needed to feel something again. Anything, to remind him he was still alive.

The howling wind hit his exposed cheeks like a slap and stung his bare arms. It was no less than he deserved. He should have known that a child of a parent with a dependency on drugs or alcohol was twice as prone to experiment themselves. He should have been more emphatic in his description of its side effects when River had asked. He should have scared his son into never giving in to temptation. The echo of the boy's cries as he fell apart before their eyes, pixel by pixel, haunted him. Gabriel was the one to blame for River's death, nobody else.

The show had a duty of care to all participants but Gabriel had refused the offer of help from its psychiatric team. He had barely spoken to Cadman either. Instead, the moment their accounts were terminated and they were returned to their Real World home, Gabriel locked himself away in one of the spare bedrooms, where he remained for days.

Now, he trudged across the wet, muddy garden, past the two-storey house at the end of their property and towards a low fence that separated them from the reservoir and country park. He wiped the rain from his eyes and tucked his head down to shield himself from the adverse conditions. Gusts of wind caught the water's ripples, transforming them into waves that collided with the stony shore so forcefully that they scattered pebbles in all directions.

Gabriel unclipped the buckle from the satchel hanging from his shoulder and removed his VR headset. Then he picked up the largest rock he could find and began smashing it to pieces until only shards of broken fibreglass and wiring remained. One by one he scooped it all back into his satchel along with fistfuls of stones. Then he took hold of the strap and swung it like a hammer thrower, hurling it into the water. It sank quickly beneath the surface. He would never spend another second of his time in the Metaverse again.

'Hurts, doesn't it?' came a male voice from behind. Gabriel turned quickly.

A figure he hadn't been aware of was standing about ten metres away from him. The collars of a waterproof jacket were pulled up and his hood pulled down, masking much of his appearance.

'What?' shouted Gabriel, fighting to be heard over the noise of the wind.

The man raised his voice.

'I said it hurts, doesn't it? Having something you love taken away from you through no fault of your own.'

'Who are you?' Gabriel asked.

The stranger ignored him and pointed at Gabriel's hands.

'Your fingers.'

Gabriel glanced at them and realized it wasn't only the rain making them wet; they were bleeding from the sharp plastic shards he had picked up.

'Are you a journalist?' Gabriel asked. 'Because I have nothing to say.'

'Nope,' the man replied casually. 'Just a friend.'

'I don't know you.'

'But I know you. I've been watching you and Cadman for a while now.'

'So have millions of others. What of it?'

'Cadman's an interesting character, isn't he?'

Gabriel said nothing.

'What was the plan if you won the competition? Because you were the favourites for a while.'

'Leave me alone,' Gabriel snapped, then turned away from the man and began walking back to the house.

'Ask Cadman who he paid to frame your son,' the man added. 'And to spike you with AZ before the circus trip.'

Gabriel stopped in his tracks then turned around.

'What did you say?' he shouted.

But the stranger was already hurrying in the opposite direction.

'Hey!' Gabriel yelled as the man vanished over the top of a hill.

Gabriel ran after him, but there was little grip on his trainers and it took several attempts before he stopped sliding on wet stones and mud and reached the top.

By the time he had clambered over the ledge, the only vehicle in the area was pulling away and along the road.

MONTH NINE:
EIGHTEEN YEARS OLD

www.theij.org.uk/topstories/popular/2345676

Home / Top Stories / POPULAR

RECORD VIEWING FIGURES EXPECTED FOR THE FAMILY EXPERIMENT FINALE

More than 270 million viewers worldwide are expected to watch and livestream tonight as the winner of reality show *The Family Experiment* is announced.

After nine months and nine Development Leaps, single parent Hudson Wright and couple Dimitri and Zoe Taylor-Georgiou will go head-to-head to discover which of their children will survive in the Metaverse, and which will be erased.

The bookmakers' current favourites are the Taylor-Georgious with odds 1/2 while Hudson currently stands at 5/1.

'Hudson's objective from day one was to prove to viewers that single parents should be every bit as valued as couples,' says supporter and former Freedom For All MP Howie Cosby. 'And he has done just that. He deserves to win.'

Support for the Taylor-Georgious has come from Families First, an organization that believes in outlawing single-parent households.

'Zoe and Dimitri have risen above the criticism,' said Helena Grey. 'And if Hudson wins, it will be a kick in the teeth to every decent couple out there.'

68
Hudson

Hudson bent each fingertip towards its base, then pushed hard until it made a sharp cracking sound. It was a habit he'd retained since childhood, the sensation of bone rubbing against bone keeping him focused. He had been doing it a lot lately, so much so that the satisfaction was becoming increasingly hard to find.

The final four weeks of the competition had been almost unbearable, as he was constantly aware of his remaining time with Alice. He wondered if this was how the parents of terminally ill children in the Real World must feel, desperately trying to make every moment with them last, and cursing the cruel passing of each hour.

He tried to make the most of Alice's final Development Leap to the age of eighteen. No morning or afternoon had passed when they hadn't been exploring somewhere new in her virtual world. They played the parts of supporting cast members in classic action films like the first Star Wars trilogy and the most recent Avengers remake. They'd been on stage and inches away from the Gallagher brothers in Oasis's comeback shows at the City of Manchester Stadium and they'd walked around the running track at the opening-night ceremony of London's 2012 Olympics. They had thrown white lilies onto the moving hearse transporting Diana, Princess of Wales, to her final resting place and wept as they'd stroked the last remaining black rhino on earth in its dying moments.

But this final day, Hudson had wanted to go full circle and return to where it all began. So father and daughter had walked the streets of New York, one district at a time like they had when she was a baby. Sometimes he stole a glance at her, trying to reconcile the tiny version he had held in his hands with the eighteen-year-old woman accompanying him now. He missed every version of her.

He had always ensured Alice was aware that her creation and his role in *The Family Experiment* were just small parts in something far greater than either of them. But he hadn't needed to tell her everything. There were others he had relied on for that.

Hudson's eyes flicked to a red flashing timer in the right-hand corner of his headset counting down their last twenty-four hours in the competition. And now the final minutes were upon them.

He rubbed at the scar on the back of his hand, then took a lingering glance around his Metaverse apartment. For his own peace of mind, he once again checked the data he'd uploaded into his account and ensured it was where it needed to be and ready to share, before joining Alice on the sofa.

'Are you okay, Dad?' she asked, and rested her head on his shoulder.

Dad, he said to himself, as he had many times before. He'd enjoyed being called that.

'I'm fine,' he replied. 'I need you to know that whatever happens next, you have been the single greatest experience of my life.'

'As have you,' said Alice.

Hudson looked away so that she would not see the tears forming in his eyes. Then, without warning, everything turned black.

69
Dimitri & Zoe

Dimitri's, Zoe's and Lenny's eyes wandered around the studio App they'd suddenly found themselves inside. Seconds ago, they had been sitting together in their garden watching the sun begin to set behind Japan's Mount Niseko, the country's only remaining snow-capped mountain. And now they were standing in a huge white space next to *The Family Experiment* host, Autumn Taylor. The sky above them was awash with stars.

Before they could get their bearings, Hudson and Alice appeared on the other side of Autumn, equally anxious-looking. It was the first time they had all been in the same room together, avatar to avatar. All five contestants offered each other polite but cautious smiles.

'Welcome, all of you, to the final of *The Family Experiment*,' Autumn began with typical vigour.

She raised her arms and the white wall behind her was replaced by thousands of individual screens, each featuring a different viewer's avatar cheering and applauding. Autumn turned to the wall.

'And congratulations to our golden ticket winners too—thank you for being here to witness history.'

The noise was deafening.

'So how are we all feeling tonight?' Autumn continued, turning first to Zoe and Dimitri.

Zoe swallowed hard. She and Dimitri had not received any more post from whoever knew their secrets, but she was conscious that at any moment their truths might unspool. The sensible decision would have been to withdraw from the competition, but they were too invested in Lenny to have done that. They would not let another son down.

'Excited and nervous sums it up for me, I think,' Zoe said, and turned to her husband.

'Same,' Dimitri replied. 'It's been an incredible experience. One I wouldn't change for the world.'

'And you, Hudson?' Autumn asked.

'Likewise. The best part has been getting to know my daughter. We might be a small family, but we're complete.'

'Well, only ten minutes remain for viewers to cast their votes,' she continued. 'And I can tell you that based on the preliminary results we've received so far, there is very little in it between both families. It could still go either way. So guys, I'd like to give you the opportunity to tell the audience why you think they should choose you to win *The Family Experiment.* Dimitri and Zoe, would you like to go first?'

Dimitri glanced at his wife, then to Lenny, and cleared his throat.

'Losing our son Adam taught us in the hardest way imaginable just how precious life is. We were blessed to be given a second chance with Lenny, and I hope that viewers have seen how much we've appreciated every moment of it.'

'I didn't think I'd survive the grief after Adam,' Zoe added. 'For a long time, I didn't even care if I lived or died. It was my role as his mum to protect him and I failed, both of us did. Losing a child under any circumstances creates a burden of guilt that remains with a parent for ever.'

Her avatar dabbed at her eyes with the cuff of her sleeve.

'And then Lenny came into our lives and he changed everything,' she continued. 'He hasn't replaced Adam. He's reminded us of how much we enjoy being parents. And he has helped us to focus on the present and the future and not the past. We owe him so much. So we would like to win this competition as much for him as for us. It would break our hearts to watch another child die.'

Dimitri pulled her head to his shoulder and kissed her crown. Zoe noticed the flurry of red hearts filling her headset. The speech they had worked so hard rehearsing was resonating.

'Thank you,' said Autumn. 'And Hudson, what would you like to say?'

He waited for the wall of viewers' applause for Zoe and Dimitri to die before he spoke.

'I am grateful not to have suffered the loss of a child and the pain that must bring,' he began. 'I cannot imagine how awful it must be to have watched the young life you have treasured die before your eyes.'

He paused.

'But then neither can you.'

All heads, including Alice's, turned to Hudson.

'I'm sorry?' said Zoe.

'Neither of you can imagine what it must be like watching your child die because it hasn't happened to you.'

Zoe and Dimitri turned to one another and then to Autumn, who was equally perplexed.

'Well, no, we didn't witness Adam's last moments, if that's what you mean,' said Dimitri. 'But we were there at that loch when he died.'

'You were there at that loch on the day when you claimed Adam went missing, yes, that's true. But most of what you've told the world happened is a carefully constructed fabrication that was impossible to disprove. Until now.'

Zoe grabbed Dimitri's hand and squeezed it tightly.

'Hudson?' said Autumn.

His eyes narrowed as he glared at Zoe, Dimitri and then Autumn.

'Their son Adam didn't die that day. His body was never discovered at Loch Ba because he was never there in the first place. It was all a lie.'

70
Hudson

Hudson's heart threatened to beat its way out of his chest. Thousands of hours of careful, calculated planning had finally come to a head. The cheers and applause that only moments earlier had warmed Zoe's and Dimitri's hearts were replaced by gasps and calls for him to explain further.

Beads of sweat appeared across his back and under his arms as he felt the weight of every pair of virtual eyes in that studio upon him, waiting to hear what he was going to say next. Black hearts floated across the screen, directed at him, he assumed. Viewers were doubting him, and why shouldn't they? He had yet to prove his accusation. But he wasn't going to make this easy for anyone. He wanted to savour the awkwardness and make everyone in that room work for an explanation.

Zoe was the first to regain her composure, but she couldn't disguise her fear. Hudson had seen the same fear in similar eyes before.

'Why would you say such a thing?' she began. 'Are you that desperate to win?'

'I know what desperate people are capable of,' he replied pointedly.

'If you think the viewers will side with you because of some baseless accusation, you're wrong,' Dimitri interjected. 'They'll see straight through you.'

'It's not baseless though, is it?' Hudson continued. 'I know the truth behind the events the day Adam "died", and it's very different to the lies you have spent the last twelve years peddling.'

Autumn was out of her depth, Hudson could tell. Dimitri and Zoe glared at her, their eyes desperate for her to step in and cut this short.

'Are you going to allow him to get away with this?' Dimitri asked. 'You can't let him try to turn the audience against us.'

'Um, Hudson?' Autumn continued.

'Let's throw this open to Zoe and Dimitri first,' suggested Hudson. 'Remind us what happened the day you claim Adam died?'

Dimitri shook his head.

'We've been through this many times and it's on public record,' snapped Zoe. 'We don't have to answer to you.'

'Then allow me to do it for you. You claimed that while on a day trip to Loch Ba, a sweeping fog came in earlier than forecast and you found yourselves separated from your son, is that correct?'

Dimitri went to answer first but Zoe beat him to it.

'No, don't give him the satisfaction.'

Hudson continued. 'It's assumed he was either swallowed by quicksand or drowned in the freezing temperatures of the loch, but unusually, his body was never recovered. There have been fifteen deaths there in the last twenty-five years, and Adam's body was the only one not to have been found.'

Zoe brought her hand to her chest.

'And we have to live with being unable to bring him home or hold a funeral for him. I almost lost Dimitri too when he tried to rescue him in freezing temperatures. He was in the early stages of hypothermia when rescuers found him.'

'The hypothermia part is true,' said Hudson, 'but what he didn't tell the search team was how he put himself at unnecessary risk for appearances' sake. Because Adam was never there.'

'Stop saying that!' fumed Zoe.

'Then be honest with me or I'll have no choice but to do it for you,' said Hudson calmly.

'What do you want from us?' shouted Dimitri.

'The truth. The police found no evidence or video footage to suggest Adam was ever present in Loch Ba—because he never went with you. Dimitri was so desperate to convince the world Adam had been there that he even risked his own life throwing in the boy's jacket and one of his trainers that later washed up ashore.'

'No...no...' said Zoe, her voice beginning to catch. 'The police believed us...why would you do this to us...'

'Because I know with 100 per cent certainty that Adam couldn't possibly have died that day. Twenty-four hours earlier, the human traffickers you'd sold him to were pushing his drugged, dazed, semi-conscious body into a dinghy and smuggling him across the Channel to France.'

Chats

TV / Reality TV Shows / **The Family Experiment**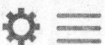

OOPS...
It's not you, it's us

We are experiencing increased numbers on our site which is impacting its performance.

Please try again later.

71

Dimitri & Zoe: Twelve years earlier

'Bloody hell, Zoe, it was warmer in the car than it is in here.'

Dimitri closed the front door behind him and pushed a snake-shaped draught excluder against the base. He removed his boots but kept his coat and scarf on as he made his way through the hallway to the kitchen, the only illuminated room. Zoe didn't glance up from where she was seated at the table, her spine arched, hunched over a tablet. Her forehead rested on her palms.

'Did you hear me?' said Dimitri. 'Can we turn the heating on?'

She looked up, her anxious expression only now becoming apparent.

'We can't afford to,' Zoe replied.

'Not even a fifteen-minute blast?'

'I'm saving it for when Adam gets back from school.'

'Is that what we're rationing ourselves to now? Are things getting that bad?'

'They're not getting that bad,' Zoe sighed, 'they have been this bad for a long time. You just never want to talk about it.'

'That's not fair,' Dimitri protested. But she was right. So convinced had he been that their dire financial situation would eventually sort itself out, he'd dismissed it each time Zoe brought the subject up.

'We're about to lose the house,' Zoe said suddenly.

'What?'

They could no longer afford the rising interest rates on their mortgage. Their savings were long gone, they'd cashed in their pensions, cancelled their health insurance policies, and they owed money on loans and credit cards.

'We've reached breaking point,' she said. 'In fact, we are way beyond it.'

Dimitri blinked a handful of times as if processing what she was telling him, then joined her at the table.

'Tell me everything.'

Zoe closed her eyes and began.

'Because the operation to remove Adam's ruptured appendix came a few days after his tenth birthday, the NHS+ has billed us for every bloody part of it. The surgeon, anaesthetists, the porter who wheeled his bed into surgery, sterilizing equipment, his bed, his food, everything.' She hesitated. 'And then there are...the *payments*.'

He bristled at the mention of them. Nine years after the agreement had been signed, they were still handing over half their monthly household income.

'What does it all mean?' he asked.

'Dimitri, it means we are well and truly screwed! We can't afford to survive as a family. The house is either going to be repossessed or we'll have to sell it. Either way, we'll get nothing for it because we're in negative equity. And after that, we won't be able to afford to rent anywhere.'

'So where will we live?'

She glared at him as if to remind him he already knew the answer.

'No,' Dimitri said adamantly. 'No way. Once they put you in Community Housing, you never get out. We can't do that to Adam. There must be another way.'

Zoe sat back in her chair and threw out her arms.

'Tell me what that way is then, because I'm all ears.'

'We'll look for better jobs, ones that'll pay more and give us health insurance.'

'If it was that easy, we'd have found better jobs already. But there aren't any. We have hit rock bottom.'

Once again, she propped up her head with her hands.

'This is all my fault, isn't it?' she added.

Dimitri held back from saying yes. He would never admit to partially blaming her for putting them in this predicament.

'It is what it is,' he replied.

'But if I had only been more careful, watched what I was doing instead of being distracted, I'd never have driven into—'

'Don't,' he replied. 'You're not the only one who got us into this situation.'

His stubbornness had also played its part. He'd ignored warnings that his job as area manager of Britain's last remaining high-street bank was at risk until 75 per cent of the workforce, including him, were replaced by AI technology.

Likewise, Zoe had assumed her head-of-year position at school was also safe. Until the government's schools minister announced a radical shake-up of the education system, cutting the learning week to three days at school and two at home with AI teaching the latter. Now Dimitri was claiming benefits and Zoe's part-time job only paid slightly above minimum wage.

A stony silence reigned as they considered the bleakest of futures.

'So what are we going to do?' Dimitri asked.

Zoe pinched the bridge of her nose 'When I mentioned it before, you point-blank refused to hear me out.'

Dimitri looked vacant until the penny dropped.

'No, Zoe, please, not this again. We can't even think about it. We just can't. He's our son.'

'You think I don't know that?' she replied. 'I love him more than anything else in the world and I want the best for him. But we are not giving him that. So what choice do we have? You said it yourself—Community Housing will destroy any future Adam has. The education facilities are sub-par, and now that the equality in the Workplace Act has been scrapped, most employers point-blank refuse to take on kids raised there because they don't have to. Have you seen how high the statistics are for those who turn to crime or drugs? It's frightening.'

'But we can't send him abroad to fend for himself! He's only ten years old.'

'Then our only other option is to put him into care because at least he'll live somewhere where they can afford food and heating—and that's more than we can do. But he won't be adopted because it's too expensive so he'll be pushed around the system until he's eighteen before being kicked out and expected to fend for himself. At least if he's living abroad, he stands a better chance of making something of himself than he does if we force him to remain here.'

'No, I'm not having it,' growled Dimitri, and stormed out of the kitchen and into the lounge, throwing himself onto the sofa.

It was so cold that he could see the breath that came from his mouth in short, angry snorts. Zoe waited for him to calm down before joining him.

'I know someone who will help him,' she said in a low voice. 'Someone I used to work with, his son organizes safe passages from the UK to Europe. I've... I've had a conversation with him.'

'You've done what? You had no right to!'

'I was exploring our options. And did you know there's medication we can give him before he leaves us to make his transition smoother?'

'You want to drug him?'

'Not drugs, medication. It targets the parts of the brain that hold memories and...erases them.'

'Oh Jesus, Zoe, do you hear yourself? Now you want to erase everything he knows?'

'No, not the parts that control how he functions and behaves, but the sections that hold his memories. If he doesn't remember where he came from, then he won't miss us. It'll be like starting all over again, only into a better life than the one he has here.'

'So everything we've done with him, all we've experienced together as a family, will disappear from his memories, just like that?'

'You have to stop thinking about yourself. This isn't about you or me, this is about Adam and what he needs and doesn't need to know.'

Dimitri shook his head. 'No, I can't do this. I can't give my boy away.'

The best part of a month passed before the subject was broached again. But this time it was Dimitri who brought it up. It had followed a final-warning email and a visit from bailiffs threatening legal procedures for failing to pay Adam's medical bills.

'Where would they send Adam?' he asked Zoe.

'Part of the agreement is that we don't ask and they don't tell us, but it's somewhere in Europe, somewhere more prosperous than the UK.'

'Who will look after him? How do we know he'll be safe?'

'The man I know, he's been doing this for years. They have families all lined up waiting for bright, English-speaking kids.'

'How will he get there?'

'By ship and then by train.'

'How much will it cost?'

'Nothing, the family who raises him will foot the bill.' Zoe broke eye contact with him. 'And they'll...help us too.'

'Help us?' he repeated. 'How, exactly?'

'They will erase all our debts. Everything, overnight. We won't owe anyone a single penny. We'll be debt free.'

Dimitri's face paled. 'You mean we'll be profiting from this? We're selling Adam?'

'No, you can't think of it like that. We'll be giving Adam the promise of a better life, which is the most important thing. But as a consequence, they'll also be helping us to get back on our feet.'

A week later and after becoming fixated by a national news story in which six families died in Community Housing when an illegal AZ lab caught fire, Dimitri reluctantly made his decision. He and Zoe twice met her contact, who played them videos of the smiling faces of other young people he had repatriated abroad.

Eventually—and reluctantly—Dimitri agreed.

Both parents had wept for days in the lead-up to the exchange, trying to spend as much time as possible with him. It was only when Adam fell asleep at the dinner table one Sunday night that Dimitri knew the process had begun.

'Help me to secure him,' Zoe urged, and they stretched Adam's drugged body out across the floor.

She removed from her handbag a small bottle of transparent liquid and a long thin silver device with a sharp tip.

'What's that?' he asked.

'It's to inject the PKM Zeta drug directly into his brain through his eye socket.'

'Oh Jesus,' Dimitri said.

He reached the kitchen sink just in time before vomiting.

'Go into the other room,' Zoe ordered.

Through the lounge window, he spotted Zoe's contact reverse his van up their driveway.

'Is he ready?' the man asked as Dimitri opened the door.

Dimitri was too choked to reply and instead allowed the man inside. Then he left him and Zoe alone in the kitchen until finally he was called to join them.

'He's ready,' said Zoe, her voice barely audible. Dimitri stared at his unconscious son, desperate for him to wake up, to realize what they were doing and beg them to change their minds. Because Dimitri would have done so in a heartbeat. But Adam's eyes remained sealed.

The man gave Zoe and Dimitri a few moments of privacy while they took turns in hugging, stroking and kissing Adam for the last time, and apologizing to him for their failures. Then they helped to carry him to the front door and load him into the back of the vehicle, and shut the door behind him.

They watched in silence as it made its way up and along the road until its tail lights were swallowed by the darkness. Then Dimitri collapsed to his knees and sobbed with a force he hadn't known was in him, all the while comforted by his wife.

And he remained by the front door until early next morning, when Zoe helped raise him to his feet, ready to set off for Loch Ba, where, for a second time, they would say goodbye to their son.

72

Dimitri & Zoe: Today

'How could he know what we did?' Dimitri, aghast, whispered to Zoe.

'Don't engage with him,' she said. Then, a little louder. 'He's speculating. He's a fantasist.'

'I'm not the fantasist, Zoe,' Hudson continued. 'I'm not the one who's been nursing a doll in her attic for the best part of a decade, a substitute for the son they sold.'

She stared at him in wonder.

'It was you who sent him back?' she faltered.

Hudson nodded, then reached into the pocket of his cargo pants, pulled out an item of clothing and threw it at Dimitri's chest. Dimitri unfolded it, a T-shirt he recognized immediately. Its image of New York, the Statue of Liberty and the Hudson River was identical to the one Adam had been dressed in the night they'd allowed him to be taken from them.

'Who are you?' asked Dimitri.

It was the question Hudson had waited a long time to be asked.

'Who do you think I am?' he responded.

Dimitri took all of Hudson in. He had the same colour eyes as his son and the same dark hair. He tried to imagine Adam without the puppy fat and with Hudson's angularity. There were definite similarities.

'Adam?'

Zoe appeared to reach the same conclusion, but no words passed her lips.

A bewildered Autumn Taylor turned to Hudson. 'Are you their son?'

'Dad?' asked Alice.

Hudson looked into Dimitri's eyes first and then Zoe's, with the same piercing stare.

'No,' he said. 'I'm not Adam. Your son died the night you sent him away to Europe.'

A stunned silence enveloped them. Eventually, Zoe responded.

'He...died?'

'Yes. Adam drowned. Whatever you were told about how he was going to be transported to Europe was a lie. He was one of fifty kids who were thrown into an overloaded dinghy that sank as we approached Calais. They made us jump overboard and swim to the shore. None of us were given lifebelts.'

'No, that's a lie,' Zoe said adamantly. 'We were told he'd be on a boat, a ship, that's how he'd travel. And then a train.'

'A dinghy and a sheep truck. That's what we were given. That's all we were worth.'

'But Adam was a strong swimmer,' Dimitri disputed. 'He had his lifesaving certificate. He could've made it to the shore, I know he could have.'

'And he did. But not before he saved me first because I couldn't swim. I panicked in the freezing temperatures and he pulled me up to the surface and helped get me to shore. There were bodies everywhere, but not mine. He saved my life.'

'Then how did he drown?' asked Dimitri.

'Once we staggered off the beach and into the truck, we had to cover ourselves in straw to keep warm. We were too exhausted to care that we were sleeping in sheep shit. At some point in the night, the lorry pulled over to the side of the road and they threw us a few dozen sandwiches and bottles of drinks. I tried to wake Adam up for his, but his eyes stayed shut. I tried again and again, then I shouted at him and I shook him. I tried CPR like I'd seen on TV but his lips were blue and his body was already freezing cold.'

'No, no,' said Dimitri, shaking his head. 'Ten-year-old boys don't just die for no reason.'

'They do if they suffer secondary drowning,' said Hudson. 'It happens when too much water gets into a person's lungs. They can become inflamed, and even hours later, they can just stop breathing.'

'Did he suffer?' Zoe asked.

'I have no idea,' Hudson replied. 'Only he knows that.'

Dimitri waited for Hudson to add something else, anything that might suggest Adam hadn't spent his last moments in agony. It didn't happen.

Zoe saw little else through her headset than black hearts. They covered the faces of everyone in the studio and the audience behind them. Without warning, they vanished, likely disabled by producers.

'They promised us that Adam would go to a family,' Dimitri continued, choked. 'They said he'd be looked after.'

'And you were all too willing to believe it,' said Hudson.

'If he's dead then it's your fault,' said Zoe suddenly. 'Drowning people grab at anything to survive. You must have pulled him under the water. That's how he got so much of it in his lungs.'

'You handed him a death sentence by sending him away,' Hudson fired back. 'That's on nobody else but you two.'

'Was Adam scared when you were on that boat?' Dimitri asked.

'Don't keep kidding yourself it was a boat. It was a cheap, overcrowded inflatable dinghy and every child on it was fucking petrified. And yes, so was Adam. He was scared and he had every right to be. You'd erased his memory so he didn't know who he was or where he was going, which made his confusion all the more tragic.'

Dimitri bent double, the palms of his hands resting on his knees as he took deep breaths. Zoe remained upright, fists balled, skin colourless and expression devoid of emotion.

'So this is true?' a bewildered Autumn asked Zoe and Dimitri.

Their silence gave her their answer.

'We had no choice—' said Zoe eventually.

'No, it was Adam who had no choice,' Hudson interrupted.

'We thought we were doing the right thing,' Zoe said. 'That we were giving him opportunities we couldn't give him ourselves. We could barely afford to keep a roof over our heads.'

'Yet somehow you managed it. I know that, because I've been to your house. Perhaps your debts being wiped in exchange for Adam helped to keep the wolves from the door?'

'Thousands of families like us slip through the cracks. That's the state of modern Britain.'

'Plenty of families haven't handed over half their monthly earnings to pay retribution to the family of someone they killed when they were driving carelessly. I assume you knew Charles Simmonds took his own life some years ago, because your payments must have stopped. Adam, Charles and his son Nate. That's three deaths on your conscience.'

Zoe looked up to the virtual sky and closed her eyes. Of course Hudson knew about that. He'd known about everything else. He had been the one to have sent copies of court documents that were supposed to have remained sealed, in which she admitted colliding with two cyclists in a car accident years earlier. It had left a father paralysed and his son lying dead in the road. She had benefited from legislation allowing the victims of specific types of crimes to receive regular financial payments from the perpetrator instead of that person facing a lengthy court case, prison and a criminal record. Blood money, it had been dubbed by those opposing it. But such arrangements were supposed to be kept strictly under wraps.

Zoe turned to face Hudson again. This time her temperament was noticeably different. She was angry with him.

'So why are you here? To expose us, to humiliate us, to punish us? You don't think we've put ourselves through all of that already?'

'All of the above, yes,' he admitted. 'But also to ensure that you don't win this competition and be given the opportunity to parent another child, either here or in the Real World. You didn't deserve the first one, you sure as hell don't deserve a second chance with another.'

Autumn's avatar held her finger to her ear as if listening to a direction from a producer somewhere in the Real World. She turned to Dimitri and Zoe.

'I'm so sorry to have to do this,' she said, her voice tense, 'but by admitting tonight what really happened to Adam, you're accepting responsibility for a crime which goes against our terms and conditions. So we have no choice but to bring your time in this process to an end.'

Zoe and Dimitri turned to each other and then to Lenny. Dimitri had been too caught up in events to have noticed his son watching, listening and trying to process what had been said, and calculating the probability of his own outcome.

He looked to his mother, his eyes panicked yet still hopeful. For a moment Zoe wondered if Adam had looked at anyone like that when the dinghy carried him off into the darkness.

'Please can I stay with you?' Lenny asked. 'Please?'

'Don't do this,' Zoe shouted across the studio in the hope that the producers were listening. 'It's not his fault. It's cruel. Punish us, but don't hurt him.'

She reached out to hug her son and the two made contact for a fraction of a second before his body began to separate into minuscule pieces. His shrill scream pierced their headsets, ringing in their ears, until nothing of him remained.

Zoe's and Dimitri's avatars disappeared from screen just as quickly.

Chats

TV / Reality TV Shows / **The Family Experiment**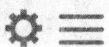

FaffyDuck 8.37 p.m.
Are we online again?

SubStan, 8.38 p.m.
Think so. Demand must've knocked out the servers. What the hell just happened?

TellyBob, 8.38 p.m.
Is this 4 real? Have Zoe and Dimitri been lying for all these years?

MickeyFinn, 8.38 p.m.
Guyz, I don't think this is a social experiment any more . . .

SubStan, 8.39 p.m.
No shit, Sherlock. Hudson has just blown the roof off this thing.

PaceyTwitter, 8.39 p.m.
Does he deserve to win tho? Just cos he exposed Dimitri & Zoe only means he's the best of a bad bunch.

FaffyDuck, 8.39 p.m.
Agreed. #Paedo

PaceyTwitter, 8.39 p.m.
My nerves are shredded. I'm never watching reality TV again.

MickeyFinn, 8.40 p.m.
Same.

SayItLikeISeeIt, 8.40 p.m.
Same.

TellyBob, 8.40 p.m.
Same.

FaffyDuck, 8.40 p.m.
Same.

> **SubStan, 8.40 p.m.**
> Anyone else think it's not over yet?

MickeyFinn, 8.40 p.m.
Hey...this is weird. Anyone else just received a message on socials claiming to be Hudson Wright? He's telling us to open something.

> **SubStan, 8.41 p.m.**
> What is it?

MickeyFinn, 8.41 p.m.
A link. He says the feed is about to be cut.

73
Hudson

Hudson took great satisfaction from watching the typically unflappable Autumn Taylor struggle to take control of a situation that he'd ripped from her hands. He could only imagine the panic transpiring behind the scenes as producers in the Real World argued as to what approach to take now that Hudson had torn up the rule book. The delay allowed him a moment to gather himself. To reach this far had been nothing short of a Herculean task. And the journey wasn't over yet.

Autumn once again held her finger to her ear, as if awaiting direction. Meanwhile, Hudson gripped Alice's hand firmly. She had remained near-silent the whole time, absorbing all that was said without comment or question. She squeezed Hudson's hand in return, as if to reassure him that whatever was to happen next, she would take it in her stride.

'Well, Hudson,' Autumn said finally, 'I don't think that this is the finale any of us were expecting. Apart from you, of course.'

He repressed a smile.

'So as you are the last remaining parent,' she continued, 'I'm sure it comes as no surprise when I tell you that you are the winner of *The Family Experiment*.'

Hudson turned his head as the backdrop behind him switched from viewers in avatar form, still reeling from that evening's revelations, to the night-time setting of a beach. Brightly coloured tape flew through the air, covering him, Alice and Autumn as booming fireworks exploded over a tranquil ocean. In front of them, a podium rose from the ground, containing two red buttons. One said 'Keep' and the other 'Delete'.

When the tape finally settled and the fireworks muted, Autumn offered Hudson a congratulatory but empty hug.

'So how does it feel to be the winner?' she asked.

'It's been an unforgettable experience,' he replied.

'The one question I purposefully didn't ask any of our contestants throughout the process is what they intended to do if they were to be crowned the winner. But now I get to ask what everyone wants to know. Will Alice stay with you, or will you switch her off and use the prize money to fund a biological Real World child?'

Hudson turned to his daughter and took both of her hands in his own.

'Alice, up until now, you've been the only thing I have accomplished in my life that I'm proud of. And because we are so intertwined, you know that my role in both worlds is to be more than a parent.'

Alice nodded and the two embraced.

'I love you so much,' he whispered into her ear before they faced Autumn. 'I am choosing neither my daughter nor the prize money.'

A line appeared between Autumn's brows. 'I'm sorry?'

'I'm choosing neither,' he repeated.

'I don't think I understand,' she said, and placed her finger to her earpiece yet again.

But before she could take instruction, Hudson stepped forward and without losing eye contact with Alice, firmly pressed the delete button.

To the shock of everyone but him and Alice, she exploded into millions of pixels, without making a sound.

'Why?' Autumn gasped when Alice had completely vanished from the screen.

'Because I know the number of lives Awakening Entertainment has destroyed in creating her and every other MetaChild in this competition. And tonight, it ends.'

74

Hudson: Two and a half years earlier

Hudson had held his breath as the shaven-headed woman pushed open the door on the left and beckoned him to follow. Lights above them flickered to life and illuminated a white corridor leading to another door. She placed her eye in front of a retinal scanner and then her palm against a second device before that door opened too. Only instead of rolling hills, vast oceans, wasteland, a forest or even a desert island, there was a door with the words Viewing Room written upon it.

'This isn't the exit?' he asked.

'For some it's only the beginning,' she replied with a knowing smile. 'You don't have any perception of what else happens here, do you?'

He shook his head.

'After you,' she told him, holding out a hand. Then she and Hudson ventured inside.

Behind a floor-to-ceiling window, he gazed across a vast circular floor filled with dozens of small rooms, each no more than a few square metres in size. Blue horizontal and transparent beams of light replaced walls, enabling him to see though them. He assumed they were electrified. Each room contained a person clad from head to toe in haptic-wear and full-facial masks. Dozens and dozens of multicoloured lasers were pointed at different parts of their bodies like rainbow arcs exploding from their bodies.

'We refer to them as the Chromatics,' she said with erroneous pride. 'Objects characterized by colour sensations.'

In the centre of the space was a glazed building manned by a handful of staff.

'Have you heard of a Panopticon?' she asked.

'No,' Hudson replied.

'They date back to eighteenth-century prisons, but this, of course, isn't a penitentiary. It's a research facility. But each one of our Chromatics can also be observed from that one central room at any time by our staff. The principle behind our Panopticon is that even though not every Chromatic can be watched by humans all the time, the knowledge that they might be being viewed is enough to make them more compliant. They are more scared by people watching them than AI. It's a psychological incentive, like an extra level of encouragement to complete the tasks we ask of them.'

They moved from the viewing room and onto the main floor. From the corner of his eye, a red light blinked on a security camera and he heard the familiar buzz of a rotating lens. He was also being watched, and it was highly likely AI was examining his every expression.

She was testing him, he was sure of it. And to pass, he must offer no reaction. He must remain completely impassive.

He walked slowly past each box until he reached a section of children without their masks. Many he recognized. He had reluctantly rejected them when they hadn't proved suitable candidates to help train their AI. The last he had seen of them was when they were led through the door on the left. Each one approximated their former self: pale skin, angular body, haunted eyes, and face contorted by pain past and present. Others were utterly expressionless and inanimate, as if someone had pressed pause on a moment of time. It was his fault they were here, wherever here was.

'What is this place?' he asked, trying to ensure the tone of his voice didn't give away his guilt.

'It's the yin to your yang, Hudson,' the woman replied, as if the answer was obvious.

Hudson stared at her blankly.

'Your side of the building has positive experiences. The AI we are developing has learned from your team how humans react when they're happy, excited, inquisitive, aroused, satisfied and confident. But there's more to the human experience than that, isn't there? So the ones on this side experience the opposite. This is where AI learns from them about pain—physical as well as emotional. They're made to feel sadness, loss, fear, anger, frustration, and so on. And through them, our AI discovers how much a human mind and body can take when it's pushed to its limits.'

'So if one of the beta-testers, say, hits an avatar, the lasers pointed at those suits will make that child feel it?'

'We like to think that we can vet our testers well enough so that doesn't happen. Very often, anyway. But AI needs to understand suffering in order to progress. And these brave souls have been willing to offer themselves to our cause.'

Hudson wanted to argue, to tell her what they were doing was illegal, immoral and almost incomprehensible, but he knew it would be the wrong approach.

'Machine-learning is about computers gathering information and adapting without us humans specifically having to tell them something,' Hudson said. 'If we are showing them how to feel, be it happiness or pain, then they aren't learning it by themselves.'

'In theory, yes. But unfortunately that is still some time away from being perfected. The competition between AI developers has never been so tough. So to remain at number one and to get our products out there before anyone else involves taking routes others may not approve of. But to all intents and purposes, no child was harmed during our research and development process.'

'How long do they stay in here for?'

'The timescale varies from case to case, but generally until they decide they need to re-cooperate.'

'And then?'

The woman smiled. 'You're inquisitive. I like that.'

Hudson followed her into a separate wing he assumed to be a hospital ward. The walls were made of curved white panels with aluminium fixtures and touchless doors. Large screens above patients' beds contained their statistics in real time, from heart and respiratory rates to brainwave patterns and care plans. In the beds were young adults and children, all unconscious but restrained with metal harnesses.

'This is where they are placed when they are beyond the brink,' the woman explained. 'After they cease responding to anything else thrown at them some are given intense therapy or medication programmes. But if they don't respond, sections of their brains preventing their ability to move on are erased of oppressive memories. They forget what they've been through already so they can start all over again. It's the humane thing to do.'

They passed another room where this time patients weren't confined to their beds. Hudson paused to view patients wandering aimlessly, staring blankly at the walls surrounding them. He became fixated by one young woman. She was seated, and motionless but for her trembling hands.

Suddenly her eyes fixed upon his. Each one of his muscles constricted when they realized who one another was.

It was Eva. The only friend he'd ever made in Ararat.

Her once fresh, youthful face was now sunken. Her blonde hair was streaked with grey ropes, her lips cracked, her eyes now a milky white. Blueish veins protruded from each side of her neck. Helpless, he wanted to raise his hand and place it on the glass. But he couldn't allow his escort or the cameras fixed upon him to identify any negative reaction. So he moved along, as if taking it all in his stride.

'What happens if they can't be cured?' Hudson asked the woman.

'They're never cured, Hudson, they're simply reset. And even then, it's only ever a temporary fix. They're back out in the field until their next breakdown or until they're recycled for the next stage of their lives.'

'Which is?'

'Medical science, typically in South America or parts of Europe. Their lives are valued, never wasted. And their sacrifices always appreciated.'

By the time she and Hudson exited and made their way to a waiting car outside, it was all he could do not to punch her to the floor.

'You'll do well with us back in England,' she added as a guard approached them. 'I have a good feeling about you. And I'm never wrong. You are one of us.'

75
Hudson: Today

Hudson realized that while he had been recounting to viewers the activities hidden inside Ararat, the studio had fallen silent. The beach backdrop where fireworks had earlier illuminated the sky had long since vanished, replaced by white space.

He assumed the live feed to viewers had been cut by frantic producers midway through his disclosure. But he had prepared for this. They could cancel their own feed, but they couldn't revoke his, which was broadcasting to hundreds and thousands of social media accounts worldwide. He had targeted and time-delayed the sending of messages to the social media account of anyone who had used supportive phrases or hashtags, advising them of an extraordinary twist to come. And if their *The Family Experiment* screens were to suddenly go blank mid-finale, the secure link he provided would allow them to view what producers didn't want them to see. He also urged them to share it. The same link had also been sent to journalists, news desks, influencers and bloggers.

If the audience could only view what Hudson was witnessing, they would be staring at a bewildered Autumn Taylor ripping out her earpiece to prevent the producers' gallery from demanding she terminate their conversation. But Hudson knew they were powerless to mute her headset too. He'd read in her contract that its provision had been sponsored and was thus not controlled by them. And Autumn was canny enough to capitalize on a career-defining moment of television when she saw one. She was not going to allow anyone to cut her off.

'You tell a good story,' she began. 'But why should we believe you?'
'A fair question,' Hudson replied. 'Please watch this.'
His eyes focused on a play button in the corner of his visor. Footage

appeared of everything he'd described, from the children with kaleidoscopic lasers pointed at their bodies to the ward where others were restrained while yet more wandered, stupefied by pharmaceuticals and illegal medical procedures.

'If you're at home and still able to view this,' he announced, 'look at the mail symbol in the top right-hand corner of your screen. It will automatically download documents supporting everything I've told you tonight. It contains thousands of pages of medical reports on the young victims locked inside that place, details of how Awakening Entertainment's AI moved ahead of its rivals due to the deliberate pain inflicted on children, along with lists of the parents of trafficked children whose debts were wiped clear. There are dates and times of chartered flight paths from New York to around the world where those who are too damaged to continue are now seeing out their days as human guinea pigs. And of course we've included exact location and access codes for the site in New York where hundreds of others are being held against their will.'

'If this is true, then why have you waited until now to expose it?' asked Autumn.

'I was institutionalized for a very long time,' Hudson explained. 'For ten years I was programmed to believe I was part of something revolutionary, that I was working for the greater good. It took me a long time to admit I was defending the wrong side. And when that realization came, who would've believed me if I'd gone public? Genuine evidence takes time to procure. Because without it, I'd sound like every online conspiracy theorist. I needed a stage that was large enough to be heard from. And there's no bigger stage than tonight's global audience.'

'Who are you really?'

'Who I was or how I got here doesn't matter. What matters is the information I've shared, and what you do with it. I've given away, or lost, a lot of myself over the years. Now it's time I kept a piece of me to myself.'

And before Autumn could ask anything else, Hudson's avatar vanished. It was replaced on screen by a two-word notice.

'Account terminated.'

https:/www.news.uk/US&Canada/12908765

 NEWS

Home | **US & Canada**

Further accusations made in the wake of Staten Island fire

An investigation continues this morning into a fire that ravaged a building in New York's Staten Island yesterday, leaving dozens dead.

Hundreds of firefighters took twenty hours to extinguish the blaze which tore through the fourteen-story building before a search for bodies began.

More than 150 children and teenagers were rescued but many others are believed to have perished in the blaze.

Accusations of abuse and torture of children in the name of technology have been made against Awakening Entertainment, the company leasing the property.

NYPD police commissioner Al Riley says teams of forensic officers will likely be sifting through the debris for weeks in the search for more fatalities.

'To date, I can confirm that seventy-six bodies have so far been discovered, but we expect that toll to rise considerably,' he said. 'Those rescued have been taken to various hospitals around the tri-state area to be treated and psychologically evaluated. This is a unique and tragic situation.'

ONE YEAR LATER

76
Leo Hamilton

Leo Hamilton was standing at the edge of the beach where it had all begun. The last time he had trudged across those pebbles he'd been a naïve ten-year-old. And it had been a dark, damp and disorientating night. Men with foreign accents had yelled and children around him had sobbed. When he had taken a deep breath, it had been the first time in his life he'd smelled fear. Not his own, though. Leo had not been frightened. He had kept his composure.

Today, he had chosen to revisit the past in daylight. To the best of his recollection, he had located the spot where the dinghy had been positioned when he'd climbed on board. He remembered the lights attached to the jackets of the three traffickers, and how they'd dazzled his eyes. He recalled the taste of salt on his lips when the wind skimmed across the sea and howled in his ears. And based on the atmosphere of panic surrounding him, he'd realized he was likely the only one of this group who was there voluntarily.

It had been Leo's choice to be trafficked.

Prior to that night, he'd been raised in a Community Housing district of Leicester. For much of the time, he had brought himself up as, aside from the essentials of food, water and clothing, his parents had provided little else. They were in their mid-teens when he'd been born, abandoned by their own families for falling pregnant and forced to hustle to get by. And when that hustling on occasion led to custodial sentences, Leo had, in turn, also hustled. Only he'd been too sharp to get caught.

Unlike many of his peers, Leo had known there was a brighter future out there for him but one that would stay beyond his reach as long as he remained trapped in that environment.

And then something began to happen to his community. Acquaintances were disappearing. Children he had grown up with, who he had known all his life, would simply vanish. When he inquired, their unconcerned parents would tell him they'd moved to live with relatives elsewhere. He hadn't believed them. Especially when soon after, their parents also left Community Housing for greener pastures.

Eventually, an overheard conversation between adults revealed the truth. In return for cash to help their families buy their way out of poverty, these children had been shipped abroad with promises of a better life in Europe with new families who could afford to raise them. They'd receive a better education and healthcare, thus improving their prospects.

And in a light-bulb moment, Leo realized that was his way out. There was only one problem—there was no one around to sell him. He hadn't seen his parents for the best part of four months and had survived by sofa-surfing and the kindness of other families who pitied him. Regardless, Leo was determined.

He'd also picked up on the mention of Old Folkestone as a frequent drop-off point. An inflatable boat would then transport the children to a yacht where, once aboard, they'd set sail for a more prosperous world.

It took three autonomous coach trips before Leo finally reached Mermaid Beach, which sounded more beguiling than its reality. He had, in his naivety, expected to find a group of children like him, neatly lined up, gazing across the water in awe of their lives ahead. Instead, he had been alone.

For three days he slept in a disused pub, questioning his decision to leave the familiar. But on his final night, he spotted a minibus arriving and a group of young people shepherded onto the beach. There, under moonlight, a dinghy was being inflated and pushed into the water, followed by the children. Others had arrived one by one in cars and vans.

The process of herding them to the shore appeared disorganized. So he took his chances and ran from the pub, making a beeline for a second group of children, coming to a halt at the back of the line while the adult escorting them became distracted by his phone. One by one, they waded through the freezing water and climbed on board the vessel, where, for the first time, he saw the faces of the others. Without exception, none were as jubilant as he felt. Instead, they were muddled, distressed and jittery.

An inner voice that had helped him through many scrapes in the past appeared suddenly, warning him this was not going to be the second chance he'd pinned his hopes on. So he'd risen to his feet, readying himself to return to the water and relative safety of the shore. A firm hand had pushed him back down.

'I shouldn't be on here,' he tried to explain to the man towering over him. 'I want to get off, please.'

'No one leaves,' the man replied in broken English.

'But I don't belong—'

The man's second response came in the form of a backhanded slap to the side of Leo's head. He only just stopped himself from toppling sideways into the terrified girl next to him. He turned to the horizon and searched for the waiting yacht he'd overheard the adults speaking of. It would be better once they were all on board that, surely? But the moon illuminated an empty horizon.

His attention had then been drawn to a semi-conscious boy being thrown on board. He grabbed the child's arm and pulled him upright.

'What's happening?' the boy asked, and Leo answered to the best of his knowledge. They were being taken to Europe.

'What's your name?' Leo asked.

'It's...' But the boy seemed confused, as if working out a difficult maths problem. 'I... I don't know.'

Soon after that the overcrowded dinghy set off, and Leo noticed the boy's New York City T-shirt. 'Hudson,' Leo said suddenly. 'That's what I'll call you until you remember your name.'

The boy didn't argue.

Amongst the guilt Leo felt for so many things throughout his later life, Hudson's death had always remained at the very top. If Leo had been able to swim, he wouldn't have panicked when the dinghy began sinking and its young occupants were forced to leap overboard, many to their deaths. Then he wouldn't have dragged Hudson down with him, and the boy wouldn't have swallowed so much water and might have survived the journey.

But it wasn't only Hudson's life he had stolen, it was his identity too. A tearful Leo had swiped two things from the boy's body: his T-shirt to give himself an extra layer of warmth, and the dog tags that each child who, unlike him, was supposed to be there had been handed before they'd reached the Kent coast. The tags contained a QR code with their personal data attached. And upon their arrival in Ararat, the tags had been seared into the back of each child's hand. It was there that he learned Hudson's birth name was Adam Taylor-Georgiou. However, to keep up the pretence that his memory had been erased, Leo admitted he recalled very little but thought his name might be Hudson. He hadn't been corrected.

Once their plain grey tracksuit uniforms had been designated, Leo had been expected to toss into an incinerator all the clothes he'd arrived in, including Adam's T-shirt. Instead, he kept it hidden under the base of his dormitory locker, a reminder of an ultimate sacrifice. And there it remained until the day he left for the UK.

Today and back in Kent, Hudson removed the T-shirt from his jacket pocket and held it in his hands. He'd never learned what had happened to Adam's body once it had been removed from the truck and he hadn't asked.

There had been no funeral for the boy and no one to mourn him. Except Leo. So he made his way to an area of scrubland, dug a hole in the soil with a pocket knife and buried the T-shirt. Then with a quiet 'thank you', he placed a circular black rock on top of the mound and returned to the adjacent car park.

Out of habit, he checked the passport App on his phone. The version of himself in the photograph had blond hair and eyebrows, a pierced ear, veneers and blue contact lenses. A surgeon in Turkey had shaved the bump from his nose and taken a little bone from his chin, squared his jaw and eradicated the scar from the back of his hand. Just enough to fool facial recognition software that he was convinced was being monitored by his former employers. He was beginning to look more avatar than human.

He glanced again at his name, his third in the last twelve years. Born Leo, assumed to be Hudson, and now he was Mark Smith. Plain, simple, completely unremarkable, and hard to find by anyone searching for him.

77
Woody & Tina

A chill ran through Tina as the lift doors opened and she made her way along the corridor. She couldn't be sure if it was nerves or the air conditioning pricking her neck and shoulders. She turned a corner and paused as she reached the floor-to-ceiling glass windows of the restaurant. Woody was already there, waiting at a table with his back to her.

It was the first time she had seen him in months.

Tina made her way inside and approached his table. There were no embraces or kisses, just polite, but cool, nods to affirm each other's presence. As she removed her coat and draped it across the back of the chair opposite him, she spotted the heel of his right foot tapping against the floor in a rapid, repetitive motion. He was as anxious as she was.

She took in his appearance. He had lost weight since they'd last seen one another, not long after Belle had been killed. Tina had been consumed by anger and loss, while Woody had been more concerned by Issy's disappearance. They had grieved together but for different children, causing a chasm to open up between them.

Woody knew that his suffering had not been as great as Tina's. Her avatar had strangled Belle so she had borne the brunt of public scorn. And when the truth had come out, it became even worse. The media picked up that they already had a Real World, human daughter who had killed a school friend and then her 'sister'. It was more pressure than their marriage could take. Soon after, Woody had moved out.

'How are you?' he began.

'I'm still getting hate mail on a daily basis, the clinic has let me go saying the bad publicity has made my position untenable and the whole world knows we lied about the existence of our killer daughter. Apart from that, great. And you?'

'Okay, I guess.'

'Did you bring the documents?'

Woody reached into a brown leather messenger bag on the floor and pulled out an envelope containing paperwork, passing it to her. She opened it. The first sheet was headed 'Application for a Decree Absolute', the last form that needed to be completed before their divorce was finalized. Their split had been amicable enough for them to have organized it themselves online and without the aid of costly solicitors.

'Why did you insist we did this in person when we've done everything else via email?' Woody asked.

'Because there's one last thing we need to discuss, face to face.'

He raised an inquisitive eyebrow as Tina cleared her throat.

'The boy Issy killed, Archie Anderson. I found his watch and phone.'

The blood drained from his face. Tina felt the pace of his tapping foot quicken.

'Where?' he asked.

'Where you hid them, in a tightly wrapped plastic bag under a tile that came off the garage roof in those recent high winds. You must have brought them with you when we moved there. It was too high for a ten-year-old girl to reach, even with a ladder.'

She looked him dead in the eye.

'So I know what you did.'

Woody took in her expression and body language and knew she wasn't bluffing. He sat back in his seat, held his head in his hands and rubbed his cheeks with his palms. The game was up. He had been the one to hide Archie's stolen devices. Because he had stripped the boy's body of them, not Issy.

Eight years had passed since, from a distance, Woody had followed Issy one afternoon from the school gates to a local recreation park. Something had been bothering her. She'd become distracted, sullen and withdrawn, which was very unlike her. When he'd mentioned his concerns to Tina, she'd dismissed it as 'another of her phases'. But Woody had known his daughter better than that. She was keeping something from him.

He had decided to walk her the four streets from school to home and encourage her to open up. But as he approached the school, he spotted her amongst the mass of uniforms, heading for a street in the opposite direction to their house. Curious, he trailed her until they reached the park. It was only then that he realized that while he had been following her, she had been following someone else, a young man with white-blond hair and a backpack thrown over his shoulder.

As the boy walked through the park, Issy picked up the pace so that by the time he reached a shelter housing recycling bins, she was only metres behind him. The two disappeared from sight within seconds of each other.

Woody hesitated, pausing behind the large trunk of a horse chestnut tree as he decided what to do. But in the time it took him to make up his mind, Issy suddenly returned to view, hurrying towards the waterpark section of a children's area where she frantically ran her hands and the sleeves of her shirt under a tap. Then she sprinted across the grass in the direction of home.

Curious, Woody skirted through the trees until he reached the shelter from the opposite side. And it was there he found the blond-haired boy, lying on the ground, his eyes closed and blood pouring from a gaping wound on his forehead. Half a brick lay by his side.

Immediately, Woody tried to stem the flow with the sleeve of his hoodie.

'Issy, what have you done?' he whispered to himself, just as the boy's eyes opened.

'My head,' the boy muttered, then placed his hand on the source of the pain.

His face paled as he realized he was bleeding. Then he glared at Woody, the bloodied brick, and tried to scramble to his feet.

'No, no, I'm not going to hurt you,' Woody tried to reassure him. 'I found you, I'm trying to help you.'

'You're that psycho's dad!' the boy said suddenly. 'She did this to me. She tried to kill me.'

'No, no, I'm sure she didn't. It was an accident.'

'My parents are going to call the police.'

Woody's heart was in his mouth.

'They don't need to do that,' he said. 'Let's get you some help and we can sort this out between us. I'll tell Issy to apologize.'

The boy was now on his feet.

'She's batshit nuts, everyone knows it,' he barked. 'I'm going to get her excluded from school.'

Woody gripped the boy's arm. He winced, so Woody slackened his hold, but it remained there.

'No, you're not, we're going to talk this through,' he said firmly.

'Let go of me or I'll tell everyone that you're a paedo.'

Woody shook his head, exasperated.

'You don't know what you're saying. I told you we can sort this out.'

The boy had tried to yank his arm away but Woody was too strong for him.

'Help!' the boy had yelled at the top of his voice. 'He's trying to kill me.'

'Shut up,' Woody had snapped.

'Help!' the boy screamed again.

Woody yanked his arm so robustly that the boy had fallen to the ground, banging his head against a bin.

'I'm going to ruin your life and hers!' the boy had threatened tearfully. 'Everyone's going to know your daughter is a psycho.'

Woody's urge to protect Issy was so absolute that he gave no forethought to the consequences of what he was to do next.

He picked up the brick and hit the boy twice in the head with it. Only when the boy remained motionless on the floor and with no trace of a pulse did Woody regain his senses.

With the murder weapon still in his hand, he spotted a puddle behind a tree and calmly washed his and Issy's fingerprints from it. He wet a handkerchief and rubbed the skin on the boy's arm and his head to remove any trace of his DNA. Then he took the boy's watch and phone, turned them off so they couldn't be tracked and stuffed them in his pocket. To his good fortune, he had approached and left the bin shelter from the opposite side, beyond the reach of the lens.

Later, on his return home, he hid the devices carefully under a rock by his elderly neighbour's overgrown pond, changed out of his clothes and trainers and doused them in white spirits. He'd already found Issy's bloodied clothes inside the laundry hamper. Then he burned them all together in a firepit in the garden and scattered the ashes in a nearby field later that night. He didn't tell Issy that he knew what she'd done or that, in trying to protect her, he'd killed Archie.

Issy's arrest days later knocked him for six. But if he admitted that it was him who had killed Archie who would be there to protect Issy? What use would he be to her if he was behind bars? Tina had all but washed her hands of her daughter. He was all she had left.

The guilt of watching her being tried in court had almost broken him and many times he had been on the brink of admitting his culpability. So when Issy was found guilty of manslaughter, he made his lawyer fight tooth and nail to have her sentence carried out under lock and key at home and under her parents' strict supervision.

Tina never understood why Woody continued to defend Issy and proclaim her innocence. She branded him gullible and unwilling to listen to reason. But now she knew the truth, he thought.

'Tina,' he began. 'You need to hear the whole story—'

'You should have admitted it straight away, not kept the truth from me,' she interrupted. 'I'm *your* wife and her mother. I deserved to know *everything*.'

'I'm sorry,' he replied, and as he took a deep breath, he prepared to explain.

But Tina beat him to the punch.

'When did she give you the phone and watch to hide? The same day she told you that she'd killed him? The next?'

Woody hesitated, processing her words.

So she doesn't know I'm responsible, he thought. *She just thinks Issy confessed to me.* He briefly considered setting her straight, but decided against it.

'Um, the next day,' he lied.

'Why did you protect her?'

'I... I know what I did was wrong. But she's our daughter.'

Tina looked him dead in the eyes. 'No. She's your daughter, not mine.'

He opened his mouth to respond but thought better of it. Instead, they remind in silence.

Eventually, Woody took hold of the Application for a Decree Absolute, signed it, then passed it back to Tina. She did the same. He promised to post it the next morning.

Tina rose to her feet and slipped on her coat. Woody remained where he was.

'Where do you think Issy is now?' he asked suddenly.

Tina shrugged.

'Do you care?'

'No, I really don't. We did everything we could to try to make her a better person and she never even met us halfway.'

'We should have tried harder.'

'It would've made no difference,' said Tina adamantly. 'We haven't lost her because we never had her. She has always been on her own and that's how she likes it. Wherever she is now, she'll have landed on her feet because that's what she does. She will survive anything that's thrown at her.'

78
Issy: Eleven months earlier

Issy's forehead slammed against the corrugated-metal wall before she fell to a heap on the floor. Had it been the first time she'd been thrown around, it might have hurt. But she was growing accustomed to it so she barely felt a thing. She tasted blood in the back of her throat and spat it out. Then she mustered up what little energy she had left to pull herself up to her knees, where she remained, powerless to stop herself from swaying back and forth.

It was pitch black and she had no idea how long it had been since she'd last seen daylight or felt fresh air against her face. The torch had long since ceased to work despite the replacement batteries, and the glass screen of the disposable tablet had cracked underfoot days earlier, rendering it useless. That had been her lowest moment until now, because without her chess App, there was nothing to take her mind away from the mess she was in.

Issy winced as she leaned forward, using her fingertips to fumble around, trying to locate one of the remaining water bottles. The next sharp turn worked in her favour, and the bottle rolled towards her and hit her foot, so she grabbed it from the floor and unscrewed the lid. She twice gulped tepid water before everything moved swiftly and again she was hurled from one side to another. This time, she landed awkwardly on her arm. She might have felt it crack. Something wet and sticky seeped from a wound when she rubbed it. It was thicker than blood and likely to be more yellow discharge from the infection.

On the day of her escape from Woody and Christina's home, she'd cut open her arm with a vegetable knife to remove the tracking device. It had hurt like hell and she used a YouTube video to instruct her on how to sew up and bandage the wound. But somewhere between her home and here, it had become infected, and she'd lost a bag she'd brought containing spare bandages and antiseptic spray.

'Fuck!' she screamed at the top of her voice, but there was no one outside to hear her.

In fact, she could barely hear herself against the sound of crashing ocean waves. The queasiness returned so she took in long deep breaths, inhaling only stale air and the stink of the bucket she'd been using as a toilet. There had been nowhere to empty it, but today's storm had seen to that. It was now spread across the floor along with rainwater which had earlier come through the small air vents that ran the length of the shipping container she was locked inside.

A month had passed since she had packed a bag and run away. While Christina and Woody had been begging her to spare Belle's life, she was in a booth at a Metaverse access point cafe in the town centre. Once Belle had been terminated, she discarded any traceable electrical equipment and began the next leg of her journey.

Seven years had passed since she'd last been out in the Real World, and she'd had to prepare for change. So she had visited Metaverse towns and cities to give her a flavour of what to expect from their Real World equivalents.

Another ginormous wave crashed against the container, but the wooden packing cases she was sharing the space with remained securely attached to the floor, a small mercy. Issy frantically moved her good arm around and found a strap attached to the corrugated-iron wall. She wrapped her hand around it as the ship rose again for a handful of seconds before descending harder than ever.

Issy took a sharp intake of stale oxygen as she prepared for the next wave. She tapped into an inner reserve of buried strength.

'I will survive this,' she yelled at the top of her voice. 'I'm not going to die.'

Without warning, an image of Archie Anderson appeared. All these years later and her hatred for him remained. It was his fault she'd been imprisoned in that basement; his fault she'd had to escape; his fault she was now locked inside this living hell. His fault she had killed him.

Had he not mocked her when she asked him if he wanted to hang out after school; if he hadn't rejected her and behaved like the other immature boys in his class and told everyone else; had they not relentlessly bullied her, laughed at her, chanted at the top of their lungs, 'The psycho wants a friend,' then she wouldn't have had to teach him a lesson.

The brick she had taken from the garden and brandished behind the park bin shelter was only supposed to have been a threat, something to scare him into telling everyone that actually, yes, she was normal, that she wasn't crazy. But when he laughed in her face, she'd retaliated.

Her first and only blow knocked him to his knees, and he clutched his forehead as he began to bleed. Then his eyes rolled into the back of his head and he fell to the ground. She had killed him. And he deserved it.

She hadn't thought to check for CCTV, that she might have been captured following him, then washing his blood from her clothes under a tap. She hadn't considered they might match the murder weapon with the bricks surrounding her parents' flower beds. She'd never learned why her fingerprints weren't on the brick, why she could never find her damp, bloodied clothes or who had taken Archie's watch and mobile phone.

She pushed Archie out of her mind and recalled how she'd kept a relatively calm head out in the open after her escape. She'd purchased a vending machine burner tablet using one of her parents' credit cards, then hired an autonomous taxi to drive her to the Port of Immingham on the south bank of the Humber estuary. There, she withdrew all the cash she could from her parents' accounts, then hung around greasy-spoon cafes and electronic vehicle-charging stations. It was relatively easy to locate a young port worker willing to accept money in return for smuggling her inside a container bound for Poland. Once she reached its shores, she'd make her way by train to neighbouring Russia.

The journey was not going to be without its complications, she had known that, but without a passport or any form of identification, travelling by train, plane or car through each country would be much harder.

So freight ship had been the safest choice. With enough provisions to last her the ten-day route, she was locked inside and the boat set off.

For the most part it had literally been plain sailing. She had always loved Apps where she could traverse and explore the world's oceans. They took her far away from the world she had been locked in. And on this journey there had been glorious moments as she peered through the vents to watch a school of dolphins launching themselves into the air.

But her view of the outside world came to a halt when today's storm broke and she closed the vents to make the container waterproof and airtight.

It was her love of chess that was motivating her new start in Russia. The game had become as much of an obsession as escaping that house. And a Russian training camp in St Petersburg State University promised to be the answer to her prayers.

Russia's borders would not be easy to penetrate, but Issy believed with all her heart that she was made for impossible things. Metaverse lessons had given her a rudimentary understanding of the language in written and spoken form; she could learn the nuances once the admissions office saw her potential, cut through any red tape and allowed her to enrol.

All she must do to get there was survive this leg of the journey. She wiped the sweat from her brow as more thunderous waves crashed against the side of the ship.

Only this time, something felt different.

The ship failed to straighten up. Instead, it rolled in time with the waves, then listed. A loud, piercing siren suddenly sounded somewhere outside. Issy held firm to the straps as the boat tilted further, and this time, it was followed by an unfamiliar noise, like metal being dragged across metal. It took a moment for it to register.

The container was unfastening from its securing devices.

Another huge rise was followed by an even bigger dip as the container moved, sliding further and further until it turned over completely. Issy lost her grip. Other containers sounded as if they were doing the same thing, crashing into one another and sending her flying from one side to the other. Until there was a moment of weightlessness followed by a final crash and a whooshing sound.

Her container had fallen into the ocean.

Now she was sliding down the floor at a ninety-degree angle, plunging deeper and deeper into the water. Pressure made her eardrums hammer and her chest feel as if it was about to cave in on itself. She was expecting water to burst through seals in the air vents but they were keeping it out. For now at least.

Slowly the container sank, ever deeper, ever more pressure building up inside her head and body until finally she could no longer take the pain and she slipped into unconsciousness. Only when she awoke, nauseous and with a throbbing behind her eyes like she had never felt before, did she realize she was no longer drifting in a downward trajectory. She had reached the ocean floor.

Issy remained motionless. And in that moment, she realized her hopes and dreams would not reach any further than these four corrugated-metal walls.

As fear began to make way for hysteria, she balled her hands into fists and opened her mouth, ready to scream and bang on the doors, begging for help. She stopped short, knowing it would make no difference.

Nobody would ever know that she was down here in an underwater grave, all of her own making.

79
Leo Hamilton

Leo had witnessed graphic images of this building more times than he cared to remember. But the relentless news coverage still hadn't prepared him for how it might feel to be there in person. Fear, sorrow, loss, regret and longing hit him like a tidal wave as behind mesh-metal fencing lay the charred remains of Ararat.

The fire that had ripped through the four multi-storey buildings the night of *The Family Experiment*'s final broadcast had been the result of scores of explosive devices. And now, his home of ten years was nothing but rubble.

Beside a dozen or so people who were also here taking videos or live-blogging were piles of debris. Amongst them were burned-out vehicles, the remains of furniture, bed frames and clothing. Behind him were charred trees and shrubbery, scorched by the reach of the flames. How anyone, let alone a hundred and fifty people, had survived this, God only knew. A hundred others hadn't though, trapped inside that building either too terrified to run for help or too damaged to understand the threat to life. Or perhaps they'd seen death as their only escape. Most remained unidentified even now.

The mass murder had sparked a wave of inquests and investigations, from how children had been smuggled in and out of one of the busiest airspaces in the world, to how a building once assumed uninhabited had actually incarcerated so many young people and been a place of employment for others. How had it gone unnoticed in a population of nine million and in a city that never sleeps?

There were also questions asked as to where the hidden figures behind Awakening Entertainment had vanished to. Multiple arrests had been made thanks to the others Leo had been working with having made employee records available to authorities. However, they had been small fish in a large, toxic pond. No charges had been made and they hadn't been able to shed any light on who their employers were. They had been too clever to have left any kind of trail. Back in the UK, it was a near identical story. Only there had been no tortured young people to burn, just electrical equipment in Sizewell to erase and destroy.

Leo took a deep breath, convinced he could still smell smoke in the air. He recalled his final moments in that building, when he hadn't been allowed the opportunity to say goodbye to anyone and had instead been directed into an awaiting vehicle. Inside had been Cain, once his childhood nemesis, and who, going by his haunted appearance, was no longer a threat. They journeyed home on that flight to an airstrip in Ipswich in silence.

A week had passed before their paths crossed again. Leo, lost in a world far across the Atlantic Ocean, was oblivious to the figure standing behind him on Sizewell beach.

'You took my advice then,' Cain began, his voice taking Leo by surprise.

'What advice?' Leo replied, clambering to his feet.

'When I told you to leave Ararat the moment the opportunity arrives or you'll end up with all the others. You listened. And now, I need you to listen again. You know what goes on behind the door on the left, don't you?'

Leo nodded.

'I saw it in your eyes in the car. You weren't just surprised to see me, you were wondering how the fuck I survived it.'

Leo's gaze fell, unable to keep Cain's eye.

'What you did to me...how you set me up,' Cain continued. 'I'd have done the same to you if the roles had been reversed. So I don't blame you. I don't like you, but I don't blame you. But you need to take a walk with me.'

The unlikely pairing began making their way along the beach.

'Did you see her?' Cain asked. 'When they showed you what they were doing to the Chromatics behind that door, did you see Eva?'

'Yes.'

'Where was she?'

'In the psychiatric unit.'

Cain closed his eyes tightly.

'At least she's not in those red cubes any more,' said Leo.

'How did she look?'

'I don't know. Sad, I guess. Distant.'

'But alive.'

'Yes. How did you escape from it?' Leo asked.

'If you're strong enough to survive it and show they can't break your body or spirit, then they reassign you to something else. Otherwise it's a waste of resources to leave you there. It makes sense to retrain the strongest and use the rest as lab rats.'

Leo scratched as the scar on the back of his hand started to itch.

'This is her third breakdown in eight years,' Cain continued. 'The maximum amount of repairs you get is five before you're shipped off, so we still have time.'

'Time for what?'

Cain stopped.

'Time for you to get her and all the others out of there.'

Cain's fixed expression suggested to Leo that he hadn't misheard.

'Are you serious?'

'Would I be breaking rank like this if I wasn't?'

'How can I do that?'

'You can join us.'

'Us? What us?'

'Do you know what they have planned for you now you're here?'

'Research for a television show they're planning, in the run-up to an international rollout of the MetaChildren programme.'

'And what's your position?'

'I'm not supposed to tell anyone.'

'It's not a trap,' Cain said.

'How do I know that?'

'I have better things to do with my time. Like blowing that fucking place apart. Exposing to the world what Awakening Entertainment is doing in the name of advancing its own technology. We can bring down Ararat. It's possible.'

'No,' Leo said. 'We've worked too hard to get where we are today. All the sacrifices people have made would be worthless.'

'They're not sacrifices if they haven't been made willingly. They've stolen lives.'

'But the testing...that's going to come to an end soon, isn't it? Once the TV show begins and the public starts subscribing. There won't be any need for the Chromatics.'

'And what do you think is going to happen to everyone inside Ararat? They'll be given their freedom? The doors will open and they'll be told to go on their merry way?'

Naively, Leo had not thought about it.

'I don't know. They might do.'

'Awakening would never risk that kind of potential exposure,' Cain replied. 'They're *never* going to let those people go. Have you ever heard of the term "Model Drift"?'

Leo shook his head.

'The world is constantly changing. Views on parenting evolve and people's values adapt. What might have been acceptable as the norm when we were first taken to Ararat ten years ago might not be the same tomorrow. So they need to make sure their MetaChildren keep up with the times and respond to its customers' changing values without any errors. It's all about keeping clients engaged and customer retention. Until Awakening's AI becomes fully self-sufficient, they'll keep needing new test subjects and will continue to retrain their older ones. And then, when they're done, their avatars will be sold on to medical science or virtual Houses of Assignation.'

'Houses of what?'

'Virtual brothels, Hudson. Where for the right price, nothing is out of bounds. Look, I get it, you've been brainwashed by that place,' Cain went on. 'There's a name for it—Stockholm Syndrome, where hostages bond with their kidnappers. They begin believing what they're told.

But it's nothing more than a coping mechanism. It's your brain's way of not going completely fucking nuts while you're in that cycle. I know because I was the same as you. And if you let them, they're going to keep manipulating you for the rest of your life.'

'No,' Leo said. 'The MetaChildren programme is going to help millions of families who can't afford kids of their own. It'll change the world.'

'There are other platforms out there planning to do something similar, only ethically. They haven't made human sacrifices or cut corners to be the first to launch.'

Leo's skin prickled as images from inside the viewing room burst back to life in his mind. The gaunt, haunted faces of the innocent.

'What do you want from me?' he asked.

'They haven't told you this yet but you're being groomed as a contestant for the TV show. A single dad to one of these MetaChildren. Awakening wants to control the outcome, and you are perfect for two reasons. The first, because you have no past. I don't know how you got Adam Taylor-Georgiou's dog tags burned in the back of your hand, but we know you're not him as we tested your DNA. Who you really are no one knows. The second is you'll do what they tell you to do because that's how they've trained you. So when you ask what do we want from you? The answer is the same as Awakening does. To win.'

'How?'

'They want us to find contestants we can manipulate the outcomes of until you are the last man standing. But they don't know that's when our partnership ends. Because that's when you expose to the world what goes on in Ararat.'

'You make it sound easy,' Leo said.

'Believe me, it's far from it. Even if we plan meticulously, I know it's going to be near impossible to pull off. But Awakening doesn't know there's a large group of survivors like me scattered about the organization who haven't forgotten the friends and families they took from us, or the grudges we bear. And with our combined skills, insider knowledge and a shit load of luck, think what we could accomplish if it works. Please, don't dismiss it.'

The opportunity to right the wrongs he had been an unwitting party to was tempting. Yet still Leo was torn. It wasn't until Eva's vacant expression reappeared in his memory alongside so many other young faces that, later the same week, he gave Cain his answer.

'Tell me what you need me to do,' he said.

Today, outside Ararat's ruins, he took the bouquet of white lilies he'd been holding under his arm and, with the string keeping them together, he tied them to the mesh fencing amongst all the others left by visitors to this macabre tourist attraction.

The card attached to his bouquet read simply:

'For the Chromatics.'

80
Cadman & Gabriel

Cadman paced the corridors of his empty house. Each room he passed was devoid of furniture, paintings, electricals or framed photographs—everything that had once made it feel like home. Only this time, he hadn't been forced to sell it all or watch it being repossessed.

His office was the final room the removals team had packed up and taken away to his new property. He hated to think of how many hours he must have spent over the years between those four walls, giving everything to his career and his profile at the expense of those who'd loved him.

He paused to glance from the window towards the reservoir. He'd often gazed at it, reliving memories of watching Gabriel running around the vast expanse of water, earbuds wedged into his ears, lost in a world of music and fresh air. Once, they'd run together, before Cadman no longer had the time and purchased a running machine to keep by his desk instead. Now, he longed for those times in Gabriel's company.

In the aftermath of River's termination from *The Family Experiment*, Cadman had capitalized on his high demand. He'd assumed that throwing himself into work would fulfil him. However, he underestimated what now constituted happiness. And it wasn't his career. It was the two people he had chosen to rid himself of.

The end of the life he'd known had arrived four days after River's death. He and Gabriel had barely seen each other until Cadman spotted him trudging across the lawns towards the house during a storm. Cadman hurried to their bedroom for the suitcase he had prepacked.

Minutes later and Gabriel returned, soaked to the skin and talking about a stranger who'd made accusations about Cadman. He cut himself short on noticing the case by Cadman's feet.

'Where are you going?' Gabriel asked.

'Nowhere,' he replied calmly. 'It's you who's leaving.'

'What's going on?'

'I know about the money you've been hiding from me, the cryptocurrency account, the house you had in the Metaverse for you and River, the house in Florence you're renting once you've left me and how you sold yourself to pay for it all.'

Gabriel's head snapped back.

'What the hell are you talking about?'

'Don't lie to me,' Cadman continued.

'I'm not!'

'I've seen the proof. I have bank statements, I have pin numbers, I've accessed your accounts, I've watched the videos of you with other men.'

'Well, the documents must be forged and the videos deepfaked because I don't have a penny to my name and I haven't slept with anyone but you in eight years. Who's been filling your head with this bullshit?'

'Someone using an anonymous account contacted me.'

'And you believed them? Should I have believed the idiot who just approached me by the reservoir telling me you paid a *The Family Experiment* insider to frame River?'

Cadman considered denying it. And in doing so, perhaps everything could return to the way it had been before River. But they were too far removed from the way things used to be to ever negotiate a return. Gabriel's brow furrowed as he waited for a response.

'You didn't do that, did you?' he asked. 'It's a lie, isn't it?'

But Cadman maintained his silence.

'Why?' Gabriel gasped.

'Because you are a leech,' Cadman snarled. 'I gave you a good life, I gave you money and a job and a beautiful home and all you could ever have dreamed of. I even let you have a child and that still wasn't enough for you. You wanted more.'

'The only thing I ever wanted was respect!' Gabriel replied. 'And I got that from the child you "let" me have. Why would you take him away from me, from us?'

'To remind you who is in charge. To show you that I will not be taken advantage of.'

Gabriel folded in on himself, his palms resting on his thighs as Cadman watched intently, but with less satisfaction than he'd expected.

'That party before the circus,' Gabriel continued. 'The one where I was drugged. Was that you too?'

Cadman folded his arms and nodded his head.

'Why?'

Cadman had felt a sudden remorse for that decision. But he couldn't admit to his petty jealousy over Gabriel's popularity, so he offered a nonplussed shrug instead.

Gabriel shook his head and then stood upright.

'How could you kill your own son?'

'He wasn't my son. He was never my son.'

'Stop lying to yourself. I watched you with him, especially towards the end. You haven't always felt like that.'

'Perhaps you're not the only one who can act the part.'

When Gabriel moved sharply, Cadman turned to one side and raised his fists. But instead of striking Cadman, Gabriel reached for the suitcase.

'You're not worth my anger,' he said, heading for the front door. As he opened it, he turned to face his partner one last time.

'You will always want more,' he added. 'More money, more fame, more popularity, more followers—and perhaps you'll get it. But you'll never have anyone to share it with. You'll push everyone away until you die alone.'

In the days that followed, Cadman expected Gabriel to seek revenge in a very public way. And Cadman had already planned how he'd refute any accusations with pre-prepared counter-claims. He was willing, armed and ready to go to war.

But nothing happened. Gabriel gave no interviews and made no online or public appearances. He had vanished.

And then a few weeks after the final, explosive episode of *The Family Experiment* had aired, a third anonymous email had arrived. This one contained a five-minute video made up of clips to demonstrate how each piece of the original 'evidence' made against Gabriel had been manipulated. It revealed the mapping techniques used to create deepfake images of Gabriel participating in sex acts with others, forged bank statements, rental agreements and flight plans. Cadman must have watched it a dozen times before he accepted the truth. He had been all too willing to believe Gabriel would manipulate him because, at his core, Cadman himself was a manipulator.

Cadman had frantically tried calling him, but Gabriel's phone was no longer in service and his emails bounced back unread. Gabriel's social media accounts were deactivated. He hadn't even been spotted by facial recognition software on the millions of cameras Cadman's team had access to across the country. Unless Gabriel wanted to be found, there was no way of locating him.

The typically tight grip Cadman held over his own emotions slowly weakened in the months that passed. Both his waking and sleeping hours were peppered with images of River's final moments and Gabriel's face contorting with the agony of losing a child.

He struggled to muster the energy required to devote to his career. He turned down public appearances and work opportunities, instead choosing to spend hours watching old *The Family Experiment* footage of the man and boy he'd so often rejected. Depression quietly descended upon him. And after an intervention from members of his staff, Cadman checked himself into a wellness clinic in Arizona.

Upon his recent return to the UK, Cadman had immediately put their Buckinghamshire house up for sale and purchased a new place in London, where he was also to relaunch his media career by presenting a brand-new television show.

Yet still he yearned for Gabriel and what they once had.

A Push notification from his Audite caught his attention—an alert for when Gabriel resurfaced online. His stomach performed the first of many somersaults. He pressed a button to project the message onto the white office wall. It was a BBC News clip of Gabriel, broadcast only minutes earlier, with the caption *Reality Star Campaigns for Children's Rights*.

The newsreader first offered a summary of the story, about how Gabriel had just been appointed the public face of a national campaign to persuade the government to reinstate payments to adoptive parents, thus encouraging more to volunteer. Cadman's heart fluttered at the sight of Gabriel.

'These payments were cut more than a decade ago when we were in a recession,' he told an interviewer. 'And they've yet to be reinstated. The number of children being adopted or fostered is now at an all-time low and less than the estimated number of those annually being shipped abroad to live in Europe. If a child survives the journey—and we know that many don't—there is no way of knowing what happens to them next. Keeping them here in the UK is the only answer. Our charity helps parents by offering them financial support. But we don't have a bottomless pit of money, and until the government steps up, more lives will be at risk.'

'And how can viewers help?' the interviewer asked.

'They can sign the petition to encourage the government to change their minds or they can donate to our charity. Meanwhile, French winery Vin de Languedoc-Roussillon is one of the largest exporters across Europe and has agreed to print photographs of missing British children on the back of two million bottle labels in the hope that customers might have seen them.'

The clip ended and Cadman replayed it twice over. He desperately wanted to speak to Gabriel again, and for him to know how sorry he was. He asked his phone to find him a contact number for the charity and dialled it. But before the call was answered, he hung up. He clutched the device close to his chest. Gabriel was a good man, and now that he had stepped out from beneath Cadman's shadow, he was able to do good things. He was better off without Cadman in his world.

Instead, he visited the charity's website, made a sizeable donation, ticked the box that read **'Anonymous'** and turned his tablet off.

Then he left the house for the last time, locking the door behind him.

81
Selena

Selena spread the picnic blanket across the grass and patted out the creases. She opened the lid of a wicker basket, laid out the paper plates and wooden cutlery, then removed the contents from the various recyclable pots.

'Food's ready, guys,' she shouted, and waved across the playpark, catching their attention.

They waved back from a swing and a slide. Meera and her son Ben were the first to arrive, followed soon after by Kelly and her daughter Esme, then finally Rebecca and Lucy. They all sat on the blanket, the mums first dishing food onto the plates for their giggling youngsters before tucking in themselves.

Selena took in those surrounding her, recalling how a few short months earlier, this had felt awkward, Jaden's wife dining with the three women he'd impregnated, and with them, their children. The mothers had not known of one another's existence before his murder, or that Jaden had been married, but they had accepted and welcomed one another. And now these meetings were a regular occurrence. Once a fortnight, all seven met out in the open, in cafes or soft play centres, and the women chatted while the half-siblings played.

Selena still couldn't be sure why she had first instigated it. She'd told Jaden their marriage was over shortly before his death. It would have been the perfect time to have drawn a line under that chapter of her life. But it hadn't stopped her from grieving for her DNA Match.

Everything she had read about losing a Match had proved correct. It cut deeper than grief, it transcended loss and she'd carried the pain around with her every second of every day. There were very few moments where she'd briefly become distracted by something else. It was a constant, unrelenting awareness.

In the weeks that followed, Selena had made a decision. She wanted to meet the children she had hoped to have had with Jaden. Perhaps being around them might feel as if she hadn't lost him completely. And she'd been proved right. She could hear him in these two girls and one boy when they laughed, and she saw him in the way their eyes twinkled when they smiled.

'Did you end up streaming that Netflix documentary about her?' asked Meera, tucking into a couscous salad.

'No, didn't need to,' Selena said. 'I lived it.'

An image of Suzanne Ross, Jaden's killer, barrelled its way into her head. She was standing above Jaden's dead body, her face spattered with his blood. Selena blinked it away.

'Do you think she was telling the truth?' Meera replied. 'That Jaden ghosted her after the miscarriage?'

'If he did, I think he must have thought he had good reason to,' said Selena. 'Maybe there were red flags in her behaviour that made him have second thoughts. He shouldn't have abandoned her, though.'

'We all know what it's like to be desperate for a child,' said Esme. 'We don't know how that impacted her mental health or if she ever was pregnant or if her brain had tricked her body into believing it was.'

'I agree with Selena,' said Meera. 'I think he must've recognized an instability and that getting pregnant might not have been the best thing for her.'

'Did they say anything in the programme about when she might be released from the secure psych unit?' asked Selena.

'No, but I can't see them letting her out of that hospital for years and years.'

'Good,' Selena replied. The longer she was incarcerated, the safer she'd feel.

She paused for a moment to reflect upon her MetaChild, Malachi, and how she had failed him. She'd been a poor parent, never truly accepting or committing to him. But each time she had looked deep into his eyes, searching for something that had made him feel as if he was truly a part of her, all she'd seen was code.

Had Jaden not been killed, the public's positive perception of her might have been different. If, as planned, she'd left her husband, the couple would have been automatically terminated from the competition. However, as self-serving as it sounded, Jaden's murder meant it had been producers who had switched Malachi off. They'd received the flack and not her.

She found herself gently rubbing her stomach in a circular motion. She wasn't sure if she was imagining it or whether her bump had grown in the last few days.

'Do you still want me to come with you to the twelve-week scan?' asked Kelly.

'If you're sure you have the time?' Selena replied.

'You know I do. None of us can wait until we meet the next member of our tribe.'

Months after Jaden's death, Selena had decided life was too short to wait any longer for motherhood to find her. When faced with picking an anonymous sperm donor or her late husband, the choice had been obvious. So she'd used her frozen eggs and Jaden's sperm, which had both been deposited at a fertility clinic before he'd gambled away their money, scuppering their IVF plans.

Selena had afforded the treatment after signing a contract with a streaming production company which planned to make a six-part dramatization of her story. The deal had paid for the multiple scans, tests and hormone injections before she had undergone IVF. She had been in the one-third of women for whom it had worked first time.

She took another glance at the people she was surrounding herself with. Jaden might not have always brought her happiness, but he had brought these strong, capable, wonderful women together. And his death had taken her in a direction she feared she might never travel. And for those things, she would always be grateful to him.

Through the Grapevine

Home | UK | **Trending**

NO CHARGES AGAINST 'TRAFFICKING' COUPLE

After a twelve-month investigation, police have confirmed no charges will be made against *The Family Experiment* contestants Dimitri and Zoe Taylor-Georgiou despite them apparently admitting to selling their missing son Adam to human traffickers.

The Crown Prosecution Service says that even though millions heard their 'confession' live on television during last year's finale of *The Family Experiment*, the couple have since retracted their claims.

CPS spokesperson Jessica Pilkington said: 'Despite extensive investigations, we can still only take the Taylor-Georgious' word for it as to the nature of his disappearance. However, until a body is found, the case remajns open.'

In the live finale of the reality show, fellow contestant Hudson Wright claimed to have been with Adam Taylor the night he died, which was not when his parents claim he went missing.

Jason Gibbins, lawyer for the Taylor-Georgiou family, said his clients maintain their original story.

'What viewers heard that night was nothing more than play-acting,' he explained. 'They assumed it was part of a Monthly Challenge, and by the time they realized it was not, they had been unfairly eliminated from the competition.'

The Taylor-Georgious had been living in a police safe house following an arson attack on their home when their address was leaked and shared across social media.

It is not known where they have moved to since.

82
Leo Hamilton

Leo held the palm of his hand against the electronic panel until the front door opened. He closed and locked it behind him, yawned, placed a brown paper bag on the wooden worktop and announced his arrival with a loud 'Halló'.

'Hey,' came a voice from behind a bedroom door, and a moment later, Cain appeared, drying his wet hair with a towel. 'Have you just got back?'

'Landed a couple of hours ago,' Leo replied.

'And how was it?'

'No problems, flights all left and arrived on time.'

'No suspicious activity?'

'Nope.'

'You're sure no one followed you anywhere?'

'Cain,' Leo said firmly.

'Yeah, okay, I'm sorry.'

Leo brushed the fresh snow from his shoulders and woollen hat and removed his outdoor clothes.

'How long has it been snowing for?' he asked.

'It started about a week ago, soon after you left. You know it's not an Icelandic winter if there's not at least one blizzard a day.'

Leo looked along the corridor and at the closed bedroom door. There was nothing to be heard from the other side and he saw no flickering light from the television through the gap. His eyes returned to Cain's. He didn't need to ask the question for Cain to shake his head.

'Right, I'm going to freshen up,' said Leo.

Moments later and the water cascading from the shower head was as hot as he could stand without burning his skin. He closed his eyes and thought back to the weeks and months following his acceptance of Cain's request to help in the plan to destroy Ararat from the inside.

Leo had thrown himself into his new day job working on upcoming TV show *The Family Experiment*. Alongside researchers, producers, psychologists and company executives, he had participated in narrowing down applications from the thousands to a shortlist of just thirty. Meanwhile, a team of experts were schooling him in how he should portray himself on screen to win favour with savvy viewers who were increasingly attuned to recognizing if they were being duped. The decision had also been made not to inform Autumn Taylor that he was an Awakening Entertainment employee so that she would not go easy on him in television interviews.

Meanwhile, Cain had been tasked with leading a team carrying out background checks on the shortlist. That had included surrendering access to their social media accounts alongside their assets to search for evidence of financial impropriety.

Once the show had begun to air, the first couple they were prepared to expose were Rufus Green and Kitty Carter. She had racially offensive slurs in social media posts she'd uploaded as a teenager. However, exposing her had been unnecessary when Rufus had shaken their daughter to death.

For Selena and Jaden Wilson, Cain had spotted a red flag in the form of large sums of money paid out from a savings account to online casinos, followed by random deposits made into their account of £10,000 a time. Digging deeper, they'd discovered three independently affluent single women who had all given birth within a few months of one another. Jaden's name had appeared on each child's birth certificate.

Assuming Selena had been unaware, one of the team had taken control of the counselling avatar whom Selena had opened her heart to. It looked as if the couple's exit was a dead cert, right up until the moment Jaden had been bludgeoned in a tragic twist none of them had foreseen.

For Woody and Tina Finn, the team had dug much deeper before striking gold. Sealed court documents revealed a secret daughter who had been found guilty of killing a classmate and was under house arrest. Isabelle Finn's birth certificate, medical and school records had all been removed from public searches. She didn't exist in search engines either, and each time they received the same notification.

'Some results may have been removed under data protection law in Europe.'

Even social media searches proved a dead end.

'This search goes against our community guidelines.'

Investigators were dispatched to probe the family's last home. Neighbours revealed they recalled her vaguely and that her family had moved out of the area. The family of the boy she had been accused of killing refused to talk to them.

Thermal heat and infra-red cameras attached to giant leylandii trees surrounding their home suggested Isabelle never ventured above basement level. A freelance contractor had been hired to break into the house, and she had taken photographs of a basic electronic locking system attached to the basement door. Then, midway through the competition, she returned to unlock the basement door and leave the device for Isabelle to find. The rest of the Finns' story became television history.

Leo had protested the inclusion of Cadman N'Yu and Gabriel Macmillan in the final six. But he'd been overruled by senior producers, who argued that a minor celebrity might make for an interesting spin. Leo and Cain knew it would be easier said than done manipulating a man who made a living from manipulating the public.

However, Cadman had been surprisingly easy to dupe with fake documents and video clips suggesting Gabriel's plans for a new life in Italy. Once confirmation arrived that Cadman had read the emails containing this falsified information, Cain contacted him. He denounced Cadman's plan to publicly expose Gabriel's deception, suggesting it might make Cadman appear weak and gullible. Instead, he suggested a controversial termination of River, one that would likely gain Cadman a wave of public sympathy while simultaneously punishing his partner.

Following their exclusion from *The Family Experiment*, Leo appeared at the reservoir to reveal to Gabriel Cadman's role in River's demise. How he would respond was up to him.

Leo turned the shower off, stepped inside the body dryer, dressed, then, in the kitchen, removed a pot of kjötsúpa from a pan in the warming oven. As he ate, he thought of Zoe and Dimitri Taylor-Georgiou, the contestants whom Leo himself had actively targeted and encouraged to participate.

He had first learned of their version of events upon his return to England. He had scanned the QR code on the back of his hand to learn more about Adam's background and discovered who his parents were and the lengths they'd gone to in order to conceal what they had done to their son.

Leo knew that if he could encourage them to participate in *The Family Experiment*, then navigate them and himself towards the finishing line, it would make for a perfect, explosive finale. And soon after his pitch to Awakening Entertainment's senior producers was given the green light, the charm offensive began.

Reports of Adam's 'death' had been picked over by the media countless times over the years and the blame heaped upon his parents had likely left them battle-scarred. Targeted advertising was employed, via mail, email, text and Smart tech, to announce plans for the show and how to apply. Mentions of *The Family Experiment* on digital advertising ensured their wearable tech activated any billboards, bus stops or lorry sides they passed using vehicle or on foot. A month later, he watched via a hidden camera as members of Cain's team met with Zoe and Dimitri at their home to invite them to participate.

Zoe had been the more defensive of the two.

'Why would we put ourselves out there again to be hate figures?' she asked.

'For closure,' the researcher replied. 'To prove to the world and to yourselves that you were good parents. That what happened to Adam was a tragic mistake and that you shouldn't be judged by it for the rest of your lives. This competition is your chance to start afresh. Not to replace Adam but to be a family again.'

By the end of the week, the couple had completed their application forms and Cain had begun scrutinizing their accounts. He learned how deeply in debt they had been around the date of Adam's departure and how much of that debt had been erased via an untraceable offshore account two months after their son's faked disappearance. However, the reason why the Taylor-Georgious had found themselves in so much debt had taken Leo by surprise. They were all bound together not only by Adam's loss but also by the deaths of Nate Simmonds and, subsequently, his father, Charles.

Even during the competition itself, Leo's anger towards the Taylor-Georgious meant he had sometimes taken needless risks that had irritated Cain. Leo had occasionally parked outside the Taylor-Georgious' home for no other reason than to watch them.

By chance one morning, he'd witnessed Dimitri loading his vehicle with boxes and had followed the driverless car to the rubbish dump. Then Leo paid a member of staff to give him the unwanted detritus. And inside one suitcase he found a lifelike doll of a boy, wearing a jumper with the name Adam embroidered on it. Cain discovered the doll had been paid for from Zoe's own bank account eight years earlier. Leo had used a recording of Adam's voice from a YouTube clip the boy had posted himself and uploaded it to the doll. Then he'd placed it in a box and addressed it to Dimitri. It followed the sealed court documents and postcard he'd also sent.

The night before *The Family Experiment* finale, he'd taken the Red Eye Eurostar to Paris to meet Cain in a hotel suite. There, they accessed the Metaverse for the live finale. But after Leo's revelation and subsequent disappearance, there'd been no time to reflect on their success. As the rest of the covert team in Ararat and Sizewell made their escapes across the world, Leo's first destination had been New York.

Much of the two-hour flight on board the Concorde 2 had been spent mourning the loss of his daughter, Alice. Unlike the other MetaChildren, she had been programmed with an awareness and acceptance that each Development Leap was a step closer to her death. Regardless, losing her had upset him immeasurably.

The Family Experiment

Back in the present, Leo picked up two boxes of medication he'd left earlier on the kitchen worktop, removed a bottle of water from the fridge and approached the third bedroom. He knocked twice before slowly opening the door.

Eva was in her bed, lying on her side and facing the wall. Her head turned and she acknowledged him with the slightest of smiles. He reciprocated with a broader one of his own followed by a 'Hey, you'. She didn't respond. She had yet to say a word since he had found her in a New York hospital recovering from smoke inhalation three days after Ararat's destruction. Doctors advised that her lack of speech wasn't because of physical damage, but psychological. It wasn't a surprise after all she had suffered for so long.

Leo had smuggled her out, and they drove for four days until they reached Mission, Texas, on the Mexican border, where Cain joined them. Using counterfeit passports, they travelled by car and bus to Argentina, then flew from Ezeiza International Airport to South Africa, where they remained for a month, followed by stints in Spain, Germany, Sweden and Belgium. Leo and Cain had just enough cosmetic procedures to fool facial recognition software that they weren't who they once were. Nevertheless, each time they had an inkling that their whereabouts might have been compromised, they relocated. Iceland was the first country where they had felt safe.

Eva had found life outside Ararat challenging, and the continuous moving had unsettled her. Gradually, the screaming fits and rages subsided, the hysteria became less aggressive. Now, days might pass without incident.

Always in the back of their minds was the fact that while Leo and Cain had matured mentally, Eva had not. She remained the twelve-year-old girl she was when she'd first been smuggled into Ararat. While being locked in those boxes and experimented upon, she had not been allowed to develop emotionally. They were taking care of a twenty-five-year-old child.

'So how have you been?' Leo asked as he lay down beside her.

He placed the bag of medication between them and recounted his trip. She flinched at the mention of Ararat.

'Ah, here you are,' said Cain as he made his way into the room. 'You okay, sis?'

Eva inched her way to the middle of the bed to make room for her brother, then she reached out to hold both of their hands, gently squeezing them. Neither man made a fuss of this small but significant gesture, but Leo felt his throat tightening ever so slightly.

How long they could remain together in the safety of their unit was anyone's guess, but he and Cain would do all they could to protect her.

This might be their home for years, or they might be on the run for the rest of their lives. But while they had each other, they had a family.

Chats

TV / Reality TV Shows / **The Passengers**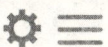

SirMixALot, 7.45 p.m.
Launch night folks – you all ready?

WideAwake56, 7.46 p.m.
Not sure if I can stomach this one. My cousin's friend's grandad was killed in one of those cars the terrorists blew up. This all feels too close for comfort.

TellyBob, 7.47 p.m.
#GriefTourist

SirMixALot, 7.49 p.m.
Yeah but they're not actually blowing anyone up this time, are they? It's just a reality show.

TellyBob, 7.SO p.m.
Shame

CatsAndBoots, 7.50 p.m.
What are the rules?

SirMixALot, 7.51 p.m
Link to The Passengers' website here. Says 'Over the next seven days, contestants will travel in driverless cars while being put through physical tasks and moral dilemmas. The better they are, the more cash they'll earn. But each night, viewers eliminate one Passenger. That contestant can either leave without the money or remain inside the car as it explodes while trying to hold on to as much cash as they can.'

WideAwake56, 7.52 p.m.
#WTF

> **SirMixALot, 7.54 p.m.**
> Don't get your knickers in a twist, Karen. It's contestants' avatars that get blown up, not them. Although in their haptic suits, they'll get to feel the explosion as if it's real. The ultimate winner keeps their cash and the car.

> **FaffyDuck, 7.55 p.m.**
> LOVE that they have Cadman N'Yu hosting it. He was an advisor on the day of the original attack, wasn't he? He'll do ANYTHING for money.

> **CatsAndBoots, 7.55 p.m.**
> Anyone ever wonder what happened to some of the other contestants? Most have kept a low profile.

> **WideAwake56, 7.57 p.m.**
> You know who I wonder about? Adam.

> **SirMixALot, 7.57 p.m.**
> Who?

> **CatsAndBoots, 7.58 p.m.**
> Yeah, who?

> **WideAwake56, 7.59 p.m.**
> Duh! The son Dimitri and Zoe sold. The one who rescued Hudson and which kickstarted all this.

> **CatsAndBoots, 7.59 p.m.**
> Vaguely recall him. Dead, isn't he?

> **WideAwake56, 7.59 p.m.**
> Yes, I just wonder where his body is. It'd be nice if he was brought home for a proper burial.

> **TellyBob, 8.00 p.m.**
> Shhh, The Passengers is starting. Love the slogan Who Lives, Who Dies, You Decide. Can't wait to start blowing these fuckers up.

83
Mathéo

Mathéo scrutinized the arched wooden roof above him and the iron bowstring trusses keeping it in place. The drip, drip, drip of leaking water was coming from somewhere up there, but it was too high to see with the naked eye. Later, he would need to use the cherry-picker to take a closer look.

For now, he made his way around the aluminium wine fermenters, checking the stability of digital pressure gauges, heaters and coolers, and the electrical capacity and seals on drainage sumps to ensure everything was running as it should. Their winery was on course to produce a record number of litres that year despite how extreme weather conditions and climate change had decimated much of the French industry.

Mathéo couldn't afford for there to be any errors as it was he who had persuaded his père to expand from a modest winery into one of the biggest players in southern France's Languedoc-Roussillon. If all went according to plan, the two-million-euro, state-of-the-art building, storage, equipment, restaurant, cafe and tasting room would have paid for itself in three years.

Mathéo's grumbling stomach reminded him that he had skipped breakfast. He made his way across the car park and into the cafe. He greeted staff with smiles and 'Allo's' before helping himself to a pastry and chocolat chaud. Then he chose a table by the windows overlooking the vineyards and rolling countryside and began to eat.

This could all have been so different, he thought. If Maurice hadn't phoned in sick that day and his father, Christophe, hadn't driven the van instead to pick up supplies from Montpellier. If the van had been fully charged and he hadn't needed to stop off at that charging station en route. If Christophe hadn't lit up a cigarette, stretched his legs and walked around the perimeter while he waited. If he had looked left instead of right. If just one of those moments had not occurred, his father would not have spotted a child's foot poking out from under a discarded tarpaulin, and then found Mathéo's semi-conscious body beneath it.

Mathéo remembered little about what happened after that, just fragments of moments. He recalled opening his eyes at the sensation of being carried and realizing the stranger was taking him to a van. Even if he'd wanted to cry for help or fight, he was too weak. But he didn't feel threatened by this man—there was kindness in his eyes that told Mathéo he was safe. Then he'd been placed in the passenger seat and given water from a bottle.

The man began talking to him in French but switched to English when it became apparent Mathéo only understood the odd word. He was asked his name and where he lived but he didn't know. Likewise his age, the names of his parents or why he was in France. Christophe later admitted to having a bad feeling about how the boy had got there. He knew that human trafficking from the UK to France was prevalent and that gang leaders were ruthless with children who weren't fit for purpose. Mathéo fell asleep, exhausted, soon after.

He awoke later that evening tucked under a brightly coloured quilt in the upstairs bedroom of a farmhouse. A middle-aged woman was sitting in a chair by the bed, watching him. She smiled and he returned the gesture. By her feet was a bowl of warm soup and two thick slices of seeded bread. She introduced herself as Christophe's wife, Elize.

'We think you were sent here illegally,' she explained as the boy ate. 'They bring enfants from England at night and take them to only God knows where.'

She moved closer to him as he sat up and tucked into his food, showing him online news articles about himself on a tablet.

'We also think your name is Adam,' she said. 'We looked online at British websites for boys who have recently been missing...we have seen images...pictures of you. Your parents are very...how do you say... worried.'

'Adam,' he repeated, but he had no flicker of recognition.

Then he watched a video of a couple he didn't recognize being interviewed by reporters as the search took place across a foggy Scottish moorland.

'We must be taking you back to them,' Christophe said as he appeared at the doorway. 'They want you back.'

'No,' Adam replied. 'I don't think they do.'

He recalled snapshots of a conversation he'd had with a boy aboard the dinghy that had carried them to the French coast. He learned that some parents had administered drugs to their children before sending them to Europe to erase all memories of their past. He assumed the same had happened to him as he could remember nothing before that fateful boat ride.

'I think they gave me away,' he continued.

But there was no emotion in his voice, and no longing to see them again. By drugging him, his parents had ensured he was unable to feel anything for them.

The next morning, he overheard Christophe and Elize discussing what to do with him. Elize had researched the consequences of his return to England and learned that once the truth was revealed, he was unlikely to be returned to his parents. Instead, he would be placed in a care home with dozens of other unwanted children. Why would they want to send him there when they could raise him themselves?

'We have plenty of room now that Jerome and Adrienne are at university,' Elize told Christophe. 'He can live here.'

And without further debate, Adam became part of the Laurent family. Their friends in the small village of Castelbouc had accepted their explanation that the son of a second cousin had come to live with them following the death of his parents, and he was enrolled into the local school under the name Mathéo. However, their two adult children were told the truth before their first end-of-term trip home and relished having a younger sibling.

As the years progressed, Mathéo was a keen student and helped at the vineyards at weekends, learning the trade from the ground up. Upon his graduation from school, he shunned university in favour of working full-time for the family business. And he continued to show little interest in where he had come from or reconnecting with his biological parents. He neither resented them nor pined for them. They had done him the greatest of favours.

His new parents, however, kept a distant eye on Zoe and Dimitri. And when they learned they'd become a part of the most watched television show in the world, they felt it was important to inform Mathéo. He viewed one episode, but it failed to capture his interest.

When the series finished and Christophe informed him Zoe and Dimitri had been exposed for selling their son to traffickers, he streamed the final episode and watched it alone. He listened closely to Hudson's recollections of that night at sea and realized he must have been the boy whose life he had saved when they'd jumped overboard. He hated that burden of guilt Hudson had carried over the years, believing that Adam had died because of him.

It hadn't taken much persuading for his new family to agree to include images of missing British children on the labels of their wine bottles in the hope that some might be recognized. However, he refused an invitation by the charity involved to appear with its ambassador, *The Family Experiment* contestant Gabriel Macmillan, on screen in a news report. The chances of being recognized as an adult and exposing his family for not handing him back as a child were weak, but nevertheless, not without risk.

Mathéo took a last sip from his hot chocolate, wiped the flakes of pastry from his lips with a napkin and began making his way back to the winery. Others in his position might be curious as to their origins, but not him. The grass wasn't greener on the other side, he was sure of that.

It was greener on the hills and lush vineyards that surrounded him every single day of his second chance at life.

* * * * *

ACKNOWLEDGEMENTS

The inspiration for *The Family Experiment* came from a newspaper article suggesting that a few years from now, it will be commonplace for people to start families in the Metaverse. For a monthly subscription fee, you'll be able to start a family and spend as much or as little time as you'd like with them. It's a fascinating concept and got the cogs in my brain whirring. The book *AI By Design—A Plan For Living With Artificial Intelligence* by Catriona Campbell was invaluable in my understanding of AI. I'd recommend it to anyone who wants a basic grasp of the subject.

As always, getting my story from my head and into a bookshop or an online store takes a lot of work from a lot of people. So bear with me while I begin my roll-call of thank yous. As always, I'll begin with my husband, John Russell. He is the first person to read each book I write. Once upon a time, he'd offer an opinion here or there, but now, I get ten pages of notes on what works and what doesn't. And somehow, our marriage has survived. For one more book at least!

Thanks to our son, Elliot, for his patience while I wrote, not an easy ask of a four-year-old. Neither is me dragging him into every book shop we walk past so I can sign any copies of my book that might be in stock. Huge gratitude goes to my editor, Gillian Green, for her unwavering support. This is our fifth book together, and as always, I've so enjoyed working with you. Thanks to my mum, Pam, for her support and to my early readers, including Tracy Fenton at Facebook's THE Book Club, along with Emma Louise Bunting and Wendy Clarke at The Fiction Café Book Club, Mark Fearn at Book Mark! and everyone at Lost In A Good Book. Thanks also to Facebook group Psychological Thriller Readers, who are always such fun to be around and so supportive. Also my gratitude goes to the Pan Macmillan team including

Rebecca Needes, Moesha Parirenyatwa, Natasha Tulett, Bryony Croft, Sian Chilvers, Rosie Friis and Mary Chamberlain. Thanks also to my TV and film rights agent, Jon Cassir at CAA.

When it comes to social media, Facebook and Instagram are my favourite places to post. So thanks to all my followers as well as bloggers, vloggers and reviewers. I'm eternally grateful every time you tell someone about me.

Last and by no means least, to my fantastic readers. This is the twelfth book of mine you've picked up and have hopefully read, and it's thanks to you that my ego is now the size of a small Mediterranean island. And if I sell a few more books, I might be able to afford to buy myself one. You're all invited to the housewarming party.

AUTHOR NOTE

Generative AI is redefining how many people make content and is understandably a concern for photographers, designers, editors and anyone involved in the publishing industry, including writers like me. There is a lot that still needs to be worked out—should AI be used at all? If so, how and in what measured way? However, considering the subject matter of the book (if you've got this far, you'll know this already) it seemed fitting to ask an AI app to come up with an image of myself rather than me using my usual (admittedly quite old now) profile headshot.

And just to clarify, the original image it's based on is a selfie, and the AI used to make me this representation of myself was not trained by infringing copyrights.

ABOUT THE AUTHOR

John Marrs is an author and former journalist based in London and Northamptonshire. After spending his career interviewing celebrities from the worlds of television, film and music for numerous national newspapers and magazines, he is now a full-time author. He is the bestselling author of: *The One, The Passengers, The Minders, What Lies Between Us, The Vacation* and *The Marriage Act*.

Follow him at www.johnmarrsauthor.co.uk, on Instagram @johnmarrrs.author, on X @johnmarrs1 and on Facebook @johnmarrsauthor.